Drew

SIOBHAN DAVIS

This paperback edition © May 2024

ISBN-13: 978-1-916651-16-6

Edited by Kelly Hartigan (XterraWeb) editing.xterraweb.com
Proofread by Final Polish Proofreading
Research and critique by The Critical Touch
Cover design by Shannon Passmore of Shanoff Designs
Cover image © bigstockphoto.com and shutterstock.com
Formatted by Ciara Turley using Vellum

BOOK DESCRIPTION

Mistakes and secrets.

My life is littered with them.

And it's not always me who pays the price.

So, I do something I swore I wouldn't do—become the monster my father raised me to be.

To shield my loved ones from the predators I hunt, I keep family and friends in the dark, but I won't apologize for protecting them.

I do what needs to be done, and I've accepted my fate.

My heart is an impenetrable fortress now, and my only pleasure comes from anonymous encounters in the private dungeon of a club where I unleash my inner beast.

Years have passed, but my thirst for vengeance never dies.

I'll tear the world apart to find the answers I seek.

No one will stop me from having my revenge.

Including the woman who took a wrecking ball to my heart.

Loving me hasn't ended well in the past. Why would this time be any different?

A Note from the Author

This book is not a stand-alone romance, and it should only be read in series order and after reading *The Hate I Feel*. This is a dark romance with mature content including explicit sexual scenes and violence. Please refer to the content warning list on my website if you have any triggers. www.siobhandavis.com/triggers

I know there are readers who are firmly #TeamJane and some who are firmly #TeamShandra. I ask you to keep an open mind when reading this book and to trust me and trust my characters. After all, I am just the conduit. My characters lead me along the path.

This book is set seven years after the Drew chapter at the end of *The Hate I Feel* (and three years after the epilogue that appeared in *Charlie*.) I have listed the main characters' ages, and their children, to help with understanding the progression of time across the series.

A few characters from my Kennedy Boys® Series and another one of my series (being vague so I don't spoil the story) appear in this book. The characters from the second series not mentioned below are all aged 30 – 34 now, and it has been over ten years since the conclusion of that series. **You do not need to have read either of these series to enjoy this book.** This is an explanation for readers who recognize these characters and might be wondering about the timeline!

MAIN CHARACTERS:

Drew, Kaiden, Abby, Charlie, Sawyer, Shandra, Jackson – 33

Xavier Daniels – 36

Demi Barron – 35

Vanessa Lauder - 34

Maverick (Rick) Anderson – 37

Joaquin Anderson – 31

Harley Anderson - 30

Zayn & Emery Anderson – 29

Roman Anderson - 28

Keven Kennedy – 39

Selena Kennedy – 36

Keanu Kennedy - 35

CHILDREN

Abby & Kai's children: Talia (10), Oliver/Oli (9), Orion/Ori (7), Amelia (6)

Jackson & Nessa's children: Ren (9), Danielle (3)

Charlie & Demi's children: Jane (11), Henry (9), Jamie (7), Charlie (4)

Sawyer & Xavier's children: Cuan (5), Aubree (4)

Zayn & Emery's daughter: Darcy (2)

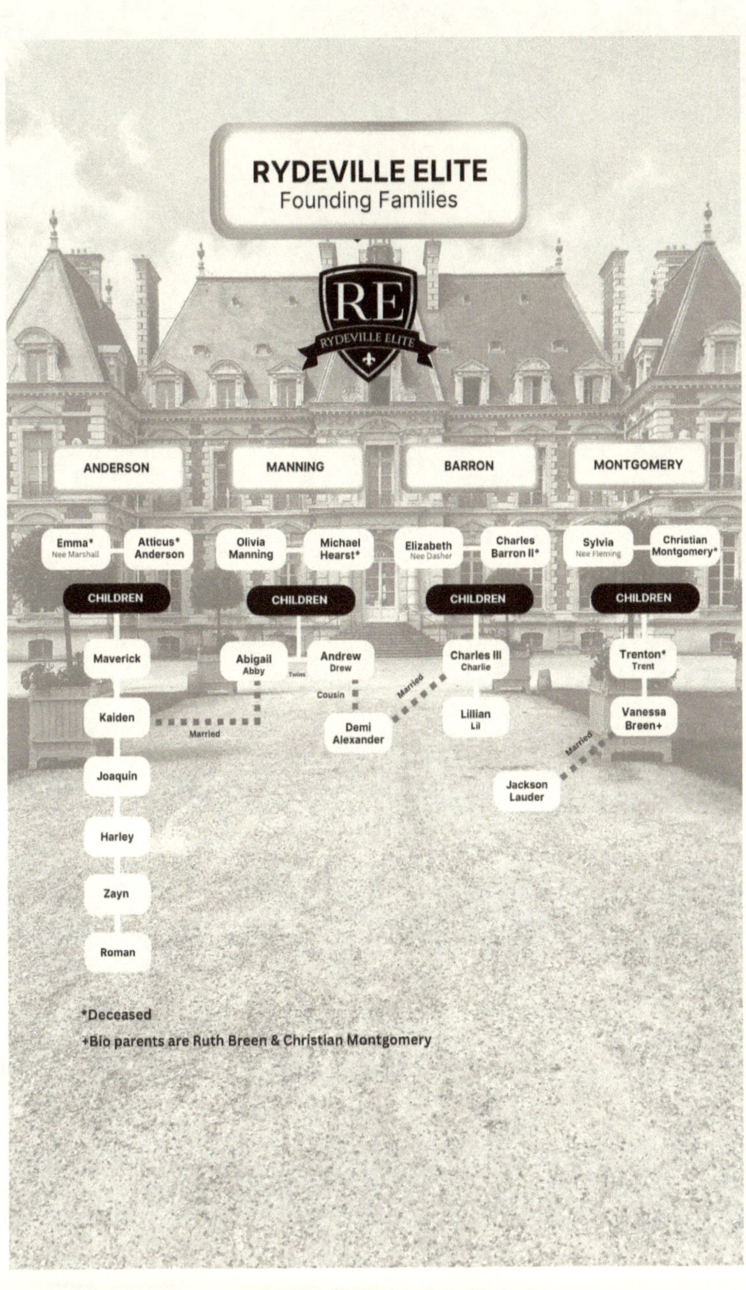

RYDEVILLE ELITE
Founding Families

RE
RYDEVILLE ELITE

ANDERSON
MANNING
BARRON
MONTGOMERY

Emma*
Nee Marshall
Atticus*
Anderson
Olivia
Manning
Michael
Hearst*
Elizabeth
Nee Dasher
Charles
Barron II*
Sylvia
Nee Fleming
Christian
Montgomery*

CHILDREN
CHILDREN
CHILDREN
CHILDREN

Maverick
Abigail
Abby
Andrew
Drew
Charles III
Charlie
Trenton*
Trent

Twins

Kaiden
Cousin
Married
Lillian
Lil
Vanessa
Breen+

Married
Demi
Alexander
Married

Joaquin

Jackson
Lauder
Married

Harley

Zayn

Roman

*Deceased
+Bio parents are Ruth Breen & Christian Montgomery

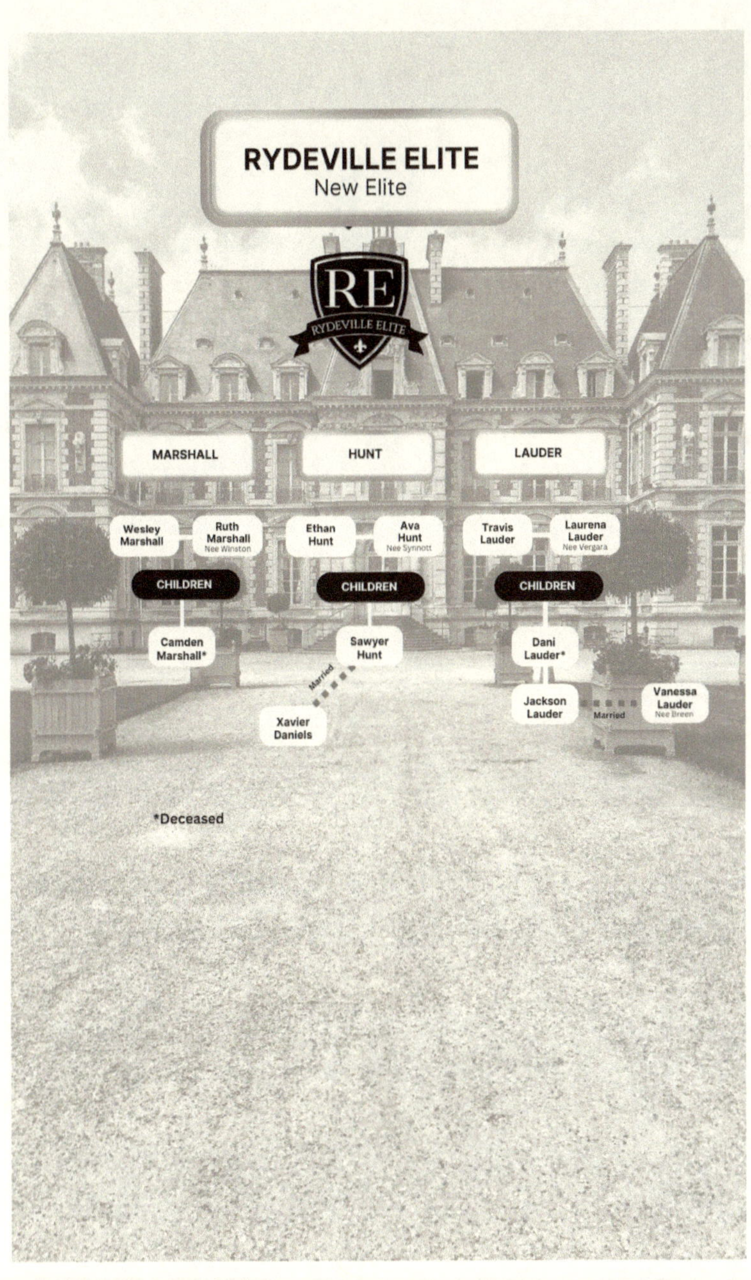

RYDEVILLE ELITE
New Elite
RYDEVILLE ELITE
MARSHALL
HUNT
LAUDER
Wesley Marshall
Ruth Marshall
Nee Winston
Ethan Hunt
Ava Hunt
Nee Synnott
Travis Lauder
Laurena Lauder
Nee Vergara
CHILDREN
CHILDREN
CHILDREN
Camden Marshall*
Sawyer Hunt
Dani Lauder*
Married
Xavier Daniels
Jackson Lauder
Married
Vanessa Lauder
Nee Breen
*Deceased

Drew

Chapter One
Drew

"She hasn't had a good week," Selena says as we hop out of the golf cart in the residential section of the facility and walk the rest of the way on foot. "Felicity has been meeting with her daily."

"I'm sorry to hear that." I drag a hand through my hair. "And I'm sorry I missed my visit on Monday. It couldn't be helped." I grind my teeth to the molars as I think of my wasted trip. It's been like this over the years. I get a breakthrough and think I'm close to finding the person or persons who set everything in motion, only to hit roadblock after roadblock and find the path closed to me. It's damn frustrating to have come this far and still not have all the answers I need.

"I know you're a busy man. She understands too."

Curtains twitch in the cabin next to the one we are walking toward, but I keep my focus on the gray door that is our destination, wondering what kind of reception I'll receive today. I can never predict what situation I'm walking into. "I appreciate you taking the time to greet me personally." Selena is crazy busy, and I haven't seen her for a while.

We stop at the door, and she turns to face me. "I know you're worried. I wanted an opportunity to talk to you. To reassure you." Her stunning face softens with compassion. "We've had other extreme cases, and those survivors pulled through. She will too." She lays a gentle hand on my arm. "It takes time. Every person is unique, just like their healing process. Recovery cannot be rushed."

"I understand, and I'm not impatient with the process or doubtful of the care she's receiving. I know Vera is in the best place. Getting the best treatment. I will continue to support her for as long as she needs me. It just hurts." I swallow a painful gulp. "To see her like this. To know..." A muscle clenches in my jaw, and I try not to go there.

Selena squeezes my arm. "My offer still stands. There is no shame in talking to someone, Drew. It would help."

"I'll consider it," I repeat for the umpteenth time. We both know I'll never take her up on the offer. Selena means well, but therapy will not quench this raging inferno continuously burning inside me.

Only revenge will quell those flames.

"I'm available to you any time you need to talk. That offer is always there too." Compassion shines from her eyes and I know she means it.

Selena Kennedy—the founder and owner of Moonlight, a facility for survivors of sexual trauma and sex trafficking—is the only person on this Earth who knows the truth. I had to tell her when I found Vera and needed help. What she has achieved through Moonlight, over the years, is nothing short of miraculous.

I'm lucky she had a place for Vera because the facility is in high demand, being the only fully immersive rehabilitation program of its kind in the US. The entire Kennedy family is lobbying the government for more funding so they can establish other similar facilities around the US. I hope they are successful. I have seen how necessary and effective these services are. Society owes it to survivors to help them get their lives back on track. Especially the ones we failed to protect as kids.

"I appreciate it," I say.

She smiles softly while rapping on Vera's door. She should be expecting me. For the past year, I have been visiting every Monday and Friday, only missing my biweekly visits if I'm out of the state or out of the country on business or chasing a lead.

The door swings open, and I subtly suck in a breath. Vera has worn her hair cropped or in a bob since I brought her back to the US from Venezuela, but she's grown it out in recent months, and it's like looking at a ghost. Her unkempt, greasy blonde locks are the exact same shade as her sister's. The same piercing blue eyes stare back at me, but where I was used to warmth and vibrancy, Vera's angry glare is a reminder they are not the same person, no matter how much they resemble one another.

Her lips curl into a sneer. "Are you coming in, or do you plan to just stare at me all day?"

Selena clears her throat. "I'll leave you to talk in private. Call if you need anything." She looks directly at Vera. "Felicity has freed up some time this afternoon if you need to talk with her again."

"Thanks. I'll probably take her up on that." Vera scratches at the reddened skin on her arm. Her tone is softer, her expression warmer, as she stares at the woman who has gone above and beyond to help her. As a sex trafficking survivor, Selena understands more than anyone, and it's why the men and women who live here seek her out more than most. She gets it, and she has come out the other side. She is the physical embodiment of what their lives can be. Proof that their abusers and kidnappers haven't taken everything from them.

I truly hope Vera can get to that place one day, but there are times when it's hard to hold on to that hope. She has been through the most horrific hell and hasn't known anything else. My heart breaks every time I think of the things she has endured.

"I'll talk to you later." Selena waves as she walks off.

Vera turns and strides into the cozy cabin without uttering another word. Closing the door behind me, I follow her inside. Each full-time resident has their own one-bedroom one-bathroom cabin with an open-plan living space with a kitchen, dining area, and living room and a small patio and garden area at the rear.

The place is a mess. Dirty dishes clutter the sink, and half-eaten food-crusted cartons line the main counter. Books, clothes, and empty candy wrappers litter the floor. I'm betting it won't be long before she's forced to clean up. Selena has previously explained how maintaining a tidy space and a regular cleaning routine are important to fight depression.

Vera flops onto the couch in her stained sweats and plain tee, yanking a black, red, and white blanket up over her legs as she fixes me with a narrowed scowl.

Clearing some papers off one of the chairs, I sit and open the buttons on my suit jacket, getting comfortable as I stare at the troubled girl sitting across from me. "I'm sorry I wasn't able to visit on Monday."

She shrugs. "I've told you I don't care. I'm not your responsibility, and I don't need you to babysit me. We're nothing to one another."

"That's not true, and you know it." I try to hide my pain as my gaze roams her delicate features.

Vera drags bony fingers through straggly strands of her hair. "Liking what you see, *An-drew?*" She enunciates the word, and it's a true talent to sound both seductive and disgusted in the same breath. She leans forward, her eyes blazing with familiar fire.

Vera seems to have two main settings—mute and angry. It's understandable, and I never blame her. I briefly squeeze my eyes shut as I think of the life she led until I rescued her thirteen months ago.

"What's wrong, Drew?" Her voice is tinged with anger-coated sweetness. "Indulging fantasies in your head?"

I flinch when her hands land on my lower thighs and blink my eyes open at the contact. Vera is on her knees between my legs, licking her lips and staring at me with a look I've seen before. "We could role-play." She waggles her brows and presses up against me. "I'm only one year older than she was when you sent her away." Her hands crawl up my thighs. "I can please you so much better than she ever could," she adds with a provocative smile.

I reach out as her fingers inch toward my crotch, holding her wrists and stalling her motion, trying my best to be gentle because I never want to hurt her.

"My mouth drives men wild." She fights against my restraint as she snarls. "Want me to suck your cock and call you Daddy? You got it. Want me to part my cheeks so you can lick and fuck my ass? No problem. Want to cut me and make me bleed? Want to punch me while you fuck my pussy? Or how about fucking me with an inanimate object? Want to shove your fist so far inside me it—"

"Stop. Please," I implore, unable to deal with this particular persona today.

A bitter laugh bursts from her lips. "Come on, *An-drew*. Don't pretend like you wouldn't like any of those things. I see it, you know. All those dark wicked desires you think you keep hidden. News flash, you aren't hiding shit. I've known men like you all my life. It's all I know." She fights against my hold, and

I lift her up by her arms and plant her feet on the ground. Then I step around the chair, putting a solid obstacle between us.

"I am not like those men," I say through gritted teeth.

"Whatever you tell yourself to sleep at night." She rubs at her arm again. "She would never have been able to satisfy you, but I could. I'm experienced in all the ways she wasn't." In a lightning-fast move I didn't predict, she whips her soiled T-shirt off, exposing her bare upper body to me. Scars and puckered skin cover her chest and stomach, and I can't unsee it before I look away.

Memories of carrying her frail, battered body in my arms resurrect in my mind, and I relive the horrors of that day over again.

I'm yanked out of my head when her chest brushes against mine. I reel back as if burned, staring at her face with mounting uneasiness. When she's angry, Vera lashes out at a world that has only ever given her pain and suffering. I'm used to bearing the brunt of her anger on those days. She's thrown this shit at me before too, but she's never stripped in front of me, and it's a new level of hell.

"Vera, please stop this." I stare directly into her eyes. "You know I am here because I care about you. You're like a sister to me, and I want to help you. I don't want anything from you but for you to heal and start living the life you should have always had." I move around her, snatching her shirt from the ground and holding it out. "Cover yourself up and stop trying to piss me off. If my being here today is upsetting you and you want me to leave, I will go."

"I can't even do this right anymore." A sob rips from her throat as she grabs the shirt. I look away while she dresses herself. "I'm useless. A washed-up whore no one wants."

"That is not true." I look up, heaving a sigh of relief when I find her clothed and back on the couch. "The things you have been forced to endure do not define you."

"Now you sound like Felicity."

I reclaim my seat, mulling over my response carefully. I have spent a little time with her therapist because I needed to be coached on how to handle Vera's explosive moods and how to behave around her so I don't trigger her or cause her any further pain. Felicity updates me weekly. It's important we work together to aid Vera's recovery. She never divulges things told to her in confidence, only updating me on what I need to know.

I never want to hurt her. Jane would want me to take care of her baby sister, and I already feel like I'm failing.

I'll just add it to the list.

I clear my throat. "I'm no psychologist, but the things you were made to do don't sum up who you are as a person. You're only nineteen. You've got the rest of your life to work out what you want to do with it. Figure out who you want to be."

"What if I'm no good at anything else?" Her eyes fill with tears.

"You will find your place in this world, Vera, and I'll be there to support you every step of the way."

"I'm sorry," she blurts as tears roll down her face. "I don't know why I did that or said those things."

"It's fine. Forget about it. I just want to help."

"Why?"

"You're family, Vera, and I take care of my family. I'm just sorry it took me so long to find you."

"I'm just glad you found me at all," she whispers, and a solemnity settles in the air.

I can only nod. I wish I had found her sooner. I wish I had been able to find Jane in time. To find Silas.

"You're my only family," she adds, staring at me like she's

staring through me. The haunted expression on her face tears strips off what's left of my heart. "I have no memories, Drew. I don't remember my parents or Jane or Silas. I can't even tell you where we went after we left Rydeville because I don't remember anything. All I have are the photos you gave me. I have stared at that album repeatedly, willing the images to conjure some memory that might help, and there's nothing."

"Don't be hard on yourself. You were only three when you left Rydeville. Most people don't have memories of their early years. I barely remember anything myself." When you add in the trauma and her drugged-up-state, it's completely under-standable. I wish she did remember something from those early days because I've hit a brick wall, and I'm fearful I may never find the last remaining puzzle pieces.

"That's 'cause you're *ancient*."

She smirks, and I smile. I'll take teasing over her tears any day. "It feels like it some days," I truthfully reply.

Her features soften, and I'm glad her anger has faded. "You must have loved her a lot."

"I did. I do," I add because my love has never died.

"Thank you." She swipes at the moisture under her eyes. "I don't think I've ever properly thanked you for getting me out of that hellhole."

"You don't need to thank me for that. I wish I'd gotten you out years earlier."

"I wish I'd been more lucid so I'd seen you burn that shit-hole and all the monsters in it to the ground." Defiance shimmers in her eyes again.

"I wish I'd had more time to torture those fuckers because they got off lightly."

Well, not all of them did. Smug satisfaction spreads across my chest as I remember my time with Rafael. I never told Vera because I wasn't sure what the knowledge would do to her, and

I didn't want to jeopardize her recovery. I handed out vengeance on her behalf, and maybe someday I might get to tell her about it.

"They can't hurt anyone else ever again. You didn't just save me and the others you rescued that day. You saved countless future victims."

"Don't paint me as a hero. Please don't do that." My tone is harsher than I intended, but the look she's giving me now is worse than the look she sported when she was trying to seduce me. Jane's little sister would not look at me like that if she knew the things I've done. The people I've hurt. The people I've killed.

I am no one's hero. Least of all hers. I'm the reason she ended up living a nightmare. I'm the one who coaxed her father into leaving Rydeville that fateful day. It was all my idea, and the Ford family paid the price for my bad decision-making.

"If the hat fits, you should wear it."

I climb to my feet. "How about you grab a shower while I clean up and order us some lunch from the cafeteria?"

Throwing the blanket off, she stands. "Nice deflection. If Felicity were here, she'd call you out on it."

And that's another viable reason why I'll never see a therapist. "Let's be grateful she's not." Vera has enough nightmares without me adding to it. I remove my suit jacket and roll my shirt sleeves up as Vera walks across the room.

"Drew," she calls out, stalling at the doorway to the bathroom.

I turn to face her, raising a brow.

"You'll always be *my* hero." She grips the door frame in her slim hands. "I just want you to know that."

Chapter Two
Drew

An unexpected, unwelcome trespasser waits for me by my car when I approach it a few hours later. "What the hell are you doing here, and how did you know where I was?"

"Nice to see you too, buddy." Charlie pushes off the side of my SUV and walks toward me.

"That's not a fucking answer," I growl, unlocking my car with the fob.

"I'm staging an intervention, and this time, you're not pushing me away."

I reach my best buddy and drill him with a sharp look. "I don't know how to make this any plainer. Butt the fuck out, Charlie. This doesn't concern you."

"You're family, Drew, and I'm done being sidelined. I can't stand by and watch you do this alone anymore. I won't." He squares up to me, daring me with a challenging look.

"Demi know you're here and why?"

"Yes," he replies, surprising me. "She is on board with this."

"Then you're both fools. I've told you a million times I'm

keeping you out of this to protect you. Go home to your wife and kids, Charlie. I don't want or need your help," I say as I climb behind the wheel of my car.

"It's nonnegotiable, asshole." He wedges his body between me and the door before I can close it. Resting his palms on the top of my car, he leans into me. "Demi wants me to support you as much as I want to. She's worried about you."

"Tell her not to worry then. It's unnecessary."

"Is it?" He quirks a brow.

"It's none of your business. Stay out of it."

"Nope." He waggles his brows, and it irritates me to no end.

"Fuck off, Charles."

"I know where you were on Monday, and you don't have to say anything for me to know this is about Jane." He levels me with a look bordering on pity, and I fucking hate it.

"My answer is nonnegotiable, and it's still no." I shove him away, uncaring he stumbles and almost loses his balance completely when I slam my door shut and peel out of there.

After I have somewhat calmed down, I call Selena and Felicity together and give them a quick update on my visit with Vera. Then I hang up and call Ezra. "How the fuck does Charlie Barron know about my trip to L.A.?"

"I've got no idea," he calmly replies.

"I fucking pay you to know!" I roar, digging my nails into the steering wheel.

"I'll look into it," he says, and I hang up.

I'm still wired when I pull into the parking lot at the cemetery on the outskirts of Rydeville forty minutes later. Grabbing the flowers I just bought, I get out and begin the trek through the large graveyard, heading toward the ornate crypt at the back, alongside the bordering wall. Tree branches sway in the light breeze as I walk along the path, transecting rows of gravestones, some kept in pristine condition, others clearly neglected with overgrown weeds, faded pictures, and chipped engraving.

The crypt I paid to have built six years ago is tucked into a corner at the rear of the grounds as far from my father's grave as possible. Every other Manning, going back generations, resides in the private graveyard on the grounds of Mom's estate. There was no way Michael Hearst was ever getting buried there. Especially not after he turned Mom's family home to ash in the aftermath of his death.

The asshole had clearly left instructions, and some elite prick had carried them out. We never found out who was behind the arson, but it makes no difference now. What matters is Mom rebuilt a home for herself on the grounds, and in a twisted way, my father did her a favor. There were so many bad memories attached to the old Manning house. Mom's sprawling modern mansion isn't tainted by that bastard, and it's the fresh start she needed.

If I'd had my way, Michael Hearst would be rotting at the bottom of the ocean right now. But Mom is clearly a better person. Despite the hell he put her through and the years he stole from her, she wanted him buried. She said it was the right thing to do, and Abby and I didn't fight her on it, even if we didn't agree. There wasn't any service, but Mom organized the coffin and burial in the cemetery. Maybe seeing the plain gravestone was something she needed. A physical reminder the monster is dead. A celebration of our victory over his evil ass.

I've been lost in thought, not realizing my journey until I'm standing in front of my love's final resting place. FORD is engraved on the section over the gated door of the crypt, summoning a lump at the back of my throat like usual. Placing a hand on the stone wall, I bow my head and close my eyes, letting my torment run free. My chest heaves as pain obliterates me from all sides. Maybe it wasn't such a good idea coming here straight from a difficult visit with Vera.

It's all too raw.

It takes me longer than usual to unlock the gate and step inside.

Stained-glass windows let in slivers of light as I move around the square room lighting the various candles. Jane loved candles. Lavender was her favorite, and every time I visited her bedroom, she had a few lit.

The lump in my throat thickens as I approach the first raised marble box, which cossets all that's left of the love of my life. "Hey, beautiful. Sorry I haven't visited in a while."

I replace the flowers in the vase on top of the coffin and sit on the adjacent marble bench. Propping my phone against the side of the coffin, I press play on our playlist. It's the last one Jane made for me before I sent her and her family away from Rydeville to their demise. Pain spears through me as I place my hand on top of her coffin. "I'm so sorry I failed you, my love. That I continue to fail you." My eyes flit to the three matching empty coffins alongside her. "I swear I won't stop until I find Silas and your parents. I promise I will hunt the person or persons responsible to the ends of time until I've made them pay."

"Jane's *dead?*" a man with a familiar voice asks from behind me.

Anger wars with resignation as I turn to face Charlie.

Shock is splayed upon his face, joining the grief that rises in his gaze.

I don't bother asking how he knew to find me here. I wasn't tailed. I made sure of it. My guess is he put a tracker on my SUV last night after I left Abby and Kai's place following a boisterous dinner with Charlie and Demi and all their respective kids. It was remiss of me not to check this morning before setting off for Moonlight. It's a testament to how fucked up I am after my disappointing trip to L.A. How much it's all really starting to weigh on me after years searching for answers.

I scrub my hands down my face and sigh. "You really don't know when to leave it, do you?"

"You're my brother, and you're in pain. I can't do nothing anymore, Drew. Especially not now." He stares at Jane's coffin for an indeterminable time, and the air is thick with unspoken emotion.

My heart feels heavy, my body bone weary, and my mind drained as I watch my friend openly grieving. Jane and Charlie weren't particularly close, but they got along and became friends in time. Charlie was there for all of it. He witnessed me falling for Abby's best friend when I was fourteen and helped me plan a strategy where my father agreed to replace my intended bride with the girl I was madly in love with. He was there to prop me up when the guilt of all I was concealing from her almost suffocated me.

Charlie drops onto the bench beside me, sliding an arm around my shoulders in silent support. We stare at the coffin as the scent of lavender fills the chilly space and flickering shadows bounce off the stone walls. The musical story of our love plays quietly in the background.

"Who were you visiting at Moonlight?" Charlie asks after minutes of silence have passed. I'm surprised he's not asking about Jane. Maybe he senses I can't talk about her death in here.

"Vera Ford."

Instant recognition flares in his eyes. "She's got to be, what, seventeen or eighteen now?"

"Nineteen."

His Adam's apple bobs in his throat. "What happened to her?"

"She was sex trafficked as a little kid. At some point after they left Rydeville. From somewhere in Cali."

Horror floods his face, and I'm guessing he's thinking of his daughter. Jane is eleven now and the oldest of his three kids. "From what age, and for how long?"

"I haven't been able to find out exactly what happened or when, but it wasn't too long after they fled. Vera was three and a half when they left, and she has no recollection of anything that happened. No memories of her parents or her brother or sister. If she'd been a year or two older when taken, she'd most likely remember some things."

"Jesus Christ." Charlie props his elbows on his knees and cradles his head in his hands. "Fuck, Drew. Fuck, fuck."

"I know." I can barely speak over the messy ball of emotion lodged in my throat. "She has suffered unimaginable things. It's all she knows of life, and the trauma is severe."

When he lifts his head, tears cloud his vision. "I hate that I can imagine the kind of things she endured. I hate this is the world we live in. I hate the things we were forced to do. I hate that Jane's baby sister has led that life." He shakes his head and looks away.

"I found her thirteen months ago," I begin explaining because there's no point holding back now. "She was caged along with fifty-seven other boys and girls in a private compound in the mining district in Orinoco in Venezuela. Most of the kids were way younger, but her and a couple of others were kept when they got older and used as recruiters."

A fresh wave of horror ghosts over Charlie's pale face. "Fuck no."

"She tried to kill herself a month after I brought her back to the US. She was skin and bones when I found her and severely malnourished. I took her to Parkhurst and stayed while she was nursed back to health and weaned off the cocktail of drugs she'd been fed for years. Getting clean meant she was more aware of what'd been done to her, what she'd been forced to do, and the things she'd witnessed. She only remembers bits and pieces because they drugged her from a young age. But she remembers enough. She broke, Charlie. She fully broke, and I was so out of my depth. I knew she needed specialist care, and I didn't want to leave her at Parkhurst. I know they have good medical programs and top-notch, ethical medical professionals employed now, but I didn't want to see her in that kind of environment long-term."

"So, you called Selena," he surmises.

We have personal connections with the Kennedys, one of the US's most famous families. My sister's brother-in-law Rick is best friends with Kyler Kennedy, and through him, we've gotten to know Keven, Selena, and other members of the family. Keven is now part owner of HADK Cybersecurity Solutions Limited, alongside Zayn, Xavier, and Sawyer.

Selena knew Dani Lauder, Jackson's sister, from their mutual time spent imprisoned on an island where both girls were forced into sex slavery. We all regularly donate funds to support Moonlight, and I knew it was the perfect place for Vera. Though I wouldn't have forced her to stay there if she hadn't liked it and wanted to.

I bob my head. "She hasn't tried to harm herself since, but it's a long road to recovery, and there have been lots of ups and downs."

"What can I do to help?"

I shrug. "Keep donating to Moonlight, I guess. I'm not sure there's anything else anyone can do." I bite down on my lip. "I feel like I've failed her. It took me so fucking long after Jane's body was returned to me to track her down, and I haven't been able to find Silas or their parents. It's like they vanished into thin air."

"Jane was *returned* to you?" Charlie's troubled eyes probe mine. "How and by who?"

"That's another story and not one for here." My eyes drift to the marble coffin. "I won't let talk of that shit taint the peace Jane has finally found." At least I hope she's at peace. I can't bear to think of anything else.

"I want to know it all, Drew. You're not cutting me out of this any longer."

Chapter Three
Athena

"Your dad's on the line for you," my executive assistant Lucy says, poking her head through my open door. I work hard to hide the grimace from my face. There goes my good mood and my weekend plans I'm guessing. I should've known he'd call my office when I ignored the calls he made to my cell earlier.

Amos Martin is not known for his patience.

"Put him through," I say before closing my door and sitting back down behind my desk. Smothering my frustration, I pick it up when the call is transferred. "Father."

"Athena." He always manages to say my name in a slightly constipated tone. Before she died, Mom loved telling me the story of how she convinced Dad to name me after the goddess who personifies wisdom, warfare, and craftwork. I'm not sure Dad was ever entirely convinced, but I guess he must have loved Mom enough at that point to let her have her way.

"I left messages on your cell." Displeasure rifles through his tone.

"I haven't checked my cell all day," I lie. "I'm finalizing a project for a big client, and I didn't want any distractions."

"I have a mission for you. I need you at the house this weekend."

"Can you not tell me over the phone? I have plans." I promised my small team I'd take them out for dinner and drinks tomorrow to celebrate finishing this project, and I was planning on visiting the club tonight for a rendezvous with the man I've been fucking this past month.

Thoughts of his rough touch, dirty mouth, and skillful cock have me salivating and squirming on my seat. No man has ever fucked me so good or captivated me enough to want more, and I don't even know his name or what he looks like.

"Unmake them. Unless you'd prefer I assign this mission to your brother?"

"I'll be there," I snap, hating he uses Arlo to push my buttons because he knows I will always concede when confronted with that threat.

"I'll send the jet. My assistant will forward the flight details by text. I'll see you in the morning." He hangs up, and I lean back in my chair glaring daggers at the ceiling.

"Fucking prick," I hiss to myself as I try to remember if I hated my father this much as a little girl or if it was purely the consequence of his controlling ways as I grew older.

I'm thirty years old with a degree from Stanford, my own home, and a hugely successful marketing consultancy business, and I am still beholden to the asshole who gave me life.

I can only think of one way to end his control.

Ending him. Period.

Tapping my fingers on the desk, I contemplate the risks involved with killing my father. If I thought I could get away with it, I would do it in a heartbeat and feel no remorse. It wouldn't only release me. It would release Arlo too, and I want that more than anything. I want to spare my little brother the life our father has mapped out for him, and short of murdering the controlling bastard, I don't know any other solution.

Except killing a man of his standing in our society would warrant serious punishment if I was discovered. At least a lengthy stay in jail. Possibly a death sentence. And removing Amos Martin as the head of our family would ensure my brother is on the fast track to take his place. The men in charge of our world are changing things, for the better, but there are some things they cannot change, and these are the cold facts.

Rock, meet hard place.

And that's before I've even considered my bitch of a step-mom. I'd have to kill Cadance too, and while she's a total cunt to her only child, she *is* Arlo's mother. He's not fond of her, but I don't know how he'd feel about me slicing her head from her shoulders. And I'm not sure he'd be understanding if I murdered his father too. Unlike me, he likes Dad. Though I wonder for how long.

My thoughts turn to bloodthirsty plans for the woman who got rid of every framed picture of my mother from our house, and my imagination has no limits. In an ideal world, I'd kill her and my father, and there would be no repercussions. Arlo and I would be free to live our lives the way we want to. Maybe my brother would leave the West Coast and come live with me in Boston. There are several top private schools in the area and I'm sure I'd have no trouble enrolling him.

My cell pings with a message from Dad's assistant with my flight details, and I'm yanked out of the fantasy land in my head back into the steaming turd that is the real world.

Time to own this shitshow.

Pushing my aggravation aside, I head out to the reception area to break it to my team that we'll have to reschedule our celebratory dinner.

"Oh, it's you," Cadance says the following morning when I appear in the kitchen of the massive house in Lowell, California, that's been in the Martin family for generations.

"Try to contain your joy, Cady," I drawl, dumping my purse on the island unit and heading toward the fridge to grab a bottle of water.

"Don't call me that. You know how I feel about it."

It's *disrespectful*. She told me that when I was thirteen and I first used the nickname. Cadance had been living with us for four months, and I already detested her. Dad had implored me to make more of an effort with my new stepmother, and I tried despite the humongous grief that hovered over me like a perpetual thundercloud.

"You need to ask permission before taking anything," she adds as I open the refrigerator door and remove a water bottle. "This isn't your home. It's *mine*." Her over-inflated pouty lips curl upward as she attempts to put me in my place.

"Wrong, gold digger. It's my father's. You're just a temporary resident." I glance at the expensive gold watch on my wrist. "I'd say it's nearing time for Dad to replace you with a younger model." I rake a derisory gaze up and down her shockingly thin body. "No amount of cosmetic surgery or starvation attempts can turn back the clock. You'll be forty in two years. I bet it won't be long before he finds a third twenty-one-year-old wife."

Distaste crawls up my throat every time I think about how easy it was for my father to replace my mother so soon after her death. It happened far too quickly, and now I'm older and not suffocating under a mountain of grief, I know he must have been screwing this bitch while my mother was undergoing treatment for stage 4 cancer and making plans with her while his wife was on her deathbed.

I was always destined to hate Cadance even if she wasn't a prize cunt. That fact just makes it easier to suffer zero guilt for loathing my stepmother and taking every opportunity to piss her off and push her buttons.

"Unlike your mother, I've taken care of myself, and I take care of my man. He has no need to bed other women when I worship his cock and let him do whatever he wants to my body. I gave him the heir your mother couldn't." She shoots me a smug look, and I see red.

"My mother was a million times the woman you are." Slamming the bottle of water down on the counter, I stride toward Cadance with venom shooting from my eyes. "She was the best mom, and you're the shittiest one."

Indecipherable emotion shimmers in her eyes for a fleeting second. Then it's gone and her hands ball into fists at her side as she sneers at me. "Your mother was a washed-up wrinkly bag of pathetic bones who didn't know the first thing about holding on to a powerful man. She—"

A strangled sound rips from her lips as I wrap my hands around her scrawny neck and shove her back up against the wall. Having an additional six inches in height on her is helpful, and I revel in the panic splayed across her face as I lift her off the ground, still holding her by the neck while I push her forcefully against the wall. "You really are a stupid cunt, Cady. How many times have I told you not to spew crap about my mother? You know what I'm capable of. You know the things I have done. The things your husband has forced me to do. I could snap your neck right now, and I'm sorely tempted."

"Thena?"

I curse internally as Arlo's newly deep voice calls out from behind me. I have worked hard to hide this side of my life from him, and as much as I'd love to throttle this bitch until all the air leaves her lungs, I don't think my brother would appreciate me strangling his mother in front of him.

Reluctantly, I let her go, and she slumps against the wall, sucking exaggerated lungsful of air down her greedy throat. A choking sound rips through the air as Cadance bends over, clutching her neck and gasping in an overly dramatic fashion.

I roll my eyes and count to ten in my head before turning around to face my brother.

"What's going on?" Arlo asks, wearing a frown. He's in sweatpants and a hoodie, and his hair is slightly damp. I'm guessing he's just returned from his usual Saturday morning training session.

"It was just a minor disagreement. Nothing for you to worry about." I smile as I walk toward my brother, the sound of my high heels clicking off the tiled floor competing with the choked sobbing sounds coming from the diva at my back.

"What did she do?" he asks in a low tone when I reach him.

"She was talking crap about my mom again."

"You're going to pay for this," Cadance says over a sob as she shoves past me, still clutching her throat. "I'm telling your father."

"Knock yourself out, Cady." He won't do anything except utter a half-hearted condemnation. Dad needs me, and while he uses Arlo to control me, he knows he won't get me to do his bidding so easily if he forced me to bow to his vain, selfish, man-stealing whore of a wife. Especially after she insulted my mother to my face.

If I was Cadance, I'd be second-guessing the power I hold over my husband's cock.

I grimace the instant the thought lands in my mind because eww.

"You should do it," Arlo says, pulling me back into the moment.

"Do what?" I ask, brushing strands of messy blond hair out of his eyes.

"Kill her."

My eyes widen at the calm way he said it and the intense look on his face. "She's your mother."

"I hate her."

"Did she do something else?" I ask, wondering if he's been concealing stuff from me. We talk or text every day when I'm in Boston, but it's not the same as being here in the flesh. I try to make it home once a month, purely to see Arlo, but he's in his sophomore year now, and he recently made varsity, which is a massive deal at fifteen. It's the middle of football season, and he has practice and away games, and I don't often see a lot of him if I am here.

So, I haven't been around as much in person, and I'm wondering if shit is going down I know nothing about.

"No. She's actually afraid of me now." A devilish grin ghosts over his mouth and his big brown eyes glitter with pride.

Ice tiptoes up my spine. "Why?"

"She can't physically push me around anymore."

Arlo had a huge growth spurt last summer, and he looms over all of us now at six two. Not sure where he got his height from as dad is at least a couple inches under six feet and Cadance is only five four. I inherited my tall frame from my mom. Looking at old photo albums of her is like looking in the mirror at times. We have the same long blonde hair, blue eyes, and slim, statuesque build.

"What happened and why didn't you tell me?"

He puffs out his chest. "You don't need to look out for me, Thena. I'm not a kid anymore. I can look out for myself."

I grip his shoulders, peering deep into his eyes, trying not to overreact. "You're my little brother. My only brother. I will always look out for you."

"Like I'll always look out for you." Steely determination washes over his face. "I know what he makes you do, and you don't have to do it anymore. It's not your responsibility. It's mine. I'm the heir, and it's time I stepped up."

Horror engulfs my insides like flames pitching through my veins. "What the hell has happened?"

"Dad told me everything, and I've been to HQ. After football is over, I'll begin my training and—"

"No! No, no, no." I grip his shoulders tighter. "He promised me you'd be left out of it until you turn eighteen and can make your own decision."

"This *is* my decision." Pain flashes in his eyes as he wrangles out of my reach.

"You're too young to make it! And you don't have all the facts." There is no way our dad would have explained all the harsh realities of this life.

"I know my own mind, Athena, and I know enough. I want this. I want it real bad."

A muscle pops in his jaw, and I'm spiraling inside. Everything I have done has been to protect him. To keep him away from this world for as long as possible. Father fucking agreed, and he's gone behind my back. Fuck the consequences. I'm going to kill that motherfucker and grab Arlo. Find somewhere we can run and hide. Or maybe I'll appeal to the board. Perhaps they'll let us go as long as I have someone else lined up to take over as head of the family.

"You don't know what you're saying!" I cry. "You don't understand what you're giving up."

"Stop saying that!" he yells, looking all kinds of butt hurt. "You keep treating me like a little kid while you get to go on missions and have all the fun."

Oh my god. What the hell has my father told him? "There is nothing fun about it, Arlo. It's dangerous, and the things

I've had to do haunt me in my sleep. I don't want that for you."

He folds his arms and levels a glare at me. "It's not about what you want. Dad needs me to do this, and I want to do it. You're just pissed because you won't get to go on every mission now."

"Arlo, listen to me." I reach forward and clasp his face in my hands, trying to keep calm because arguing won't solve anything. All it'd do is alienate him and have him turning to our father. "Dad has manipulated me my entire life, and he's going to do the same to you. I'm trying to protect you. Whatever he's told you, I guarantee it's not the full truth."

"Dad wouldn't lie to me."

I understand why Arlo feels this way. Unlike his relationship with his mother, Arlo has a great relationship with our father. Of course, I know it's Dad's way of buttering him up for this very situation. He's been grooming him for years without Arlo realizing it. I thought I had more time, but I was a fool. Right now, I'm regretting sheltering my brother so much. He's so incredibly naïve, and I must accept some of the responsibility. I should have told him before Dad got to him, but there's still time to reach him. We have a bond he doesn't have with anyone else.

Footsteps echo on the floors out in the hallway, and I know I don't have much time. My eyes dart over Arlo's shoulder, checking the coast is clear before I whisper, "I will tell you everything. I'll hold nothing back and answer any of your questions if you hold off on making concrete plans."

His eyes light up with natural curiosity. "You mean that?"

"Yes. I would never lie to you." Unlike others I know. "Don't go anywhere. I'll find you after I've spoken with Dad, and I'll explain it all."

"Okay."

Grabbing his head, I press a kiss to his brow and vow to keep him safe. There is nothing I won't do to protect my brother. I'm prepared to make the ultimate sacrifice if it comes down to that.

As my father enters the kitchen, wearing a disgruntled look I'm used to, I swear I'll find a way to murder the prick if it's the only way to save my brother. Even if I die doing it.

Chapter Four
Athena

"Let's talk." Dad drills me with an impatient look.

I warn my brother with my eyes as I step back. Arlo nods, and I rein my fear in knowing he won't do anything rash until we have spoken further. I push it from my mind for now, needing my wits about me for this conversation with my father.

"How was practice?" he asks Arlo.

"Good. Coach is happy."

My father's smile is genuine, his pride in his only son authentic. I have never been on the receiving end of such smiles, irrespective of my achievements, because I was born the wrong sex. For years, having an heir to take over was all he spoke about. The day Arlo was born was the best day of his life.

Fear creeps up my spine again, and I wonder if I'm the naïve one to believe I could ever save Arlo from his fate.

"We'll talk in my study," Dad says, refocusing his attention on me.

I give my brother a quick hug and grab my purse, walking out alongside my father.

"Must you goad Cadance all the time?" he asks as we stride side by side toward the rear of the house where his large study resides.

"She goads me too, and I've told her talking shit about my mother is not acceptable, but she continues to do it."

A sigh cleaves from his lips. "She can't help it. She's a naturally jealous woman."

My eyes pop wide. "It's not jealousy, Dad. It's called being a complete cunt."

"Language, Athena. My god."

"Come on, Dad. Don't act like I'm three."

"You represent this family, and no child of mine will act so uncouth."

"That's a bit rich considering the things you force me to do. You have no problem getting me to seduce men of your choosing with said cunt, but I'm not allowed to mention the word?"

He scrubs his hands down his face. "You test my patience too much."

"I could say the same," I reply as he opens the door to his study.

He steps aside to let me walk in first. "We're too alike," he says, and I almost choke on my tongue. "We're bound to clash on occasion."

That's putting it mildly.

I take a seat on one of the high-backed leather chairs in front of the roaring fire, smoothing a hand down the front of my red pantsuit as he fixes drinks.

"I know I haven't always done right by you, Athena," he says, and I'd fall over if I wasn't already seated. "And it's possible I've been far too hard on you," he adds, walking over to the fire and handing me a whiskey glass. "But I am proud of you. No man I know has a daughter who comes even close to matching you for beauty, intelligence, and skill." He claims the seat beside me, placing a brown paper folder on the coffee table and raising his glass to his lips.

I stare at him as I swirl the amber liquid in my glass, wondering how many of these he's had already today. Before I can fall into the trap, I remember the kind of man he is. He's sucking up to me because he knows Arlo has told me. And my ire is back. "I am the woman you forged me to be, Father. Let's avoid pretenses. You have used my brother to control me, and I did it because you promised you would leave him out of this until he's eighteen, but you lied." I glare at him before knocking back a large mouthful of my scotch.

"I had no choice. My hand was forced."

I sit up straighter as prickles of apprehension cascade over my flesh. "In what way? What don't I know?"

"This is why I needed to speak to you in person. We have a problem, and the board has asked me to handle it." He puffs out his chest, proud as a peacock, and I'm trying to work out why the board would trust him of all people if they had some top-secret mission.

"The board has specialist teams to handle high-level missions. Why come to you?"

"This is very sensitive, and it dates back to Rhett Carter's time."

Mention of that man sends shivers ricocheting all over my body and not in the same way my sex-club fuck buddy does.

"They want no one to know about it," I surmise, and he nods.

"I was there when this happened, so I have a vested interest. The board knew I'd want to be involved. And they know you are efficient and discreet. That you'll get the job done with the least amount of noise."

"What exactly are they asking of me?" I inquire before taking a sip of my drink.

Dad taps the top of the file on the table. "It's all in there, but the short version is there was a situation years ago with an illegal sex trafficking ring run on the down-low by Carter in South America."

I know what he's referencing. I've made it my business to know as much as I can about our world. Information is power, and I spend every second of my free time researching and learning. "I know about it. I thought it was shut down."

"So did we, but it seems we were wrong. There were pockets still in operation, and our fear is there could be more. Some asshole is sniffing around, looking into things he has no business interfering in." His eyes narrow to slits as he grips the edge of the chair. "We don't need that kind of heat."

"You want me to kill him," I say before knocking back the rest of my drink.

"Ultimately, yes, but first we need you to get close to him. To spy on him and find out exactly what he's up to, what he knows, and who he has told. We need to destroy all evidence he might have acquired. If he isn't stopped, he's going to draw too much attention. This can't come out. It will have serious consequences. This goes all the way to the top. So, the approach is two-pronged. To shut down the rest of these operations and to find out what this elite bastard knows. When we know it's safe, you will end him."

"Why should I do anything you ask now you've broken your promise and drawn Arlo in?"

"Because his life is in danger."

All the blood leaches from my face. "Explain," I snap, feeling the whiskey sloshing uncomfortably in my stomach.

"This asshole has been compiling information on certain families, including ours. We don't know what he intends, but he is targeting heirs. The board is sufficiently worried, and I was told Arlo had to be initiated and trained."

Shit must be real if the board is making those kinds of demands because granting kids free will and decision-making powers is a big part of their mantra. They would only dictate Dad do this if they genuinely believed Arlo's life was at risk. In light of this information, I can't fight to keep him out anymore. He needs to understand what is going on, what he's up against, and to have the requisite skill set to defend himself. Arlo is proficient with a gun, and he attended Krav Maga classes for several years, so he isn't completely vulnerable. But the kind of skills and cunning he needs to operate in our world is lacking, and he's going to require intense training to catch up.

"I want to help. I can train him."

"You live in Boston." Dad's lips tease at the corners as he lifts the glass to his mouth.

"I can work remotely from Lowell," I say, mentally rearranging projects as my mind churns. "I hired and trained junior consultants for this very reason." I had to have backups because Dad often calls me out on missions at short notice, and I didn't want my business to fall apart because I was MIA for days or weeks at a time. I'm glad I invested time and money in my small team, so they can hold the reins while I get my brother up to speed.

"You're needed in Boston. That's where the mark is." He lifts the file and slaps it onto my lap. "Everything you need to know is in there, either printed or on the digital key."

I flip open the folder, staring at the familiar face staring back at me from the profile page. Drew Manning is a handsome psychopath with his messy, dyed dirty-blond hair, calculating, sultry brown eyes, high cheekbones, sharp jawline dusted with dark hair, and full lips I'm certain are expert in delivering pleasure.

"You've got to be shitting me, Dad." My eyes lift to his. "Manning isn't your run-of-the-mill asshole elite bastard. There is still talk of what he did to that MC when he was only fifteen. He's the monster you warn kids about, and he should not be underestimated."

Dad's brows climb to his receding hairline. "You know him?"

I scoff. "Not personally, but did you really expect me to move to the East Coast and not investigate any potential threats in the area? I know all the criminal entities operating in New York and Boston. The elite were top of my list."

An almost proud smile crests over his face. "It's such a pity you weren't born a boy."

"I'm not even going to dignify that bullshit with a reply."

"It's a compliment, Athena."

"It's a fucking insult! The fact I'm a woman shouldn't make any damn difference!"

"It's the way of our world, and you should be grateful for the opportunities I've given you. Most women are married off and under their husband's thumb by your age."

I suppose I can be grateful for that small mercy. Though I'm sure my father will turn his thoughts to that now he's bringing Arlo into the fold. If Amos thinks he's going to force me into marriage with some sap, purely to strengthen ties, or for traditional reasons, like most of the arranged marriages in our society, he can think again. I don't want to get into it now though. This bomb he's just dropped in my lap requires my sole attention.

"Drew Manning is not just any mark, Dad. He's a cold-blooded killer with sharp instincts. How do you expect me to get close to a man like that without him getting suspicious?"

"You're presenting a proposal to him at Manning Motors

on Tuesday. They're rebranding, and your company is the perfect fit for the project."

"I can't prepare a professional proposal in three days! I don't even have the brief!"

"It's all on the key, and you don't need to worry about it. My contact has already prepared the perfect proposal. Just tweak it a little, and show up looking sexy and confident, and you'll have him eating out of your hand." He scrutinizes my hair with narrowed eyes. "You'll need to dye your hair."

"What?" He's never made any such demands of me in the past. If the mission is to seduce some target, he's always left it up to me. I am particularly skilled in that area.

"He doesn't date blondes."

"He doesn't date, period." Drew rocks up to corporate and social events with a different woman on his arm every time. He's never photographed with the same woman twice, and he's never been known to have a girlfriend.

"I was trying to be polite. He won't fuck you if you're a blonde, so dye your hair."

Dad can get fucked. I'm not dying my hair. I've traded enough of my soul to do his bidding.

He doesn't get my hair.

"This won't be an easy task, and it's going to take time."

"I'm aware, but don't take too long. Remember your brother is a target. Right now, we don't know why. You are doing this to protect Arlo and our way of life. Don't fall for anything that manipulative bastard might say. He's the enemy, and he needs to be taken down."

"I don't need reminding. I'll riddle his hot body with bullets before he has a chance to get anywhere near, Arlo. That is a guarantee."

Chapter Five
Drew

"Harder," she moans as I bring the leather paddle down on the lower part of her ass and the tops of her legs. My cock jerks, leaking precum when she cries out as it makes contact with her sensitive flesh. Her ass must be reddened and stinging because I've been hitting her for longer than usual tonight. We could move to the bondage room, the orgy room, or voyeur room, and I could salivate over the marks I regularly leave on her body. Except I like it here in our own private dark dungeon on the lower level of the prestigious club.

Not being able to see is the only downside to fucking in the dark. Of course, it has advantages too. Being forced to use my imagination—to visualize the marks I leave on her body—is the biggest turn-on, and it never fails to get me going.

The thrill of not knowing who I'm fucking adds to the appeal as well.

Maintaining my anonymity is another big draw.

For years, when I first started coming to this elite sex club in the city, I fucked women in the open and very quickly gained notoriety. It got to the point where any time I showed up, I was besieged by women begging me to fuck them, and it quickly got irritating.

Now, I fuck in private, preferring to keep my activities to myself and my partner of choice.

I usually alternate partners every couple of months, but I'm tempted to keep Vixen for longer. Her body turns me on like no other. The way her hot pussy grips my cock is addictive, and I have to invoke massive self-control when I drive my dick in her tight asshole. The woman has no gag reflex either, easily swallowing all of my nine inches.

But mostly it's her craving for pain with her pleasure that gets my juices flowing.

"Again, Beast," she purrs in a sexy throaty voice.

I'm tempted to ask if this is punishment for something that's happened, but that would be crossing a line. This is about sex. Mutual pleasure and pain, and we don't bring our personal lives into it.

I hit her a few more times on her ass and her legs while stroking my straining cock in a leisurely manner, wanting to hold back for as long as possible.

She's whimpering and panting as I lean over the spanking bench, covering her warm body with my own. Fisting her long hair in my hand, I tug her head back and press my lips to the pulse point on her neck before moving them to her ear. "Do you want more, slut, or are you ready for my cock?" I bite her earlobe, and the startled cry sends lust shooting through my veins.

"Fuck me, Beast. Fuck me so hard I'll be feeling it for days."

I reach under her body and palm one large soft breast. "Is there anything on your list you don't want to do tonight?" Sometimes, she'll mention she's not in the mood for a particular kink.

"Nothing is off-limits tonight. Hurt me good. I want to feel pain."

"Use your safe words. If I go too far, tell me." I use a classic traffic lights system with the women I fuck at the club. Green to keep going, amber to slow down or check in, and red to stop.

I yank on her nipple, twisting and pinching it as she writhes underneath me. My erection digs into her ass, and I wet my lips in anticipation. "You're such a perfect slut. I'm going to hurt you real good, sweetheart, and you're going to love it," I growl, wanting to sink my teeth into her neck and mark her good. But no visible marks is one of the conditions of our agreement.

Sometimes, I chuckle at how PC this place is. Things were so different in the past. Back then, the elite sex clubs only catered to male needs. Women were playthings. Told to spread their legs and open their mouths while filthy animals ravaged their bodies and wreaked havoc on their minds. Under Robert Huss's leadership, the elite is vastly different. I have no doubt there are underground clubs, serving the traditionalist core who have mocked the advancements and our move to more legitimacy, but they are the minority now.

Here, I sign agreements with every new fuck partner in advance so we both know boundaries and limits before we get down to screwing. It's been freeing in a way I hadn't expected. There isn't much I won't do, and there are only a few things I insist on: complete anonymity in the dark, fake names, no kissing on the mouth, regular testing, condoms, and no blondes.

"I'm ready," she says, and I lick the side of her neck before I slowly move down over her gorgeous body.

There is something intensely intimate about learning a woman's body from touch alone. Without sight, I'm forced to concentrate on other senses. My palms roam her toned curves as I trail a leisurely path down her body, molding my hands around the dip in her waist and over the slope of her hips. My mouth explores the muscular planes of her back as I nip and bite my way down her soft skin. My teeth sink into the fleshy globes of her ass, and I slam my arm over the backs of her thighs to hold her in place as I devour her ass, biting her tempting flesh and sucking on it in a way I know will leave obvious marks.

I part her thighs while I feast on her ass, driving three fingers into her pussy, growling into her skin as her slick heat latches on to my digits. The noises she's making are the best aphrodisiac, and my dick is swollen with need. I roughly pump my fingers in and out of her wet cunt, adding another digit and stretching her wide.

"Rougher," she pants, and I move off the bench, removing my fingers and standing between her thighs.

"Ass in the air," I command, working my dick in my hand as she gets into position. I pull her down to the edge and thrust her ass up higher. Then I shove four fingers back inside her cunt, thrusting savagely as I pinch her clit with my free hand. She cries out as she moves back against me, working in tandem with my fingers, before shattering, screaming as she comes, jerking her hips and coating my fingers with the evidence of her arousal.

I withdraw my fingers and lift her off the bench, shoving her to the ground on her knees. Fisting a hand in her hair, I bring her face to my dick and force my fingers into her mouth. "Suck. Taste yourself." She licks my fingers eagerly, moaning as she cleans her cum from my digits, and it's hot as fuck. I remove my fingers and force her mouth wide.

"Keep it open," I command as I twist her hair around my hand and manipulate her movements. When her warm breath fans the tip of my dick, I slam into her mouth, fucking her with brutal thrusts as I pull on her hair and shove her face right into my crotch. She gargles around a mouthful of my dick, greedily slurping and sucking, and I close my eyes, arching my head back as I savor the sensation of her skillful lips wrapped around my shaft.

Before I come, I pull out of her mouth and command her to remain on her knees while I grab the things I left on the table earlier.

She yelps as I attach the nipple clamps to both her breasts. "Problem, slut?" I ask, yanking her head back by her hair.

"No, Beast."

"Turn around, stick your ass in the air, and part those cheeks for me, bitch."

A surge of fresh lust washes over me as the air stirs, and I know she's obeying. "Don't change position until I tell you." I wrap the hair tie around her hair in a high ponytail, giving it a few sharp tugs. She moans, and it's like a siren's call. My need to fuck her into the ground is almost insurmountable. Moving her hair out of the way, I fix the collar around her neck, tightening it to the max before I pull the attached chain to the side, letting it sit on the ground for now. Then I kneel on the padded ground behind her, spreading her thighs wider as I run my hands up and down her upper legs, grazing my nails against her silky flesh as my good little slut stays in position.

I roll a condom over my hard length as I wonder about this woman who seems to crave pain as much as I do.

What demons haunt her dreams?

What things does she want to forget?

Warming lube in my hand, I drizzle it between her parted cheeks and all over my cock and my fingers. I spend a few minutes teasing her puckered hole, stretching it as I smack her ass with my hand. Bringing my cock to her hole, I put the tip in as I lean down and grab the chain. I pull it back, holding it loose as I leave my dick where it is, letting tension build in the air.

Her thighs tremble against my legs, and I sense the fearful

expectation, the heightened anticipation as she waits for me to fuck her. When I can stand it no longer, I drive into her ass in one fast savage thrust, and her screams bounce off the sound-proofed walls as I fuck her hard. I yank on the chain, pulling it tight around my fist so her head is pulled back while I slam into her over and over. Strangled sounds pepper the air while I tug repeatedly on the chain and dig my nails into her hip while I pound her tight ass.

All sense of humanity leaves me as I let go, fucking her with brutal intensity. Usually, I like to wrap my hands around her neck and choke her, but I didn't trust myself today. Knowing I'm meeting Charlie tomorrow night to tell him everything has had me on edge all weekend. I'm wired and not in full control. I don't want to accidentally kill her while riding my cock.

Those thoughts keep me grounded in the moment as I destroy her ass while tugging on her neck, pulling her hair, and leaving bite marks all over her shoulders and her back.

I fuck her pussy after her ass, pressing her head down to the mat and keeping a solid grip on her neck as I let rip on her warm cunt. She cries out, pleading for mercy as I bring her to the edge of orgasm several times before I take pity on her and let her come.

With one last wild thrust, I roar as my release thunders through me, filling the condom with ropes of cum.

I pull out and remove the collar and clamps and cradle her in my arms while she drinks a bottle of water. "Are you okay?" I ask, smoothing a hand down her hair.

"I'm fine," she says, moving off my lap, and I let her go. "Thanks, Beast." Surprising me, she leans in and kisses my cheek before dragging her fingers through the scruff on my chin and cheeks.

I hate that I don't hate it.

"I needed that." Her voice is softer, sounding different.

"Yeah." I can relate.

No more words are spoken as she walks away, heading into the pitch-dark female changing room. The lock clicks shut, and then a trickle of light filters out from under the door.

I stay on my knees on the floor for a while longer. My temporary distraction is gone now Vixen has left, and my thoughts are crowded with long-ago memories of an angel with long blonde hair and the biggest blue eyes.

I wonder what Jane would think of me now.

And not for the first time, I wonder if there would've been a forever for us if she'd known the true nature of the beast she was in love with.

Chapter Six
Athena

"Come in," the older woman says, opening the door to a decent-sized office and ushering me inside. Her smile is tight as she drags her gaze slowly over me from my navy and red stilettos to my fitted designer navy pantsuit with white silk blouse and up over my vibrant red lips, carefully applied make up, and my sleek, thick blonde hair tied in an elegant chignon and pinned in place with a dazzling diamond clip. My mom's pearls wrap around my neck, and I'm wearing the matching bracelet around my wrist.

I took time and effort with my appearance, deciding on a modern classical look that is sophisticated and understated sexy. I know I look good, but you could never tell from the expression on Belinda Markham's face.

"Do I have something on my face?" I ask, thrusting my shoulders back and eyeballing the shorter woman with faux confidence.

I'm not the type to get nervous pitching to clients, but I'm on edge today for a variety of reasons. While hot sex with the mysterious dark beast helped to deflect some stress, his touch isn't capable of performing miracles.

Since my long conversation with Arlo on Saturday, I've been struggling to focus. My brother is determined to throw himself headfirst into our world, and nothing I said deterred him. So, I've got to accept it and work out new ways to protect him. Starting with ending this threat Manning poses.

Too much is resting on today's presentation, and I feel ill-equipped because it's not my pitch and I've had the sum total of ten hours of sleep since I left Cali late on Saturday night. Apart from my club visit, I've been working around the clock for the past two days tweaking the prepared presentation I was given, trying to give it some unique touches. I have also read everything I could find online about Manning Motors and its CEO, but I definitely could have used more time. Usually, I come to these things fully prepared and feeling completely in control, knowing I can handle anything that crops up because I have explored every possible question and objection.

Today, I'll be winging it, and I don't like taking chances even if Dad says it's a foregone conclusion. My business reputation is at stake, and I can't afford to fuck up. Winning this contract is too important, and Arlo's life may depend on it.

The constipated look disappears from Belinda's face, and she emits a sigh as she closes the door. "Forgive me, that was rude. You don't have anything on your face," she adds, gesturing me toward the chair in front of her desk. "You look professional and polished."

"Then what's the issue?" I ask because I know there is one. I take a seat as instructed, setting my purse and briefcase on the floor at my feet.

"Didn't your father explain about blondes?"

My eyebrows crawl up my brow. "That was serious?"

Honestly, I didn't give it much attention, and it hadn't crossed my mind since my father mentioned it.

"Yes."

I drill her with a look. "Are you telling me Drew Manning would refuse the perfect candidate for a job because she has blonde hair?"

"No. I—"

"Then what's the problem? As VP of marketing, surely, this hire is ultimately your call?" Father made out like this presentation was only a formality.

"It is, but he has final approval. Rebranding the organization is a big deal. This project will take months to conclude and it requires working closely with our internal team. Your father made it clear he wants you working from our offices, which means Drew will see you every day, and that's where the problem lies."

"What does he have against blondes?"

"I'm not quite sure, but he's never seen with blondes, and any time we hire models for official photoshoots, his instructions are always *no blondes*."

What is it with men and their no blondes rules? Is this a Boston thing? Beast had that listed on his requirements. Truth be told, that clause made me sign the agreement. Deny me something, and I'll always challenge you. We meet in the dark, and we've agreed on complete anonymity, so it's not like he'll ever find out I broke one of his terms.

For a fleeting moment, I wonder if Beast and Manning are one and the same, but I dismiss the thought as quickly. That would be too coincidental, and I don't believe in coincidences. In a city the size of Boston, it's not inconceivable there are two men with aversions to blonde-haired women.

"Then I guess I'll just have to blow him away with my intelligence and charm so he overlooks the fact I'm a blonde."

"At this point, it's our only play." She rubs at her temples, and I wonder what my father is holding over her to force her to do his bidding.

"I'm good at what I do, Miss Markham, and I want this job on its own merit not just because my father wants me here."

"You wouldn't be here unless you were. I have worked tirelessly to climb the career ladder at Manning Motors, and no amount of blackmail would make me fuck up at the office." She leans back in her seat and studies me again. "I have researched your work and spoken to all your previous clients. They speak incredibly highly of you and your team."

"That is good to hear. I pride myself on being the best, and I dedicate one hundred and fifty percent to every project. I won't be slacking on this project. I'll give it my all."

"Good. I expect nothing less." She glances at the expensive watch on her slim wrist and stands. "It's time."

I rise to my feet and grab my things before following her out of her office, along a wide corridor, and around the corner to a row of meeting rooms. She stops in front of mahogany double doors and turns to look at me. "Mr. Manning is incredibly smart, and he doesn't suffer fools. He can sniff out imposters in no time. Answer honestly. While you need to impress him, it's okay to admit vulnerability. It's far better than telling a lie."

I nod as I force the butterflies swooping into my chest to take a hike.

I've got this.

There is no other outcome that is acceptable.

Lifting my head, I keep my back straight and my smile gracious as Belinda knocks on the door, and a man with a deep voice tells us to come in. Two men and one young woman are seated on one side of the long glossy black table with their backs to the impressive floor-to-ceiling window that highlights the view of downtown Rydeville in the near distance. Manning

Motors relocated from the original HQ on the outskirts a few years ago when their growth necessitated a larger premises.

"Right on time as usual, Belinda," the older man with the salt-and-pepper hair says, wearing a smile as he gets up and walks toward us. "You must be Athena Lewis," he says, extending his arm toward me.

I shake his hand firmly, maintaining eye contact as I smile all while I feel Manning's eyes boring a hole in the side of my head. "I am. It's a pleasure to meet you, Mr. Grant. Thank you for the opportunity to present to you all today."

"Let me introduce you to our CEO," the chief marketing officer says, letting my hand go.

I draw in a subtle breath as Drew Manning climbs to his feet and walks toward us. His presence instantly dominates the room, and it's like the air particles separate to let him pass through. Dark energy fills the space, and it's impossible to look away. His eyes are glued to me as he approaches, his intense inspection causing all the fine hairs on the back of my neck to lift. The air is thick with tension as he stops a couple feet in front of me.

He stares at me, his gaze darting from my eyes to my hair, and a slight frown mars his smooth brow.

Up close, he is completely captivating in a way few men are. The pictures I have seen of him online and in the file Father gave me do not do him justice. Gone is the almost preppy look he sported post college when he first took up the mantle at his family business. Now, he looks like the quintessential bad boy with his artfully messy dark hair streaked with blond, the facial hair lining his chin and sculpted jawline, the bulging muscles barely contained behind his designer black suit, and glimpses of ink crawling up one side of his neck and sneaking out from under the sleeves of his shirt. But it's the intensity of his heated stare and the wickedly dark promise behind those sultry brown eyes that cements it.

Lust coils low in my belly the longer he stares at me without saying anything, and I wonder what it would be like to be the sole focus of his attention. I bet he's obsessive when he wants something and he doesn't back down until he gets it.

Mr. Grant clears his throat, claiming both our attention, and whatever that was is now broken. Belinda's boss offers Manning a semi-apologetic look when his daggered gaze settles on the older man.

Manning turns back around, pinning that intensity on me again. He slowly extends his arm, holding my eyes captive the entire time. "Drew Manning," he says in a sinfully sexy voice that sends shivers cascading up my spine. "Thank you for taking the time to present to us today."

His large warm palm glides against my smaller less callused one, and he grips my hand in a solid handshake. "Thank you for the opportunity to pitch for your business. AMC Solutions would be honored to work with Manning Motors." It's a miracle the words came out of my mouth because I'm struggling to maintain composure in the face of his overwhelming presence.

I knew Drew Manning was a powerful dangerous man, but if I didn't, this greeting would have confirmed it.

How can anyone get work done around here with him? I bet the women in the office cream their panties at the sight of him every day.

"Now all the sucking up is done, shall we begin?" he asks, his lips tipping up at the corners when I realize I'm holding his hand prisoner.

I withdraw my hand, just about managing not to blush like a schoolgirl. "Sounds good."

"This is my personal assistant, Hilary." He tips his head at the young redhead with the quirky purple glasses.

Hilary hurries around the table to shake my hand. "Nice to meet you, Ms. Lewis."

"Likewise, and please call me Athena."

"That's an unusual name," Drew says as he holds out a chair on the opposite side of the table for me.

"Thank you," I say as I drop into the plush gray velvet chair. "It was my mother's choice. She picked it when she was a little girl." Drew pushes my chair in and Belinda takes a seat beside me, hooking up a laptop to the screen at our backs. "She was insistent if she had a daughter she wanted to name her Athena. She was a big fan of Greek mythology as a child and an avid reader."

"If I'm not mistaken, Athena was the warrior goddess and a counterpart to Ares," Drew says, reclaiming his seat across from me as I extract my notes from my briefcase.

"She was also the goddess of craftmanship and known for her inventive mind," I reply as Belinda tees up the presentation.

"And which are you?" he asks, tipping his head to one side. "The creator or the destroyer?"

"You're assuming I'm either of those things because of a name bestowed on me long before I was ever born?" Incredulity drips from my tone.

"I'm not assuming anything."

His brown eyes pin me in place, and momentary fear freezes me in my seat.

Does he know who I am?

Is he aware this is a setup?

No, he can't know. It's impossible. I use the name Lewis professionally to hide my real name, and the experts in our world have carefully crafted a false identification and history for me in the event anyone starts looking. Our people are masters at this stuff, and there is no way he knows who I really am.

I allow myself to relax a smidgeon, forcing my fear deep down inside.

He continues staring at me, and it's unnerving. Belinda kicks me under the table as she slides the laptop in front of me.

"If I had to choose between those options, I'd think the answer is obvious, Mr. Manning," I say as I rise to my feet. "I invent strategies that enable businesses to achieve their growth plans and unparalleled success." I fix him with a broad smile. "I build. I don't destroy."

Unless you threaten me and mine, and then all bets are off.

Chapter Seven
Drew

She's got bigger balls than most of the men in this building. I like she's not easily intimidated, and she's clearly as intelligent as she is beautiful, but we won't be hiring her. It might seem ironic or hypocritical, but I despise nepotism, and it's obvious Markham or Grant, or maybe both of them, have worked on this pitch with Athena, and I already know they're going to push for her firm to win the coveted contract.

I don't usually let personal bias or emotion dictate business decisions. That's a slippery slope. But there is something about this woman that gets under my skin, and I can't have her around for the next six months.

Athena progresses effortlessly from slide to slide, speaking passionately about our values and her ideas for rebranding the business—if they even are *her* ideas—and how it will align to our goal of growing revenue by twenty-five percent in the next three years.

She carries herself with poise, but there's a stealthy catlike resemblance to the way she moves that has me intrigued.

Though she's focused on her presentation and she rotates eye contact to watch us for cues ensuring she has our attention, her predatory gaze scans her surroundings, drinking everything in with a subtle cunning lens that implies there is a lot more to her than meets the eye. Confidence infuses every movement of her body, but there's a stiffness there too, like she's primed and ready for an ambush and jonesing to take any detractor down.

She fascinates me more than any woman has in a long, long time.

She definitely has to go.

When Athena brings her presentation to a close, I join our CMO in asking her questions, but I don't drill her like I have the other candidates who pitched for our business because I'm too busy to waste any more time on this. I plan to leave early tonight, to get ready for my meeting with Charlie.

"I think we'll leave it there," I say, locking eyes with her gorgeous blue ones.

She truly is stunning with the most exquisite face and a body made for sin. The suit she's wearing is expensive and elegant and not overtly sexy, but it hugs sumptuous curves begging for a man's touch. Images of paddling Vixen's ass resurrect in my mind, and for a fleeting second, I replace the memory with Athena, imagining her spread out on a spanking table, her ass cheeks flushed from my touch.

I meet plenty of hot women in my line of work, but I can't say I've ever visualized paddling their asses in a business meeting.

I'm surprised at the strength of attraction that ignites the space between us, and I wonder if she's felt it too. Charlie would say it's because she reminds me of my love, but that's not it. Usually, any resemblance to Jane sends me running for the hills, but she has the opposite effect on me. For the first time in a very long time, a woman has sated my curiosity, and I'm tempted to find out more. She might share some physical traits with Jane, but that's where the familiarity ends. If I had to guess, I'd say Athena Lewis is a career ballbuster who eats men for breakfast, chews them up by lunch, and spits them out by dinner.

The power play would be intense, but I don't mix business with pleasure, and I don't bring complications into the workplace. Besides, I sense there's something she's hiding, and I think Ms. Lewis would be nothing but trouble, and I need that like a hole in the head.

"If you have any follow-up questions, feel free to email me directly," Athena says, yanking me out of my head. She passes a business card to all of us.

"Thank you for your excellent presentation. We'll be in touch." Chairs are pushed back as we all stand. I lean across the table and shake her hand one final time.

"I would love the opportunity to work on this project for your company, Mr. Manning. I guarantee, if you award me the contract, I will pull out all the stops to ensure the delivery is exemplary and the project comes in on time and within budget. No one will work harder for Manning Motors than me."

I can tell she means that, but it's too slick, too practiced, and it only confirms my suspicions.

"I appreciate that," I say, offering her a tight smile as I dismiss her. "Ms. Markham will see you out."

Hilary leaves to go back to her desk to begin typing up the notes while I discuss the presentation with our CMO. Belinda returns five minutes later, and it's like a two-for-one assault as they push me to hire her, but I'm adamant she's not the one for the job. After a very heated discussion, I tell them my preference and request they get the paperwork drawn up, and then I leave them with scowling faces to return to my desk.

A couple of hours later, I'm finishing up a review of the

monthly departmental budgets for next month when Hilary rings through to my office.

"I'm sorry to interrupt you, Drew, but Ms. Lewis is here to see you." She lowers her voice. "I told her you're tied up all afternoon, but she said she was fine to wait, and she's just sitting out here. What do you want me to do?"

I assume she's been told she didn't win the contract and this is some last-ditch attempt to convince me to hire her. "Tell her my schedule is full, I don't have time to see her, and stalking me will not win her any favors."

"Okay. I'll tell her, boss." Hilary emails me a few minutes later to confirm Athena has left.

I'm later leaving than planned, so I'm rushing to my car in the underground parking lot under the building, slightly distracted with dark thoughts of tonight's meeting, which is why I don't spot the blonde bombshell waiting by my car until I'm almost on top of her.

"I believe my assistant relayed my message," I grit out, clicking the fob and opening the rear of my Lexus SUV.

"I apologize for cornering you like this, Mr. Manning," she says, striding toward me as I deposit my coat and briefcase inside the cargo space alongside the two sturdy gray boxes containing various supplies.

I close the door as she stands beside me, looking only mildly apologetic.

"This is extremely unprofessional. The decision has been made. Act gracious and accept it."

"I think you're making a mistake."

I snort out a laugh. She's got balls, all right. "I think I know my business better than you."

"Of course, you do, but you don't know mine. I'm sure you think I'm small fry compared to Genesis Marketing, but they won't give you the dedicated focus a project like this needs.

They'll assign a large team who will spend more time pushing paper and talking about strategies instead of getting the job done. They rotate teams around several clients, and you'll have different people coming and going. It's not an efficient process and they won't bring the project to conclusion on time and within budget. I guarantee if you hire me you will be my sole focus. My team's too. I won't take on any other big projects. This contract will have our complete attention. I'm prepared to put my money where my mouth is."

I quirk a brow, trying to decide if this passionate display is genuine or all part of the setup.

"If I don't complete the project on time and within budget, I will forfeit my fee. My entire fee."

She comes from money. The suit and the pearls confirm it. She can afford to work for free, so it's not exactly selling it to me. "Why do you want this contract so bad?"

"Are you kidding?" Her eyes pop wide. "Manning Motors is one of the most successful automotive companies in the US, and it's the oldest. Managing a project like this will do wonders for my business. It will open doors currently closed to me. It has the power to transform my career and that of my team."

"So, you just want to use me?" I smirk, leaning against the side of my car.

"It's not like you won't be getting anything out of it."

I like she doesn't deny it. "Careful, Ms. Lewis. Those words could be easily misconstrued." I push off the car, straighten up, and eyeball her. She's only a few inches shorter than me in her heels. Her big blue eyes radiate determination, and I admire that about her.

Fire dances in her eyes. "Careful, Mr. Manning. That could easily be misconstrued as an inappropriate proposition. Whatever would HR say?"

"HR would do as I say, and I don't proposition women." I

move in closer until there's only a sliver of a gap between our bodies, and the tips of my shoes nudges hers. "I don't have to, sweetheart." I press my mouth to her ear. "They come crawling to me."

"Wow. Your arrogance is astounding." She tips her head back a little, and our eyes meet.

"It's not arrogance if it's true."

"It's very unattractive in case you weren't aware." She brazenly holds my gaze, not moving an inch, even though I know grown men who have shit their pants this close to me.

If she only knew who she was challenging, she wouldn't be so brave.

"And you think I give a shit, why?"

"I know men like you. Men who think women only exist to serve them. Men who buy into their own press, but it's all bullshit."

"It doesn't sound like you keep the best company, Ms. Lewis, and insulting the man you're begging for a job is not a smart strategy either."

She steps back. "I've changed my mind." She levels me with a sharp look. "I don't want to work for a misogynistic prick who loves to lord his self-proclaimed superiority over everyone."

"And I don't want to hire a woman who uses her contacts to cheat her way into a contract she doesn't deserve."

She barks out a laugh. "One would think you didn't have a clue about how business deals are done. News flash, Mr. CEO. Networking is the blood flow of industry. And if you really want to know, it wasn't my idea." Her nostrils flare as she loses her cool demeanor.

"Whose idea was it?"

"My father's," she hisses, and a weird feeling settles on my chest.

"What has your father got to do with this?"

Derision washes over her face. "He shares the same misogynistic views you do."

"I don't have a single misogynistic bone in my body."

"Keep telling yourself that if it helps you to sleep better at night."

I shrug because I'm not about to have a stupid argument over something that is nonexistent.

She moves to go past me. "This was a mistake. Good evening, Mr. Manning. Good luck with Genesis Marketing. You'll need it."

Chapter Eight
Drew

"Where the fuck are we going?" Charlie asks from the passenger seat of my SUV as I turn off the road and drive through the open gates of the private entrance that leads to the old, abandoned hotel situated thirteen miles from Rydeville.

"You wanted to know, and the best way is to show you," I supply as my cell pings with an incoming call. I press the button to accept Blackwood's return call. "About damn time," I growl.

"You're not my only client." His voice rings out through the car speakers.

"I'm the only client that matters."

"Your arrogance never fails to astound me," he replies in a droll tone.

"You're not the first person to tell me that today," I admit, and Charlie snorts. Silence descends for a few beats. "It's okay," I tell my contact. "Barron is with me, and he's about to find out everything."

"Good. That's good. It's long overdue."

"Don't have a fucking clue who you are, but you talk sense," Charlie says as I navigate along the bumpy driveway, maneuvering around potholes and bits of the old fence that litter our way.

"Ezra is my PI and personal hacker," I explain, turning the windshield wipers on as the heavens open, tipping sheets of rain from the sky.

"I want to be there when you tell Daniels, Hunt, and Anderson." Charlie chuckles.

"They will never know," I say in a clipped tone, casting a quick glance at my buddy. "You promised you'd keep this confidential."

"And I will."

"I mean it, Charlie. I'm not dragging anyone else into this. It's too fucking dangerous." I take a sharp left at the end of the bumpy road, driving more smoothly along the tree-lined lower part of the driveway now we're on asphalt.

"I don't agree, but I gave you my word. I won't say anything to the others. The only people who will know are me and Demi."

Charlie has changed so much. There was a time he was as secretive and stubborn as me. I'm still shocked he tells his wife everything.

I wonder what it'd be like to not have to hold anything back. To have someone accept you and love you completely knowing every dark broken part of you.

"I've got another call to make," Ezra says as we approach the front of the old run-down hotel. "What do you need?"

"Find out everything you can on Athena Lewis. She runs AMC Solutions. And find out if there is any connection between her and Belinda Markham or Walter Grant."

"Leave it with me." He hangs up as I drive around the side of the sprawling three-story once plush stately home that was converted to a hotel fifty years ago. At one time, it was a sought-after destination for rich socialites, obnoxious celebrities, and elite assholes with money to burn.

"Who is Athena Lewis?"

"The second person who called me arrogant today. As well as a misogynistic prick with a self-proclaimed superiority complex."

Charlie chuckles again. "I like her already. When can I meet her?" He is typing on his cell while keeping one eye on me, watching as I pull the red fob out of the glove compartment.

"She's no one," I say, driving into the covered parking lot attached to the back of the building.

"She's clearly someone if you're ordering intel on her."

"She's someone I crossed paths with who has raised suspicion. I don't like to leave any stone unturned." I drive deep into the parking lot, slowing down as we approach the fake wall I had installed shortly after I bought this place.

Charlie whistles under his breath. "She's gorgeous." He stabs me with a look. "And blonde."

I glance at his phone, spotting the AMC Solutions logo on the top of the page he's perusing. "What's that got to do with anything?" I ask, coming to a stop in front of the apparent dead end.

"That's what I'd like to know." Lifting his head, he pockets his phone and stares at me.

"Don't read into it, and this isn't the time." I press the fob and the wall starts to rise.

Charlie blinks repeatedly as he watches the wall lift revealing the hidden part behind it. "What the hell is this place, Drew?"

"Mission central." I drive forward into the remodeled

modern parking lot and park in between two black vans. I press the fob again, and the wall-like shutter closes behind us.

Charlie doesn't say anything else as we climb out, silently following me as I flip on a flashlight and open the side door. I haven't reactivated any of the power in the main part of the hotel because it needs to look derelict so it doesn't draw attention. He walks at my side as we stride along the dark, chilly hallway, inspecting the paint peeling from the walls and the threadbare dirty carpet under our feet.

"This must have been something else in it's heyday," he says when we emerge from the dank hallway into the wide lobby.

Italian porcelain tiles that were once white and gold cover the entire floor, barely visible underneath a layer of grime and debris. Overhead, the original ornate chandelier still presides over the magnificent room coated in a layer of dust and an abundance of cobwebs. Behind the old reception desk, a gold-framed mirror dangles precariously on the wall, tipped down on one side, the mirrored element rusted and cracked. Velvet couches and glass coffee tables are dotted around the space, broken and sharing the same general air of neglect as the rest of the space. The pièces de résistance are the wide sweeping staircases on either side of the desk, curling upward to the next level. The traditional-style gold banisters are in better condition than the rest of the hotel.

"I'm sure it was." But this isn't our destination. "Come on." I jerk one shoulder, urging him to follow me as we step behind the reception desk and enter the former staff door. We walk through several rooms until we reach the old kitchens.

"I'm totally confused right now," Charlie says, watching me reach for one of the overhead cupboards.

"It'll all make sense in a minute." My grin is wide as I yank down on the secret lever and step back, taking my buddy with me as the entire front of the kitchen cupboards swings forward with a loud creaking noise, revealing the hidden entrance behind it.

"Fuck, Drew. This is some next-level shit." Charlie's grin matches mine as we step forward. I flick the light switch on, illuminating the stairs descending to the basement level. As soon as we're both on the stairs, I hit the button to seal the entrance behind us.

The steps light up as we go down into the hub of the building and my home away from home. When we hit the ground, I turn left and approach the thick steel door, standing in front of the retinal scanner and letting it do its job. The lock unlatches with a loud click, and I yank down on the handle, pulling the heavy door open. "After you." I waggle my brows and smirk at the look of shock splaying across my buddy's face. Didn't think there was anything that could shock Charlie after everything we have seen and done.

I wait until the door has shut behind us before typing in a code on the wall-mounted control panel and turning the power on. Lights switch on automatically throughout my basement lair, and the underfloor heating will soon have the place nice and toasty.

"Let's grab a bite to eat first," I say, heading toward the kitchen. I point out rooms as we stride along the wide corridor passing a myriad of doors on the left. "Living room. Office-slash-war room. Surveillance room. Bathroom. Bedroom. Bedroom. Gym." I open the second-to-last door, which leads to the kitchen, and he trails me inside.

"You've got to give me some answers."

"What do you want to know?" I ask, heading toward the coffee machine and switching it on.

"How long have you owned this place?" he asks, hopping up onto a stool at the island unit.

"I bought it the year we graduated RU. Spent a year fitting it out. Another year putting in security and surveillance systems and doing a few other modifications. That's when I hired Ezra Blackwood, and he helped with the heavier technical stuff."

"I can't believe you did all this by yourself and that none of us knew."

I shrug as the coffee machine churns to life, grabbing two mugs from the mug stand. "I did what I had to do."

"Is this where you go when we think you're away on business trips?"

"I do travel with work but not as much as I've led you all to believe. Sometimes I am holed up here. Other times, I'm overseas following a lead."

"When did you start looking for her?" he asks as I grab a couple frozen pizzas from the freezer.

"I need to start at the beginning. From when I sent her away." I grind my teeth painfully as pressure sits on my chest. I tried to prepare for this night. I spent my Saturday night at the fight club, expending a ton of pent-up emotion, and hours fucking Vixen Sunday night at the club in an attempt to destress and exert my control. While it helped, I'm still on edge. Dredging up the past will not be easy, but I promised Charlie I'd bring him in, and I'm a man of my word. If he's going to do this with me, he needs to know everything, and that means I can't hold anything back. He needs to know this story from the very beginning.

Chapter Nine
Drew

Charlie watches silently as I turn the oven on and slip the two pizzas inside. I pour us both a coffee, half considering switching it for bourbon or scotch, but getting drunk won't help, so I soldier on.

I claim the stool beside him and take a mouthful of the strong coffee as I prepare to spill my deepest, darkest secrets. An alert pings on my phone, and I open it up, checking the image of the hill at the back of my property, wondering what might have set the motion detector off.

Charlie glances over my shoulder. "Is that here?"

I nod, relaxing when I spot the red fox skulking through the brush on top of the hill. "I have hidden surveillance cameras, motion detection sensors, drones, and infrared alarms all over the exterior property in all directions. The feeds are displayed on multiple screens and monitors in my surveillance room, and all tapes are backed up to the cloud and never erased. I also own the house up the road, and I have a small team of men on standby in case of emergencies. All are ex-military and highly trained. They monitor the feeds constantly and alert me if there is anything suspicious."

"Has anyone ever come here snooping?" he asks, and I shake my head.

"No one knows about this place. I mostly come here at night, and I have fake plates on the car I switch out every time in case anyone should notice me arriving or leaving."

"It seems you have thought of everything."

"I didn't have a choice. The information I have uncovered is dangerous in the wrong hands."

"Tell me."

Ignoring the acid churning in my gut, I start spilling my guts. "That night, when I went to Jane's dad, I told him everything that was going on because I needed him to understand the severity of the situation. I needed him to leave immediately, and I knew if he had the brutal truth he would go. Family was everything to him." Charlie nods, already knowing this part. "He said he had a place to go, and he was starting to explain, but I stopped him. I told him not to tell me anything. That it was safer I didn't know."

I swallow thickly over the lump in my throat. "I told him I was getting a new cell and email and shutting the old ones down so Jane couldn't contact me. I knew she'd try, and I couldn't leave any way for anyone to trace her whereabouts. I sent four men with them for protection, gave them burner cells, and told them to send a coded weekly text letting me know everything was okay. They knew the only time to call was if there was an emergency, if someone had made them, and there was a threat to their lives."

"When did they call?"

I'm not surprised he's jumped to that conclusion. "They didn't." I get up as the oven timer goes off, pulling plates and napkins out of the cupboards before removing the pizzas. "I had weekly texts for years. Sometimes they sent me photos of Jane even though I hadn't asked for them. Man, that was hard. I wanted to go to her so badly."

"It's no wonder things never progressed with Shandra. I knew you were still pining for Jane, but this must have killed you, man."

Charlie is the only one who knows what happened—or didn't happen—with Abby's other friend. "It did. Every time I got a photo, my heart shattered all over again." I slice the pizza as I talk. "I was so tempted to find her, but the elite threat had not gone away even though most of the assholes were dead. Atticus was still MIA when we graduated RU, and though Hamilton was in jail, we all knew he was still playing an angle. When Zayn and Roman showed up, it confirmed Hamilton was continuing to use our loved ones against us, and it was still way too dangerous to go for her, so I began making active plans. I wanted to be ready to go get her when the time was right."

Setting the pizza, plates, and napkins on the island unit in front of my buddy, I turn and grab two bottles of water from the fridge and reclaim my stool.

We dive into the food, both of us ravenous, and my story stalls while we eat. When we're done, I wipe my mouth with a napkin, drain the rest of my water and stand. "I want to show you my office."

Charlie climbs to his feet and joins me as I exit the kitchen and step out into the hallway. "I got close to Huss on purpose. Spent a year getting to know the guy and having him checked out to ensure he was the good guy we all believed him to be. When I knew I could trust him, I told him about Jane and her family. I asked for his help in finding her and bringing her safely back home."

"Did he help?"

"He did. At first."

Charlie arches a brow as we approach our destination.

"He was warned off seven years ago, and that's when his involvement ended." Stopping at my office door, I stand in front of the scanner. It scans my eye, and I press my thumb on the finger pad, and once my identity is verified, the door unlocks, granting us entry. "He thinks I gave up then too, but fuck that. This isn't over until I find the bastard who sent Jane to her death and take him apart, piece by piece, before I end his miserable existence."

"We'll find him." Determination is etched upon his face, and I'm grateful he forced my hand. I was close to breaking and having him on board makes all the difference. I should have told him years ago, but I didn't want to be a selfish prick. Truth is, this has felt like such a lonely crusade without him and the others.

I open the door and step inside, quickly followed by Charlie.

"Holy shit, Manning." His eyes are bugging out of his head, and I think I've shocked him again. I know what this must look like. This is the second biggest space I had built down here.

Photos, articles, travel and location information, and key pieces of intel are tacked to a whiteboard covering the entirety of the large rear wall. The long wooden table in the middle of the room holds maps, coordinates, and other paperwork. Computer equipment resides on the desk abutted against the wall on the right, and the wall on the left houses floor-to-ceiling shelving. Boxes of research line the shelves, all labeled and dated. Tucked into the remaining wall on our left, just inside the door, is a leather couch, coffee table, and liquor cabinet.

Charlie strides toward my evidence board, and I move to fix us some drinks. I definitely need alcohol for this next part. Pouring a generous helping of bourbon into two glasses, I take them with me as I walk toward my buddy. I hand Charlie one, standing silently beside him as I drag my gaze over the familiar faces pinned to the board. Rage infiltrates my veins as I look at some of the men involved in Jane's kidnapping and sale. The fact all of them are now dead does little to appease me.

I take a mouthful of my drink and then start talking. "Huss promised he'd help keep Jane and her family safe if they returned to Rydeville, so I called the men who were with the Fords," I begin explaining, and Charlie studies the board while listening. "None of them picked up or answered any of the texts I sent requesting an address." Bile travels up my throat. "That's when I knew something wasn't right."

"This was, what, a year after we left RU?"

I nod. "I was twenty-three, and it had been over five years since I'd last seen her. I was done waiting. I just wanted her back."

He clamps a hand on my shoulder before returning his attention to the board and keeping his ears pricked. "When my messages started bouncing back, I knew the burners had been destroyed and I'd been played, but I didn't know for how long. I was in a complete panic. I had no fucking clue where she was, and I regretted not asking her dad to put the information some-where secure for a future time when it would be safe to come back."

"Don't beat yourself up, Drew. You were only fucking seventeen, and you had to make a split-second decision to protect her. You did the best you could."

"I made all the wrong decisions, Charlie. I should never have sent Jane away. I see now what I couldn't see back then. Keeping her by my side was the best way to protect her." I knock back the rest of my drink, relishing the burn as it glides down my bitter throat.

"Hindsight is a wonderful thing. I made tons of mistakes too, and I get it. This need to punish yourself for fucking up continuously." Pain flares in his eyes. "My mistakes cost my father his life."

"And mine cost Jane hers."

"No." He grips my shoulders, eyeballing me with a lethal look. "The only person responsible for Jane's death is the man who delivered it. It took me a long time to accept that Hearst was responsible for my father's death."

I'm so glad me, Abby, and Mom all legally changed our names to remove Hearst from it.

"A part of me will always feel somewhat responsible even if I know your father would still have killed mine without my interference," Charlie adds. "He knew he was plotting with Atticus against him, and my dad signed his death warrant the day he partnered with Anderson."

"It doesn't actually matter anymore," I say.

"Of course, it does. You're not living, Drew. You're barely existing. You've got to stop punishing yourself and—"

"We're getting sidetracked. Did you come here for answers or to conduct a therapy session?"

"You're such an asshole sometimes."

"Only sometimes? I'll take that as a compliment." My grin is wry and short-lived.

"I'll drop it for now." Charlie's attention returns to the wall. "What happened after you lost contact with your protective detail?"

"I began investigating, but I needed help. I literally had nothing to go on. I had no clue where the Fords had gone after they left Rydeville, and it swas obvious immediately I was out of my depth. I thought long and hard about asking Hunt and Daniels, but they were newly married, and I knew I'd be putting them in danger. Plus, I knew it would be unfair to ask Xavier to keep another secret from Abby, and I couldn't do that to him, so I began recruiting my own team. Huss put me in touch with Ezra, and together we hired tech specialists to help with research and ex-military soldiers who would accompany me on missions. Later, we hired people on the ground in different jurisdictions once we began tracing their steps. Lawyers, soldiers, PIs, etcetera."

"I'm seriously fucking impressed. I think your talents are wasted at Manning Motors."

I shrug. "It helps to keep me sane. I need some normalcy in my life, or I'd give in to the dark and never lift my head into the light."

He slowly bobs his head. "Yeah, I can relate."

I move to the left, trailed by Charlie, to the start of the board and begin pointing out maps, flight paths, car rentals, and accommodation receipts. "We have retraced their steps, but it's been painstakingly slow, and it's taken years. They didn't travel a direct route. They used a combination of private jets and cars and different fake names in every location."

"I'm not surprised." Charlie runs a hand across the back of his neck as he examines the information. "Ford was elite. Part of the inner circle and wealthy. He knew how to cover his tracks."

Chapter Ten
Drew

"I've cursed him for years for doing such an awesome job."

"So, if I'm reading this right," Charlie says, poking his finger at the first map. "They went from Boston to Memphis, stayed there a few days before moving to Nebraska. Had another pit stop and then drove to Boise, Idaho."

"Then after another little sojourn in Idaho, they drove to Cali, and that's where the trail ends."

He arches a brow. "You think that's where they stayed?"

I bob my head. "That is my best guess because the trail is dead after that. And it was just after I placed them entering northern Cali that I was ambushed and warned off."

Abrupt silence greets my words. Charlie slowly turns to face me. "Want to say that again?" he asks in a lethally calm voice.

A chuckle escapes my lips without warning. "It's been a long time since I've seen that look. Kinda makes me melancholy."

Charlie blinks. "Who took you, and please tell me they're resting in a shallow grave?"

"I wish." I turn and stride toward the couch needing another whiskey.

Charlie follows, dropping down onto the couch while I fix us new drinks.

I sit beside him and hand him a glass.

"I received an anonymous text at Talia's third birthday party."

"I remember you leaving in a hurry and trying to stop you." He glares at me. "Goddamn it, Drew! I wanted to come with, and you refused."

"We've been over this," I drawl, taking a drink. "I didn't have much time to prepare, which is how the pricks managed to subdue me. There were four of them. All trained."

"Elite?"

I shrug. "I don't know, but from what I've learned since, I don't think so. I think they were something else entirely."

"VERO?"

I shake my head. "I don't believe so though I could be wrong."

"One call to Diesel would fix that."

"And put what I'm doing on his radar? No thanks."

Charlie's brow puckers. "Who else could it be?"

"I don't know, and we're getting sidetracked. Whoever they are, they told me they knew what I was investigating and to drop it. To let her go, or I'd be sorry. I agreed and made a deal with them so they'd let me go. They offered me closure, but it was vague as fuck. I didn't do anything obvious for months while I waited for some sign, and then I got it."

I gulp over the lump in my throat. "I was sent coordinates to a warehouse down by the docks. Took a team in case it was another ambush." I bark out a harsh laugh. "It was but more of the emotional kind."

"They sent you her body," he quietly says, and I'm grateful he said the words I couldn't say.

"Someone had taken care to wash her and dress her in fresh clothing, and she was in an expensive casket." My voice cracks, and I clear it as Charlie places his hand on my shoulder. "But they couldn't erase the scars and marks covering her exposed skin, the burst blood vessels in her eyes, nor disguise how thin her hair was or hide her malnourished bones. When I removed the scarf from around her neck, I discovered bruising and finger marks, and the swelling indicated a broken hyoid bone." I almost choke on the next words. "When I inspected the rest of her body, I found knife marks all over her chest and—"

I pause to draw a deep breath. My hand shakes while holding my glass. I pull myself together, reinforcing the walls around my heart, and forge on. "Her vagina was hacked to pieces, her ass all cut up."

His eyes close, and I raise a shaky hand to my mouth, swallowing more bourbon. "I'm so sorry, Drew. You shouldn't have had to endure that pain alone."

"I fell apart after that," I admit in a dead tone. "Grief is too flippant a word for what I went through. I told everyone I was in London those six months because I needed to be hands-on as we set up the UK office, but it was a lie. I barely stepped foot in our new building, leaving it all to the management teams." I hang my head, breathing deeply and feeling that pain as if it was yesterday.

Charlie squeezes my shoulder.

"I was barely functioning. I knew what it meant, and I was plagued with nightmares of the things she must have endured. I was consumed with guilt. I promised Jane I'd always protect her, and I failed. Worse than that, I betrayed her with Shandra. I fucked around with another woman while the love of my life was trafficked and abused."

"It was one time, Drew, years after Jane had gone, and you stopped it before going all the way because of your love for Jane. That is the last thing you should feel guilty about."

"I wasn't exactly thinking logical thoughts back then, and I still hate myself for the way things were between Shandra and me."

"You might have given off a few mixed signals, but you were always straight with her. You're not to blame if she built it up to be more than it was. I still think you should have set Abby straight about that part."

"I have never wanted to come between Abby and her friend."

"Enough time has passed, and Shandra is dating Rick now. Demi says it's serious."

"I'm happy for them, and I hope it works out. Shandra deserves to be happy."

"Rick does too. He went through hell with Rebecca."

Rick's ex-wife is a piece of work. Kai never thought they were right for one another, and none of us were surprised when the marriage failed.

"It's water under the bridge now, and you should at least let Abby know the truth of what happened between you two."

"I can't. She'll only ask questions about Jane." I finish my drink and set the glass down on the coffee table.

Charlie levels me with a stern look. "I think she deserves the truth. You weren't the only one who lost her. She was Abby's childhood best friend."

"How can I tell her this?" I claw my hands through my hair and lean back against the couch. "It would devastate her."

"She will always wonder if you don't."

I turn my head to look at him. "I don't think that's a bad thing. Let Abby imagine her off happy somewhere. Married with kids and living her best life. It's what would've happened if she'd never fallen for me."

"I think Abby would still want to know. If you think she hasn't considered the worst, you don't know your sister."

"Thinking and knowing are two different things."

"At least if she knew the truth, she could process her emotions, grieve for her friend, and support you. She worries about you so much. Abby is not dumb. She knows you are hiding secrets, and she suspects they're to do with Jane. You're not fooling anyone."

"I'm not arguing with you about this again. I'm not telling the others. End of."

Air whooshes from his mouth as he raises his palms in the air. "Okay, okay. I don't agree, but I'll let it go." He lowers his hands to his lap. "What happened after London?"

"My grief and guilt gave way to rage and a burning need for revenge. But I had to lay low because those assholes had warned me to drop it. I built the crypt and poured time and money into following the trail discreetly, but it's like once they got to Cali they disappeared into thin air."

"Surely one of them popped up somewhere on facial recognition software?"

"You'd think so, right? Yet there is nothing, and I've come to two conclusions. One, whoever Ford went to is involved in whatever happened to the family, and he's powerful enough to have completely covered his tracks, or two, Mathers and Hamilton were involved, and they used Zayn's reverse-engineered facial recognition software system to wipe all trace of the Ford family ever having been in California."

Charlie's brow furrows and then smooths out. "Zayn shared

his system with Hamilton and lied about it when we asked," he correctly surmises.

"It was during the time he was suspicious of all of us, and after we earned his trust, he just forgot to mention it. When I was drawing a blank, I spoke with him. Asked him outright if any other elite had access to it, and he confirmed Hamilton did."

"But you said earlier you didn't think the elite were involved."

"We can't find any concrete trace to the elite, and those guys who ambushed me were something else. Some other entity. Either they were involved and they sent me Jane's body to stop me from uncovering evidence of their guilt, or they know who's responsible and they're shielding them. It's possible they were contacts of Hamilton's and he was involved, or maybe providing the reverse-engineered software was the limit of his participation."

"Is that why Hamilton was assassinated? To bury that knowledge with him?" Charlie asks.

"It's possible, but Hamilton had plenty of enemies. As did Atticus. It could have been for any reason." Whoever took both men down has managed to avoid detection. The FBI worked with the Italian police, but the assassin was never found, and no one was ever arrested for Hamilton's prison murder either.

"True." Charlie sinks into the couch, looking deep in thought. "We may never find all the answers."

"Then I'll never find any peace." I prop my elbows on my knees and sit forward. "I won't rest until I find the person responsible and end him."

"Where are you at now with the investigation?"

I explain how after lying low for a couple years after those guys warned me off I began following up leads that led me to Venezuela. How I led several missions deep in the heart of the

Orinoco mining valley, rescuing trafficked victims, killing their kidnappers, and burning their compounds to the ground. How I discovered Vera was at one of them and went in to rescue her.

I stand and lift one shoulder. "This brings us right up to speed. I know now that Jane ended up in Orinoco though I don't know which compound she was at. They don't exactly keep records. We have pieced together a rough timeline, and it seems like it happened approximately seven or eight months after leaving Rydeville. What I don't know is how she got to Venezuela from the US. I was hoping if I discover the how I can find the who and then work back to identify where the Fords stayed in Cali.

"I got a tip-off a month ago about a guy who worked for a shady shipping firm at Cabello port in Venezuela. We had a talk"—I smirk, remembering that interrogation with fondness—"and I got a name out of him. This American guy works for a transportation company who ferries stolen kids from the port in Bolivar to southern Orinoco and from there via road to the different compounds. The guy has been in the business for years, so it's likely he'd know something. He'd been in hiatus for a few years after I shut down most of the compounds, but it appears some brave fucker has decided to reclaim the territory and this dickhead came out of retirement."

Charlie follows me as I exit the room and take a left. "I flew out to Venezuela last week and apprehended the guy, but it seems like another dead end." I walk past the kitchen to the solid black door at the very end of this side of the basement. "Either the guy genuinely knows nothing or he's been trained to withstand interrogation."

The retinal and fingerprint scanner confirms my identity, and I push the door in, descending the stairs with Charlie hot on my heels.

"A basement within a basement," Charlie murmurs as we

go down. "You're just full of surprises, old pal." He claps me on the back.

"I'm about to make all your dreams come true, Charlie boy." A wicked grin spreads over my mouth. When my foot hits the ground, I turn and face my best friend. "Want to come play torture the bastard with me?"

Chapter Eleven
Drew

We head into the changing area, and I hand Charlie a set of black boots and black overalls. After hanging our clothes in the lockers, we head out of the bright light into the darkened dungeon.

"How many prisoners are currently enjoying your hospitality?" he asks as we walk past four rusted iron doors, making a beeline for the door at the end of the corridor.

My chest rumbles with silent humor. "Just the one, but we've been at full capacity plenty of times in the past."

"You work alone or with help?"

"Mostly alone, but I pull in reinforcements as I need them. Most times we've had to blow the compounds to kingdom come with all the monsters trapped inside, but if we can grab a few of the bastards to take home for questioning, we do it. None of them know who's controlling it from the top, but we've gotten enough intel over the last few years to piece things together." We stop at the door. "Torturing the sick pricks helps keep me sane. If I didn't slake my bloodlust on these assholes, the slow nature of our progression would have made me crazy years ago."

"There is no feeling close to the feeling you get gutting a motherfucker." Charlie agrees, grinning as we share an excited look.

"Feels like old times." A familiar surge of adrenaline courses through my veins.

"Yeah." His grin fades a little. "Those weren't always fun times though."

"We made the best of them," I remind him as I punch in the code on the door. Taking the masks from my pocket, I hand him one. "For the smell." I offer him a set of plastic gloves next.

Putting our masks and gloves on, we enter the room together, and I shut the door and flick the light switch on.

Charlie's hungry gaze roams the room with mounting interest. "Nice work, Manning," he says, whistling low under his breath as he takes in the remains of the other men this cell has housed over the years.

"I like to keep them here. I find having a visual image of their fate helps to loosen tongues a lot quicker."

"Fuck." Charlie's eyes lift to the naked man staked to the wall in front of the prisoner. Dried blood coats his patchwork skin, and we stop for a minute to critique my handiwork. "Nice touch with the nails through his balls and his nipples."

"I had fun with that one. He screamed like a little girl, and I thought it was fitting he died choking on his chopped dick as I fed it to him."

"Poetic. I like it."

"It wasn't enough. That prick is the one I mentioned earlier. He was turning a blind eye to all the trafficked kids coming into the Cabello port for years, accepting payoffs to say nothing." His putrefying remains tickle my nostrils even through the mask, and I'm glad he suffered before death even if he deserved so much more. "I should have given him the Rafael treatment."

Charlie tips his head to one side. "What's that?"

"Rafael was the only guy we managed to get out of the compound Vera was at. He confirmed she had arrived there when she was *four*." It's part of how we were able to piece the timeline together.

Charlie's face pales. "Fucking hell." He scrubs his hands down his face.

"He didn't take long to break." A muscle pops in my jaw, and renewed rage flows through my veins as I stalk toward the pile of bones in the corner. Bits of flesh still cling to the bone, but the piranhas did their job well. "I won't repeat what he told me they did to her because it's too sick to repeat. I went full-on beast for his torture. Slicing, cutting, burning, hacking. Bribed a few sick pricks into fucking him, and they tore his asshole up real good with their cocks, broken glass, baseball bats, and a few other choice objects. I let them cover him with cum, shit on him, piss on him." I waggle my brows and grin. "I have a video if you ever want to watch."

"Sounds like some light entertainment to watch with my wife."

We both crack up laughing, and I cast a glance at the naked prisoner tied to the wooden chair in the middle of the room, but he's still passed out. I worked him over good last night.

"Then I made Rafael watch as I used a chainsaw to rip them limb from limb after they had served their use, constantly reminding him this was his fate. I dragged his death out for six months. I beat him, starved him, sliced little pockets of skin, let him get to the brink of death, and then I had my men feed him, put salve on his wounds, give him water and false hope. When he was well enough, I did it all over again. Did that a few times until I had the final scene prepared. Then I dropped him into a sealed tank with five hundred piranha who'd been starved for weeks and basked in his agonizing screams as they tore into his patchy flesh with their jagged teeth. It took less than ten minutes for them to kill him."

"I always thought the piranha kill was an urban legend."

"The conditions have to be right, but it works. They picked the flesh clean from his bones. It was a highly entertaining, virtually evidence-free way of offing the asshole."

"You got that on film too?" His lips curve into a smile.

"Damn straight." I flash him a wide grin. "You can have a back-to-back movie night with Demi."

We chuckle again. "I can't believe you didn't let me in on the fun."

"You've got it good, Charlie. Don't let the dark suck you back in."

"The dark is a part of me, Manning, the same way it's a part of you. Not indulging it doesn't make it go away. It just remains hidden."

"They really fucked us up, didn't they?"

Charlie shrugs. "Probably, but maybe we always had it in us, and they just coaxed it out."

"It's the age-old nurture versus nature debate." We turn around, and I rake an appraising gaze over the dungeon. It's a typical old-school interrogation cell composed of grubby brick walls and a stone floor with no natural light or ventilation. The stains of human misery cling stubbornly to the ground as we walk toward the unconscious prisoner. The place is cold enough to freeze my balls off, but that's the intent.

Charlie walks to the table, inspecting the variety of tools with an approving smile.

He picks up an electric drill, and the euphoria crawling through my veins is the best kind of high next to sex. I walk to the prisoner and slap his face a few times to wake him up. He starts cursing at me in Spanish, and my smile grows wider as I contemplate how I want to play this today. This is his last opportunity to give me something useful before I end the motherfucker.

The buzz of the electric drill is music to my ears as Charlie approaches holding it in his hand. His pupils are dilated, his face alive with the promise of retribution. He presses the power switch on and off, and the intermittent buzzing of the drill has the beast in my pants stirring with violent arousal. "I'd like you to meet my friend, Charles Barron III, Luis," I say as Charlie steps around the chair and stands beside me in front of the man.

"*El pendejo*," he hisses, and a broken tooth falls loose from his mouth, bouncing off his battered naked body and pinging on the hard ground.

Charlie digs his thumb into a festering wound in his shoulder. "That's not very polite."

Luis howls in pain as Charlie rummages in the wound, flashing a devilish grin I haven't seen in ages.

"Luis isn't very polite," I say, walking to the table and grabbing my knife. The serrated edge is perfect for cutting and lifting the flesh from his bones. "He refuses to answer my questions." I trail the tip of the knife down his arm, slowly digging it into his ice-cold flesh. "Refuses to give me the name of the originating port."

There are transporters that leave L.A. for Venezuela regularly, but I can't just assume that's how Jane and Vera were sent overseas. We have researched manifests of the L.A. port for two years from the time the Fords left Rydeville but couldn't find anything out of the ordinary. We need a name as well as the port of origin. There are several other US ports that sail to Venezuela, and they could have left the States via any of them.

It's like searching for a needle in a haystack without something to work from.

I crouch at his feet and begin removing the patch of skin from just above his ankle bone. Luis screams, attempting to thrash around, but Charlie stands on his foot, holding him in place while I cut a nice even square of his flesh. The drill buzzes to life again, and the sounds ripping from Luis's mouth as Charlie drills into the kneecap of his other leg is sweet, sweet rhapsody.

"We need music to work to," Charlie says, reading my mind. Blood splatters his face and mask as he ceases drilling to open his cell. He props his phone up on the table, and I give him a "hell yeah" as his death metal playlist kicks in.

Between us, we carve up the sick prick, working companionably just like the old days. When I have a few choice pieces to work with, I lock eyes with Charlie and nod. He sets the drill down as I stand and admire the succession of holes in Luis's right leg, running from the knee to his foot. Blood gushes from the wounds, but they're only surface level. Charlie wouldn't end his life so easily.

The music stops, and Charlie comes back to my side. His black jumpsuit is slick with blood, his face dripping in the stuff, and he looks completely in his element.

I hold the bloody skin patches in my hand as I lean down over Luis. His face is contorted in pain, and his eyes are wet with tears. "If you're not going to fill your mouth with the words I need to hear, I'll find something else to fill it with."

"News flash," Charlie says, jabbing a finger over his shoulder at the man crucified on the wall. "He filled the last guy's mouth with chunks of his cock."

Luis isn't quick enough to hide his panic, and I chuckle. "I'll go easy on you at first." I hold up one of the squares I took from his leg. "It's your choice. Tell me what I want to know, or start chomping, asshole."

"Please, I don't know anything."

"Wrong answer, dickwad." Shoving the bloody, fleshy lump between his lips, I clamp his mouth closed with my fingers and keep it sealed as he tries to spit it out. I hold it like that for a few seconds as he freaks out, his terrorized eyes widening with panic. Charlie grips his cheeks and arches his head back as I open his lips and push the flesh down with the handle of my knife to really drive it home. "I think it's better if you chew."

A gargling, choking sound fills the air, and I press my knee into his groin to hold him in place as I swirl the flesh around his mouth. Charlie and I exchange a look, and we sit him up straighter, plucking the mangled lump from his mouth and tossing it away. Can't have him choking to death and ruining all our fun. "This is your final warning. Give me information, or we'll chop up every part of your flesh and drip feed it to you." I grin at my buddy. "I think we'll try his ass next."

"Feed shit to a piece of shit. I like it."

I waggle my brows and grin. "More poetry in motion."

"Don't, don't!" Panic threads through Luis's tone. "I'll tell you what I know if you promise to put a bullet in my skull."

Charlie's dark laugh bounces off the wall. "Can you believe this motherfucker?" Charlie turns the drill on and drives it through Luis's nipple. "Who the fuck said you had any bargaining rights?"

"Men who get into bed with predators don't deserve any leniency," I say, slicing his other nipple off with my knife.

Luis shouts and roars, and tears leak from his eyes.

It's beautiful to behold.

"But it's your lucky day, fuckface." I carve a line in his cheekbone. "I'm a busy man, and I don't have hours to waste," I lie, "so I'll agree to your deal, but don't try to fuck with me,

Luis. If you do, I'll take your punishment out on your precious *abuelita*."

Resignation floods his eyes. Finally. A fresh wave of adrenaline surges through my veins.

"There is a gringo in L.A. who oversees the shipments. I spoke to him on the phone a few times. I only have a first name."

"What is it?"

"Miguel."

I stab my knife into his gut. "What did I say about lying to me, Luis?"

"I'm not lying," he says in between sobs.

"That's not enough." Charlie restarts the drill, and Luis begins hyperventilating. I slap him a couple times. "We need something more."

"I don't have anything more," he cries.

Charlie and I share a look. Time to cut our losses.

Charlie brings the drill to his other knee while I move to the table and pick up the chainsaw. Darkness swallows me whole as I charge it up, and the raw, grating sound soothes a little of my pain. This has been the story of this journey. Get a great lead, followed by a dead end, and I'm tired of waiting for the ultimate revenge. Tired of not knowing who did this to my love.

Luis is screaming and crying as I approach him with the chainsaw as Charlie is drilling holes in Luis's right knee, going deeper this time.

"Wait," he whimpers. "I remembered something."

I take my finger off the button. "Out with it."

"He's a grandfather. I remember two or three years ago he was talking about the baby. Couldn't stop gushing about her. He said her name was Sophia."

It's not a huge help, but maybe Ezra can do something with

it, and at least we have confirmation the shipments are coming from L.A.

"Anything else you remember?" Charlie asks, bringing the drill to Luis's crotch.

He shakes his head. "I told you what I know, now shoot me."

"An opening has just appeared in my schedule," I say, "and now I have time to kill."

"Literally," Charlie jokes.

I turn the chainsaw back on and flash Luis a deadly grin. "Guess it's not your lucky day after all."

Chapter Twelve
Athena

"I told you I have it handled," I say through gritted teeth as I finish getting dressed in my usual mission attire— long-sleeved black top, fitted black pants, and black boots.

"There wouldn't be anything to handle if you hadn't made a mess of the presentation," my father retorts in a snippy tone.

"I didn't make a mess of the presentation. My pitch was perfect."

"You didn't listen to me. I told you to dye your damn hair," he yells down the phone, and I hold it away from my face. It's rare Amos loses his cool, and I give myself a mental pat on the back for rattling him this much.

"I didn't lose the contract over my hair. I lost it because it was blatantly fucking obvious my presentation had been prepared by his VP of marketing. If you had given me more time, I would have come up with my own pitch, and my connection to Belinda would not have been made. If you want to blame someone, blame yourself."

"He needs to be stopped, Athena, before he hurts your brother."

"That asshole is getting nowhere near Arlo. You have my word." I check my gun is loaded before securing it in the holster at my hip. "While being at his office would make this easier, I can still spy on Manning from outside his organization, which is why I've got to go. I'm tailing him tonight."

I haven't told my father I'm in L.A. because he'd only insist I fly to Lowell later to give him a briefing. Hopefully, it won't be a wasted trip. I have a contact at the airport who tipped me off that Manning had submitted a flight log for this weekend. I was curious enough to travel here last night, holing up in my pad in downtown L.A. while I prepared for my surveillance mission.

I was at the airport nice and early this morning, and I watched Drew Manning and Charles Barron disembark the Manning Motors private jet with a six-man team of bodyguards. All were dressed in smart suits, and they certainly looked the part. Only a trained eye could tell they are all guns for hire. Ex-military. Highly specialized killers who know how to get the job done discreetly.

Excitement charges through my bloodstream, and liquid lust pools in my core. The thought of beating that arrogant jerk at his own game is the greatest turn-on.

"I need you on the inside so all angles are covered."

An exasperated sigh flees my lips. You'd think I was constantly letting my father down, not delivering successful mission after successful mission. He seems particularly antsy about this one, and I know Arlo is the reason why. Some of my ire dissipates at the thought. My father does love my brother, and I'm glad he's pulling out all the stops to protect him even if I'm still pissed he went behind my back to reel Arlo in. "Dad, trust me. I've never let you down before, and I'm not about to start now. I'm working a play. Drew Manning will be eating his words and begging me to take this contract before Thanksgiving. You can hold me to that."

"I will. Goodnight, Athena." He hangs up before I can reply.

"Asshole," I murmur as I stand in front of the mirror and fix the short black wig over my golden-blonde hair. Missions are the only time I conceal my hair because it draws too much attention when I need to fade into the background. The wig is styled in an angular bob and actually suits me. Maybe I should dye my hair jet-black.

I check I have all my weapons, my keys, my lock-picking kit, and my burner cell before grabbing my helmet and snatching my black jacket and leaving my apartment.

I tap out a text to the man in my employ sitting in the hotel bar.

> Me: Any update?

> RX: No change

Tucking my cell into the inside pocket of my jacket, I zip it up before carefully pulling the helmet down over my head, ensuring I don't mess up my hair. Then I climb onto my motorcycle, kick-start the engine, and floor it out of there.

I'm waiting in the alleyway alongside the five-star hotel where Manning and Barron are staying this weekend, wondering if they came all this way just to get drunk at the bar, when my cell pings with a new text.

RX: On the move

Me: Follow and advise

I watch my screen with impatience for the next ten minutes, waiting for a further update. When it comes, there are two accompanying photos of black Range Rovers with fully tinted windows. I text the plate numbers to my tech guy and request updates.

I usually always have Andreas on standby when I'm out in the field. There are cameras all over the streets of L.A., and it's easy enough to follow a vehicle. Andreas will also run a search for cell phone signals and track those closest to the vehicles. In the past, we've been lucky when he's hit the jackpot, and it's made surveilling our mark easier. Increasingly, I'm using drones, but there are so many of them in the skies of L.A. that it's challenging to stay concealed. Manning and Barron are shrewd players, and I need to take extra precautions.

RX: Coming your way

Me: I'm on it. Hold position.

I start the engine and wait for their vehicles to pass before I pull out onto the busy street. It's past eleven p.m. at night in the city that doesn't sleep, and traffic is still a bitch. I hold well back so they don't make me, knowing Andreas will send coordinates to my phone if I lose sight of them.

Traffic flows more freely as we move away from downtown, driving south on the highway. I maintain a reasonable distance behind them as we drive for a further twenty minutes, and when they don't take any of the exits, I think I know where we're heading.

It's harder to follow and remain hidden when we reach Long Beach. I'm expecting them to either drive straight to the separate port here or drive farther to the main one at San Pedro Bay, but they veer left, heading toward the industrial section of Long Beach.

Andreas is watching them via the street cams, so I stop on a side road and wait for a couple of minutes. When the coordinates come in, I drive into the large industrial sector where several well-known businesses have warehouses. I spot the two Rovers parked behind a gray warehouse, and I pull in behind the adjoining warehouse and kill the engine. Removing my night vision binoculars and balaclava from the storage area under the seat, I drape the binoculars around my neck and stuff the face covering in my pocket before propping my helmet on my bike and setting out on foot. I use the flashlight on my cell to guide my path because the fuckers who own this space clearly didn't budget for lighting.

I arrive in time to see Manning and his crew creeping along the back of the warehouse, heading toward the one next door with the lights on. All the men are dressed in dark combat gear and heavily armed as they sneak forward.

I follow at a reasonable pace, sticking to the shadows as I creep up on them. Two of the men are sent up ahead to scout the area around the lit warehouse. Ardent Shipping is written in patchy white lettering on the side of the building. I tap out a text to Andreas to run a quick check on the company before using my binoculars to zoom in on the men Manning sent ahead, watching them slap a few tech devices around the perimeter of the building. I duck down as one of the men sends a stealth drone into the air, directing it toward the tall narrow window at the top righthand side of the building.

I'm guessing their high-tech gear comes courtesy of HADK Cybersecurity, a specialist security company established initially by Sawyer Hunt and Xavier Daniels. They changed the name and rebranded after Zayn Anderson and Keven Kennedy came on board as co-owners. When it comes to running covert illegal ops, it pays to have super-smart tech geniuses for best friends.

After the drone returns along with the two scouts, they form a circle and begin talking in hushed whispers. It seems obvious they plan to bust into the warehouse, and I'd like to know what's inside, so I turn back the way I came, darting to the right and jogging around successive warehouses as I loop around to the Ardent Shipping warehouse from the rear left of the structure. From this angle, I'm hidden from Manning and his crew. I look up and smile. The gods are certainly looking out for me today. My lips curve wider as I walk toward the fire exit and my way in. Stretching up, I slowly and quietly pull the ladder down.

There's a fire in my belly and a charge crackling in my veins as I scale the ladder and climb all the way to the top. The small door that leads inside is locked, but it only takes me a few minutes to jimmy the lock and slink inside.

I'm hidden in the roof space, surrounded by a godawful musty smell and several brown boxes. I sneak a peek in a few of them, finding nothing but packing materials. Raised voices from down below tickle my eardrum, and I inch closer to the box nearest the edge, hiding behind it as I gingerly poke my head out.

Down below, a group of men surround an older man with a long straggly gray beard. He appears to be arguing with a tall man sporting a nasty scowl and a large beer belly. They are too far away to hear what they're saying but not far enough when the tall man whips out a gun and shoots the old man clear through the eyes. The pop rings in my ears, and it's lights out for the bearded man before he's even hit the ground.

Manning chooses that moment to make his appearance, bursting into the room with his men from two different angles. In what was clearly a planned strategic attack, his men take out the warehouse guys in quick succession before they've even had time to reach for their weapons. I didn't even have time to record it on my cell. Only two men remain standing. The tall man and a second younger man who bears a striking resemblance to the man standing at his side.

No wonder the board is scared. These guys operate like Luminaries, and they are considerable foes. If I had my rifle, I could take Manning out now, but I wouldn't make it out of here alive. As much as I respect the guys who lead our world, I'm not ready to die. Not before I've truly had a chance to live. Besides, killing him would be premature. I need to discover what he knows and who he's told. Blowing Manning's head off now, while hugely appealing, would only cause a different problem. I need to bide my time and gather as much intel as I can. Then it will be Ares, Baz, Knight, and Jase's collective decision how to handle it.

Manning and Barron quickly disarm the men and secure their wrists with cuffs. Words are exchanged before Manning pistol-whips the tall guy, and he crumples to the ground like a sack of potatoes. The younger guy protests, earning him a punch in the face from Barron. He loses consciousness, falling on top of the older man on the ground while Manning starts issuing orders. I watch him through my binoculars, fascinated with the cold calm expression on his face as he commands his team. A couple of men leave the warehouse while the others begin searching the place. I figure I'll wait until they're gone before making my exit, but that decision is taken out of my hands when I hear footsteps climbing the stairs toward my hiding place.

Shit! There's not enough time to leave, so I do the only thing I can. I pull the balaclava over my head and jump up, grabbing the ceiling beams and using them to haul my body up. I fit my feet into the roof cornices while plastering my spine to the flatter roof panel and gripping the two beams ahead of me. Then I pray to the gods and cling to the roof for dear life while the stocky man with dark eyes and a shiny head checks the area and inspects the boxes. A line of sweat rolls between my breasts as I hold my breath and wait for him to finish his inspection.

I close my eyes for a brief second, offering silent thanks as the guy leaves and begins climbing back down. I wait a good while, to be sure the coast is clear, before carefully unfurling from the roof. My foot lands on something lumpy, and I almost lose my balance. I thrust my arm out, holding on to the side wall to steady myself. I frown as I stare at the slightly raised section of the floor.

Goose bumps sprout on my arms as I bend down to examine it. An ominous sense of foreboding washes over me, but I'm still shocked when I lift the loose edge of the flooring sheet and make a horrific discovery.

Wide, glazed blue eyes stare up at me as I clamp a trembling hand over my mouth. I have met a lot of monsters in my line of work, but it takes a particularly sick, depraved creep to stuff a little girl into the floorboards of a warehouse and leave her to rot because no one would find her here unless they stumbled upon her as I did.

Pain fills every empty space within me as I'm reminded of all the evils of our world. Our leaders have worked tirelessly for years to shut down child trafficking, but as soon as you cut off one head, another one grows. It's a never-ending cycle, and the world is full of too many sick pricks.

Her skin has a bruised-like complexion, and it's starting to swell, confirming she's been dead at least three to four days. She's small and petite with a thick head of white-blonde hair tied up in a pink and white ribbon. She wears knee-high white socks and glossy black pumps. Her pretty pink dress is torn at one shoulder, and the doll she's clutching in one arm is missing its head. But it's the round bullet hole in her forehead that has me welling up. Bile swims up my throat, and nausea pitches through my stomach. I take a picture of her with my cell as I contemplate my options.

I can't leave her here. Someone out there is frantically looking for this little girl, and they will need closure. Tapping out a message to Andreas, I ask him to send a crew to collect a body at the scene, and I prepare to wait.

Doors open and close downstairs, and I crawl back behind my box, watching as Manning's men load the two unconscious men into the cargo space at the back of one of the Rovers while Drew and Charlie pepper the other bodies with bullets, ensuring no witness is left alive.

Except for me, of course, but they don't know that.

After they leave, I crawl back to the little girl, take her cold hand in mine, and sing her a lullaby. Rage comingles with sadness as I sing lullaby after lullaby, my frustration so intense I wish I could scream until my lungs feel like they might burst and my throat is scraped raw.

I make a silent promise to myself.

If Drew Manning has anything to do with abducting and murdering little kids, I will slice his cock from his body and feed it to him in little pieces before ripping his heart from his chest with my bare hands and watching him bleed to death at my feet.

Chapter Thirteen

Drew

"You look pale and tired," Mom says the instant she opens the door to me.

"Gee, thanks, Mom," I say, slipping inside her house when she stands aside to let me enter. "You look great too."

She closes the door behind me as the sound of multiple voices filters down the hallway from the main living area. Mom scheduled an early dinner because she wanted the kids to come too. Don't get me wrong, I love my nieces and nephews and my little cousins, but it's a bit like feeding time at the zoo when we're all together. When Lauder, little Anderson, and Hunt and Daniel's kids are added to the mix, it's complete mayhem. But they're not here today, so my ears should survive the evening.

"Don't be a smart-ass." She musses up my hair. "I'm just worried about you."

"There's nothing to worry about."

"Sure, there isn't." She loops her arm through mine. "You work too hard, Andrew. You need to make time for fun too."

"Trust me, I have plenty of fun," I say, sporting a smirk as I think of my next playdate with Vixen, which is happening tomorrow night, and reminiscing fondly over the torture session Charlie and I indulged in with Luis last week.

"I'm not talking about those kinky women you hook up with. I mean making time for a real relationship."

I arch a brow as we stall at the end of the hallway, wincing as one of the kids emits a high-pitched squeal that feels like it's piercing through my skull. "Kinky women?"

She musses up my hair again. "I know about that sex club you go to." Her mouth pulls into a grimace, and I can imagine where her mind has gone.

"It's not what you think, Mom. It's not like the elite clubs of the past. It's professional, and everything is fully consensual. Women have control, and it's empowering."

"Maybe we'll sign up." Abby leans against the curved archway that leads into the main part of Mom's house.

"At least I know who blabbed now."

"It wasn't me." Her lips tip up at the corners. "Mom has Kai wrapped around her pinkie. She coaxed it out of him."

"Only because I want you to meet a nice girl and settle down."

"That's not in the cards for me, Mom, and you need to stop butting in. I'm happy with my life. I don't need a woman to complete me, and now you know about the club, you can rest assured I am not short of female company when I need it."

"Sex is not the same as love and companionship."

"Uncle Drew!" Oli shouts, racing toward me and snatching my hand. "You're just in time. We're bobbing for apples."

My nine-year-old nephew hops from foot to foot, literally vibrating with excitement. He's a hyperactive little dude who rarely sits still. Oli is constantly looking to be entertained, and he is never short of quickly rotating interests and passions. He's a lot like Jamie in that regard. Charlie and Demi's middle son is a lovable little rogue. Talia—Kai and Abby's eldest— tries to baby her younger siblings. She is the quietest of their four kids and very mature for her age while Ori, their youngest son, is so laid-back he's practically horizontal. But he's a sensitive soul too, and he feels things deeply. Amelia, my youngest niece, is a bubbly little cutie who reminds me of her mother. She has a naturally inquisitive mind, and she's constantly asking questions, just like Abby as a child.

They're great kids, and I love spending time with them.

As long as I can hand them back when I'm leaving.

"We're making chocolate apples too, and we all have a pumpkin to carve," Charlie's eleven-year-old daughter Jane says, grabbing my other hand. Her warm fingers curl around mine, and I smile at my little cousin. We share a special bond that is everything to do with her name and also not. She's a sweet kid and a bit of a mother hen like Talia with the younger ones.

"And we're gonna do the monster freeze dance," Talia adds, winding herself around my legs and looking up at me with puppy-dog eyes she knows will get her anything she wants. "Mom said we had to wait for you to get here 'cause you're the best at it."

"Did she now?" I narrow my eyes at my troublesome twin.

Abby smirks into her wineglass.

"Come on!" Oli tugs on my hand. "I want to get there before Henry gets all the apples!"

I let the kids drag me into the room, saying a quick hi to Charlie, Demi, Kai, and Mom's best friend Sylvia, who are all seated on the couches in front of the roaring fire, before the kids pull me into the kitchen where all the pre-Halloween activities are taking place.

Mom and Abby help with the supervision as the kids dunk

for apples and then make a mess coating others in melted chocolate and rolling them in sprinkles. I swear there is more chocolate on the kids' faces and fingers than on the apples. I carve a pumpkin for baby Charlie as he's only four and too little to do it by himself as Demi helps and Abby works with Ori on his.

Then Mom shoos us out of the kitchen so she can plate up dinner. Sylvia helps her while Abby and Demi get the kids settled in front of some cartoon movie on the TV. Finally, I get to drop down beside my brother-in-law and grab a beer.

Kai clinks his bottle against mine. "Good to see you, man. I was beginning to think you were avoiding me."

"I probably should for blabbing about the club. You do realize she's going to up the ante now?" Mom is determined to find me a woman no matter how many times I tell her I don't want one.

"Why'd you think I told her?" He doesn't even attempt to hide his grin.

"Asshole," I mutter as I smile.

"It's not a bad idea though," Kai says, wearing a more serious expression. "Don't you get sick of sex with random women?"

"You make it sound like such a chore," Charlie says, smirking.

"That's what it seems like to me."

"Only because you were pussy-whipped at seventeen," I remind him.

"Best thing that ever happened to me." He glances lovingly at his wife and kids, and I love seeing it. Kai is a great husband and father, and he makes my sister really happy. It's all I ever wanted for her, and I'm glad she got the life she dreamed of.

But it's not for me.

Not anymore.

"You've got it good," I agree.

"You could too." Kai eyeballs me. "Abby wants to set you up with this new woman who joined her yoga class last week. She just moved into the area, and according to Abby, she's smoking hot and—"

"Not interested." I cut him off with a warning look. "I've got my own smoking-hot fuck buddy at the club, and she meets all my needs. Tell your meddling wife to butt out."

"Olivia isn't the only one who worries about you, Drew," Kai says, lowering his voice. "Abby knows why you're doing this and—"

"I came to dinner to catch up with everyone and spend time with the kids, not to be harassed with unwanted opinions. Drop the subject of my sex life and give me a break. I know you all care, but you need to stop interfering. I'm never getting married, and I won't ever have kids, and that's not changing any time soon."

"She would hate that for you, Drew," Abby says in a soft strained voice as she perches on the edge of the couch beside me. "Jane would want you to be happy even if it wasn't with her."

"Stop," I snap, glaring at my sister. "I'm not talking about this."

"You have to sometime." Abby rests her head against mine. "I know this isn't the moment, but we're discussing it, brother. This has gone on long enough."

"Speaking of things to discuss," Kai says, clearing his throat and looking ten kinds of awkward.

They all exchange knowing looks.

"What don't I know?"

"Shandra and Rick got engaged." Abby probes my face for a reaction.

"That's great news," I truthfully reply. "I always thought

there was something between them, and he deserves happiness in his life after the shit show that was his first marriage."

Kai's shoulders relax. "He was worried how you'd react."

I frown. "Why?"

"You know why," Abby says just as Mom calls the kids to the table. It's like a stampede of elephants as the seven kids race across the room, all vying to be first to sit down. You'd swear there were twenty kids here from the noise level alone.

"Shandra and I were never a thing, and frankly, it's none of my business who she dates or marries. If she's happy, I'm happy for her."

Dinner is a boisterous affair, and after we finish eating, all the adults join the kids in performing the monster freeze dance. Abby records it and posts it on her Insta story, using it to promote her children's dance studio. She still operates out of the same building in Rydeville, close to her old ballet studio, but now she has two smaller premises in the two surrounding towns. She could probably expand further, but she's already far too busy with her existing business and the kids, and she likes to be able to take on more of the family responsibility at times when Kai is working nonstop on a commission or preparation for a show. When he's less busy, he picks up more of the slack, and they seem to have a good system going.

"Uncle Drew?" Charlie Junior tugs on my hand. "Will you play soccer with me, Uncle Kai, and Daddy?"

"Sure thing, little dude." He's been obsessed with soccer since I gave him a Messi signed jersey shortly after Lionel signed for Inter Miami.

I kick the ball around the garden with my little cousin, shooting the shit with my friends, grateful the subject of my lack of love life has passed.

At least until I'm leaving.

Abby insists on walking me out to my car after I've hugged

all the kids and said goodbye to the adults. "Are you really okay with Shandra and Rick's news?" she asks as we stroll along the hallway toward the front door.

"Yes." I stop just before the door and turn to face my sister. She's almost a foot shorter than me and so petite I often joke I could put her in my pocket. What she might lack in stature, she more than makes up for with strength of character and personality. Abby is a ballbuster, and she makes no apologies for it. She's also fiercely loyal and incredibly protective of her family and all those she loves. She has tried not to force my issues, and when all that shit was going down with Shandra, she didn't interfere. I respected that, but I think it's time to set her straight.

"I think it's time you know what went down between us."

Chapter Fourteen
Drew

"Agreed." Abby purses her lips.

"I'm not talking about Jane," I warn her.

I've been mulling over Charlie's words, thinking maybe he's right. Maybe it is better that Abby has full closure, but it's not that straightforward. If I tell her, then I'll have to tell everyone because there's no way she'll keep it from Kai or Xavier, and then it will do the rounds until everyone knows the truth.

I can't forget I'm keeping them out of it to protect them, so the Jane news just can't come out. At least not yet.

"You're going to have to at some point."

I purposely ignore responding, so I don't end up promising something I can't fulfill. "Let's take a walk in the garden," I suggest, grabbing her coat from the coat closet and handing it to her. I step outside and retrieve my black woolen coat from the back seat of my car.

Abby is all bundled up in a coat, hat, and gloves when we set out on the main walking trail that leads around the edge of the front garden, heading toward the wooded area at the back of the vast estate.

"Did you ever love Shandra?" she asks, just putting it out there in a way I've always admired about my sister.

I shake my head. "No. We were only ever friends. I was incapable of loving anyone when Jane already had my heart."

"And now?"

"Nothing has changed."

The saddest expression is etched on her face. "It breaks my heart that you and Jane didn't get your happily ever after."

"I can't go there, Abby."

"Does everything have to be a big secret?"

"I know I'm secretive and it bugs you, but I hold stuff in for a reason. I'm just trying to protect you."

"I know, D, but I miss how close we used to be. You used to tell me everything."

"Our lives have gone in different directions, and I'm protective of what you've built with Kai. Your happiness means more to me than my own."

She slams to a halt, tugging on my arm and glaring at me. "That is the biggest load of bullshit I have ever heard!" She digs her fingers into my arm. "Your happiness should matter more to you than mine. That's your greatest flaw, you know," she says, and the anger fades from her face as her features soften.

"We're on to my flaws, great," I drawl.

She smacks my chest before looping her arm through mine, and we resume walking. "You'll do anything for your loved ones, constantly putting their needs above your own, and while it's commendable, D, it's not right. You can be selfish. You *should* be selfish. You only get one life, and it's too short to waste it doing things you think you should be doing instead of being happy."

"Just because my idea of happiness is different than yours doesn't mean I'm not happy, A."

She stops again and looks up at me. "Tell me to my face, Drew. Tell me you're one hundred percent happy with your life, and I'll drop it. I won't mention a word of it again."

I'm so tempted to lie, but I try not to do that with my sister. There was a time I had to lie and keep stuff from her to protect her from our father, but after all that shit went down with the elite, I swore I wouldn't lie to her again. "I never said I was one hundred percent happy. I think that's a fallacy anyway."

"It's not. I'm one hundred percent happy with my life. Probably more."

"Then you're lucky because I think it's an anomaly."

"I think that's more bullshit, but I don't want to argue. The gremlins will need to be tucked into their beds soon, so my time is precious. Tell me about Shandra."

"Only if you promise you won't tell her what I say. I never want to hurt her."

"I don't like keeping shit from my friends, but you're my twin, Drew, and you come first. I will keep your confidence."

Warmth floods my chest, and I wrap my arms around my sister, holding her close. "It's you and me against the world, little bug," I whisper like we used to when we were kids after we thought Mom died, and we were grieving while our asshole father continued living life like it was only a minor speedbump. All we had back then was one another, and I tried to be the strong one, mopping up Abby's tears and holding her while she cried herself to sleep every night for months.

"You're the bestest brother in the whole entire world, and I love you so much," she whispers like she used to back then.

"I love you more than anyone on this planet, Abigail Anderson. You will always be my person."

"And I will always be yours. I want you to know there isn't

a damn thing you could tell me that would ever change my mind. I've got your back, big bro, even if you keep all your secrets hidden from me." Tears fill her eyes when we break apart. I hate that my actions have caused her pain but protecting her has to take priority.

Abby grabs my hand and drags me over to a wooden bench in front of Mom's rose garden. We sit close, and I wrap my arm around her shoulders, tucking her in beside me to ward off the cold.

"Shandra was a great friend to me after Jane left Rydeville," I begin explaining. "We grew closer after she became my fiancée, and I didn't feel so empty when she was holding my hand or sitting in my lap or snuggling up to me. I didn't realize she was reading more into it. I thought it was clear I was pining for Jane. That Jane was the love of my life." I rest my head on top of Abby's. "I didn't mean to lead Shandra on, but I guess that's what I was doing."

"Did something happen between you before graduation?"

"Shandra kissed me. She caught me totally off guard, and I didn't handle it well. It felt like such a betrayal to Jane. I pushed her away. Told her I was in love with Jane and she'd only ever be a friend to me. I was too harsh, and she was upset."

"That's why you two didn't speak for months."

A heavy sigh leaves my lips. "Yeah. I tried to apologize a few days later when I realized how it must have seemed to her, but she didn't want to listen."

"But you clearly patched things up over the summer because I remember you guys hanging out a lot, and she later told Nessa you guys had dated."

I ease back, eyeballing my sister. "We never dated. That was all in her head."

Abby frowns.

"Shandra extended an olive branch," I continue explaining.

"She said she was sorry for pushing me. She understood I was grieving and needed time. She asked if we could be friends. I said yes but it'd never be anything more because I wanted to be crystal clear with her so there was no further misunderstanding. She said she was fine with it, so we hung out. Went to the movies and the diner a few times and hung out at the beach on occasion. She even dragged me shopping this one time. Shandra is cool, and it was fun. Being with her helped me to forget all the shit we were dealing with back then, but it was never anything romantic for me. It was just two friends spending time together as far as I was concerned, but she built it into more."

I scrub my hands down my face. "We started RU, and she was getting very touchy-feely again. It made me uncomfortable. I was still feeling guilty over letting her kiss me, but she reassured me it was all friendly, so I relaxed and stopped getting so worked up over it. Then we went to a party one night. I don't think you and Kai were there. Anyway, she was drunk, and she tried to kiss me again. This time, I stopped her before her lips touched mine. She was upset, but I put her to bed and told her we'd talk the next day. When I dropped by to take her to brunch, she laid into me. Said she wouldn't wait for me forever and I needed to stop chasing a ghost."

"What?" Abby's brow creases. "I can't believe she said that."

"It was in the heat of the argument. She later apologized, but we really got into it. I told her nothing had changed for me. Jane was still it, and I'd only sent her away to protect her. I said all I could offer her was friendship."

"I really thought there was more to it than that."

"Everyone did, and the only reason I didn't say anything was because I didn't want to embarrass Shandra, but if I'd known she was telling people we were dating, I would've set the record straight. I eventually told Charlie, but he was the only one who knew the truth."

I wet my dry lips, hating to admit this, but I don't want Abby thinking it's all Shandra's fault, and I promised her honesty. "I did fuck up though." Abby's brown eyes, so similar to my own, stay latched on mine as I explain. "The night of Nessa and Lauder's Hamptons wedding. I was going through a hard time. It'd been so long since I'd seen Jane, and I was drowning. I drank too much, and when Shandra asked me to dance, I didn't refuse her. It got a bit...heated, and we went to her room. I—"

Abby slaps her hand over my mouth. "Spare me the lurid details."

My lips twitch in amusement. "Let's just say it quickly got out of hand, but I stopped things before it got too far. When I realized what I was doing, the guilt was instantaneous. I told Shandra it was a mistake and I could never betray Jane. She was understandably upset. She screamed and threw her heels at me, and I ducked out the door before the crystal decanter could hit me in the head."

"Poor Shandra."

"It was a dick move, and I still feel like a piece of shit to this day."

"It would've been worse if you'd slept with her and then told her it was a mistake," Abby muses. "Though either way, it was hurtful."

"She didn't speak to me for ages after that. Then I finally got her to agree to meet. I wanted to apologize again and see if there was any way we could patch up our friendship because I hated the way we'd left things. And it was causing tension in the group. But she stood me up, and we never had that talk. We're polite with one another now, but we're not friends, and I don't have a clue what is going on in her life except for what you tell me."

"That makes me sad for both of you. She was really hung up on you, Drew. I think she legit loved you at one point. I seriously thought you two had a real thing. I'll admit I was shocked because I remember how you were with Jane. But I didn't begrudge you your happiness or judge you for it."

"I thought I was doing the right thing because I spelled it out plainly on several occasions. I thought she understood we would never be more than friends. I didn't intentionally lead her on, but I see now I gave her mixed signals."

"I don't think either of you are to blame. You just wanted different things, and remember how everything was always so much *more* when we were teenagers? Especially for girls. We read into every little thing. I can see how Shandra might have misconstrued the situation."

"I never wanted to hurt her. I actually really like Shandra and I miss her friendship, but it was clear we couldn't have any kind of relationship after what happened at the wedding."

"We're all older and supposedly wiser now." Abby grins. "And she's in a good place. Maybe this is the perfect opportunity to clear the air."

"Can't say it's on the top of my priority list, but if the opportunity presents itself, I'll talk to her."

"Thanks for telling me." Abby pulls me into a brief hug.

"I didn't tell you back then because I didn't want to make things awkward for you or mess up the friendship you guys had."

"I always knew that, and it just proves my earlier point." She waggles her brows and stands. "We should head back. The kids are probably grouchy and testing Kai's sanity by now."

We walk side by side back toward the house, both lost in thought. "Oh, I almost forgot," Abby says a few beats later. "Is there any chance you're free the first weekend in January to babysit the kids?"

"You'd trust me with the gremlins?" I've had them for the odd sleepover in the past but never for a full weekend.

"I'd trust you with my life, so yeah. I wouldn't ask if we weren't stuck. Kai has a meeting with some hotshot gallery owner in L.A., and he wants me to come with so we can make the most of the trip. Mom is away on her Mexican cruise that week, or I'd ask her to take them."

"It's fine, A. Of course, I'll take them."

"What about work?"

"If anything crops up, I'll just reschedule it."

"You're sure? They're a handful."

"I'll plan a few excursions for the daytime and tire them out. It'll be fine. It'll be fun."

She cracks up laughing. "Famous last words, big bro. I hope you know what you've signed up for."

Chapter Fifteen
Athena

Excitement winds its way through my veins as I take the elevator down to the basement level where the private dungeons reside. My regular fuck sessions with Beast have become the highlight of my week. Not only is he a hot fuck, he's a fantastic distraction from the shit show that is my life at the moment.

I've been on edge since the warehouse stakeout. Finding that little girl really rattled me. And I don't say that lightly. I know the kinds of evil there are in this world. I have confronted it head-on for most of my life, thanks to the society I live in. But there is nothing more impactful than seeing the evidence face-to-face. I can't get her out of my mind.

Ariana DeSousa.

She was only six years old. Taken from a playground in the blink of an eye when her mom's back was turned in conversation with another woman. Her parents are distraught, I'm told, but grateful an anonymous tip led them to recover their only daughter's body.

It should never have happened, but part of me is glad for

whatever caused her death before she'd been ferried overseas and her life became a living hell.

It's only made me more determined to find out what Drew Manning is up to. Dad made it sound like he has some kind of vengeance plan against the Luminaries or maybe he is going after his competition in the trade. The latter doesn't seem likely now. I have pored over every scrap of evidence I can find on Manning, and there is nothing that says he's the kind of man who would be involved in sex trafficking or harming kids. He's no saint, none of those elite bastards are, but he tends to turn his violent charm on sinners not innocents.

In fact, Manning and his friends took down the elite years ago, and they were instrumental in lobbying for reform when the entire elite organization was restructured more than ten years ago.

Is it possible he's working to stop them?

If that's the case, why has the board asked Dad to take him down? Surely, they would support his efforts if he is one of the good guys? Unless they want to be the ones to handle it, and they prefer outsiders are not involved?

What if they're trying to bury this?

That thought sits like sour milk in my stomach. The board has fought hard to make changes in our world, and I have supported them because I always believed they were trying to do good. But what if they've changed? What if they are gunning for Manning to hide these evil deeds?

I'm conflicted and not sure who or what to believe.

All I know for sure is it's not making much sense.

I should probably tackle Dad about it, but something is telling me not to say anything for now. I'll continue following Manning and gather more intel, and maybe it'll be clearer then.

I can't figure out what is going on, but I will get to the bottom of it.

The elevator pings when I reach the lower level, but the doors don't open. Which means there is someone else in the hallway. It's all operated via heat sensors, and the doors will only let me out when the hallway is empty. I'm glad they take anonymity seriously. If Beast found out I broke one of his terms, it'd likely be the end of our fuckfests, and I'm not finished with the man yet.

I'm not sure I ever will be.

No man has ever fucked me to within an inch of my life and had me begging for more. His hands are magical, and I'm putty beneath his skilled touch.

After a couple minutes, I'm released from the elevator, and I'm grinning to myself like a loon as I walk to the private dungeon Beast reserved and tap in the code that admits me to the female changing area. Removing my clothes, I hang them up on the hooks and slip off my heels. Then I pee, brush my teeth, run a comb through my hair, and rub scented coconut oil into my naked body, grateful I found time to visit the salon this week for waxing and pampering.

Standing in front of the mirror, I admire the lingering bruising on my skin. My pussy pulses with liquid lust as I imagine the fresh marks he'll leave on my body tonight.

When the light over the door turns green—indicating he's in the dungeon—I don't waste a second, my desire to feel his hands all over my body charging my steps as I move forward. I press the button at the door, and the light dies behind me. Only then does the door open with a loud click, and I step into the pitch-black room.

"On your knees, whore," he says from close to my left, making me jump a little at his nearness.

I drop down onto the padded floor without hesitation. Sex is the only time I willingly and happily bow to a man's command. Part of the allure is handing the responsibility for my pleasure to another. In here, I don't have to make any decisions or carry the weight of any burden. There is no stress. Only indescribable pleasure. He knows what my limits are, can read the signs from my body, and he tells me what to do understanding my desires fully.

I love shedding the responsibilities that weigh so heavily on my soul.

It's the greatest form of freedom.

"Such a pretty slut," he growls, wrapping his hand around my hair and tugging on it sharply. He yanks down hard, and my head lifts, my neck stretching. "Suck." He forces my mouth apart before plunging his cock between my lips in one violent thrust.

I suck him enthusiastically, concentrating on giving him pleasure as my body purrs and sings, and there are no other thoughts in my mind.

"Fuck, you're so good at that, but I want to come in your pussy first."

His dick leaves my mouth with a loud pop, and he lifts me carefully to my feet. "Hold still and look at the floor."

I do as I'm told, moaning quietly as his hands sweep over my body. His touch is feather-soft at first, more tender than any time before. "Your body is exquisite," he says, which might seem strange since we've never seen one another in the flesh. But learning a person's body through touch alone is one of the most intimate things I've ever experienced. I don't know if every experience is like this in the dungeon because this is the first time I've tried this, but I'm addicted. Obsessed. Hungry for more.

His hands move to my breasts, and he cups them in large callused palms as his touch grows rougher and more familiar. "I want to eat these," he growls before dipping his head and sucking one breast into his hot, wet mouth. He isn't gentle, sucking and biting my breast while his free hand tugs at my other boob and flicks my hard nipple. He alternates between them, and it takes massive effort not to sway on my feet. It's as if there's a direct line from my tits to my pussy because I'm dripping with need, and we've barely gotten started.

I almost weep when his attention leaves my breasts and heads south.

"Hands on my shoulders," he says in a wickedly dark tone that lifts all the fine hairs on my body. "And stay quiet."

I could come from his voice alone.

There is something about it. Some instinct hovering at the back of my mind, but before I can examine it, his mouth presses against my flesh, and all logical thought evaporates.

Beast drags his teeth along my stomach and down lower. He sucks on the thinner flesh at my hip bone while I cling to his shoulders and try to remain upright. His touch does the most amazing things to me. Knowing he is marking me where no one will see ratchets my lust up a level. This is our secret, and it's one I have come to cherish. I love seeing the reminder of our sessions imprinted on my skin for days afterward. It helps to keep it constant in my mind, and I'm regularly daydreaming about my mystery man.

Burying his nose in the top of my pussy, he slowly drags one hand up the inside of my leg, and I stop breathing as his fingers sweep over my inner thigh. One finger runs a line up and down the crease to one side of my cunt, and I almost cry, such is my need. My pussy aches as he toys with me, touching my thighs, his fingers moving close but never quite touching.

I bite down a whimper when he presses his face to my crotch and holds still. "I can smell how much you want me." He lowers his face, pressing his nose between my pussy lips, and my legs tremble. "Hold still."

My nails dig into his shoulder when he parts my folds and inhales deeply. "Such a dirty, filthy slut."

God, those words should not turn me on, but they so do.

"How badly do you want me to fuck you?" he asks, sliding one long finger inside me, and I almost die on the spot.

"Bad," I croak, barely able to speak when he adds another finger.

He chuckles. "So eloquent."

"I lose all coherence when you touch me," I truthfully admit.

"Glad the feeling is mutual," he says, and his words do funny things to my insides.

"I'm going to fuck you with my mouth, and you're going to come all over my face when I tell you."

"Yes, Beast."

"Oh, Vixen," he says, adding a third finger and stretching me. "I'm going to have you screaming louder than ever tonight."

His tongue drives into my pussy, and I can only hold on as he devours me with his tongue, his lips, and his fingers. I could come in seconds, but I hold back until he tells me to let it fly, and I fall apart all over his face as the most intense orgasm wracks my body.

His tall shadowy figure looms over me as he reaches out, trailing his sticky fingers over my jawline and my cheekbones. "I bet your face is as beautiful as your body," he says before prying my lips open and shoving his fingers inside. "Suck, whore. Taste how good you are."

After I've licked my essence clean from his fingers, he leads me to the St. Andrew's cross propped against the wall and ties me to it by my wrists and my ankles. When we used this before, I was tied with my stomach to the cross, and he whipped and fucked me from behind. Tonight, my back is to the cross and I'm facing him as he drags a leather flogger slowly down my body, taking his time, his explorations gentle as he warms me up.

I scream as he whips the flogger hard against my pussy and then my breasts. He works up to full intensity, and my juices are dripping from my cunt and gliding down my thighs as he hits my chest, my upper arms, my stomach, pussy, and upper thighs.

Stopping abruptly, he sinks to his knees and removes the ties from my ankles. He stands and walks off, and the only sound is my anticipation ringing excitedly in my ears. I hear the flogger being tossed on the ground and the telltale sound of a foil packet being ripped open. "Safe word," he says in a deep sensual voice, and a delicious shudder works its way through me.

"Green," I rasp, more than ready for what he is planning next.

He says nothing, creeping stealthily toward me, and it's only the slight distortion of the air that warns me of his presence three seconds before he lifts my legs, bends my knees, and ruts his hard thick length inside me in one violent thrust.

I scream his name as he presses my legs into my chest and fucks me like the wild beast he is. His warm breath fans across my face, and for a fleeting moment, I have the urge to break another one of his rules. To crash my mouth to his and know if his lips taste as good on my upper lips as they do on my lower ones.

But I don't give in to temptation. There isn't much he has ruled off-limits, and it would be disrespectful to take something he's not willing to give. So, I shake off my disappointment and concentrate on the feel of his big dick slamming in and out of my warm cunt as he fucks me like he believes the world is ending.

We stay for hours. Way longer than usual, but I don't

complain. I'm drunk on his touch and addicted to his hands and his cock. He cradles me in his arms for longer, running his hands firmly but gently over my body, easing worked muscles, soothing my soul, and I know it'll be difficult leaving him tonight. He feeds me chopped fruit and chocolate and makes me drink two bottles of water.

As much as I don't want to go, there is no point delaying the inevitable. Our relationship has boundaries for a reason, and reading more into our arrangement would be foolish. I attempt to get up off his lap, but his arms tighten around me. Only when I promise I'm good does he release me.

My legs wobble as I stand, and every part of me is tired but completely sated. "Night, Beast," I whisper as I head toward the door to the female changing room.

"Don't drive, Vixen," he calls out. "I can call a car to come pick you up."

"Don't worry, I've got it handled." I always use a car service when I visit the club because he generally works my body to the point of exhaustion.

"See you next week. Sweet dreams, my sexy Vixen."

His words work their way through skin and bone, burrowing deep, and if I'm not careful, I might catch feelings for this man.

Chapter Sixteen
Athena

Note to self: never conduct surveillance here in mid-November without a rainproof heavy jacket and gloves. At least I have my balaclava and a hat to bear some of the brunt of the bad weather. Torrential rain blows in every direction as strong winds whip through the air at this elevation. As biting rain slaps me from all angles, I'm seriously questioning my sanity.

Why the hell did I decide to do this tonight?

Because Manning is at a charity event in the city, and I knew he wouldn't be coming to his secret hideout, so it was the perfect opportunity to do some snooping. Except it wasn't as fruitful as I'd hoped.

My teeth are chattering, and my hands are stiff with cold as I climb into my car, turn the engine on, and crank the heat to the max. Removing my backpack, I place it on the floor in the back before climbing into the back seat to get changed. I pull my wet clothes off and toss them in a sodden heap on the floor. After toweling off, I change into yoga pants, sneakers, and an oversized hoodie and crawl back behind the wheel, feeling a little more human.

Reaching for my flask, I pour a large amount of coffee into my travel mug and wrap my hands around it, siphoning heat into my chilled bones. I'm sure most would say I'm exaggerating, especially since it isn't even winter yet, but my Cali bones aren't equipped for the cooler temps in Massachusetts and more frequent propensity for rain.

I slurp my coffee and chew on some trail mix as I lean back in my seat and stare at the old hotel down below, wondering what the hell Drew Manning is using the place for. My best guess is it's where he brings people for interrogation, but I'd like to verify it with my own eyes.

After Manning and Barron returned from L.A. three weeks ago, I trailed them from the airport back to here. Since then, I've been following Drew as often as possible, and he has come here several times. He nearly made me one night, so I've been alternating cars and motorbikes and mixing things up so it's not obvious someone is shadowing him.

I place a call to Andreas, and he picks up on the second ring. "Did you get the photos I sent?" I ask as I dump the rest of the coffee from the flask into my mug.

"I'm running them through my system now."

"He has the place locked up tight, and I can't see any way in without being detected." I'm itching to break in and explore, but it's too risky. I had to duck and dive to avoid his cameras picking me up as I scouted the property from this vantage point on top of a hill that faces the rear of Manning's property. Assuming it is his. "Did you get confirmation of the hotel owner yet?" I ask my techie friend.

"I'm still working on it. Whoever did this knows what they're doing. If it's Manning, he's covered his tracks well."

"Okay, keep digging and keep me posted."

"Will do. Do you still want to me hold off on that Genesis Marketing guy?"

"Yes, for now. They're fucking up without our interference. If that changes, I'll let you know."

Belinda is keeping me updated on the project at Manning Motors and it's a shit show. I had found an in—a guy in their employ with a nasty secret he'll want to keep. I was planning on blackmailing him into sabotaging the project, but the idiots are doing that without my involvement. Belinda is pushing to have them fired, and I'm expecting Manning to eat humble pie any day now.

In case he's too stubborn to make the call, I have other ideas on how to force his hand.

"Stay safe, Thena," Andreas says, and I'm smirking to myself as I end the call.

Setting my mug in the cupholder, I put the car in gear and drive away. I'm careful as I drive down from the hill and out onto the road, checking there is no traffic to prove witness to my presence and no one watching as I push out onto the asphalt and peel it out of there.

"You need to back down and let me do what I do best," I hiss into the phone as I inspect my reflection in the mirror one final time.

"It's been over a month, Athena, and you're making no progress."

"It takes time. Like I said from the outset, Dad, a guy like Drew Manning requires careful handling. I won't be much use to you if I'm dead, and that's what'll happen if he makes me."

"We don't have time." He sounds really rattled, and I'm starting to smell a rat.

My gut is telling me there is something else at play here, and I don't ignore my instincts. They have always served me well in the past.

"Your brother's life depends on it."

But does it? I really don't see how or why Drew Manning would come after Arlo. This whole thing reeks, and I'm determined to get to the truth. Which means I need to play ball for now and not let Dad know I've become suspicious of his motives. Or maybe it's the board whose motives I should be wary of.

"I give you my word that within the week I'll be working at Manning Motors and on hand to snoop from the inside."

"See that you keep it," he says before hanging up.

"Ugh." I take deep breaths to calm down as I slip my cell in my purse. I can't show up at the restaurant in a foul mood because my father is a giant jerk.

Twenty minutes later, I pull into a parking space on the street just across from the Mexican restaurant where I'm meeting my new friends for dinner. I add another layer of vibrant red lipstick to my lips before slicking some gloss over them and dragging a comb one final time through my hair. I styled it straight, and it falls in glossy sheets over my shoulders and down my back. I chose a plain fitted black dress with black and gold heels for tonight, wanting to look classy without having tried too hard.

I know I look good. Let's see if my date thinks so.

Grabbing my coat and my purse, I get out of the car and head across the road.

I'm struggling to contain my grin as the maître d' leads me through the busy restaurant toward the table by the wall where the other five people in our party are already seated. I can't wait to see his face when he sees me. This is technically my first ever blind date, but what Abby doesn't know is it's not really blind because I already know and have met her brother.

"Here she is," Demi says, noticing my approach. She turns around in her seat to smile at me.

Three, two, one.

Drew's sultry brown eyes whip to my face, and I've got to hand it to him; he's got one hell of a poker face. Apart from the slight twitch to one eye, one would think he's completely indifferent to my appearance. His gaze rakes me from head to toe, lingering a little on my hair, and his eye twitch worsens, but it's subtle, and only someone watching closely would spot it.

"I'm so glad you could make it," Abby says, standing and leaning in to hug me. I bend down and return her embrace before we break apart. "This is my husband, Kai." She points at the hot guy sitting across from her whose features I'm already familiar with from my research. "And this is Demi's husband, Charlie," she adds, jabbing her head at Barron who is seated on Kai's left while the man of the moment is seated on his right across from the only empty chair at the table.

"It's lovely to meet you both," I say, claiming the vacant seat as Abby sits back down to my right. "Your wives have been very welcoming since I moved to the area."

"Stalker much?" Drew says, drilling me with a dark look.

"What?" Abby's brow puckers as she looks between us.

"Well, isn't this a surprise," I lie, smiling graciously at him, and it's taking huge effort to contain the smug grin dying to run free.

Drew snorts. "At least own it, Athena."

"Wait. You two know one another?" Demi asks.

I look down the table at her. "I pitched for a contract at Manning Motors a while ago. Drew turned me down."

"Desperation is never a good look on anyone," Drew replies before raising a glass of red wine to his lips and drinking from it. His gaze flips to my hair, and he seems to zone out for a few seconds before snapping out of it.

The way his throat works as he drinks shouldn't be hot, but it is. And I'm not imagining how those long slim fingers would feel caressing my body. The Manning Motors CEO looks good enough to eat in a crisp black shirt and pants. The top few buttons of his shirt are open, showcasing the ink on his chest. He's made an effort to tame his hair, but it still falls sexily across his brow. The stylish layer of stubble on his chin and cheeks is a little heavier than the last time I saw him, only begging for my fingers.

"I know what you're implying, but you're wrong. I don't have a single desperate bone in my body, and I don't play games to get work."

"Names weren't exchanged, Drew. You know that." Abby sends a warning look her twin's way.

"It's good you two are already acquainted," Demi adds, curling her fingers around her wineglass. "Cuts out that initial awkwardness."

Anderson and Barron are staring at me with narrowed, suspicious eyes, and protectiveness practically oozes from their pores. I can't help but admire them for it.

"Remind me, Athena, how you know my wife?" Barron asks in a chilling tone.

"We met at yoga class," I coolly reply, smiling at the waiter as I gesture for him to pour me some wine.

"And when exactly did you move into the area?" Kai asks.

"A month ago," I confirm before raising my wineglass to my lips and taking a sip of the lush full-bodied wine.

"Right after I rejected you." Drew runs the tip of his finger around the rim of his glass while he attempts to intimidate me with another dark look. "That isn't shady at all," he drawls.

"Not that I owe you an explanation, but I won a new

contract with a pharma company. They have their HQ a few miles outside Rydeville. They need me at the office regularly, so I have moved temporarily to the area."

When Manning checks that out, it will stack up because the guy who runs the global pharma company is from a Luminary family, and he owed me a favor. "I could have commuted from the city, but I liked Rydeville when I visited for our meeting." I shrug before fixing him with a killer look of my own. "I didn't realize I needed to seek permission to move here."

"Stop this," Abby snaps in a low tone. "All of you."

"You're acting like total assholes," Demi agrees.

I knew there was a reason I warmed to these two women the minute I met them. And while I did sign up for the class with the intent of orchestrating a meeting, they approached me first when they noticed a newcomer, and every interaction I've had with them since has been completely genuine. I might have contrived to meet them, but our burgeoning friendship is sincere.

I've never had proper female friends. At school, I hung around with girls from Luminary families because it was expected, but none of those so-called friendships were ever more than surface level. After I graduated, those friendships quickly fell away, and I've been too busy working in the intervening eight years to form any lasting friendships.

Not that I'll be able to keep Demi and Abby, and it isn't smart to get attached, but it's almost impossible not to with those two.

"I can leave if you like." I stare at the man across the table.

"Drew." Abby's tone brooks no argument.

"Stay." Drew leans across the table, and the spicy, heady notes of his cologne waft around my face, tickling my nostrils and tempting my libido. A seduction mission has never been more appealing, and that thought concerns me. "Unless you have ulterior motives, then you know where the door is."

I'm opening my mouth to reply when his face pulls into a grimace, and he curses. He glares at his sister. "What are you, five again?"

"You're being a dick to my new friend, and a kick in the shin is the least of your worries if you don't quit it."

"I'll go," I say, climbing to my feet. "I don't want to cause issues in your family." I smile at Abby. "Thank you for inviting me, and I'll see you on Monday."

I've only made it halfway across the room when Manning catches up to me like I hoped he would. When his hand lands on my bare elbow, fiery tingles dance across my skin, igniting an inferno inside me. His eyes drop to where his fingers are pressed against my flesh, and he removes his hand in a flash like it offends him. "Don't leave."

His eyes bore into mine, and it's like being ensnared in a hunter's trap. At this proximity, I have a front-row seat, and he's truly magnificent up close.

It's not just that he's drop-dead gorgeous. Drew Manning exudes power and control with an undercurrent of lethal danger lingering under the surface, constantly waiting to break free.

He's intense.

Magnetic.

And unlike any man I've ever met, and I know lots of powerful, dangerous men.

It's impossible not to feel the strength of his presence. It's almost as if he commands the air around him. Like it bows before him. I'm aware of several eyeballs glued to his delectable form, and I don't blame the women of Rydeville for drooling because he's definitely drool-worthy.

"I apologize for my rudeness," he says, snapping me out of my momentary daze.

I focus on the task at hand, playing the part I was born to play. "I'm aware of how this seems, Mr. Manning, but I assure you it's entirely coincidental. If I'm making you uncomfortable, I'll call it a night. I like Abby, and I swear I have no ulterior motives." At least not where his sister is concerned.

"I believe you," he lies, but it's a convincing one. He offers me his arm. "It's only a meal. There's no need to make this into anything more." His eyes flit to my hair once again, and his Adam's apple bobs in his throat. I'm determined to find out why he's blonde-adverse. Men like him don't admit weaknesses, and this one slaps me in the face every time I meet him. If it's the clue to understanding this complicated man, then I'll find out what's behind it.

Chapter Seventeen
Drew

I escort Athena back to the table and pull out her chair. She slips onto it, thanking me. I share a look with Kai and Charlie as I reclaim my seat, glad they are picking up the same vibes I am. Or maybe it's just they always react suspiciously to anyone new in their wives' lives. Abby is no sucker. My twin has sharp instincts, so perhaps we're all overreacting, but it's better to be safe than sorry.

I already had Athena fully investigated, and it came back clear, but my gut is telling me she's up to something, and I think it warrants a second look. I tap out a quick message to Ezra before pocketing my cell and focusing on the conversation around the table.

"I'd like to know how you managed to get your twin to agree to a blind date in the first place," Charlie is saying.

"She played dirty, Charlie." I briefly lock eyes with Athena. "She called in the big guns."

Kai smirks. "Olivia is determined to find you a woman."

Mom seems hellbent on matchmaking, and I suspect she was the driving force behind this blind date. "She's wasting her time, and you are too." I eyeball my sister just as the server arrives to take our orders.

"So, Athena," Kai says after the server has gone. "I'm curious about something."

"You can ask me anything." She smiles prettily at him, and it's hard to drag my gaze from her plump red lips or avoid thinking about them wrapped around my cock.

"Why are you on a blind date? I find it hard to believe you have any trouble getting a date."

"I'm flattered, but the truth is I rarely date. Since I graduated college, I've concentrated on my career. My business consumes me, and it hasn't left much time for anything else."

That appears to be true. Most all of her past relationships seem to be short-lived, but there is a pattern. She definitely has a type—older, wealthy, successful businessmen appear to be her jam.

I definitely fit the mold, but if she thinks I'm biting, she's sorely mistaken.

"Wow, sounds like someone we all know," my sister says with more than a little sarcasm.

Anderson chuckles, and Barron's lips twitch.

"There is nothing wrong with being devoted to a career. Marriage and kids are not for everyone," I say.

"Touché." Athena's eyes twinkle as she smiles at me. "My father is constantly criticizing my single status. He'd love me to give him some grandkids, but it's not part of my plan. No offense," she adds, looking between Abby and Demi. "But kids aren't in the cards for me."

Abby's mischievous eyes flit to mine before tripping to Athena. "It's like you were made for my brother."

"Firecracker." Kai levels his wife with a look. "Stop shit stirring."

"What?" She is the picture of innocence as she eyeballs her husband. "I'm just pointing out the facts."

"Do you have any siblings who can fulfill your father's grandkids wish?" I ask, already knowing the answer.

Her features soften, and her face lights up in a pure unguarded moment. If I thought she was beautiful before, it's nothing on how she looks now. Her big blue eyes fill with love as she says, "I have a brother, but he's only fifteen, so I hope he won't be giving my dad any grandkids for a long time."

"What about your mom? Is she harassing you for grandkids too?" I carefully watch her reaction, seeing the light instantly flee her eyes.

"She died from cancer when I was thirteen."

"I'm sorry." I mean that sincerely. I know what it's like to lose a mother; even though ours was alive all along, we grieved her death for years.

She shrugs, but I see the pain etched upon her face. "My dad remarried a few months after she died, and then Arlo came along a couple years later, and he saved me in so many ways."

I sense there is a lot more to the story, but as much as I'm suspicious and trying to gather intel, I won't prolong her agony.

"So, how's the rebranding project coming along?" she asks as we eat our meals. The other four are engaged in their own conversation, and I hear Xavier's name pop up.

"Good. Everything is progressing nicely." Truth is, it's a shit show, and I'll have to make a call on it soon. At first, I was concerned Belinda had orchestrated the disaster in a bid to have me change my mind, but I'm keeping a close eye on it, and the fuckup is all on Genesis Marketing. I hate to admit Athena was right, but it's looking that way.

"I'm glad it's working out." On the surface, her smile is authentic, but there is just something about her I can't put my finger on. Something that has alarm bells ringing in my ears.

"Really?" I quirk a brow as I cut the last piece of my steak. "That's not what you said the last time."

"I'm trying to be polite. I made my thoughts clear on Genesis Marketing the last time we spoke."

"You made your thoughts clear on several things," I remind her before popping the steak in my mouth.

"I haven't seen anything tonight that contradicts my beliefs." She places a piece of fish in her mouth and chews.

"So, you still think I'm a misogynistic prick with a superiority complex?"

"Aren't you?" She quirks a brow, tossing her long blonde hair over one shoulder, and I hate how my eyes are drawn to the motion.

"You think you know me, but you don't have a clue who I am."

"Enlighten me then." She sets her silverware down on her empty plate.

"Why should I bother? I won't ever see you after tonight. It seems like an unnecessary waste of energy."

She laughs dryly, and something about it seems familiar. "I knew the forced politeness wouldn't last long."

"Let's cut the crap." I set my silverware down and push my plate away as I lean across the table and lower my voice. "My sister tries to see the best in everyone. It's a trait I hugely admire because she doesn't trust easily for valid reasons. But I'm not so easily convinced. I know this was a setup, and I've indulged it for my sister because I would burn the world down for my twin."

She stretches across the table, moving her head closer to mine. "As someone who would do the same for her brother, I respect that, but whatever you think this is, I assure you you're wrong." Those blue beauties peer directly into my eyes, and either she's telling the truth or she's the best liar I've encountered.

"I don't believe in coincidences, sweetheart."

Her brow puckers a little before smoothing out again. "I really don't care what you believe. I know the truth. It's no skin off my back if you want to imagine I have an agenda." Her eyes blaze with fire, and my dick stirs unhelpfully in my pants. "Your project would have looked good on my company's résumé, but I haven't lost any sleep over not winning it. Truth is, I got an even better contract." She eases back, spearing me with an irritating superior expression. "I should probably thank you, Mr. Manning. I only took the second meeting because I happened to be in town for your presentation. Guess it all worked out well in the end for both of us."

The look she gives me tells me she knows I'm full of shit. My fingers twitch with the need to call my head of HR and tell her to fire Belinda's ass, but I resist because I learned a long time ago not to make decisions based on heightened emotions.

"Walk her to her car," Abby hisses when we're outside the restaurant a couple of hours later.

"Don't leave," I warn my sister. She's getting a piece of my mind tonight. "Let me walk you to your car," I say to Athena, deliberately cutting across the conversation she was having with Demi and Charlie.

"That's unnecessary." Things have mostly been tense between us all night, and I think she's as glad as I am that this *date* has come to a close.

"It wasn't a request."

She huffs out a laugh. "I don't take orders from you." Ignoring me, she turns to kiss Demi on the cheek and then

Charlie as well. "Great to see you, Demi, and nice to meet you, Charlie."

Abby shoves past me, giving me one of her signature daggered looks before she hugs her friend and bids her goodnight.

"She's gonna bust your balls," Kai mouths at me before he leans in to kiss Athena's cheek and say goodbye. You'd swear my brother-in-law didn't know me at all. Of course, my twin is going to bust my balls even if I have reined myself in tonight just for her.

"Goodnight," Athena says one final time, making eye contact with everyone but me.

"What am I? Chopped liver?" I say, deciding to call her out on her bullshit.

Her nostrils flare as she turns her attention to mine. "It's been...interesting, like always, Mr. Manning. I do hope things continue to progress well with Genesis." She flashes me a knowing smile.

Bitch.

"As I hope things progress well for you with your consolation contract."

Her lips purse, but she lets me have the last word, checking both sides of the road before heading across it.

"It's no wonder you're single." Abby scowls at me.

"I'm single by choice, and no amount of matchmaking by you or Mom will ever change that fact."

"Did you have to be such a dick to her?"

"I think Drew was very restrained tonight," Charlie says.

"I did that for you," I tell my sister, letting my anger run free now the source of it is gone. "Like I even agreed to this farce in the first place for you, but I'm done with your meddling. A blonde, Abby? Seriously? What the hell kind of fucked-up game are you playing?"

"Watch your tone, Manning." Kai slides a protective arm around my sister's shoulders as he warns me with his eyes to back down.

"I'm not apologizing for Athena having blonde hair and blue eyes. That's your demon to battle, and it's high time you did. I set this up because I like her, and I genuinely think you would too if you just open yourself up to possibilities."

"I don't trust her, and I don't think you should either."

Abby steps right up to me with pain filling her eyes. "I know it's hard for you to trust anyone, Drew. It's hard for all of us, but it's no way to live your life. You have shut everyone and everything out, and Jane would hate this. She wouldn't want this for you."

That doesn't warrant a reply because I'm sick of having the same conversations with my sister. Why can't my family and friends just let me be? It's like they won't rest until I'm bound to some woman. Why don't they understand that isn't a magical cure-all?

Unless they can resurrect the dead, there is no cure for me.

I don't deserve happiness. Not when my actions stole that from Jane and her family.

My penance is to spend my life alone, and I've made my peace with it.

"There is something about her that doesn't add up," I tell Kai, ignoring my sister.

"I thought you had her checked out and she was clean," Barron says.

"You what?" Abby plants her hands on her hips with a look of outrage on her face.

I actually like my sister isn't naturally suspicious anymore. That she isn't bitter and twisted like me, but the old Abby would've been as wary of Athena as me, and she would've been on the phone to Daniels asking him to check it out.

"I conduct full background checks on everyone I plan to do business with," I explain.

"So, you ran background checks on every single person who pitched for this contract?"

"Yes," I lie, rubbing the back of my neck. I'm not admitting I only verified the companies, not individual employees, because then I'll have to explain why Athena was singled out, and it's not a question I can answer. The truth is, I ran a background check on Athena because she unsettles me, and it freaks me out.

"Why? We don't have anything to worry about anymore. The evil elite are dead, and things are different." Now, her eyes narrow in suspicion. "Unless the threat isn't gone and it's one of your little secrets?"

"You really believe I wouldn't tell you if I thought you were in danger?" Disbelief threads through my tone because I can't believe my sister would think that.

A heavy sigh cleaves from her lips. "I know you would, but if you don't want people jumping to the wrong conclusions, maybe you should open up and tell them the nature of the secrets you're keeping."

"The world isn't rid of evil just 'cause we took a few monsters out, Abby."

I can almost see the wheels churning in her mind. "So, you're taking down monsters? Is that what you've been doing in secret all these years?"

"Something like that." I shuffle awkwardly on my feet, shooting a quick glance at Charlie.

"Then I don't understand why you won't just tell us." Her eyes plead with mine.

"If it was something you needed to know, I would."

Demi blatantly glares at me, but I pretend I don't notice.

"It's late," Kai says, tucking my sister under his arm. "And I think we've busted Drew's balls enough for one night."

I shoot him a grateful look.

"I love you," I tell my sister, staring her directly in the eyes. "You're my world, Abby, and I know you mean well, but you've got to drop this and let me live my life the way I want to. You might not approve, but it's *my life.*"

Slowly, she nods. "I really thought you'd like her. She's smart and hot and snarky. She's perfect for you."

Maybe in another lifetime, I might agree.

"Night, little sis." I kiss her brow and clamp a hand on Kai's shoulder as they walk off.

Demi and Charlie parked around the block behind my car, so we walk together. "You need to tell her about Jane," Demi says when we are out of earshot.

"I don't want to hurt her."

"She suspects the worst already, Drew." Demi takes my arm and looks up at me. Compassion is splayed across her face. "She knows if Jane was alive you'd be with her. She sees your pain and knows what's causing it. She hasn't pushed because she is waiting for you to tell her in your own time, but the longer you leave it, the harder it is for her. Please just tell her. Tell her everything. You have shouldered this burden alone for long enough."

"Everyone is happy, and I want to keep it that way. None of you want to get pulled into this shit."

"Your happiness matters too, Drew." She squeezes my hand before leaning back against her husband.

Charlie is quiet, studying me with knowing eyes.

"I think you'll be happier if you tell everyone what's going on," Demi adds. "You have protected and supported us for years. Let us do that for you now."

Chapter Eighteen
Drew

I'm still mulling over Demi's words as I drive to Moonlight to pick Vera up for our graveside visit. It will be Vera's first time seeing her sister's final resting place. I ran it past Felicity and Selena after Vera asked me on Friday, only agreeing after they endorsed the request.

I punch the button to call Ezra while I drive. "Did you run that check on Athena Lewis again?" I ask the instant he picks up.

"Yep. I don't know what you want me to tell you. I didn't detect anything out of the ordinary."

"My gut is telling me she's up to something."

"Then I think your solution is obvious."

I groan, knowing what he's going to say next.

"Fire Genesis Marketing and hire Athena's company. Put her right under your nose where you can see exactly what she's doing."

"She'll fucking gloat," I grit out as I take the next exit off the highway.

Ezra barks out a laugh. "You'd do the same in her shoes."

"Yeah, and I know you're right, but even pretending I was in the wrong pains me."

"You've got issues, dude."

He doesn't know the half of it. "Did you get any more leads from the surveillance tapes?" I ask.

"There really is nothing to go on. Whatever vehicle he used was out of the range of the cameras, and the footage we do have is blurry. The weather was not our ally that night."

"I don't understand how this could happen. I'm always careful, and no one has ever come sniffing around the hotel before."

"You did say you thought someone was following you a couple of weeks ago. My guess is you are right and whoever this person is trailed you there."

"Why now?"

"Maybe you're getting too warm."

"Perhaps. I've got to go. Keep me updated."

I hang up and call Charlie. High-pitched crying greets my ears as he answers.

"Bad time?" I ask.

"Give me one sec," he says, and I listen to the sound of his footsteps as the noise grows more distant in the background. A door closes, and there is blissful silence. "You still there?"

"Yeah. Sounds like a warzone there." I chuckle.

"You're not far off the mark. Abby is here with the kids, and she has Darcy in tow because Zayn and Emery have their first ultrasound today."

Little Anderson's wife is expecting their second child. Something they only announced a couple weeks ago. Emery is due in mid-April, and my mom is over the moon. In every way that counts, she's a mother to the Anderson brothers, and two-year-old Darcy already calls her Gramma. It's sweet, and I'm happy for Mom. She's always at her best when surrounded by her grandkids.

"Darcy stole Charlie's soccer ball, and he pushed her into the grass. She hasn't stopped crying since. Then Charlie felt bad, and he started crying too."

"And my sister wonders why I don't want any kids," I scoff. "You're a braver man than me, Charles."

"What's up?" he asks as I exit the highway onto the main road a couple miles from Moonlight.

"Ezra didn't get anything from the surveillance tapes, but it's clear someone is on to me."

"It's got to be Ardent Shipping. We should have burned the warehouse and made it look like an accidental fire."

"No point lamenting it now. I need to up the pressure on Miguel. I'm done playing nice."

"Tell me when and where, and I'm there."

"Tonight at ten. I'll come by and get you and we'll go together."

"Okay. I better get back."

"Later." I hang up just as I reach the entrance to the facility.

"Wow, this is fancy," Vera says, stopping outside the crypt and running her eyes all over it. She was quiet in the car on the trip here. Lost in thought, no doubt.

"Your sister was a queen in life and an angel in death. I felt it was fitting."

She stares at me strangely before moving toward the gate. I open it up and help her inside, lighting the candles as Vera slowly walks toward the area at the back with the four mounted marble caskets. Her hands shake as she places her flowers in the vase. I walk over and add mine after removing the last bunch I brought, which are now withered. I put them in the compost bin at the door before sitting on the bench behind Vera to give her some privacy.

"I hate that I can't remember her," she says in a soft voice that is barely more than a whisper. She moves to the other caskets. "And I hate I don't know what happened to my brother or my parents. Those bastards took so much from me. My identity. My freedom. My self-worth. My family."

"I'm going to find who did it and make them pay."

"It hurts, Drew," she says over a sob. "It hurts so much. All the time. It's never-ending." She turns to me with tears streaming down her face. "Make it stop," she chokes out.

"Come here." I pat the bench beside me.

Vera slides onto it and dissolves into heart-wrenching tears. I wrap my arms around her, holding her close as she cries. The empty organ in my chest emits a few aching thumps, slapping against my rib cage as my own pain breaks through the walls I've erected. My eyes sting as I stare at Jane's coffin, and I can relate, in part, to Vera's sentiments. The pain is always with me. I carry it every second of every minute of every day.

"Drew." Her eyes are glassy and swollen as she looks at me.

"It's okay." I reassure her. "I've got you."

In an unexpected move, her lips press against mine and begin moving. Instantly releasing her, I jump up and create distance between us, sure my horror is written all over my face. "Vera, no."

"Please don't be like this." She scrambles to her feet, swiping more tears from her cheeks. "I love you, and I know you love me too." I back up as she walks toward me. "I know I can never be her, but I see why she loved you so much. You saved me, Drew, and I don't have anyone else in my life who cares about me like you do."

I press my arms to her shoulders, holding her back as she tries to reach me. "I do care about you, Vera."

"Then be with me. Show me what it's like to be with a man who hasn't paid for me."

Acid churns in my gut, and I feel ill-equipped to handle this situation. "You're like a little sister to me, Vera. I remember you as a baby. Jane and I used to take you for walks in the park when you were still in diapers and in a stroller. Stop," I say in a stricter tone as she tries to bypass my arms and get to me. "I don't want to hurt you, Vera, but I don't have those kinds of feelings for you, and I never will. Your sister has my heart for eternity."

"I'm okay with that," she says, her tears drying out. "We can just fuck and leave feelings out of it, but don't turn me down, Drew. Please, I need you. I need sex."

Fuck my life. How is it when I try to do the right thing by women it always ends up backfiring on me? "I'm not having sex with you, Vera. I am your friend, your family, and I will always be here for you, but only in that capacity."

"Fuck you," she hisses, shucking out of my hold and storming past me. "You don't get to reject me and keep me. I'm done with you. I never want to see you again." She races past me, and I lose a couple of minutes locking up before I go after her.

She's fast on her feet when she needs to be, and she's almost to the cemetery gate when I catch up to her. "Vera, stop!" I say for the umpteenth time.

"Get lost, asshole. I hate you."

"Tough shit." I jump in front of her, careful not to touch her. "I'm responsible for you, and I promised Selena I would get you home safely."

"That's not my home!" Venom spews from her mouth and

her eyes as she scratches her arm. "I don't have one, remember? You made sure that was taken from me."

It's not technically true. The Ford family home is ready for Vera whenever she is able to live independently. My attorney handled all the paperwork after I found her. It's been renovated to freshen it up, and I have live-in caretakers looking after the place. A husband-and-wife team. Housekeeper and gardener.

"I'm well aware of my failings," I say, pressing the fob and unlocking my car. "Let's go." I jerk my shoulder forward as I stride through the gates.

"I'm not going anywhere with you," she shouts after me.

I turn and walk back to her. "If you want to do this the hard way, that's fine by me. I'll call Selena to send someone to come get you, and until then, I'll be stuck like glue to your side. Hate me all you want, Vera. It's your right and I deserve it, but I won't let you fuck up your recovery because of me."

"You can't keep me there. I'm not a prisoner."

No, I can't force it, but I could get a seventy-two-hour psych hold in the hospital and from there have her committed, and she'd be forced to undergo a more traditional therapy route that would be worlds away from the resources and treatments available to her at Moonlight. I would hate to do that to her, and it's a last-resort option, but I won't hesitate to push that button if it's necessary. I won't let Vera self-destruct, and I won't stand by and watch while she succumbs to drugs and other addictions.

"No, you're not a prisoner, but we both know Moonlight is the best place for you right now. Please don't jeopardize your health and your recovery. You've fought too hard to throw it all away now. When you're ready, your family home is waiting for you, and I will take you there if that's what you want."

"My family home?" Her voice cracks.

"The house in Rydeville where you grew up." She has a

large bank account too, but I'm not mentioning that yet. Felicity explained it's not a good idea as access to cash can be problematic for trauma survivors, the temptation to suffocate their pain in alcohol or drugs being too strong.

"Can I see it?" All the anger and hostility has fled her face again.

"I'll talk to Selena and Felicity."

"Okay." She walks toward my car scratching her arm with her head hanging and her shoulders slumping, and I feel like the biggest asshole.

We don't talk on the drive back, and I have the child locks on because I don't trust her in this volatile state. Vera is liable to do anything right now, and I'd never forgive myself if anything happened to her while in my care. I let her pick music on my cell, listening in strained silence while Vera stares out the window with her knees drawn to her chest.

In a lot of ways, Vera is mature beyond her years because of the life she's endured. Yet, in other ways, she is still a little kid because she missed out on the normal growing-up experience. It kills me.

She hops out of the car when we pull into the parking lot beside the main building at Moonlight, not uttering a word as she runs off to grab a golf cart to take her back to her cabin. I stare after her with pain in my heart.

I have a conversation with Felicity, explaining what happened at the crypt, and she promises to talk to Vera. She tells me I need to distance myself from Vera while she processes her feelings and works on her recovery. She is concerned I'm a danger to her mental health while she's this unstable. She also suggests we table the visit to the Ford family home until Vera is stronger.

It feels like I'm abandoning Vera, but after today, I can see I'm causing more harm than good. I trust the experts to know what is best, and I agree on the condition it's fully explained to Vera. I don't want her feeling completely rejected or thinking I'm staying away because I'm angry or upset with her over what she did today.

I head home in a super foul mood and swim fifty lengths in my indoor pool, but it still hasn't sated this dark storm churning inside me. I'm tempted to message Vixen to meet me at the club, but I worry I'd hurt her with the mood I'm in. So, I head to one of the underground fight clubs I like to frequent instead and take my frustrations out in the ring.

Chapter Nineteen
Athena

I smother my triumphant grin as I knock on the CEO's door bright and early on Monday morning.

"Come in," he calls, and his wickedly delicious tone sends shivers tiptoeing up my spine. I pause for a second as my thoughts wander to Beast. What is it about controlling men with their sexy voices that is my personal aphrodisiac?

I open the door and stride inside in my black pants suit and high heels. "Good morning, Mr. Manning. I just wanted to let you know I was here."

"Sure you didn't come to gloat?" he asks, leaning back in his chair as his eyes drink me in. He looks incredible in a white dress shirt with a vibrant blue tie and black pants. The matching jacket hangs on the back of his leather chair. His desk is super neat with one small tray of paperwork, a laptop, two framed family photos, and a paper cup I'm assuming contains coffee.

"That would be childish and petty," I reply, walking toward the desk.

"It would, wouldn't it?" He arches a brow, pointing at the empty chair in front of his desk with his pen. "Take a seat."

I sit down in front of him and straighten up. "Thanks again for the opportunity."

"You already said that on the phone, and there's no need for formalities. You can drop the whole Mr. Manning thing too. We don't stand on ceremony here. We call everyone by their first names, and I try my best to know everyone who works in this building."

"That's a pretty tall order."

"It is, but it's important to me."

"Am I allowed to ask why?"

"You can ask. Not sure I'll answer." He stands and walks to the window, shoving his hands in the pockets of his pants. Silence fills the space between us, but it's not the uncomfortable kind. I wait him out, studying his form while he gathers his thoughts. His broad shoulders fill his white dress shirt in a drool-worthy manner, the material clinging possessively to his muscular biceps and arms. My gaze roams lower over a toned butt I'd love to sink my teeth into and muscular thighs I imagine digging my nails into as he rails me from on top.

Drew Manning is sex on legs, and I bet he knows how to use that muscle between his thighs to drive a woman insane. I'd say a night with him is something no woman ever forgets.

"I'm not sure how much you know of our history," he says, talking to my reflection in the glass. "But Manning Motors has been in my family a long time."

I am more than aware of that fact. I have absorbed every scrap of intel I could find on this company while I was biding my time.

"I never got to know my grandfather, but he's somewhat of a legend around here. He was known for his appreciation of the people who worked for the company." He turns around, propping his butt on the side of his desk as he talks to me, and he has my full attention. "He was a man of the people, and everyone loved him. I firmly believe a huge reason for the success of the company at that time derived from that fact. He valued every employee. Gave them his time and his attention. Ensured they were well paid and well taken care of. Employees stayed long-term, and people vied to work here because of the great working environment."

"That's quite the legacy."

"It is. Unlike the one my own father left." His face turns dark, and I'm guessing everything I have learned about Michael Hearst is true.

"My father wasn't a good man, and he almost single-handedly destroyed my grandfather's legacy. The company I inherited was a shadow of what you see today. It has taken years to try to turn it around, and the work is far from over. I do my best to adhere to my grandfather's legacy. To be the kind of leader he would be proud of. I owe it to our employees to drive this business forward, to continue pushing to be market leaders, to grow our profit base so I can reward the people who helped to make it happen."

"That's very commendable, and your passion for the business is clear. You're a good man, and they are lucky to have you at the helm." I throw the bait out on purpose.

His lips curve at one corner. "If you knew me, you'd realize the irony, and trust me when I say I'm not a good man."

I tip my head to one side. "Why would you say that?"

His eyes bore into me as he slides back into his seat. "I have my reasons," he says, pulling his shields back up.

"And you're not going to elaborate."

"I want you to understand we're family at Manning

Motors, and I protect my family. If anyone fucks with it, I fuck with them right back."

It's a blatant threat, and I wonder what is driving his suspicion. Is it my connection to Belinda or something else? He was pretty hostile on Friday night. "Message received, Drew, though I'm unclear why you felt the need to make it."

"This rebranding is important as are the reasons behind it. I want our customers to feel like family too, and that family element needs to be incorporated in the new brand."

Great deflection, Mr. Manning. He really should consider going into politics. "I've already got some strong ideas I think will work." I had a month to work on this project, and I'm well ahead of the game. Not that anyone here will know it. Having work done in advance ensures I can duck out at times when I need to follow our illustrious CEO to uncover the double life he's leading.

"Impress me, Athena. Don't make me regret this."

I work late Monday night so I can explore the building without looking over my shoulder. Of course, there are security cameras everywhere, so I can't go crazy, but I memorize noteworthy things like the area on the top floor where the IT department is housed and the security room. I made a point of bringing coffee to Hilary, Drew's PA, and I intend to strike up a friendship. I want to get a hold of Drew's schedule, and it'll be easier to crack into her PC instead of having to break into the IT system. I'm also hoping she has keys to his office somewhere in her desk because he locks his office every time he leaves, and that makes me think there is something in there he doesn't want anyone to find.

Drew drops by my office on Tuesday to look at the designs I

mocked up, and we discuss a few tweaks with Belinda and Walter. I leave early that day, citing a personal appointment, heading straight from Manning Motors to Moonlight for my interview with Selena Kennedy. Stopping at a gas station on the way, I put my green contacts in and cover my blonde hair with my short black wig.

Manford Media is one of the US's foremost media conglomerates, and their Luminary status came in handy. Andreas coordinated everything, ensuring my profile appeared on the newspaper website when Selena called the HQ in Lowell to verify my identity and interview request. Of course, I'm here under a fake name and wearing a disguise just in case she mentions anything to Drew.

I'm itching to know why he came here on Sunday. I tried following him, but he almost made me, and I was forced to drop the surveillance and head off in a different direction. It would be so much easier if I could bug his cell or his car, but it's far too risky.

"Thanks for meeting me," I say, shaking Mrs. Kennedy's hand. "I know you're a busy woman, and I appreciate you taking the time to talk to me."

"Publicity is important, and I rarely turn down interview requests," she says, leading me into a homey office with a plush carpet and copious plants. Bypassing the desk, she guides me to a seated area in the corner where a tray with cookies, mugs, sugar, cream, and a coffee pot awaits us on the coffee table.

"Well, I'm grateful you gave me your time. I'm new to the paper and keen to make my mark. Bringing sex traffickers to justice is something I'm passionate about."

"Have a seat," she says, smiling warmly. "I find newbie reporters to be the most passionate about our cause, and I'm glad we share similar goals."

This woman should be given a Nobel Prize or a sainthood

or something. The work she has done here is phenomenal. And she's so humble about it. "I know your backstory, and I just want to tell you how much of an inspiration you are to me and so many other women." I mean that wholeheartedly.

"Thank you, Irena. That means a lot to me."

"Why do it?" I ask, taking out my pen and notepad. I've got to make this look real. "You endured hell, and surely being around other survivors must bring it all back to you? Why subject yourself to that?"

"Coffee?" she asks.

"Yes, please. Black, no sugar." I help myself to a cookie as she fixes my drink. I didn't stop for lunch, and I'm famished.

"Moonlight has given me purpose," she explains, handing me a mug. "For years, I couldn't speak about what happened to me. It was only when I began talking about it that I truly began to heal. I was lucky because I had a loving family, a loving boyfriend, and the resources to get help. Not every survivor is that fortunate. The idea had been brewing in my head for some time, and when Keanu came back into my life, he gave me the encouragement to make my idea a reality. His entire family backed me, and we had the support of hundreds of donors. Now, we're trying to lobby for government funding so we can set up more facilities. Unfortunately, there is high demand for our services, and it shows no signs of slowing down despite the efforts being taken to stop human trafficking."

We drink our coffee and eat cookies while we chat, and I make an effort to take notes so it looks legit. After thirty minutes, I finally find the opportunity I've been waiting for.

"A lot of local businesses support our facility, and we couldn't exist without them," she says.

"My cousin works at Manning Motors, and she told me they organize an annual charity event with all the proceeds going to Moonlight."

"Drew Manning is a big supporter of our work and a generous donor. He's one of the kindest men I know."

"I heard he visits frequently. Does he teach one of your programs?"

"I'm afraid that's confidential and not something I can discuss."

"Oh, of course. I didn't mean to pry."

Yeah, right. She doesn't have to confirm it for me to know Drew doesn't teach here. Andreas ran a check on street cameras going back three months, and he told me Drew visits most every Monday and Friday. If he's not here to teach, it means he's visiting someone.

But who?

I was hoping I could get a name, but that was delusional. Selena is never going to betray any client like that.

I could ask Andreas to hack into their systems and find out, but I draw the line at invading trauma survivors' privacy. Plus, I know Selena's brother-in-law Keven Kennedy personally oversees IT security at the facility. As a former FBI agent and a current co-owner of HADK Cybersecurity Solutions Limited, he is not someone to mess with, and I can't risk getting caught.

"I'd love to give you a tour myself," she says, rising to her feet. "But I've got a family event tonight, and I need to leave."

"It's no problem. I'm appreciative of the time you've given me." I gather my things and follow her to the door.

"I have arranged for one of our team to show you around our community if you have some additional time."

"That would be great." I want to see it for myself, and I plan to make an approach to the board to ask them to apply the relevant governmental pressure to ensure Selena gets her funding.

There's a knock on the door just as we reach it. "This must be them now," she says, opening it. "Oh, it's you."

"That's not the kind of greeting I was expecting, wife."

Selena laughs and pulls her husband into the room.

Keanu Kennedy is as hot as the rest of his brothers, and he only seems to get more attractive with age. She leans up and kisses him, and it's definitely the kind of kiss that should happen in private. I feel like a third wheel standing awkwardly to one side, but I don't blame her. If I had a man like that, I'd kiss him any chance I got.

"That's more like it," Keanu says when they surface for air. He reels her in close, pecking her lips one final time before patting her ass and turning to grin at me.

"That was rude of us. My apologies, Miss?"

"Hall." I thrust out my hand. "I'm Irena Hall. A reporter for *The California Times.*"

"Nice to meet you," he says, shaking my hand. "I was overseas for the past week on a business trip, and I drove straight here from the airport because I couldn't wait a second longer to see my wife."

"That's so sweet." A pang of longing accosts me from nowhere, causing me to momentarily frown.

"I have the best husband in the world." Selena places her hand on his chest. "He always makes me feel like a princess."

"A queen, my love. You're nothing short of a queen."

"I couldn't agree more," I say, swooning at the way they are staring at one another.

At one time, I used to wish for a love like that. Until my father decided to manipulate me into doing his dirty work and I lost most control over my life.

"I'll escort you to meet Clara for your tour," Selena says, but I wave her away.

"Please stay. Just tell me where to go, and I'll make my way there."

I'm deep in thought as I walk down the long hallway

toward the main lobby where Clara is waiting for me. I'm one hundred percent certain now that Drew Manning is targeting sex traffickers to take them down. I think it's personal for him. So, why the fuck are Dad and the board hellbent on eliminating him? If they asked me to deliver his intel so they could handle it themselves, I would understand. But they want him dead, and the million-dollar question is why? Unless he *is* targeting the heirs. Of course, they'd have to neutralize that threat.

Why would Drew go after the boys who are in line to succeed their fathers in our world? He doesn't even know there's a higher power. Few elite do, so what am I missing? Something stinks to the high heavens about this entire mission, and I'm going to find out what is truly going on before I hand anything over.

I won't sentence Drew Manning to his death unless I'm convinced he deserves it.

I'm so lost in thought I'm not watching where I'm going, and I almost collide with the thin blonde girl as I round the corner. "I'm so sorry," I say, reaching out to hold her arm before she falls.

"Don't touch me," she hisses, pulling her arm back before a huge sob wracks her frail form.

Her eyes are the bluest eyes I've ever seen, but they are awash with pain. The kind that speaks of untold horrors and deep-seated agony. Her agony is visceral, and my heart hurts for this stranger. I can only imagine the kinds of things she might have endured.

Removing a packet of tissues from my purse, I silently hand them to her.

She sniffs, staring at me with suspicion as she whips the tissue packet from my hands and proceeds to blow her nose.

Why does she seem familiar to me? I'm very sure I've never met her before.

"Can I do anything to help?" I ask as she dabs at her eyes, feeling completely useless when faced with this level of pain.

"Unless you have a time machine or you know any lobotomists, I don't see how you're any fucking use to me," she says, shooting me a filthy look before pushing past me.

Chapter Twenty
Drew

The hallways of Manning Motors are eerily empty as I lock my office door and head out. I am nearing the elevator when I come across Athena, typing away on her laptop in the office that was assigned to her with the door open. I pause in the doorway, admiring the look of fierce concentration on her face as she's lost in whatever she is working on. "What are you doing here on a holiday?" I ask.

"Jesus, fuck," she rasps, slamming a hand over her chest as she whips her head up from the screen.

Her breathy voice stirs some hidden memory, and I frown, trying to pinpoint what about it resonates with me.

"You scared me almost to death. Do you make a habit of creeping up on people?"

"Not usually," I lie, "and sorry." Her chest is heaving, her breaths exaggerated, and my lips lift in a smile.

"Liar. I bet you were that kind of brother. The one who loved jumping out from behind trees and doors and scaring the hell out of your sister just for shits and giggles."

A chuckle rumbles my chest. "You couldn't be more wrong." That stuff was way too tame for me, and we stopped being playful kids the second our mom was taken from us. "I've always been the one protecting Abby from that kind of shit."

She leans back in her chair, and soft, wavy, blonde hair floats over her shoulders and down her back. She's dressed casually today in jeans and a sweater with minimal makeup on her face, and she's never looked more beautiful.

"I always wanted an older brother," she says, chewing on the corner of her lip. "I used to wish for a brother like you. Someone to look out for me and make all the bad shit go away."

"What bad shit?" My frown returns as I wonder who has hurt her. Then I wonder why the fuck I care. I might not have discovered any dirt on Athena Lewis, and searching through her system activity logs hasn't identified anything suspicious, but I still don't trust her. I've watched the cameras. I've seen her prowling around my building. To innocent eyes, she is a curious newbie roaming our hallways, taking it all in. To a trained killer like me, she's staking the joint and plotting a plan of attack.

I'm onto you, Miss Lewis, and it's only a matter of time before I figure out what your game plan is.

"I'm talking in general terms."

"You never answered my question," I say, chuckling as she stares blankly at me. "What are you doing at work on Thanksgiving?"

"Thanking my boss for giving me a job."

I roll my eyes. "You don't expect me to buy that, do you? You had a job. You didn't need mine, remember?" The little minx used it to bargain for double the contract fee, citing damage to her reputation from walking away from a client mid-project. Maybe it's true, but I'm calling bullshit. I've seen her bank balance, and she's not short of cash.

"Okay, you got me." She sits up straighter. "It's too far to travel home for one day, and I didn't want to take any more time off. I'm already one month behind, and I'm determined to finish this project on time."

"You could have worked remotely for a couple days. I'm not an ogre. It's the holidays, and you're entitled to a break."

Her eyes latch on mine, holding me captive, and it's like being sucker-punched in the nuts. Her gaze is usually so guarded but not now. Now, she's shielding nothing, and I'm intrigued by this woman who may or may not want to do me harm. "Truth is I didn't want to go home. My brother isn't there, and he's the only good thing about my family."

"Go on." I encourage her with my eyes.

"My father is very controlling," she supplies. I got that impression when she said he was misogynistic. "And we rarely see eye to eye." Emotion washes over her face, and she grips the arms of her chair tight. Her eyes flare with anger, and her tone is bristling when she speaks. "My stepmother is an evil cunt, and if she wasn't Arlo's mother I'd have—"

"What? Don't stop before you get to the good part."

The walls go back up, and she flashes me a tight smile. "Let's just say we have never gotten along and leave the rest up to your imagination."

"I have a very vivid imagination."

"I'd say."

"What does that mean?" I push off the doorway.

She shrugs. "Keep your panties on, Drew. I wasn't insinuating anything. Just that men in your position have sharp minds, and I imagine vivid imaginations are the norm."

She totally just tried to play me, and her guards are firmly back in place. But she let me in for a second, and I want to see more of that. She might let something slip if I can get her in a relaxed environment. I don't stop to question my decision the second the idea lands in my head, choosing to just run with it. "Pack up your things and come with me."

Brief alarm shimmers in her eyes before she disguises it. "Why?" Distrust underscores her tone.

"No one works at Manning Motors on Thanksgiving, and no one should spend the day alone. You're coming home with me."

She blinks repeatedly. "Why would you do that? You don't even like me."

"I never said I don't like you."

"You don't have to. I read it in your body language, and you weren't exactly welcoming last week at dinner."

"I don't like being caught off guard, and you can't blame me for being suspicious given how we met."

"Fair enough, but that still doesn't explain why you'd want to bring me to your place on Thanksgiving."

"Not to mine. My mom is hosting Thanksgiving at her house. And I already told you why I'm inviting you. It doesn't sit right letting you go home to an empty apartment. Abby would string me up by my balls if she knew. She'll love to see you. Demi too."

"I don't know, Drew." She runs a hand through her hair. "I can't just show up unannounced and uninvited."

"*I'm* inviting you, and I'll call my mom on the way. There is always way too much food, and we can easily fit one more in. It'll be fun. Although I should warn you it'll be like a zoo with wild animals-slash-kids racing around the place, a bunch of my asshole friends, and their nosy significant others, and if I rock up with you on my arm, my mother will fall at your feet and worship the ground you walk on because she'll think we're dating and you've tamed me."

She cracks up laughing, and it does something funny to my

insides, which I do not like. I'm considering rescinding my offer when she closes her laptop and stands, grinning widely. "Why didn't you say that in the first place? It sounds incredible and I'd love to join you."

Athena

Drew is rummaging through the drawer in my coffee table when I emerge from my bedroom wearing a black-and-red-patterned fitted dress and black heels, which I hope is suitable for Thanksgiving with his family. Maybe I should have called Abby and asked her what to wear, but I'm probably making a big deal out of nothing. "What are you doing?" I ask, snatching my wool coat from the back of the stool in the kitchen part of my open-plan living space.

"Trying to find something personal. There is no part of your personality showcased anywhere in this apartment."

"Well, nosy, I have only been living here five weeks, and it's a rental. I didn't see the point in moving my stuff from my place in Boston when I won't be here long-term."

"I get that, but buy some flowers or plants, a few cheap colorful cushions or throws, something to make it less sterile."

"Are you always this rude?" I ask, flipping open my compact and applying a clear gloss layer over my signature red lips.

"Is it rude if I'm telling the truth?" I feel his eyes drilling holes in the side of my face as he watches me.

I close the compact and pop it in my purse, making eye contact with him. His eyes are becoming very familiar to me, and there is something warm and inviting that draws me in.

"You're either extremely arrogant, narcissistic, a total ignoramus, or socially inept. I haven't worked out which yet."

He barks out a laugh. "Insulting the boss to his face takes balls, Athena. I can't decide if I'm impressed or if I should fire you."

"We're not in the office," I remind him, putting my purse down so I can put my coat on.

"Allow me." He darts forward, taking my coat and holding it out for me.

I look back at him, and our eyes connect again. My heart thumps against my chest cavity, and butterflies swoop into my stomach as I slide my arm through one sleeve. His attention doesn't stray from my face as I slide my other arm through the second sleeve. Not even when he moves around to my front and begins buttoning my coat.

My mouth is dry, my panties anything but.

"You are always representing Manning Motors even when not in the office."

I bite on the inside of my cheek to stifle a moan as his fingers brush against my boobs through the coat as he slowly buttons me up. I'm physically and figuratively melting in my coat as an inferno flares to life inside my body. He is so close and far too tempting with his sultry voice and his confident hands as he finishes buttoning my coat and ties the belt at the front.

His mouth tips upward as he watches me before his gaze lowers to my lips for a fleeting second. He jerks back, the smirk falling off his face. "Don't you agree?"

"What?" I blurt, confused and turned on and wondering why the fuck I just let him do that.

Amusement returns to his expression. "That employees always represent their company in and out of the office?"

"I agree management expects that, but I doubt many employees would concur." I snap out of my fugue state and grab my purse, removing my keys. "And in case you've forgotten, I'm not an employee. I represent AMC Solutions. Any bad behavior reflects back on my company, not on yours."

"I disagree. You're running a high-profile project that has significant visibility. Any bad behavior while contracted to my company would reflect poorly on us too."

"If you're so convinced I'll behave badly, why hire me in the first place?" I challenge, lifting a brow.

"Are you saying you're behaving badly already or likely to do so at some point before the contract ends?"

"If you have something to say, Drew, just say it."

"I thought we were speaking hypothetically." He rubs a hand along his chin as he stares intently at me, and this feels like some kind of test.

"You speak in riddles. It's a miracle your company is so successful if this is how you normally conduct yourself."

Another laugh rumbles from his chest. "And the insults just keep on coming." In a fast move I don't predict, he steps right up to me and grips my chin lightly. "Who are you, Athena, and what are you hiding because I see the secrets cowering behind your eyes."

Heat rolls off his body and washes over me. His closeness is unnerving, but I'm guessing that's the point. If he's hoping to intimidate me into giving up my agenda, he'll be sorely disappointed. It will take a lot more than that for me to trust this man.

I don't believe he's bad, but he's done bad shit, and he's caught up in bad shit, and he clearly has suspicions about me, which is not good.

I wonder what gave me away. It's a slip-up I can't afford.

He's looking for something, and it's an opportunity to steer him down a different path and also plant these seeds.

"Have you guessed my dirty big secret, Drew?" I purr in my most seductive voice as he lets go of my chin.

His brow puckers, and I wonder what I said to cause that frown.

I lower my shields, allowing old emotions to flood my face so I can draw upon them. "The truth is I'm lonely. I don't have many friends, and the only family I truly have is my brother. I've sacrificed everything to build my career, and I wasn't fully honest that night at dinner. I do want more. Not the kids part. That's not in the cards for me."

I slide my hand up his chest on purpose, trying to conceal my mirth because I know this will have him running and screaming for the hills. "But I want love." My eyes drill into his as my hand creeps higher up his body. I'm not sure he's even realized I'm doing it. I pause for a second to trap the laughter dying to burst free. "I need a man, and you're the first one to catch my eye in a very long time." My hand curls around his neck, and I press my body up against him. "So, there you have it, Drew. My dirty big secret is I have a crush on my asshole boss."

He lets go of me so fast it's comical, and I can't control my laughter when I see the look of absolute horror on his face. I convulse as wracking waves of uncontrollable laughter rock my body. So much for keeping the pretense. I'm not sorry I went there even if he ditches his plans to take me with him. That look on his face right there was worth it.

"You're an evil bitch, Athena Lewis."

"Oh, come on, admit that was funny."

"If it was payback for almost giving you a coronary earlier, consider it achieved."

Drew

"The idea of me having a crush on you almost gave you a heart attack? Wow. I don't know if I'm flattered or insulted."

"You're a handful, Miss Lewis." Planting his hand on my lower back, he urges me forward. "And I'm warning you now, if you even attempt to joke about that at my mother's house, I'll put you over my knee and spank your ass in front of everyone. Let's see how funny that'd be."

Chapter Twenty-One
Athena

"This place is incredible," I say as Drew drives us through high wrought-iron gates along a winding driveaway lined with majestic trees and manicured lawns. Tall walls keep prying eyes out, and I spot security cameras and barbed wires all around the perimeter. I know what happened to Olivia Manning, and the heightened security makes total sense.

"It's been in my family for generations," he explains, and it's the first time he's spoken since we left the store fifteen minutes ago. He's been brooding over my prank, and I'd love an inside look in his head to know exactly what he's thinking. "But the original house burnt down years ago, so Mom built a new one."

"I read about that." His gaze narrows on me, and I roll my eyes. "You are such a suspicious man, Drew Manning, and keep your eyes on the road. I'm sure your mother would not appreciate us crashing in her driveaway." I run a hand through my hair. I wore it wavy today and didn't bother straightening it when I was at home. "I studied your company and you before I came to present. It's important to me to have a full picture of my client and the project. There is a lot about your family online. I read all about the elite and the stuff that went on at Parkhurst. Your father sounds like a nasty piece of work, by the way."

"He was a total prick. One of the happiest days of my life was the day he died. I'm only sorry I wasn't the one who put a bullet through his skull."

"That was Montgomery, right?" It's been well documented. "He sounded like another piece of shit."

"He was a monster. The worst kind."

"Lucky some good Samaritan did us a solid and removed that evil from the world. Funny how they never discovered what happened to him. Montgomery just vanished into thin air, presumed dead after all this time." I watch him for any physical tells, but there is nothing, which is true talent. I know he wasn't there when Lauder, Anderson, and Hunt murdered Montgomery, but he definitely knows the truth. I'm not surprised he's loyal to his friends, and I meant it when I said they did the world a favor. It's a better place without Christian and his brutish son.

"I don't care, and I don't think anyone lost any sleep over it."

"What is your dirty big secret, Drew, and don't say you don't have one because I see it in your eyes too."

"How about you tell me yours, and I'll tell you mine," he says as he pulls the car up in front of a gorgeous expansive modern building.

"Touché, Mr. Manning."

He climbs out and rounds the hood of the car as I reach into the back seat for the flowers and champagne for his mom and the candy for the kids. It's the best I could do on short notice.

Drew

Drew opens my door, taking the flowers and the bag with the champagne and candy before helping me out. He looms over me by a few inches, and I love it. So many men come up short when I wear heels, and tall men always make me feel sexy. His chin lowers as he leans down, pressing his mouth close to my ear. "I get the feeling your dirty big secret is more of a dark big secret."

Shivers crawl all over my body, and I grip the side of the door as my legs threaten to go out from under me.

"Most women would grimace at the things the world knows the elite have done, but your eyes shine with excitement. Why is that?"

He straightens up, and I eyeball him as I give him this truth. "I'm not like most women."

The door opens, ending our conversation, and I'm glad because it was getting dicey. I take the flowers while Drew keeps a hold of the bag.

"I came to warn you," Abby says, smiling broadly as we walk toward her. "Mom is like an excitable kangaroo on speed since you called."

"Awesome," Drew drawls, placing his hand on my lower back.

"Hey you." Abby stretches up to kiss my cheek. "We're so happy you could join us. If I'd known you had no plans for Thanksgiving, I would've invited you on Monday."

"I didn't want to make a big deal."

"Well, you're here now," she says, hauling me inside. The door closes with a bang behind Drew. "I don't know if Drew warned you, but it's crazy when everyone is here."

"He mentioned that."

"And my mother is fixated on finding Drew his one true love. He hasn't brought a date to any event in a very long time, so she's reading more into this. Don't take it personally."

"I've been prewarned, and it's cool." I look back at Drew, grinning. "I was just telling Drew—"

"Don't you dare," he growls, cutting across me.

"That I have a dirty big crush on him, and I've been doodling his name all over my journal and planning a massive fairy-tale wedding and—"

He clamps his hand over my mouth, stalling my words. "You're certifiable, or maybe I am for bringing you here."

Abby wears an inquisitive expression as her gaze dances between her brother and me. "At least you're not snapping at one another. This is progress." She waggles her brows and grins.

"Your lipstick is smudged," Drew says in a clipped tone like his sister's words really irritated him, or maybe mine did it.

Before he can stop me, I dart in and press a firm kiss to the underside of his jawline, leaving a visible mark. "There." I beam at him as he looks at me like I'm the antichrist. "Now there's an explanation for it."

Abby grabs her twin's free hand so he can't rub the mark away, dragging him down the hallway while I walk on his other side, snorting a laugh at the look of thunder on his face.

"Look who's here!" Abby shouts to be heard over the noise in the large open-plan space. My jaw trails the ground as I count the bodies around the room. Holy fucking shit. There are at least twelve adults and ten kids by my calculation. With us, that's twenty-five. It's crazy. Who are all these people?

"Uncle Drew!" a chorus of little voices says, and warmth fills my chest as I watch the kids descend en masse on Drew and surround him.

"We're missing a few," Abby explains. "Our friends, the Lauders, are in New York with Jackson's family today."

Everyone knows who Jackson Lauder is. He's been

crowned champion four times during his career, and it's not over yet. "He's the Formula 1 racer."

"He's so amazing," Abby gushes. "We're all very proud of him." She loops her arm through mine, tugging me toward the kitchen where two older women are busy cooking. "Two of my brothers-in-law are missing too. Harley got married recently, and he's at his in-laws, and my youngest brother-in-law, Roman, is a top model. He's signed to Keanu Kennedy's modeling agency, and he lives in Milan with his Italian fiancé. They don't celebrate Thanksgiving in Europe, but we spoke to him this morning, and Leonardo's family is throwing a big family dinner in Roman's honor, which is so sweet."

Olivia Manning turns around at the sound of Abby's voice, and her face lights up like a thousand suns when she spots me. "You must be Athena. Oh my, look how gorgeous you are."

The other woman glances at me over her shoulder, smiling as she stirs a pot at the stove.

Olivia practically skips toward me, taking my hand and pulling me away from her daughter. "A beautiful name for a beautiful woman. My son is a lucky man."

"He definitely is," I say, deciding to just go with this. It's going to really wind Drew up, and I'm giddy at the thought of pissing him off all day. Which is probably super mean because he was considerate in inviting me, but oh well.

I never claimed to be an angel.

Her squeal of delight almost bursts my eardrums.

"You are so wicked," Abby whispers in my ear. "But I love it, and you're officially my new best friend."

The smile cresting over my face is genuine as I wink at Drew's twin. It feels so good to have a partner in crime.

"These are for you," I say, handing the flowers to Olivia. "Drew has some other stuff I brought."

"There really was no need, but this is so thoughtful." Olivia buries her head in the petals before grinning at me.

"If I'd known in advance, I would have baked something. Before my mom died, she used to give the staff the day off on Thanksgiving, and we always cooked everything from scratch. It was the same at Christmas. I miss those traditions."

"I take it your cunt of a stepmother doesn't cook," Drew says, staggering into the kitchen with a cute little redhead clinging to his leg.

"Andrew!" Olivia shrieks, placing her hands over the little girl's ears. "Watch your language around the little ones."

"Shit. Fuck. Agh." He thrusts the bag at me, looking clearly rattled, and I can barely contain my glee. This is gonna be so fun. "Sorry, I forgot."

"You need to remember." His mom drills him with a look.

"I'm so sorry," a striking woman with dark red hair and bright green eyes says rushing into the kitchen. "You know Darcy is half in love with you, Drew," she teases, trying to coax her daughter away from Drew's leg.

"Join the club, girl," I say, holding my hand out to the little girl for a high five. Her soft little palm smacks against mine as she giggles, and she's the most adorable little thing.

I love kids.

So long as I can give them back at bedtime.

Abby cracks up laughing, and I join her when I see the lethal expression on Drew's face. He would definitely give Voldemort a run for his money.

"This is very generous," Olivia says, peeking into the bag as I hand it over, oblivious to the toxic vibes her son is emitting.

"Thank you for having me."

She puts the bag down on the island unit and reels me into a brief hug. "I'm so happy you're here." She holds my hands and beams at me, and I feel a teeny-tiny bit guilty because she's genuinely happy at the thought her son has me in his life. "Drew is so secretive, and he tells us nothing, but I had a feeling there might be someone special." She reaches out and pinches his cheeks. "Now your anger makes so much sense! You should've just told me you had a ladylove!"

A very unladylike snort escapes my mouth, and I do believe Drew Manning would shoot me in my obnoxious mouth if he thought he'd get away with it.

"I'm glad I can stop my matchmaking efforts now. It was starting to stress me out," she says, patting her son on his reddening cheek as her eyes zero in on the lipstick mark on his cheek. Her smile widens. "You've got a little lipstick there, honey. Hold still," she says, grabbing a tissue from the box on the island unit and wiping it away. "I love the red lips, Athena," she says, waggling her brows at me. "It really suits you. I've heard some men love it when a woman goes down on them with red lipstick, if you catch my drift."

Abby howls with laughter, and I clutch her arm as I crack up laughing. My stomach is starting to hurt.

"Jesus, Mom." Drew scrubs his hands down his face before charging toward the refrigerator with flared nostrils and steam billowing from his ears. "I need a beer or ten," he mumbles.

"Don't forget you have to drive me home later, sweet cheeks," I call out.

Darcy's mother looks between Abby and me with slight confusion as we fall around laughing again. At this rate, I'll have a permanent bellyache.

Honestly, I don't know how Olivia hasn't figured it out yet.

Drew glares at me behind his mother's back, childishly flipping me the bird before storming out of the kitchen into the main living space.

"He's got that grumpy bad boy look down pat," the other woman says as she walks toward me with a warm smile. I recognize her. Sylvia Montgomery. She was married to that asshole Christian. "Those men are all the rage in romance novels," she adds, extending her hand. "I'm Sylvia. It's lovely to meet you. Abby and Demi have been telling us all about you."

"It's lovely to meet you too, and I might need some romance recommendations."

"Book boyfriends are always better than real life," Sylvia says.

"Kai is better than all the book boyfriends put together," Abby protests as a cute little boy with dark hair and dark eyes rushes into the kitchen and wraps his arms around her.

"Mom, Oli said I'm a stinky fart face and he's trading me in for Henry. He said I have to live at his house and Henry will be living in my bedroom." He looks up at her with glassy eyes. "He can't do that, can he?"

"No, sweetness." Abby kisses his brow. "You're stuck with us, I'm afraid." She hugs him close and bellows, "SOS, Caveman."

Kaiden gets up, mid-conversation, and strides into the kitchen. "What's going on?" he asks, looking between his son and his wife.

"Your mini-me is stirring S-H-I-T again."

"I can spell, Mom." The boy looks up at her with a "duh" face. "You just said a bad word."

"Sorry, Ori." She messes his hair. "I'll put a dollar in the swear jar when we get home."

Kai crouches down low. "What did Oli do this time?" His son explains, and I watch love bleed from Abby's and Kaiden's eyes, and it's beautiful. "Okay." Kai stands and grips the little boy's hand. "Let's go talk to your brother and clear this up. Then maybe we can play soccer before dinner?"

"Yay!" Ori jumps up and down, his previous melancholy all but forgotten.

"He's a miracle worker," Abby says, staring dreamily at her husband as he goes off to referee between their two sons.

"It certainly seems like he usurps book boyfriends."

"He so does. I'm a lucky bitch." She loops her arm in mine again. "Come on, let me introduce you to the others."

Chapter Twenty-Two
Drew

"There you are, sweet cheeks," Athena says, dropping onto my lap uninvited. "I got you another beer." She hands it to me before smoothing the creases in my brow with her thumbs.

My skin tingles from her touch, adding to the general aggravation I've been feeling all day. No matter how many times I tell everyone we are not together and this is all one big joke to her, they refuse to believe it. I know my friends are just going along with it to wind me up, but Mom actually buys into it, and she's going to be upset when she finds out it's not real. Somehow, it'll all be my fault even though I have not encouraged this one little bit.

"Don't frown, darling," Athena adds, moving on my lap in a way that is not helpful.

My dick has struggled to get the memo today, and I've been hiding semis and stiffies from the kids all afternoon because she keeps touching me and pressing up against me and treating me like her own personal chair. "If the wind changes, your face will be stuck like that."

"Athena," I growl, grabbing her hips and warning her with a sharp look. "I'm close to my breaking point, and I really wouldn't test me any further if I were you."

Her warm breath fans across my ear as she leans in and whispers, "What if I want to be punished?"

"Trust me, you don't want that," I say before knocking back a mouthful of beer. If I had her somewhere private, I would paddle her naughty ass until it's bright red before fucking her into next week.

My thoughts shock me, and I knock back more beer, unwilling to analyze them.

"You don't know what I want." She squirms on my lap again, and I curse under my breath.

"And I'll never find out," I say in case she's buying into any of this.

"If you say so." She purses her lips and grins as she plucks the beer bottle from my fingers and takes a swig from it.

Joaquin smirks at me from his seat on the couch across from me, and I snarl at him. It's usually just the two of us who are dateless at family events, but he doesn't seem to mind being the only solo male here today. Charlie, Demi, and Xavier have been riling me up all day while Sawyer is scrutinizing Athena like she's some alien species. And I get it. I don't do this—even in jest.

I haven't spoken much to Shandra and Rick, apart from a brief congratulations when we first sat down to eat. I've picked up Shandra's curious stares a few times though, which makes me a little uncomfortable.

I don't know why I thought it was a good idea to invite Athena or why I'm going along with this bullshit.

Her arms wind around my neck, and her tits are all up in my face as she drapes herself around me and buries her face in my neck.

My body stiffens all over. "What are you doing?"

"Smelling you," she says, audibly sniffing me.

Charlie is sitting beside me, and he heard every word. He's laughing and holding his stomach, and I visualize punching him repeatedly in the face because it's the only way I can calm myself down.

Athena abruptly sits up. "What is that cologne?" she asks, wearing a deep frown.

"What's it to you?"

"Nothing." She wets her lips and shakes her head before scrambling off my lap and standing. "I'm going to head home."

I should feel relieved. I mean I *am* relieved, but there's disappointment there too that I don't understand. "Let me call you a car," I say, rising to my feet. I've had too much to drink to drive her home, and I'll probably just crash at Mom's tonight.

"I can call my own car."

"You're my guest. I'll make arrangements while you say goodbye. I'll meet you at the front door."

I stand outside while I wait for her, welcoming the cold as it whistles around me. I brought Athena here today to learn more about her, but it backfired in a major way. All I learned is she has a good sense of humor and she's great with strangers. She bonded with all the kids and the adults. It's easy to tell she comes from money because she carries herself with grace in social settings. However, as much as I admire that in her, I'm not used to being played, and she has pissed me off a lot today. Even if I can admit it was funny as fuck at times. I'll try to remember that when I'm consoling Mom because I already know she loves her, and she's probably planning our wedding in her head.

"Fuck." I rest my head back against the wall and close my eyes.

"Did I go too far?" she asks, and I open my eyes and push off the wall.

"Yes, but don't start acting all remorseful now."

"I wasn't planning to," she says, shivering a little. "I own my shit."

I pull the collar of her coat up to ward off the chill. "The car will be here any minute."

"Thank you." Her eyes penetrate mine, and my heart does this funny little twisty thing. "I had the best time today. I love your family and friends, and all the kids are adorable," she says as my phone beeps to alert me to the car at the front gate.

I check the image on my phone before automatically opening the gate and granting the driver entry. "You're good in unfamiliar settings."

"Consequence of growing up how I did. Dad mixes in wealthy circles. There were always parties and charity events, and I was schooled in how to behave from an early age."

"Sounds a lot like how we were brought up," I admit, keeping an eye on my phone as I watch the car drive toward us.

"Then you get it," she says, cupping my cheek.

I gulp heavily as her touch seeps through my skin and into my bones.

"You're very lucky, Drew. You have so many people who love and care about you."

Gravel crunches behind me as the car pulls up.

"Thank you for letting me be a part of your family today, and while I should probably apologize for torturing you, I won't." Her mouth presses against my ear. "I liked pretending with you." Her smile seems sincere as she stares at me. In an unexpected move, she brushes her lips against mine in a fleeting soft kiss. "Goodnight, Drew. See you at the office."

I'm in a bit of a daze as I watch her get into the town car and drive away.

"She has you tied into knots," Charlie says, materializing at my side. I didn't even hear him come out.

"She has an agenda." My lips are still tingling from that barely there kiss.

"Then maybe you should go along with this. Get close to her and find out what she's up to."

"Perhaps." It would make sense, and it wouldn't be the first time I've fucked a woman to uncover her secrets.

"I think we should make one last effort with the two pricks," he says. "How about tomorrow night?"

I nod. "Agreed, but if they don't give us anything, we cut our loses and work out where we go from here." My lips kick up at the corners. "They have enjoyed my hospitality for long enough."

Charlie chuckles. "Not sure what it says about me, but I'm having more fun than I've had in years."

"I swear I won't tell Demi."

He punches me in the arm. "I have plenty of fun with my wife. You know what I mean."

"From one violent asshole to another, yeah, I do."

"It feels good to get my hands bloody for a good cause."

"I need closure," I say, shoving my hands in my pants pockets.

"I know, buddy." He clamps his hand on my shoulder. "We're getting closer. I feel it in my bones. We'll get the answers."

"Thanks for forcing my hand. I couldn't go on without you."

"I'm glad to help, and I've got your back, Drew. Whatever you need, it's yours."

I pull him into a quick hug. "Come on back inside. I'm freezing my balls off out here."

Shandra is waiting in the hallway when we reenter the house. "Hey, Drew. I was hoping we could talk?"

"Sure."

"I'll see you in a bit," Charlie says, smiling at Shandra as he walks by.

"Let's talk in the library," I suggest, and she nods, smiling shyly as she falls into step beside me.

"Have you set a date yet?" I ask.

"Not yet, but we don't want to wait, so it'll probably happen before next summer."

"I'm happy for you," I say, holding out the door to the library for her.

"Thank you," she says as I follow her inside. Kai and I had started the fire in here earlier, and it's toasty warm in the room now.

"Drink?" I ask as I head toward the liquor cabinet.

"Not for me."

Well, I'm sure I'll need alcohol for this talk, so I fix myself a large whiskey and join her by the fire.

"I owe you an apology," she blurts as I lower into the chair across from her.

"I'm pretty sure I'm the one who needs to apologize."

"I hate the way things were left with us, and I hate the awkwardness between us these days. It wasn't always like that."

"No, it wasn't." I cross an ankle over my knee. "I was depressed after Jane left, and you were an incredible friend to me, Shandra. You got me through those early days, and I valued your friendship highly. I'm sorry it got so messed up. I know I gave you mixed signals, and it wasn't fair."

"I wasn't fair to you either, Drew." She tucks a strand of hair behind her ear as she stares me straight in the eye. "I knew you were pining for Jane, and I knew how much you loved her. I was at school with both of you. I saw your love story firsthand.

I was so happy after my engagement to Trent ended and I was matched with you. I didn't expect anything at first, but then I got to know you, and somewhere along the way I fell for you, and I convinced myself I could have what you had with Jane."

"I'm sorry if I led you to believe that was a possibility. The truth is I was broken and incapable of loving anyone else. Jane still owned my heart. I had sent her away to keep her safe because the elite threat was considerable. Even if there was something between us, I was never going to put you at risk."

"Of course not. You've always been super protective of those you love, and I see that now in a way I couldn't back then. You were brutally honest with me about it, Drew. You told me repeatedly we would never be more, but I was the stubborn idiot who thought she could change your mind. I clung to hope where there was none, and I pursued you when I should have just accepted the friendship you were offering and let it go."

"I shouldn't have let things get that far the night of Jackson and Nessa's wedding, but you caught me at a real low point. It's not an excuse. I'm just trying to explain how it happened. I didn't treat you right, and for that, I am truly sorry. I never meant to hurt you, Shandra. That was the last thing I wanted."

"I knew, deep down, you weren't into it, Drew. You wouldn't let me kiss you, and that should have told me everything, but I was refusing to read the signs. You're not the only one to shoulder the blame for that night. I pushed for it knowing you didn't feel the same way about me. I was still clinging to stupid hope, thinking if we had sex everything would be different. That you'd see me in a different light and want me. I won't lie. When you stopped it before we crossed that line, I felt so rejected and unworthy. It hurt a lot, but even then, I still loved you. I didn't give up hope for a long time. It took me years to get over you."

Shame crawls over me like a dark cloud. "I didn't know

that, and I'm sorry things weren't different. If I didn't love Jane, maybe they might have been."

"But you did, and I can't fault you for that. I knew you loved her. I knew you were missing her. I chased something that was never there, and that's on me, not you. I built it all up in my head, read so much into the tiniest thing, but that is on me, not you."

"We were kids, Shandra. What the fuck did we really know?"

She bobs her head, sending bouncy curls tumbling around her pretty face. "It's so much easier to look back at it now and see where everything went wrong. I cringe now when I think of some of the things I said and did. I fully believed it at the time, but I see it all so differently now. I'm sorry if I added to your pain at a time when you were already going through so much."

"It's water under the bridge, Shandra, and I never blamed you for anything. I hope you know that. I just felt bad because I knew I hurt you, and it was never my intention."

"I'm really glad we cleared this up." I can visibly see the stress leave her face.

"Me too, and I'm very happy for you and Rick. I always thought there was something there."

"I think there was too, but we were both hung up on other people."

"Timing is everything, and Rick is a good man. He will love you good, the way you deserve. I would never have been capable of loving you properly. I would never have been good enough."

"Don't say that." She reaches out and squeezes my hand. "You're a good man too, Drew, and you deserve to be happy." Her eyes probe mine. "I don't know what happened with Jane, and I know you don't like talking about it. But whatever it is, it's not your fault. No one could have loved her more. If that's what's holding you back from moving on, please let it go." She stands as I swirl whiskey in my glass. "What I have with Rick is true, deep, passionate love, and it's the best feeling in the entire world. I really want that for you. I watched you with Athena today, and I know it was supposedly a big joke, but I saw something between you. There is a spark, a connection. It's none of my business, and you don't have to say a word, but if there is something there, don't fight it, Drew, and don't run away from it." She leans in and kisses my cheek. "Love is as scary as it is exhilarating. Opening yourself up and sharing everything you are with another person is terrifying, but the reward is so worth it."

She walks toward the door, stopping and turning around to deliver these parting words of wisdom: "Don't shut her out, Drew. Know you are worthy and let her in. What have you got to lose?"

Chapter Twenty-Three
Athena

I'm parked up on the hill on my bike, scanning the hotel grounds with my night vision binoculars for any sign of Drew or Charlie, but there is nothing, nada, zilch, and I'm frustrated. They went into the hotel hours ago, and I've never wished I was a fly more desperately in my life. I'm dying to know what's going on and I hate being in the dark.

At least today wasn't a total wipeout. There was only a skeleton staff at the office, and Drew didn't show up until after lunch, so I managed to sneak around Hilary's desk, and I found a spare set of keys to Drew's office. I got a duplicate set made on my lunchbreak, and I put the keys back where I found them. Now, I just need to find a way to get into the security system to turn off the cameras so I can get into his office and search it.

I'm not sure going to his mom's house yesterday was a good idea. I was melancholy the rest of the night at home. I loved the whole day, and I can't remember the last time I was that happy or had that much fun. Thanksgiving in Lowell hasn't been fun since Mom died. I sunk into a bit of a funky mood when I got back to my apartment. I couldn't stop thinking about my life and all the things I thought I'd have at thirty.

I have always known I was unhappy, but I had never admitted it to myself.

Now that I have confronted the stark reality of my life, I don't know what to do with it.

The irony is Drew thinks the joke's on him after yesterday, but the truth is the joke's on me.

I have my brother, my business, and a hot guy who fucks all coherent thoughts from my head.

But that's it, and most is transient.

I'm at risk of losing my brother to the Luminaries, my business is really just a way to spend time and a cover for my missions, and what I have with Beast is temporary. He will move on soon to another woman, and I'll be left with a big void in my life because I already know I'm done with the sex club when our agreement comes to an end. He has ruined me for all other men, and I won't be able to go to the club without wondering who he is and thinking about whoever he's currently fucking.

So, yeah, I'm the loser, and Drew is the winner because he has multiple people who care about him, a career he seems to love, and a goal to eradicate the world of evil pricks.

I can't even say I do good because I'm just my father's lackey, and most of my missions are personal to him. Like seducing the son of a rival to get inside intel he can use to destroy their business. Or killing some asshole who double-crossed him and made him look bad. And worming my way into competitor companies so I can steal their new products and he can launch to market before them.

The roar of an engine claims my attention, yanking me out of my depressive inner monologue, and I mentally beat myself up for missing them leaving. Down below, Drew's black SUV trundles down the bumpy driveway, so I kick-start my bike and tear off down the hill. I tap the side of my helmet twice to call Andreas. "They're on the move."

"The drone is activated, and I'll send you the coordinates."

"Stay on the line. I'm on the bike tonight."

"Yes, ma'am."

"Shit!" I yell as I come over the last bend and spot Drew's SUV blocking the exit. I'm going too fast to pull back, and adrenaline surges through my veins as I charge toward them. "I need another route home," I yell as I calculate my chances of crashing if I go kamikaze over Drew's car. I don't see how I've got any other option if I want to avoid capture. I'm glad I always dress in black and wear a disguise when on surveillance. At least he won't be able to make me as long as I can get away from him.

"Stop," Drew barks out the side window, lifting a gun, and pointing it at me.

"Thena!" Andreas roars in my ear, but I block him and Drew out as I accelerate toward the bump in the path, using it to launch myself up and over the car. A shot rings out as I sail over the SUV, but I ignore it, putting my fate in a higher power and concentrating on a steady landing.

A car horn blares at me as I land on the main road behind the SUV, the vehicle swerving right to avoid hitting me. My heart is thrashing against my rib cage, and a line of sweat rolls down my back as I straighten up and take off. Behind me, the screeching of tires on asphalt confirms Drew is preparing to give chase, and I'll only have a short window to outrun him.

"I have a route. Keep straight, and then take the second left," Andreas says with clear urgency.

I put the pedal to the metal and thrust forward, glancing at the mirror as Drew rights his vehicle and drives after me.

I curl the bike low to the ground as I take the left before

straightening and driving down the long road, pushing the bike to its limits as I hear the roar of an engine creeping up on me from behind.

"When you get to the junction at the end, take a left," Andreas says. "It will bring you up along the far road behind the hotel, and there's a slip road from there to get onto the highway. They won't risk chasing you where there are other cars and cameras."

"Fuck!" I snap as a shot comes whizzing by my head. "Please tell me that drone is armed and you can shoot back."

"I didn't think we'd need a combat drone. I'm sorry," he says, and I swerve to the right as another shot comes dangerously close to my left leg.

"How much further?" I shout.

"Another seven hundred and fifty feet."

Pain sears through my upper left arm as a shot ricochets off the side of my bike and hits me. I lose control, spinning wildly to the side and crashing through a low fence onto private property. Andreas is shouting, but I can barely hear him over the pain radiating through my arm and the ringing in my ears.

"Thena!" he roars as my bike bumps along plowed fields, and I struggle to keep it upright with my injured arm.

"Please tell me there is a way out of here."

"They're coming after you, and there's no way off the property at the rear. There's a forest to the back of the barn you're approaching on your right. Ditch the bike and find somewhere to hide. I'm going to fly at them to distract them so you can get away. I'll send a team to get you out. Just find a hiding place and stay put."

I manage to hold on until I get to the barn, and then I fling myself off the bike, rolling into a tumble, and springing up on my feet. I stash my bike and helmet in the barn under a heavy sheet behind a tractor and hightail it out of there, popping my earpiece in so I can stay connected to Andreas.

My arm throbs like a bitch, but I'll deal with that when I find somewhere to hide. I stumble over debris on the forest floor as I race through the woodland with adrenaline pumping through my veins.

"The drone is going down, Thena, and I need to detonate it. I can't let it fall into their hands. Besides, it should scare them off. They'll know the cops won't be long on the scene after the explosion. Keep your burner on so the team can find your location."

"Affirmative. Thanks, Andreas. Over and out." I hear a pop as the drone explodes, but I don't risk looking back. I take off running, pushing my limbs to extremes as I race through the woods, navigating around trees and trying not to panic knowing they must be giving chase by now.

There is no structure or area large enough to hide, and my only bet is escaping up into a tree. It's dark, and the forest is copious, so unless they are extremely lucky, they won't have time to find me. I'm sure it won't take long for the cops to show up. The owners must have heard the detonation and called it in.

I find a large oak tree with a thick trunk and lots of branches with adequate foliage. That should do. I waste no time scaling the tree, ignoring the burn in my arm as I haul myself up from branch to branch, climbing as high as I can before I find a thick branch perpendicular to the trunk that can carry my weight. I wedge myself in tight and stretch my legs along the branch, focusing on my breathing as I try to calm down. I remain utterly still, breathing only through my nose as I sit it out.

A crunching down below alerts me to their presence, and adrenaline spikes in my blood. I'm praying their tree-climbing skills are rusty. In case they're not, I slowly and carefully remove my gun from the holster at my hip and hold it in my good hand, preparing to use it if I need to.

"We've got to go," Barron says in a deep voice. "The cops are only three minutes out."

"I know you're out here somewhere," Drew says in a deadly voice dripping with menace. "I don't know what you want, but if you don't back off, next time, I'll shoot to kill. Consider yourself warned."

I don't move a muscle for ages and keep completely still as they leave, the cops come and go, and the owners prowl the forest, shouting obscenities and threats of violence. After what seems like forever, the team shows up, stating it's safe to come down and confirming they have my bike. I'm careful as I climb down the tree, clutching my bloody arm, and offering up thanks for small mercies because this night could have ended a whole lot worse.

My arm is still aching like a bitch the following Friday, and I would've had to cancel Beast again, for the second week in a row, if he hadn't canceled on me first.

I've been popping pain pills and working remotely from home every day this week except for today. I only came in because Hilary mentioned in her email that the boss was in back-to-back meetings this morning and out this afternoon, so I figure it's safe to show my face at Manning Motors.

I trick Hilary into leaving her desk and sneak into Drew's calendar and print out a copy of his schedule.

I leave the office at lunch, choosing to eat at an upscale Italian restaurant a couple of blocks away from work, so I can study his schedule without the risk of anyone catching me. I am in a booth at the back of the room, tucked against the main front window, devouring the mouthwatering spaghetti with sausage pasta dish when two men slip into the booth across from me, and I almost choke on the food in my mouth.

"Don't choke on our account," Ares says, filling my glass with water and handing it to me.

I gulp back the water and try to steady my pounding heart. These powerful men showing up here cannot be a good thing. Shock comingles with fear as Ares Salinger grins wickedly while Baz Stewart fixes me with the full extent of his heavy stare, confirming I am deeply fucked and in so much trouble.

Chapter Twenty-Four
Athena

"Let me guess, you were just in the neighborhood and this is a complete coincidence because there is no way the Pride & Wrath and Lust & Envy Luminaries would lower their illustrious selves to seek me out," I say, deciding irreverence is a great strategy in the current situation.

"I see you still have a reckless streak," Ares quips.

"I call it stupidity," Baz supplies, daring me to challenge him with an arrogant look.

Ares grabs my pasta bowl and slides it across the table in front of him.

"Hey, I'm still eating that!" I protest.

"Not now you aren't." Ares smirks as he plucks the fork from my hand, and I briefly visualize stabbing him with it.

"Pregnant women have killed for less you know," I grumble. That pasta was delicious, and my belly is only half full.

Ares stops mid-chew for a few beats, and I smirk as that little dig hits home. His wife is currently pregnant with their third child, and if he steals Ashley's food like he just stole mine, I don't fancy his chances of making it to the birth.

"Salinger stealing your pasta is the least of your worries, Athena, now isn't it?" Baz arches a brow.

I lift my hand to summon the server as I ask, "What is this about, and did you really come all this way to talk to me?"

"How's your arm?" Baz inquires, his gaze lowering to my left upper arm where a bandage covers my injury under the long sleeve of my woolen sweater dress.

"Fine."

"Want to tell us why you made such a rookie mistake?" Ares asks in between mouthfuls of penne pasta.

"Can I order another bowl of that pasta to go, please," I tell the pretty waitress when she arrives at our table.

"Of course. Coming right up." She writes it down on her pad, trying to pretend like she's not ogling the two tall, muscular, super-hot assholes sitting across from me.

"Answer me," Ares says after she's gone, drilling me with a look. "Is Manning distracting you from your mission?" He licks his fork in an exaggerated manner, his meaning clear, and I roll my eyes.

"Does Ashley know you still have the mentality of a teenage boy?"

Ares chuckles. "Ashley benefits enormously from my teenage mentality. Ask her if you don't believe me."

"Ugh, I'm sorry I went there. How is your mom?"

"She's doing great. She said to tell you hello and it's been way too long."

"It has. Tell her I'll call her when I'm next in Cali."

"If you're quite done with the small-talk bullshit pleasantries, we came here for a reason," Baz says.

"He's grumpy because he's in the doghouse at home and not getting any," Ares says before shoveling the last of *my lunch* in his mouth.

"Shut your face." A muscle clenches in Baz's jaw as he glares at Ares, and I wonder if there is trouble in paradise.

"As amusing as this is, I need to get back to work, so let's wrap this up. I know why you're here, and I swear I won't mess up again. He didn't catch me, and I was in disguise, so he doesn't know it's me. I have his schedule"—I point at the papers in front of me—"and his office keys. As soon as I figure out how to disable the cameras, I'll sneak in and take a look around. I know I made a schoolgirl error, but it won't happen again, and to answer your question, no, I'm not distracted by Manning."

"I'm impressed you managed all that without pausing for a breath," Baz drawls.

I shrug. "What can I say? I'm just impressive, period."

Baz smirks.

"About Manning." Ares pushes his empty bowl away and grabs a napkin.

"I promise I'm focused on the mission, and I won't let you down."

"What exactly did your father ask you to do?" Ares asks.

My brows scrunch in confusion. Why is that relevant? They're the ones who requested this mission. Anyway, I'll humor them. "He asked me to spy on the mark, find out what he's up to, what evidence he has collected on the stuff that went down in Venezuela, and who he has told. He said the board wants to review the evidence first before making the final call."

Ares and Baz exchange a look.

"What?" I lean my elbows on the table and drag my gaze between them. "Is something else going on?" I don't express my suspicions even if I am on good terms with both men. They are still part of the board who governs everything, and until I know more, I'm keeping my suspicions to myself.

"Continue as you are," Baz says.

"But we want you to send a copy of the evidence directly to

us." Ares slides a small square card across the table to me, pointing at a URL written in ink on one side. "Upload to that link in the cloud, and we'll pull it from there. Only use a secure device."

It's insulting he feels the need to state the obvious.

"We want a weekly report," Baz adds. "Send the first one this weekend, and we want to know everything you've learned so far. Hold nothing back."

"This remains between the three of us," Ares says. All hint of playfulness is gone from his tone and his expression.

"What about my father?"

"What have you told him?" Baz drums his fingers on the table as he eyeballs me.

"Nothing so far."

"Keep it that way." Ares's gaze bores into mine. "Unless that's a problem."

I don't need to think about it for long. "It's not."

"Good."

"The mark isn't to die," Baz says.

"You take orders directly from us now," Ares says.

"Okay. Got it."

Baz moves to get up.

"Wait." Both men look at me, and I take a calculated risk. "My father said Drew was targeting heirs and Arlo was in danger. Is that true?"

Baz and Ares share another loaded look before they refocus on me. "Don't worry about your brother," Ares says. "I give you my personal guarantee that Arlo will be safe. I promise, Athena. No harm will come to him."

Relief washes through me. "Thank you." I'm a little embarrassed when tears stab the backs of my eyes.

"Call us directly anytime if you need to." Baz hands me a

card with two handwritten numbers on the back. "From a secure line, and don't give this to anyone else."

"Of course."

They stand up from the booth and I get out too as my lunch break is over.

"Stay safe, Thena, and watch your back," Ares says.

I lean in and kiss his cheek. "You too and thank you for coming here to talk with me. I know how busy you both are, and I appreciate it."

Drew

"I want to know who the fuck those pricks are," I snarl, glaring at the photo of Athena kissing some strange dude on the cheek wishing I could reach inside it and pepper his smug face with bullets. He's ripped with piercings and ink, and he looks like a thug—if thugs wore a seventy-thousand-dollar Patek Philippe watch and the latest Gucci high-tops.

Ezra clears his throat. "You've done nothing but snarl and spew threats ever since Anton uploaded these photos to the cloud. Are you sure there isn't something going on between you and Athena?"

"No!" I snap, glaring at my tech friend through my phone screen though it's not him I'm angry with. "I don't like being played. That bitch is clearly up to something, and I want to know what."

"And that's all it is? Because you sure seem pretty invested and—"

"Stop busting my balls, and get to work," I growl. "I want their names before I get on the plane this evening."

I hang up, tossing my cell on my bed, and work on finishing

my packing, grumbling under my breath, now in a super foul mood.

After my weekend bag is packed, I work out in my home gym for an hour, needing to calm down before I drop in to see Mom. I need to do damage control after last week because she hasn't stopped blowing up my phone with pictures of potential wedding venues and dates. I will throttle my sister when I see her because she's encouraging this bullshit, and if I don't set Mom straight, I'm liable to throw myself out of the plane while we're en route to Bulgaria.

I hit my punching bag so hard the chain rips from the ceiling, covering me and the floor in chalky debris. Guess that's what I get for imagining the faces of those two assholes while I was venting my frustration.

I've just stepped out of the shower when Ezra calls, and I hope he's got good news for me.

I press the accept button, but I don't get a chance to speak as Ezra's panicked voice filters down the line. "I'm fucked, we're fucked, this is some next-level shit you've got me mixed up in, and they're going to fucking kill me. This is why I stay behind my screen. I never wanted to put myself in danger, and I'm going to die. We're going to die, it's—"

"Stop," I bark. What the hell is going on? Ezra is as cool as they come, and nothing rattles him. I have never heard him freaking out like this EVER. "Calm down, man, and tell me what's happened."

"I'm leaving." There's a loud crash in the background. "I need to go into hiding for a while. I bet they're coming for me. Oh fuck, who'll mind my cat?"

"*Who* is coming?"

"I don't know." Heavy breaths tickle my eardrum, and I think he's in complete meltdown mode.

"Where are you, and I'll come get you."

"No! Don't come here. They might not know about you."

"Location. Now," I snap. I have no clue where Ezra lives and works. Anytime we have met in person, it's been at the hotel or a coffee shop or a bar in the city.

"There is no point in both of us being in danger."

"This isn't open for discussion. Send me the coordinates, Ezra. I'll be there as soon as I can."

Chapter Twenty-Five
Drew

I pull up in front of a dingy bar in the city forty minutes later after having run every fucking light on the way here. I called Ezra several times to ensure he hadn't run, and to try to get him to calm down before he has a damn heart attack. I still don't know what has happened, but I'm guessing it's something to do with those photos.

I find him tucked into a booth in the back, cradling a gray and white cat in his arms and nursing a half-drunk beer. "Talk to me."

"I'm sorry for freaking out, but I'm scared, man."

I lean across the table. "Nothing is going to happen to you. I guarantee it. You can stay at the hotel. No motherfucker is getting to you there. I've put my men on high alert, so they'll be extra vigilant. I have a car and men on the way here. They'll take you to the hotel and get you settled."

His features visibly relax. "Thanks, Drew. I didn't know where to go or what to do."

"You've had my back for a long time, Blackwood, and now it's my turn to have yours. You can stay as long as you need to."

"Are there, uh, any other guests staying there right now?" He pushes his glasses up his nose.

I smirk. "The last guests departed last night."

"Of course, and good. I'm not sure I'd be able to sleep with any of those sick pricks on the premises."

Now probably isn't a good time to mention I'm expecting new guests after my weekend trip.

"You can use my stuff to work, and if you need any other equipment, send me a list and I'll organize it for you."

"I can't use my system because it's completely fucked." Ire mixes with fear in his gaze.

"Tell me what happened."

"I uploaded all the photos Anton sent us to my secure facial recognition software system, the one I built blocking Zayn's code so nothing is off-limits to us. But the instant the first pic loaded, my screen went black, and then everything died. It was like poof, and then all my screens went down, every piece of tech blacked out, and an alarm rang out, followed by a flashing message across all the screens. It said a warrant was issued for my arrest for breaching national security and they were coming for me."

"Who the fuck are these guys? They sure as fuck are not politicians." And how the fuck does Athena know them?

"I don't know, but if they find me, I'm a dead man."

I check my messages, noting the text from my man confirming they are here. "Come on. Your transport is outside." I throw a fifty on the table and grab one of his bags while he grabs the other. The cat meows and snuggles into Ezra's chest. I'm tempted to tell him my hotel is an animal-free zone, but the dude is terrified, and if the cat helps soothe his nerves, I'd be a prick to force him to leave him behind.

I step outside first, keeping Ezra behind me as I scout the

area for anything suspicious, but it's clear. I lift one shoulder, urging him to follow me to the Range Rover parked at the curb.

One of my men climbs out of the passenger seat and walks to the back of the car, opening the cargo area. From here we can see an armed man sitting in the back behind the driver.

"Don't upload those photos anywhere, Drew," Ezra says, placing his bag inside the car the same time I do. "Keep them in the cloud and personally show them to Daniels and Hunt."

I open my mouth to protest, but he shuts me down before I have the chance.

"You need to know who these men are and what the threat is. You cannot do this alone. I know you didn't want to involve your friends, but this changes things. Kennedy is ex-FBI. He might know who they are and what you've gotten tangled up in. You're a smart man, Drew. Do the smart thing."

I wait for Ezra to leave with my men before climbing behind the wheel of my SUV and pulling out my burner cell. I call Charlie on his and quickly fill him in.

"I don't like this," he says.

"You don't have to come this weekend. I understand."

He scoffs. "I'm still coming, but I think Ezra is right. Talk to Sawyer and Xavier. Let them decide if we need to pull Keven in. I worked from home today, but I can be in the city in an hour."

"Stay put. I'm only ten minutes away, and I'll dial you in when I get there."

"This is the right move, Drew. They'll be mad you concealed all this, but they won't hesitate to help, and right now, I think we need all the help we can get."

"I thought you were heading overseas on business today?" Hunt says as we walk from the reception area of HADK Cybersecurity Solutions Limited toward his office.

"My flight doesn't leave until tonight, and something just came up."

"I'm surprised you called." He peers at me in that serious intense way of his. "We know you have Ezra Blackwood on retainer."

Shock skitters through me as I walk into Hunt's office.

"I think you've managed to shock the unshockable Andrew Manning," his husband says over a chuckle.

Xavier Daniels and Keven Kennedy are seated at the round table to one side of Sawyer's large office. The blinds are drawn, and Hunt shuts and locks the door behind us.

"How the fuck do you know that?" I ask when I finally pick my jaw up from the floor.

"There are rumors on the dark net," Kennedy says, getting up and shaking my hand.

"What kind of rumors?"

"Relax, dude. It's nothing to do with all the secrets you're hoarding. His name came up on a recommendation board, and someone noted he had done work for you." Xavier drags his hand through his messy blue, purple, and silver hair.

He stopped wearing it in a faux hawk years ago. I think he's too busy feeding kids and hustling them out the door to the babysitter in the mornings to worry about styling his hair.

I jerk my head in acknowledgment at him. "No little Anderson today?"

"He's taking Darcy to see Santa with Emery. We'll update him later," Hunt says, claiming the seat beside Kennedy.

I drop into the empty chair beside Xavier. "I need to call Charlie."

Daniels and Hunt share a look. "Barron knows?" Hunt asks over a frown.

"I took Charlie into my confidence a few weeks ago."

"Now I'm all kinds of butt hurt," Xavier says, pouting.

"He forced my hand. It wasn't by choice. I've been trying to keep all of you out of my shit."

"Is that why you turned to Blackwood instead of asking for our help?" Hunt asks.

I nod. "You guys are the best, and it wasn't an easy call. At first, I thought of just bringing you both in and leaving the others out, but I couldn't ask you to lie to everyone, and I really didn't want to force you to keep another secret from Abby, Xavier, but she can't know."

"Sorry, dude, but that ship has sailed." Xavier leans forward on his elbows. "The secrecy officially ends now."

"We all suspect you've been on a quest connected to Jane," Hunt says. "We have a pretty good guess why."

Compassion splays across all three of their faces.

"Abby has guessed Jane is dead, Drew," Xavier says in a somber tone. "We all do. Not to sound harsh, but Abby's concern is mostly for you. She loved Jane dearly, but she was a childhood friend, and so much time has passed. We are all different people now. Your twin will be sad if that's the truth, but it won't devastate her as much as you throwing your life away over misplaced guilt already does."

I'm tempted to get up and storm out, but I need their help. I need to know who these men are, who Athena really is, and what the fuck they want with me. I'm guessing it's all tied up with my investigation, but I need proof, and my friends are the only ones who can possibly get me that proof now.

So, it's a healthy dose of humble pie for me.

I work hard to leash my anger and remember their concern

comes from a good place. "We can argue about Abby another time. I don't have much time."

"Give us the CliffsNotes version of what you've been doing all these years," Kennedy says, and I start filling them in. None of them interrupt me, listening carefully as I explain.

"We were afraid that might have been the case," Hunt says. "Keven spent a lot of time hunting down sex traffickers when he was with the FBI."

"It's like a ten-headed monster. You chop a couple down, and more instantly grow back," he says. "It's a massive global issue, and it contributes billions every year to the dark economy."

"Most people disappear forever," Xavier says. "That you have managed to trace some of the path is truly remarkable, but you need to prepare yourself for the fact you may never get all the answers."

"That's not acceptable to me, and I won't stop even if I die trying."

"What led you to us today?" Hunt asks.

"Call Charlie, and I'll tell you." Hunt dials him in from home, and I clear my throat and explain what happened with Ezra earlier today.

"Show me the photos," Kennedy says as I log into the cloud and open the file. I hand him my phone first, and he flips through them, giving nothing away. "I don't know these men," he says, looking up at me as he passes the phone to Hunt. My heart sinks until Hunt says, "We know one of them."

"Give me that." Xavier snatches the cell from his husband's hand. "Holy shit. It's Ares."

All the hairs lift on the back of my neck. "Ares, as in the god of war?"

"The match to Athena," Xavier says, instantly getting it.

"Could they be siblings?" Keven asks.

"Ares only has one sister, and her name is Lilianna," Xavier supplies.

"How do you know him, and who is he?" I ask, digging my nails into my pant-covered thigh.

"Ares is one of Ashley Shaw's husbands," Xavier says. "Ashley is Sydney's cousin. We met all of them at Sydney and Jared's wedding, but I've known Ares for years. We met in college, and then he hired me to help him with a personal matter."

Keven blinks a few times. "*One* of her husbands?"

"They're in a committed polyamorous relationship," Hunt says. "They've all been married for years."

"Is the other guy her husband too?" I ask.

Xavier shakes his head. "No, though he does look a little like Jase."

Xavier and Hunt share a look.

"What's that look for?" I ask.

"Jase has an older brother," Hunt says. "That could be him."

"I'd suggest you call Ares and ask him about this," Keven says, scrubbing a hand over his smooth jawline, "but given what happened to Ezra, we need to think carefully about our next move."

"What line of business is this asshole in?" I ask, crossing one ankle over my knee.

"He is an asshole, but he's one of the good guys," Xavier says. "He works for his family business though I'm not sure exactly what he does. The business is vast, encompassing many companies though their main business is finance. His mom is the CEO. You'll know her, Charlie. She's Daphne Salinger."

"Salinger Finance and Investment Banking Limited is one of our main competitors," Charlie says. "I've met Daphne several times, but I've never met her son. If he works there, he mustn't have a key role."

"At least you have additional incentive for taking this guy out." I crack my knuckles.

Xavier jabs his finger in my face. "No one is taking Ares out."

"He's out for my blood," I say in a clipped tone.

"We don't know that for sure," Hunt coolly says. "All we have right now is a connection to Athena and proof he's someone important."

"Someone *extremely* powerful," Keven corrects, eyeballing all of us. "Someone who I'm guessing is involved in a lot more than just the family business."

"What are you thinking?" I ask.

"Remember when I was running the FBI investigation after the Parkhurst bombing?" he says, and we all nod. It's not like any of us have ever forgotten the events of that day. "I shared my frustrations with you at the time. I hated how a few men were made scapegoats while most got away scot-free. We knew they were being protected by higher-ups, and I always got a sense there was something else at play. That this was bigger than the elite."

I sit up straighter in my chair. "There's another entity, and they're the ones really calling the shots." Keven nods as a few things click into place in my head. "We know there was someone working with Charlie's dad and Anderson's dad back in the day, someone we were never able to identify, but we assumed it was Mathers or Hamilton or both of them, but what if it wasn't? What if it was this group?"

"And what if they're the same ones who warned you off seven years ago?" Charlie says. "Could these men be part of that crew who ambushed you?"

"I wouldn't rule anything out at this point." I claw a hand

through my hair as excitement skates through my veins. We're onto something. I feel it in my bones.

"My dad said something strange to me once," Charlie adds. "It was during senior year. He referenced how the elite were a global organization, which isn't true because our history confirms it's strictly restricted to the US. I presumed he meant the elite had global connections and this could be it. Whatever or whoever this group is, if they are more powerful, it would stand to reason their network is worldwide."

"And if your dad was mentioning this at a time when he was working to take down my father and return order to the elite, it makes sense that their silent partner was a part of this organization."

"I'm not discounting those theories," Hunt says, "but it's all supposition. We could be forcing square pegs in round holes."

"It feels right though," Charlie says, and I'm nodding even though he can't see me.

"I agree. This feels like we're on the right track, but how can we prove it?" My gaze bounces between the three men around the table.

Xavier looks at Sawyer. "We're long overdue a catch-up with Ares. Let me call him and tell him we're coming to Lowell with the kids."

All the blood drains from my face, and Kennedy notices.

"What is it, Manning?"

Xavier and Hunt whip their heads around.

"The last sighting I have of the Ford family was in northern California. In a place called Prestwick, which is only a few miles from Lowell."

Chapter Twenty-Six
Drew

You could hear a pin drop in the room until Charlie speaks. "It can't be a coincidence. You were warned off shortly after you made that connection. Ares must be involved. He knows what happened to Jane and her family, and maybe he told you to drop it out of courtesy to Daniels instead of putting a bullet in your skull."

Xavier squirms in his seat as his brows pull together in a frown. "If Ares is mixed up in this, it's for a good reason. He's not the bad guy."

"How well do you truly know him if he didn't confide any of this to you? You don't even know what he does for a living, for fuck's sake." My knee bounces up and down. "He's been bullshitting you, Daniels."

Fire blazes in Xavier's eyes. "I know Ares would never be involved in sending anyone into sexual slavery because his sister was kidnapped when she was a kid and sent to one of those hellholes and I was helping him find her."

Tense silence bleeds into the air.

"Maybe he wasn't involved, but he knows who was," Charlie says, breaking the charged silence.

"Why was he trying to stop me then?"

"That's if Ares was one of the men who ambushed you," Hunt reminds me.

"Think about it," Xavier says, drumming his fingers on the table. He stares off into space as his brain churns. "If this organization is some super-powerful secret society, isn't it reasonable to consider they have their own traditions and laws just like the elite? What if there is an order to how things need to be done and you were getting in the way of that?"

"Hunt is right. There is too much guesswork to these theories. We need concrete proof, and it seems like Ares is our best bet," Kennedy says. "If Xavier trusts him not to be the bad guy and him warning you off could have been an attempt to keep you protected from this, Manning, then I think you can at least ask him to tell it to you straight."

"I don't want your family placed in harm's way." I drill a look at Xavier as he's the one I'll have to convince. "You haven't grown up in these circles like Charlie and I have. Loyalty is a transient thing in our world and theirs too I'm betting. You might think you know Ares, but if he's involved in this organization, then you have no clue what kind of man he truly is."

"He won't hurt us." It's no surprise Xavier stubbornly defends him.

"I'm not taking that risk," Hunt says, glancing at his husband with a look that says it isn't up for debate. "We'll go alone. Abby can watch the kids."

"Okay." Xavier readily agrees because he won't take risks with their children, and if Hunt has concerns, he won't disregard them as easily as he'd disregard them when I say it.

"One other thing," I say. "Athena's from Cali." I'm trying to make the rest of the puzzle pieces work and wondering if that's her connection to Ares. "My background check said L.A., but what if that's a lie? What if she's part of this other entity along with Ares and that other asshole in the photo? Given what happened with Ezra today, it's not inconceivable the intel online is fabricated to throw me off the scent."

"She was sent to spy on you," Charlie says. "Probably because you were told to drop it and you didn't."

Xavier frowns, looking hugely troubled.

"Ares and Athena are not common names," Hunt says. "Maybe they're cousins."

"Or maybe the society is descended from Greek gods and every asshole has a stupid name," I blurt, unnaturally pissed off for reasons I don't want to examine.

Xavier grins. "I think someone's caught feelings."

I flip him the bird. "The only feelings I have in relation to that woman are frustration and rage. For her sake, I hope I'm wrong about all this."

"Drew, you need to get going unless you plan to reschedule our trip?" Charlie says.

"No. Everything's all lined up in Bulgaria, and we may not get another chance like this."

"Why don't we see what we can dig up on Athena," Keven says as Hunt and Daniels begin whispering with their heads bent, "and I could meet with my old SA. We're on good terms, and he's completely trustworthy. I can feel him out and see if he knows anything about this other group or Ares and the other man. I'll also find out what the latest intel is on sex trafficking in Venezuela in case it offers any leads."

"Sounds like a plan," I say, pushing my chair back and standing.

"I'm coming with you," Hunt says, getting to his feet.

"Fuck no."

He smirks. "Funny you think you can stop me. I'm either

getting on that plane with you and Barron or I'm hiring my own jet and coming after you."

"And you're okay with this?" I stab Xavier with a look.

"I'm not my husband's keeper. Drill Sergeant is capable of making his own decisions. I'll work with Keven and see what we can find out while you're gone, and I'll place a call to Ares and arrange a meeting for next week. Maybe we can all go."

"It's a solid plan," Charlie says, "and maybe this Bulgarian play will give us the other answers we need."

"I'll meet you at the airfield," Sawyer says, grabbing stuff from his desk drawer.

"Don't be late or we'll leave without you," I say, making my goodbyes and hightailing it out of there.

"You have got to be fucking kidding me!" Anger explodes from my head as I charge across the asphalt toward the private plane I've hired to take us to Europe, scowling at my brother-in-law as he stands chatting to Sawyer Hunt looking relaxed and chill like we're going on vacation instead of infiltrating a dangerous criminal gang.

Dropping my bag at my feet, I yank my gun from the back of my pants and jab it in Hunt's skull. He stops talking mid-sentence, looking sideways at me. "What the fuck have you done?" I hiss, pressing the muzzle in tighter to his head.

"Whoops, he's angry," Kaiden says, and I swing the gun in his direction, pointing it at his head.

"You won't shoot me."

"Keep smirking, asshole, and we'll be testing that theory."

"If anyone has the right to be angry, it's us." Kaiden loses the smirk, wrapping his wrist around the gun and pushing it away. His nostrils flare as he waves his finger in my face. "You're a fucking selfish prick, Drew Manning. Did you even stop to consider your twin before you went running off to South America and Europe and who the fuck knows where without fucking backup?"

I glare at Hunt because he clearly told Anderson everything I divulged earlier when I specifically said I didn't want anyone else to know.

"Did you ever contemplate what it would do to my wife if you died hunting these pricks?" Kai continues, shoving me in the shoulders as the gun hangs listlessly in my hand. "Have you any idea how much she worries about you? How much it hurts her that you've shut her out and you refuse to tell her anything? She can't even ask you about Jane because you get all huffy and she feels like shit if she causes you pain." He shoves me again, and I stumble back a few feet.

I wouldn't let anyone else push me around like this.

Only Anderson gets a free pass.

Kaiden's love for my sister is this giant, shining, glorious, wonderful thing. I don't have to worry about Abby anymore because I know her husband would kill for her without a second's hesitation. He's beaten guys up before for daring to even look at her. No man has ever loved a woman as much as Kaiden Anderson loves my sister, and I love the guy for it. Which is why I'm letting him have his say. Plus, I know I deserve it.

"And have you thought about what it would do to the rest of us, you dick?" he adds, grabbing the back of my head and pressing his brow to mine. "You're not my blood, but you're still my brother, Drew, in all the ways that count." He thumps his closed fist on his chest. "Like Hunt and Lauder and Daniels and Barron." He grips my shoulders hard. "Brothers stick together. They don't shut one another out."

"It's time to stop being a martyr," Hunt says just as Charlie arrives wearing a grin.

"When's Lauder arriving?" he asks, chuckling at the expression on my face.

"He's not," Hunt says, the same time Kai says, "He's in Abu Dhabi for a race."

"Good. That guy still gets on my nerves," I lie because I'm grumpy and he's an easy target when he's not here to defend himself.

"You're so full of shit." Kai grabs me into a headlock. "I hope there are plenty of motherfuckers to beat the shit out of in Bulgaria. Otherwise, your ass is mine, Manning. You deserve a good beating for pushing us away for so long."

"I was trying to protect you, fuckface." I ram my fist in his ribs, and he stumbles back with an oomph.

"Gentlemen, the pilot would like to inform you of our imminent departure," the air steward says, poking his head out through the door of the plane. "You need to take your seats."

"We're coming." I grab my bag and follow the others on board.

"Where does my sister think you are?" I ask Kaiden a few minutes later when we're in the air and all nursing whiskeys. The planned attack isn't happening until tomorrow night, so we can drop our guard a little tonight. I wanted to get to town early, to scope out the place, meet the men I've hired on the ground, and be there to greet the crew of ex-military men on my permanent payroll when they land in Bulgaria tomorrow.

He looks sideways at me as he speaks. "She knows where I am. She knows it's a mission, but I didn't give her any specifics. I figured you'd want to be the one to tell her."

I didn't want Abby to know, but there's no point fighting the inevitable. "I'll tell her when we get back."

He clamps his hand on my shoulder. "I'm so fucking sorry about Jane. What happened should never have happened, but it's not your fault, Drew."

Everyone is starting to sound like a broken record, and I'm getting sick of hearing it.

Thankfully, he doesn't push it any further.

"Fill us in on the mission," Hunt says from his seat directly across from me. Charlie is sitting beside him, facing Kai. "What are we walking into?"

"Charlie and I were *entertaining* a couple of traffickers at my hotel base. A father and son duo. They were giving us jack shit until I found the perfect incentive." I pause for a second, exchanging a look with Barron. I'm not proud of using Miguel's granddaughter to force him into spilling his secrets, but it worked. I didn't hurt the little girl or her mother. They were both sleeping the entire time. We just had to show up with them and that was enough to confirm our threat to sell them into slavery was not an empty threat. Miguel and Miguel Junior sang like canaries after that.

I clear my throat. "Anyway, they told us that when kids age out in Venezuela they are transported to Europe, to places like Spain, Italy, Portugal, France, Germany, The Netherlands, and Bulgaria, where there's demand for well-trained adult slaves."

"Some of them go up for auction, and they're bought by rich pricks with big country houses," Charlie says.

"I thought Jane had been sent to Venezuela because the trail led there, but Miguel remembered her. He said pretty blonde Americans always fetched a high price." I almost choke on the words, and Miguel almost choked on his cock when he said that. I would have killed him before we got all the intel if Charlie hadn't pulled me back.

"She was sent from L.A. to South America purely to throw Drew off the scent," Charlie continues.

I clear my throat and get a grip. "All trades coming through this route into Europe are managed by this guy, Emil Petrov. He's the handler and everything goes through him. It's a massive operation, but it's run like a business. Miguel swore he would have records, including the name of the person who sold Jane from the US side."

"A guy like that will be heavily guarded," Hunt says.

I glare at him. "Do you think I'm a moron?"

"Is that a rhetorical question?" he replies.

"Fuck. You."

"No thanks. I only let one cock pound this ass."

I stare at him for a couple seconds before barking out a laugh. "Fuck, Daniels has really rubbed off on you."

"In more ways than one," Charlie adds.

"Here I thought you were a couple of cold-blooded killers. Instead, you're a pair of lame-ass comedians," Kai deadpans.

"I'll take the laughs where I can get them. God knows they've been few and far between in recent years." The mood instantly sobers, but the tense atmosphere is broken when my cell pings. Extracting it from my pocket, I frown when I see the incoming call from the head of security for Manning Motors.

"Boss," he grunts into the phone when I pick up. "I'm sorry to disturb you after hours on a Friday, but we've had a bit of an incident in the office I think you need to be aware of." My fingers dig into the armrest of my chair as he explains, and anger is mushrooming inside me with every spoken word.

"I'll handle it," I say when he's finished telling me everything. "Send the video to my cell."

"Fuck!" I throw my glass at the wall, feeling no relief when it smashes upon impact on the floor.

The air steward looks petrified as he comes rushing out of the cabin where he's been hiding.

"Leave it!" I snap.

"Yes, sir. Sorry, sir."

"What's happened?" Kai asks, swirling whiskey in his glass.

"Athena was snooping in my office this evening after everyone had left for the weekend. She somehow acquired keys and managed to disable the security cameras across my entire floor, but she didn't know about the secret cameras in my office." I tip my head at Sawyer because it's their tech I have installed. It evades modern tech detectors, so even if she searched for cameras, they wouldn't have shown up on any scanner.

"Fucking bitch." I clench my hands into fists. "She's been acting all friendly with my PA, and I'm guessing it was on purpose. She must have stolen the keys from her desk. No one else has a set. Now, I'll have to fire Hilary, and she was a damn good assistant."

"She's not worth shit if she made such a rookie mistake," Hunt says, crossing his feet at his ankles.

"Is there anything in your office she was looking for specifically, do you think?" Charlie asks.

"I can't imagine what it might be. I only keep work-related stuff in the office. There is nothing related to my extracurricular activities at Manning Motors, and any confidential stuff I do have is locked in my filing room, and only retinal access gets you into it."

My phone pings with a video message, and the guys crowd around me as we watch the recording. Sure enough, she runs a device around the room for bugs and cameras.

"Take a pic of that," Hunt says. "I'll send it to Xavier and Keven and see if they recognize the tech."

I send him the still, and we watch as Athena moves around

my room quietly and efficiently, checking my shelves, picking the lock on my desk drawers, and inspecting the contents. She inspects the walls for hidden panels, finding my safe, and frowning when her tech doesn't open it. I exchange a smile with Hunt, grateful he's my friend.

Athena's frustrated frown pulls a smile from my lips as she stands in front of the door to my filing room, scowling as she realizes she's not getting in there. The video ends when she creeps back out into the hallway, pulling the door shut behind her.

I turn off my phone and put it back in my pocket, running through options in my head.

"She is trained," Charlie says.

"It's obvious," I agree. "But she's not exactly being careful."

"I'm beginning to think your theories are correct when it comes to her," Hunt says.

"Abby will be super pissed to discover she's a spy," Kai says. "She really likes her."

"Let's not sentence her yet," Charlie says. "If Xavier believes Ares is one of the good guys and she's working for him or with him, then she might have a legit reason for doing the things she's doing."

"For her sake, I really hope she does," I grit out.

Chapter Twenty-Seven
Athena

The cavalcade of cars and SUVs splits into two as they drive out through the gates of the large farm on the outskirts of Sofia where Manning, Barron, their friends, and hired guns have been holed up since I arrived this morning. I was playing catch-up after discovering Drew's overseas trip on his schedule. There was no other information, and he didn't travel via the Manning Motors jet, which is how I knew this must be some top-secret mission. Andreas came through for me, and he found their transport and route plan, and I left four hours after they did.

I had to tap Luminary resources to get help on the ground in Bulgaria because I would never have found their location otherwise. I'm not sure how he managed it, but Ares sent me the coordinates to this place, and I've been staking it out ever since.

Drew and his friends left for a few hours this evening, just as it was getting dark, and I trailed them to the mountains, watching as they sent drones out over the grounds of a vast walled estate nestled deep in the woods.

For that reason, I follow the five vehicles that turn left in the direction of the mountain rather than the ten that turn right, heading in the direction of the city. I can't be in two places at once, and I can't see through tinted-glass windows, so I'm banking on Drew returning to the fortress in the hills.

The intel Andreas and I discovered confirmed the property is owned by a member of the Bulgarian mafia who is known as a drug runner and trafficker with his fingers in all kinds of pies. Ares told me to watch my back and to call in reinforcements at the first hint of trouble.

My unassuming little black car struggles to climb the steep hills leading to the Petrov mansion, but I finally make it to the turnoff that leads to the old brick water tower now used as an art gallery and entertainment venue. It is closed for the winter months, making it the perfect location to spy on Drew and his crew from a close, safe venue.

I make quick work of disarming their alarm system and busting the lock to get inside. Hefting my heavy bag over my shoulder, I climb to the top, panting when I reach my destination from the exertion. My shoulder is stiff, and my arm is still a little sore even if my injury is healing well.

I set up quickly, pushing the rusted window open and lining my rifle up. The angle is perfect from this vantage point. Ares made it clear I wasn't to hesitate to protect Manning and his friends if things turned dicey. I'm more than a little confused, but I know not to disobey or question orders from a Luminary, and I totally plan on having a conversation with Salinger when I get back. He needs to give me more. I need to know exactly what is going on because it's blatantly obvious this mission is not what I've been led to believe it is.

An explosion in the distance claims my attention a few minutes later, and I run across the floor and open the window at the back of the tower, spotting the fiery plume of smoke billowing into the sky. It's come from the direction of the city, and this has Manning written all over it. "What are you up to, Drew?" I ponder out loud as I trek back to my window and lie down on my mat on my stomach, pressing my eye to the scope in time to see several men rush out from a side house behind the walls of the Petrov home and jump into armored vehicles. The tall wooden gates protecting the fortress open a minute later, and the vehicles speed away over the mountainous terrain, descending the hill as they head toward the city.

"It was a diversion," Andreas says in my ear. "They just blew one of Petrov's drug supply warehouses sky-high."

"That was risky," I say, watching as Manning's men creep stealthily toward the gates. "And it will draw a lot of attention. I hope the gamble pays off."

Manning's guys fix a couple of circular devices to the front gates after they have closed and fall back. Nothing happens for ten minutes, and then they blow the gates apart, and fifteen heavily armed men, in a combination of black and army fatigues, swarm the property. They are all wearing balaclavas, Kevlars, and night vision goggles, so I can't tell who anyone is.

A few guys shoot out the lock on the front door of the house and race inside while the rest of the men remain outside, locked in combat with Petrov's men as gunfire breaks out. Motion-sensor lights pop to life, one by one, offering me a perfect view as the battle wages. None of Petrov's men are wearing goggles or masks, and it's easy to take out a couple of them before they pop bullets in Drew's crew. It's bedlam down there, so I'm trusting I got away with the hits without anyone noticing.

Manning's men exit the house just as the gunfire dies out, dragging two men across the asphalt and dumping them on the ground in front of the small stone fountain.

"Can you get me audio?" I ask Andreas as Drew rips his goggles and balaclava off.

All his men begin removing their face coverings, and Barron forces the two men to their knees as Drew looms over them like a thunderstorm hellbent on wreaking havoc.

"Give me a sec. I had rerouted the audio and visual drone feeds on Ares's instruction, but I can add us to the audio feed so we can listen."

"Ares is watching this go down?" He didn't mention that.

"I assume so."

Barron binds the men's hands behind their backs before tying rope around their ankles, securing them in place. The rest of Manning's crew surround their leader as he stares at the two men.

"Where is Aleksandar Petrov?" Drew asks in a chillingly dark tone.

The men respond in their native Bulgarian.

"We know you all speak English," Drew says, folding his arms and warning the men with a sharp look.

"Fuck you, yank." The man sneers and spits, his spittle landing on Drew's boots.

Drew pulls him to his feet and slams his fist in his face, knocking him to the ground. Drew and Charlie exchange a look before side-eyeing the second man who is trying to put a brave face on, but the dude looks like he just shit his pants.

Charlie kneels and wraps his arm around the man's neck before nodding at his best buddy. Drew spits on the man's face before pressing his booted foot firmly down on the man's left knee. Drew jumps on his leg a couple times, grinning as the man howls in pain. "Ready to talk now?"

More Bulgarian spews from the man's lips, and Drew casually shoots out his other kneecap before pulling a knife from his calf and slashing at the man's legs through his clothes.

Drew grabs the man's shirt and lifts him a few feet off the

floor. "Last chance, fuckface, tell me what I want to know, or I'll make chopped liver of your sniveling ass."

"I'll die before I tell you." He pants, his words littered with pain. Beside him, the second man is visibly trembling, and his face has turned pale.

"Very well. Don't say you didn't ask for it," Drew says dropping the man back to the hard ground.

"He's a fucking monster," Andreas says as Drew tears the man's clothes off and goes to town on him with a knife, slashing and stabbing him from his chest, down through his stomach, his dick, his muscular thighs, right through to his legs and feet.

While Drew is making mincemeat of his flesh, Barron is choking the man to the brink of death and then releasing him so he's fully aware of every injury being inflicted.

"He's fucking beautiful," I retort, knowing it's all kinds of sick to be aroused watching a man carve up another.

"You have issues."

"I know," I readily admit, silently fist pumping the air as Drew drives the knife repeatedly into the man's chest, wallowing in the blood and flesh covering his clothes as he violently murders the man long past his ability to breathe. "But never forget these men are far from innocent. They work for Petrov. They know what he does. The misery he inflicts on other humans. Manning is doing the world a favor wiping one more prick from existence."

"I'll tell you!" the other man shrieks, bending his head and bowing toward Drew. "I'll tell you where Petrov's son is!"

"Speak and I'll spare your life," Drew says, yanking the man's head back. "Lie to me or try to trick me, and I'll do worse to you." Drew's face and gorgeous hair are streaked with blood, and he has never looked more fucking sexy to me.

I want to straddle his powerful body and impale myself on his cock while we bathe in the blood of our enemies.

I know. I know.

Issues.

"There is a secret room behind the shelving unit in the library. Alexsandar will be hiding there."

Anderson and Hunt take off with two men, disappearing inside the house as Drew issues orders to the rest of his men.

Drew's friends return a few minutes later with a tall, lanky teenage boy. He looks terrified, but he's trying to project confidence not fear. "My father will gut you for this."

"He can try." Drew grins at the boy as he raises his gun and shoots the man on the ground through the head. He slumps forward, instantly dead, but that doesn't stop Manning from peppering his body with bullets.

The boy barely flinches, and it's clear he hasn't been sheltered the same way my brother has. The thought of Arlo has me moving my rifle in Drew's direction. Manning might be a perfect sexy beast, but I won't let him hurt that boy. It's not Alexsandar's fault he was born into this life, and until he's old enough to make his own decisions, I refuse to hold him accountable.

"I'm not going to hurt you," Drew tells him as if he senses the threat to his life coming from the water tower. "I'm taking you so I can bargain with your father for information I need. You don't need to be scared. You will be well taken care of."

"Oh shit!" Andreas's panicked tone causes goose bumps to sprout over my arms.

"Holy fuck," I hiss, spotting the armed men creeping up on the house from outside, hidden behind the tall stone walls. I have no clue where they have come from, but there are more than enough to outnumber Manning, and things are about to get real.

"Warn them!" I scream.

"It will take me too long to hijack the audio!"

I don't stop to consider the consequences. There isn't time. I just act, shooting the first man as he makes it to the gate, instantly alerting Drew to the danger.

Shouts ring out as men look in this direction, and then all hell breaks loose as Drew's men start firing, and both sides take potshots at one another. It's difficult to know who the enemy is now without the goggles and face coverings, so I train my rifle on Drew and his friends, watching their backs and taking out assholes who try to creep up on them.

Drew is like a dark angel, moving with grace through the enemy as he cuts them down effortlessly with his gun. When his bullets are gone, he uses his hands and his knife, and they are no less effective. Drew Manning is a lethal killing machine, and it turns me on like you wouldn't believe.

As if I needed more reasons to admire him.

He's just snapped the neck of one guy when another jumps up from behind him, seemingly out of nowhere, and wraps his beefy arm around Manning's neck. I don't hesitate to pull the trigger, putting a bullet straight through the asshole's skull, and his hold on Drew is gone as he slumps to the ground.

Drew's gaze lifts to mine as if he can see me through the tower.

"You need to get the fuck out of there, Thena," Andreas says as the same thought occurs to me. "They have it under control now."

"I'm on it," I say, efficiently dismantling the rifle and stowing it and my mat in the bag in record time. I quickly scan the area, ensuring I've got everything, and then I run through the door, descending the winding staircase as fast as I can.

"Talk to me," I say when I reach the ground level, sprinting toward the door. "Is it safe to exit?"

I press the button in my ear. "Andreas, can you hear me? Is it safe to leave?"

Radio silence confirms I've lost our connection and I'm on my own.

"Shit, shit, shit." I considered my chances of getting out of here undetected slim with Andreas's help. Without it, the odds are slashed to negligible.

I pull my face covering and night vision goggles on and remove my handgun from its holster. Gripping the door handle tight, I remind myself of all the times I've gotten myself out of tricky situations.

I don't pray for help because there's nothing anyone can do to help me now.

This is all on me.

Chapter Twenty-Eight
Drew

"Stop right there," I say, pointing the gun at his face as he appears in the doorway of the old water tower.

It's dark as shit with no outside lights but I can just make out the gun he points at my chest.

Tension bleeds into the air.

"You're outnumbered," Barron says, stepping up on my left while Anderson and Hunt step up on my right.

"Dump the bag and throw your gun to the right. Then raise your hands in the air," I say.

His arm doesn't falter, his weapon still trained at my head, and I arch a brow. "I suggest you don't test me. Disarm. Now. And don't try anything."

I can't see his face, but I can almost feel the venom shooting from his eyes as he drops the bag and tosses the gun aside. Charlie grabs the gun, and I stride forward to grab him.

Piercing pain shoots through my groin, and I drop to my knees in agony as he darts past Anderson and Hunt in their shocked states and takes off running. "Get him," I roar, clutching my dick and balls as nausea churns in my stomach.

Anderson and Hunt race after the man while Charlie grabs the bag, and I hiss through gritted teeth. "What the hell kind of pussy move was that?" I pant.

"You just answered your own question," Charlie says, offering me a hand up as Anderson and Hunt reappear with the asshole.

"Houston, we have a problem," Hunt drawls.

"A pussy problem?" Charlie says with humor lingering in his tone.

I straighten up, ignoring the dull ache between my thighs as it all clicks into place. Striding toward Hunt and Anderson, I flip the flashlight on my cell phone and direct it at the prisoner being held between my two friends. "Get rid of the mask and goggles."

Hunt restrains her as Anderson removes the balaclava and goggles.

I mask my shock as I stare at her insolent face.

Who the fuck is this girl?

"You have a lot of explaining to do, Athena." My cold tone matches the cold expression on my face.

"Bite me, Drew," she coolly replies, blowing wispy strands of hair out of her eyes.

Anger trickles through my veins, and I want to put her over my lap and smack the defiance out of her. "Hold her arms out," I command.

"Get your fucking hands off me," she hisses as I start searching her body for weapons.

"Trust me, I'm taking no joy from this," I lie, brushing my hands over her chest, the sides of her breasts, her stomach, back, and ass. Pushing her thighs apart, I cup her crotch through her pants.

"Liar," she seethes. "Unless you're actually stupid enough to believe I've shoved a weapon up my cunt."

"Stranger things have happened." I run my hands up and down her legs, quickly unstrapping the knives I find tied to both calves. I toss them to Charlie and stand. "She's clean."

Anderson and Hunt lower her arms to her sides, still holding on to her in case she tries to run again.

"Don't move," Hunt says, extracting an earbud from her ear. Flicking the flashlight on his cell, he inspects it up close with a frown. "Where did you get this?"

She smirks at him, firmly keeping her lips closed.

"What is it?" Anderson asks.

"Some kind of communication device, but I have never seen one like it," Hunt says, slipping it into his pocket before he turns her head, checking her other ear. Finding it empty, he runs his flashlight slowly over her body, plucking a circular black disc from her shirt. His frown deepens as he stares at it. "I'm guessing this is some kind of microphone. I'll take them back and check it out."

"You really don't want to do that." Athena's smirk grows wider.

I step right up to her, gripping her chin in my hand and arching her head back. "Who are you working for and why?"

"Right back at you," she coolly replies, and my brows climb to my hairline.

"We don't have time to do this here," Charlie says. "We need to go now."

"Hold her," I tell Anderson while I grab Athena's bag and rummage through it.

"That's mine, asshole," she says, not even attempting to wriggle out of Anderson and Hunt's hold.

"Consider it payback for rifling through my office," I snap, removing a set of handcuffs and some rope. I walk around my buddies and pull her hands behind her back, clamping the handcuffs around her wrists before tying her ankles together with the rope. She doesn't fight, and I appreciate it because we need to get the fuck out of Dodge before we all die. The plane I have on standby won't wait forever. Especially if the Bulgarians reach out to the Serbians for assistance.

"I'll get you back for this," she says as I toss her over my shoulder and secure her with my arm across the back of her thighs.

"Stay quiet unless you plan to die out here."

She doesn't reply, and we take off running, heading down the narrow driveway where our car is parked.

"Open the trunk," I say when we reach the car.

"Drew, I—"

"Don't want to hear it, Anderson."

Charlie opens the trunk, and I shove a glaring Athena inside. She's shouting abuse at me, so I grab the packing tape I used on Petrov's son and slap a piece over her mouth to shut her up.

Then I slam the trunk closed and hop behind the wheel as Charlie rides shotgun and the other two climb in the back.

"Was that really necessary?" Anderson asks.

"Yes," Charlie and I say in unison.

I eyeball Kai through the mirror. "We have a thirty-minute drive to the border, and we can't risk being stopped on the way because we have a woman prisoner in the back."

"You think rocking up to border control with a woman tied up in the trunk is better?" Disbelief underscores Kai's tone.

"Our contact at the border has been handsomely remunerated to turn a blind eye to everything."

"Let's hope that's true because you look like a reject from a horror movie," Hunt says.

Thankfully we make it through border control with the rest of our men without incident, and I've had confirmation from the men in the city they got away with no casualties. They're all

Bulgarian nationals, and they'll lie low until the heat dies down.

"I'd love to be a fly on the wall when Petrov realizes we kidnapped his only son and heir," Hunt says.

"Let's not gloat yet," Charlie says, looking out the window at the mountains as we speed along the border highway. "We still have a two-hour drive to the airfield at Nis."

Kai clears his throat when we're an hour away from the airport. "She could be choking back there. You should at least check on her."

"I'm not stopping. It's too risky."

"You could stop over there," Hunt says, pointing at a little side road up ahead bordered with dense trees.

"No."

Tension is thick in the air as I put the pedal to the metal and try to focus on getting us to the airfield before the authorities or Petrov get to us. But it's difficult not to think about the woman tied up in the trunk.

I'd had an instinct about her from the start, and I was right. Except I don't know whose side she's on. Athena helped us back there, and I'm conflicted. Is she an enemy or an ally?

She was planted in my business as a spy, and it's obvious she is the one we caught sneaking around the hotel. Fuck, I'm pretty sure I shot her. Acid crawls up my throat, and knots form in my stomach at the thought of hurting her. I grip the wheel tighter, fighting the urge to stop and check on her.

Athena is clearly skilled, yet she's taken silly risks. Why? It doesn't make sense.

But at least I have her where I want her now, and she's damn well going to give me answers.

Provided she's not dead in the trunk, the devil on my shoulder whispers in my ear.

I punt the asshole away, but I seem to have developed a

conscience from somewhere because fear crawls up my spine, and I don't stop to second-guess myself as I pull off the side of the road into an old, abandoned gas station, driving into the covered side area so we're hidden.

No one says a word as I grab a bottle of lukewarm water from the console and climb out. I round the car and pop the trunk. Relief slams into me when a pair of stunning blue eyes glare out at me. I lean in and rip the tape from her mouth.

"Motherfucker," she hisses in a throaty voice.

"Open your mouth."

She narrows her eyes before her gaze lowers briefly to my crotch.

I smother a snort of laughter. "Mind out of the gutter, Athena." I lift the bottle and wave it at her. "I'm guessing you're thirsty."

Beads of sweat dot her brow, and the fine hairs around her face are damp and curly where they've come loose from her ponytail.

"How do I know it's not poisoned?"

"Guess you'll just have to trust me."

"That'd be a big fat no," she scoffs.

"We don't have time to debate. Do you want the fucking water or not?"

"Yes," she hisses. "Remove the handcuffs, and I'll drink it myself."

"Not a fucking chance." I heave her up a little, keeping my arm around her back as she sits up. Then I lift the opened bottle of water to her lips and tip some into her mouth.

"More," she croaks, and we stay like this until she's finished the bottle. "Where are we?" she asks as I set her back down.

"We crossed the border into Serbia. It's forty minutes to the airfield where I have a plane waiting."

"Leave me tied up if you have to, but at least let me sit in the back."

"There isn't room."

"I can sit on someone's lap." Her eyes flare with challenge.

Over my dead body is she sitting on Anderson's or Hunt's lap. "Nice try but no." I move to close the trunk.

"Wait, please." Her eyes beseech me. "At least untie me. I swear I won't try to escape. I have zero desire to be trapped in this country alone."

"I'll untie your feet," I say, not trusting her words fully. She obviously has resources and contacts and that fucker Ares on speed dial. She wouldn't be alone for long.

I unknot the rope from her ankles, staggering back and falling flat on my ass when her leg snaps out and she kicks me in the face with her booted foot.

Pain spreads across my nose and cheeks, and when I touch my face, little drops of blood coat the tips of my fingers.

"You deserved that," she says, grinning gleefully as I climb to my feet and glare at her. She is lying on her side, making no move to run off, so maybe she was telling the truth, but I've got no more sympathy to give.

"Fuck you, slut," I bark.

Her eyes widen as I slam the trunk down with force. I kick the side of the car a couple times before I slide behind the wheel.

"That went well," Kai says as Charlie hands me a tissue, fighting a smile.

"Shut your face, Anderson, or I'll shut it for you," I snap, stuffing bits of tissue up my nose to halt the blood.

I tear out of the old gas station and get back on the road, digging my fingers into the steering wheel.

"She's definitely hot for you," Anderson says less than two minutes later.

"What part of shut the fuck up didn't you understand?" I growl, eyeballing him through the mirror. "And how the fuck did you come to that conclusion?"

"Do you want me to answer or shut the fuck up?" Kai says, and a snarling sound rumbles from my chest.

"You have insane chemistry with her. We all saw it at dinner and during Thanksgiving."

"We argue nonstop," I blurt, cursing my stupid mouth. I should be ending this conversation not entertaining it.

"The hate sex will be awesome," Hunt supplies.

"You could always tie her up and paddle her ass," Charlie says, deciding to throw his lot in with the others.

"Or choke her out," Kai adds.

"I vote for flogging," Hunt says.

"I vote for borrowing Athena's rifle and blowing a hole in each of your faces so you can't spout any more shit."

"Denial is not just a river in Egypt," Hunt says.

"Great, we're throwing clichés around now. Just kill me and put me out of my misery."

Charlie chuckles. "If you think about it, she's perfect for you."

I stare at him like he's just grown wings. "Are you insane? She's been lying and manipulating me from the get-go."

"I said what I said." Charlie gloats, and I flip him the bird. His expression turns solemn. "She saved your ass back there."

"She saved all our asses," Kai acknowledges, rubbing the back of his neck.

"We were toast when those reinforcements arrived. We only got away because she gave us an advantage," Hunt reminds me.

"I can't work out if she's an enemy or an ally or if it's interchangeable depending on the circumstances," I admit.

Drew

"So, let's ask her," Kaiden says. "I reckon it's cards-on-the-table time for all of us."

Chapter Twenty-Nine
Athena

"Can you take these off now?" I ask when we are finally up in the air, lifting my bound wrists. "And I need to use the bathroom." Pain shoots through my arm from my injury, and I wince.

"You're hurt." Kai frowns from his seat across from me.

"Her wrists are bleeding," Hunt says, but I barely even feel that pain. I haven't taken pain pills in hours, and my arm is throbbing like a bitch. It's possible I might pass out from a combination of pain, dehydration, and starvation.

"Don't try anything," Drew warns, reaching over from the seat beside me and unlocking the cuffs.

"What the hell do you think I'm going to do forty thousand feet in the air?"

"Cut the sass, or I'll gag you again," he says, standing and helping me to my feet.

"Get off. I can go by myself." I move out to the aisle.

"Not a chance, sweetheart." Drew eyeballs his friends. "Order food and drinks and keep an eye on the prisoner."

I glance over at the teenage boy, sitting beside Charlie in

the group of four seats on the right of the aisle. He's cuffed to the arm of the chair closest to the window, scowling at the large man with a gray crewcut sitting across from him with a menacing smile.

"Don't hurt him." I jab my finger in the air. "Touch one hair on his head, and I'll gut you like a squealing pig the minute we land."

"She's a tad dramatic," Drew says, taking my elbow.

"A bit like someone I know," Kai pipes up, and he's fast becoming my favorite person.

"No one is hurting the boy," Drew says. "Get him some food and drink and a blanket if he's cold."

"Yes, boss."

"Move." Drew motions me forward with his eyes, and I chew on the inside of my mouth instead of giving in to my desire to chew *him* out.

He opens a door at the end of the plane, letting me step into the bedroom with en suite shower room first. Drew locks it before turning to face me. "Strip."

"Excuse me?"

"I want to see your arm. How bad is it?"

"It's fine," I lie as my arm aches anew.

"Off with the shirt, or I'll do it myself."

"You're such a bossy fucker," I say before peeling my dirty top off, biting down hard on my lip with the pain the motion produces in my injured arm.

Drew cusses under his breath. "Your stitches have opened."

My eyes follow the small trickle of blood seeping down my arm.

"I'll live."

My eyes catch his gaze raking over my black sports bra and my flat stomach. "My eyes are up here, Drew."

"I'm aware." The heat in his eyes sends my insides into a tailspin.

"I'll run you a shower and find some clothes for you to change into," he says, brushing past me. He takes up most of the space in the bathroom as he leans in to turn the shower on.

I strip out of the rest of my clothes, leaving my underwear and bra on as I watch him root around the small cabinet under the sink. "You have everything you need in there," he says, stepping back out into the bedroom.

His eyes are like heat-seeking missiles blazing a trail up and down my body as he drinks me in from head to toe.

The air is super-charged, and butterflies are swooping in my chest while delicious knots of lust coil low in my belly.

"If you're finished ogling me, I'd like to take that shower now."

He steps wordlessly to one side so I can pass, and we both pretend I don't see the bulge tenting his pants.

"Athena," he says as my fingers curl around the door.

I arch a brow.

"Thank you for what you did back in Sofia."

There is no doubting the sincerity in his tone or his expression, and it does something weird to my insides. "I'm just glad I was there."

Our eyes meet and hold, and I have a sudden uncharacteristic urge to rush out of the bathroom and fling my arms around him.

Instead, I close the door, shed the rest of my clothing, and step in the shower.

When I exit the bathroom a while later, there are clean clothes on the bed along with a bottle of water and a plate of sliced fruit. I dry off and get dressed, folding the boxers and gray sweatpants several times around my waist so they stay up. The long-sleeved shirt is several sizes too large for me, but it's cool against my flesh, it smells fresh, and the material is thick, so my nipples won't go saluting anyone. I pull the socks on and forgo my boots for now. I am halfway through eating the fruit when there's a knock on the door. "Come in."

Drew walks into the room, carrying a first aid kit. His gaze tracks over me from my damp hair to the man's clothing I'm wearing, and a possessive fire dances in his eyes, making me wonder if these are his clothes. He sits on the bed beside me, setting the kit down before unfurling the item in his palm. "Charlie had this in his pocket," he says, holding the glittery pink hair tie out to me. "It's his daughter's. He thought you might need it."

"That's thoughtful." I pluck it from his palm, and fiery little tingles brush over my skin from that fleeting contact. I lift my arms to pull my hair up, and a dart of pain shoots through my left arm. I bite down so hard on my lip I draw blood.

"Let me." Drew's gruff tone sends shivers tiptoeing over every inch of my flesh. A prick of blood stains the sleeve of my borrowed shirt as I lower my arms and admit defeat. "I, ah, should probably tend to your arm first," he says, gluing his eyes to the widening bloodstain on the shirt.

"I've got it."

His eyes pierce mine, calling me out on the lie. I'm suddenly conscious of how close we are and noticing he's freshly showered too. He had cleaned his face when we first got on board and attempted to fix his bloody nose, but his hair is damp, and his black cargo pants and black short-sleeved T-shirt are new, and I'm guessing there is a second shower somewhere else on this plane. It's a lot bigger than most private planes, but there are twenty people on board, so it's necessary.

"Let me help." His fingers dance lightly across my face, and I'm in so much trouble with this man. My eyes drop to his tempting mouth, and I would love nothing more than to lose myself in him. Drew Manning in a suit is a sight to behold, but this more casual version heats my blood to the boiling point. Somehow, he seems more *him*. Like I'm seeing a side of him he doesn't show to many, and there is nothing more attractive to me. He's so gorgeous, and I bet every naked inch of him is equally beautiful and sexy. It's a long flight back to the US, and sex would be a perfect distraction.

Without saying a word, I move to pull my top off, but Drew takes over, slowly and carefully peeling the shirt away until I'm sitting bare-chested before him. To give him credit, he doesn't look at my breasts or the hard nipples waving hello, gently taking my arm and inspecting the injury with a frown.

"I'm sorry," he says, shocking me. I don't think a man like Drew Manning apologizes very often.

"For what?"

He opens the medical kit and removes a small vial of rubbing alcohol, some gauze, and paper stitches.

"For injuring you and for locking you in the trunk."

Anger mushrooms in my chest like a bomb just detonated inside me, and I'm fuming all over again. "I saved you, and you repaid me by acting like a complete asshole," I snap.

"You followed me out of the country, and I don't trust you. I did what I thought was right in the moment, but I never intended to hurt you."

"You could've let me sit in the car or put me in a different vehicle with one of your men. You didn't have to shove me in the fucking trunk!"

"I said I'm sorry."

"Well, I don't forgive you."

"Fair enough."

"I'll never forgive you for it."

"You've made your point."

"Good. Don't forget it." I glare at him, but my anger is already fading.

"I really am sorry. I shouldn't have let anger and frustration cloud my emotions and inform my decisions."

"Okay, enough with the apologies. It's making me ill. Shout at me or give me one of those grumpy glares so this stops feeling weird."

His eyes jump to mine, and he smiles. A real genuine boyish smile, and I get a glimpse of what he must have looked like when he was younger, and I'm ensnared. What is Drew Manning doing to me? I have the worst case of emotional whiplash when it comes to him, and my emotions are ping-ponging all over the place. This guy seriously messes with my head. Presently, I'm floating through the clouds outside the window, mesmerized by this enigma of a man.

"I'm not gonna shout, even if I'm still angry with you." He presses cotton wool to the rubbing alcohol while maintaining eye contact with me.

"I get that." All floaty feelings evaporate when he swipes my arm to clean it, and I hiss through gritted teeth.

"But I don't like that I hurt you. It pains me to see you in pain knowing I caused it."

"You mean that."

His sinful brown eyes hypnotize mine, and we're leaning toward one another without realizing it.

"Yes." His brow puckers. "It's confusing as fuck."

A laugh tumbles from my mouth, and his gaze lowers to my chest for a nanosecond before he looks away. "That makes two of us," I quietly admit, having no clue what is happening here.

"Hold still," he says, dabbing the cotton wool against my arm again. "I need to patch you up and get your clothes back on before I do something we'll both regret."

"Speak for yourself," I blurt before I can shut my mouth.

His eyes drill into mine, and I barely remember to breathe. "You don't know the kind of man I truly am. If you did, you'd reclaim those words in a heartbeat."

"I know enough, Drew." I reach out and cup his face, and my heart melts behind my chest when he closes his eyes and leans into my touch. "I think the things I saw today were glimpses into your soul, and none of it scared me away."

His eyes pop open. "Then you're as fucked up as I am."

My lips curl into a wide smile. "Guilty as charged."

His eyes sink to my mouth for a few delicious anticipatory seconds. When he averts his eyes and returns to my arm, I try to dampen the surge of disappointment swelling in my chest, reminding myself I still don't know what this man's goal is, and he could still be a threat to my brother.

The thought is instantly sobering.

We don't speak as he seals my wound closed with paper stitches and cleans the torn bloody skin at my wrists, wrapping gauze around both of them. He keeps his gaze on my face as he helps me back into the shirt before walking behind me to gather my hair and pull it into a messy bun on top of my head.

The feel of his hands in my hair is so incredibly good, and I'm high from the experience.

"What?" he asks, dropping back down on the bed beside me and fixing me with a curious expression.

I snap out of the daze his touch put me in. "Most men wouldn't know how to do that."

Pain flickers in his eyes for a fleeting second. "Abby and I had to fend for ourselves for a long time as kids. I used to help her with her hair." He shrugs but the movement looks stiff. He pauses for a second before adding, "I had a long-term girlfriend in high school, and she loved me messing with her hair."

Girl, I'm with you. I could die happy as long as his fingers are combing through my hair.

Hang on. Wait a sec.

A light bulb goes off in my head.

"Was she a blonde?"

He averts his eyes, and after a few tense beats, it's clear he's not going to answer. But he doesn't need to. His silence speaks volumes and tells me all I need to know. Whoever this girl is, she's important, and what happened with her has had a lasting impact on Drew. I'm even more intrigued than ever.

Who is she? And more importantly, *where* is she? Could all this be somehow connected to his childhood love?

My mind churns ideas as awkward tension lingers in the air. Drew has been locked in his thoughts since he mentioned her. I can almost see the wheels turning in his head. "How come there is nothing about her online?" I ask, trying to get him to open up more. "There isn't a single photo, not even from prom."

His head whips up, his eyes narrowing to slits.

Oh, that got a reaction out of him all right. "Don't pull that bullshit." I send him a daggered glare as I wave my finger in his face. "I know you ran background checks on me too. You're far from innocent."

He stares at me for a few beats before saying, "I didn't go to prom, and there are no photos of Jane and me because I wiped everything online to protect her."

I open my mouth to ask the obvious question, but he cuts across me, making it clear the subject is closed.

For now.

"I have some pain pills out in the cabin." He stands and offers me his hand.

"If you distrust me, why are you being so nice to me now? Why do you care?"

"Besides it being the right thing to do, the human thing to do, and it's what my sister would want, I honestly don't know."

His brow puckers. "I just know I hate seeing you hurt, and there is some innate need within me to take care of you. Don't ask me to explain it because I can't."

As declarations go, it's hardly up there with the best, but I think I get what he's saying. I'm feeling those things too and I wonder if he's as scared of them as I am?

I place my hand in his and he pulls me to my feet. There is barely any space between us, and the air is crackling with electricity and so many unspoken words. As I stare at this confusing man, I know I am in serious, serious trouble because I feel deep intense things for him.

I don't fully understand how I got to this point.

Or how to get myself out of it.

Chapter Thirty
Drew

"The pilot says we'll be landing in twenty minutes," Hunt says, returning from the bathroom. "You should wake Athena."

"Let her sleep," I say, fighting a yawn. When Athena fell asleep shortly after eating and taking her pain pills, I carried her into the bedroom and tucked her in under the covers, staring at her sleeping form for way longer than I should have.

Something has altered between us again. I feel like I'm on a runaway train and there's no way to get off even if I wanted to.

"She's been sleeping for hours." Kai rubs his hands down his face. None of us have managed to snatch more than a couple hours of sleep even with blankets and comfortable recliner seats.

"She's injured, and I think the pills knocked her out."

"How do you want to play this when we land?" Charlie asks, jerking his head at the sullen teenage boy staring out the window.

"We'll take him to the hotel, and Ezra can watch him while we get word to his father," I say in a low voice.

"Even if we give the boy back unharmed, you've gained a dangerous enemy," Hunt says, fastening his seat belt.

"I've been thinking maybe Athena can help us with that."

Kai arches a brow.

"Whoever she's working for, or with, is clearly well connected. Let's give Petrov something else to worry about so he forgets all about me."

"You're assuming a lot," Athena says, appearing in the aisle. Her hair is still up in a messy bun, but wispy blonde strands frame her stunning makeup-free face, and I'm instantly mesmerized. Charlie vacates the seat beside me so she can take it. "Thank you." She offers him a smile, and a growl tumbles from my mouth.

Anderson's lips twitch.

"How are you feeling?" Charlie asks, dropping into the seat across the aisle from us.

"Good." Her arm brushes against mine as she sits.

I lean over and buckle her seat belt. "We're landing soon." She shivers, and I drape my blanket over her body before lifting my hand to summon the air steward. "Get me water, a snack, and some pain pills."

"Please." Athena smiles at the man as he gulps and nods before scurrying away.

"Assuming what exactly?" Hunt asks, crossing his feet at the ankles.

"That the men I work for aren't already aware of Emil Petrov and the role he plays in the European trafficking network, for one. Secondly, that they'd be willing to do Drew a favor."

"Who are they, and why were you sent to spy on me?" I ask as the plane begins its descent.

"I'm not at liberty to say on either count."

I pierce her with a dark look. "You're giving me the answers I need, Athena."

"Or what, Mr. Manning? You'll lock me away in your hotel and torture me?" She smiles sweetly, and I'm seconds away from putting her over my knee and spanking the arrogance out of her fine ass.

"I am particularly skilled at getting answers from people who don't want to give them. I'd suggest you stop baiting me."

"I'm aware of your specialist skills, Drew, and I hate to break it to you, but you don't scare me."

Kai chuckles, but I ignore him. "You think you know me, but you don't have a clue what I'm capable of or the lengths I'll go to to obtain the answers I seek."

"This is connected to Jane, isn't it?" She stares me straight in the eye. "She's the reason you don't fuck blondes. She's the reason you're targeting sex traffickers. What happened to her?" Compassion splays across her face as my heart beats furiously behind my rib cage.

"It's none of your business," I say in a clipped tone as I look out the window as the plane moves closer to the ground.

"Why are you targeting my brother?"

My head whips around. "What?"

"Arlo," she says. "Do you mean him harm?" There's a fierceness in her gaze as she eyeballs me.

"Of course not. I have no beef with your brother, and I'm not targeting him. Is that what your boss told you?"

She shakes her head. "It's what my father said."

"Who is your father?"

"Amos Martin," she says without hesitation, and I'm glad she's being honest about some things.

"Not Lewis?"

She shakes her head again. "Lewis is a fake name to hide my true identity."

"I don't know your father." I look across at Charlie, and he shakes his head, his brow puckered with the same confusion I feel.

"Well, he seems to know you, and for some reason, he wants you dead."

Ice replaces the blood in my veins as the wheels touch down on the runway. "Who is your father, Athena?" I snap.

"A powerful man. More powerful and well connected than you or any of the elite," she replies, but she's not gloating. She looks as troubled as Charlie.

"Is he involved in sex trafficking?" Anderson asks.

"No. My father is not a good man, but there are limits to what he'll do. He wouldn't put innocent children at risk. We are governed by a specific set of rules, and our leaders work hard to eradicate the sins of this world. Trafficking of any kind is outlawed."

"Forgive me if I'm not convinced," I say as the plane pulls up toward the private hangar. "Are you from Lowell?" I ask even though I'm pretty sure I already know the answer.

"Yes."

A pregnant pause ensues as I try to figure this out. It can't be a coincidence. Athena's father is somehow involved. Am I getting close to the truth and he plans to kill me so it doesn't come to light?

"We have a welcoming committee," Charlie says as the plane draws to a standstill. I peer outside, spotting three black SUVs seemingly waiting for us. There are multiple figures standing around the vehicles, but it's too hard to tell who they are from this angle. Sunrise isn't for another hour, and the lights on the outside of the hangar are the only illumination.

I keep Athena behind me as we descend the stairs, insisting she take the blanket with her. It's fucking cold and she's shivering. When we reach the ground, I tuck her in close to my body and wrap my arm around her shoulders. I'm surprised she doesn't rebuke my touch; instead she leans into me, and I'm careful not to exert pressure on her injured arm.

"Xavier?" Disbelief threads through Hunt's tone as he spies his husband standing with four strange men.

Make that two strange men.

My eyes narrow at the two men who were with Athena at the restaurant, and I tuck her in closer to my side. The bigger of the two notices the movement, and he smirks. My lips curl into a snarl as we face off against one another.

Daniels walks toward Hunt, quickly inspecting him from head to toe before grabbing him into a hug. "I'm glad you all got home safe. I was worried."

"I told you I was fine," Hunt says, pressing a firm, hard kiss to his lips before breaking their embrace. "What's going on?"

"We need to talk," Ares says, pushing off one of the SUVs and coming toward us.

"Did you even leave?" Athena asks as he approaches us.

"Manning put a wrench in our plan." The asshole drills me with a cutting look.

"Sorry to inconvenience you, Salinger, but feel free to run along home now."

He barks out a laugh. "I should have put a bullet in your skull seven years ago."

"Drew." Hunt's tone conveys clear warning, but fuck that.

I push my face all up in Ares's face. "I remember you. Once an asshole, always an asshole. I owe you a pistol-whip to the head."

"Well, this got out of hand fast," a dark-haired man drawls as he walks over to us. He looks like the other guy from the restaurant, and I'm guessing this is that Jase guy Daniels mentioned.

"Are you really surprised?" the blond man says, stepping in

between us. He stares at Ares. "I thought you wanted to wrap this up fast to get home."

"He pisses me off." Ares flexes his biceps and cracks his knuckles.

"Trust me, the feeling is mutual."

"We're moving now," the fourth man says. He's the other guy from the restaurant. "It's too risky to talk in the open."

"Take the kid and stash him in the safe house," the blond says to a couple of armed goons standing on the other side of one of the SUVs.

"Like hell you are." I hold Athena's hand as I step up to this controlling douche. "He's my prisoner, and he's coming with me."

"You can trust Knight," Xavier says. "Come with me, and I'll explain everything on the way."

"You're riding with us," Ares says to Athena.

"Fuck no." My arm slides around her back, and I pull her into my body again. "She's not going anywhere with you."

Ares emits a deep chuckle. "Someone has gotten attached."

I prickle at his words, but I don't let her go or contest it.

"Am I still your prisoner?" Athena asks, claiming my attention.

"No, of course not."

She wrenches out of my hold. "Then I'll make my own decision. You don't speak for me."

Pain rips through my chest as she walks over to Ares. Their heads bend as they lean into one another, talking in hushed tones. My hands ball into fists at my side as I stare at them, visualizing creative ways to kill the motherfucker.

"You're in deep shit, my friend," Anderson says, clamping his hand on my shoulder. "She has you by the balls."

I grind my teeth to my molars, trying to talk myself out of teaching that asshole a lesson when he places his hand on her back and presses his mouth to her ear, smirking as he eyeballs me.

"He's happily married," Anderson reminds me. "And purposely winding you up. Don't give him an inch. You're Drew motherfucking Manning, and I don't care who that jerk is; he's got nothing on you, man."

His words work like a charm, and a familiar neutral mask shields my true emotions from others.

Athena steps back, nodding before returning to my side. "I'll come with you."

"Did your boss give you permission?"

She rams her clenched fist into my solar plexus, momentarily winding me. "I make my own decisions. Don't make me regret this one."

Ares chuckles, and I really hate that guy. I don't care if Xavier vouches for him. He's a total dick.

Athena and I get into Xavier's car with him and Hunt while Anderson goes with Charlie. My men split off into different vehicles to head home. The four dicks go in one SUV while their men take my goddamned prisoner in another.

"What did he say to you?" I ask Athena when we're buckled up side by side in the back of Xavier's car.

"Not to disclose anything until we're at the house."

"What house?"

"Anderson's," Xavier confirms as he drives off, following Charlie's SUV.

"What's going on?" Hunt asks before I can form the words.

"Ares showed up at our place yesterday and filled me in on a few things."

"Where are the kids?" Hunt's strained tone conveys his concern.

"With your parents. I knew we'd need some time to handle

all of this, so I called them, and they were more than happy to take the kids for a sleepover."

Hunt reconciled with his dad a few years ago after his parents made the move from New York to Boston to be closer to their grandkids.

I pop my head between the console. "What about my nieces and nephews?"

"Olivia has them." He eyeballs me through the mirror as we exit the private airfield onto the main road. "I filled Abby in, Drew. I know you wanted to be the one to tell her, but it couldn't wait. She's up to speed and waiting on all of us to arrive."

I slump back in my seat and scrub my hands down my face. "On a scale of one to ten, how pissed is she with me?"

"She's not pissed at you, Drew. She's pissed at a world that would do that to Jane. She's angry you're punishing yourself. You shouldn't be paying the price for something you had no control over. Mostly she's sad and worried about you."

Athena threads her fingers in mine and I cling to her hand like a limpet. I turn to look at her, seeing nothing but compassion flaring in her eyes. "I can see it's painful for you, but I'd like to know. What happened to her? Where is Jane?"

All the fight leaves me as I stare at the beautiful blonde pleading at me with her eyes. The walls come tumbling down, and it all comes out. There is little argument for holding back now everyone pretty much knows. No one speaks or interrupts as I tell Athena everything. Her thumb makes soothing circles on the back of my hand as I purge it all, and though it's not the first time I have told my story, it's cathartic this time.

"God, Drew." She cups my cheeks with both hands when I stop speaking just as we turn down the road toward my sister's house. "I am so sorry." She pulls me into her arms, and I go readily, snaking my arms around her back and holding her tight. "For everything Jane went through and all you're still going through." She strokes her hand up my back before her fingers curl into my hair, and it's amazingly comforting.

My eyes shutter as the car comes to a stop, and I feel so incredibly tired. Tired of chasing monsters and fighting the demons in my head. I just want it to stop. To know inner peace even if it's only an illusion. Doors open and close as we remain locked in our embrace, and I cling to her and her calming presence that has silenced the screaming in my head.

"We'd better go inside," she says, easing back a little. She kisses my cheek. "But I'm here for you, and I'm going nowhere, okay?"

I dance my fingers across the soft skin of her face. "I don't deserve your kindness."

"Perhaps." She shrugs as her eyes light up at my touch. "But I'm too fucking tired to keep fighting you, and now I know the story, so much makes sense."

"I don't want you to pity me. I fucking hate seeing pity in anyone's eyes."

"You don't need to explain." She grips my face in her palms again. "I see you, Drew Manning." She brushes her mouth against mine. "I see every deep, dark, hidden part of you, and it doesn't scare me away. It draws me closer." Her eyes shine with emotion. "I *see* you, Drew, and I like what I see." Her lips curve in a gorgeous smile. "And that's my true dirty big secret."

Chapter Thirty-One
Athena

"Thank God you're okay," Abby says, pulling me into her arms when we step into the hallway of her house. "I was so worried after Xavier showed up and told me everything."

"You should hate me."

"I might yet." Her attention turns to her brother as he closes the door and moves around me. "What happened to your nose?" Abby frowns at the swelling around his nostrils.

"I kicked him in the face when he refused to let me out of the trunk." Drew levels me with a look that says I'll pay for that, and I grin. "Just keeping it real, sweet cheeks."

"Then you deserved it." She gently prods his nose until he swats her hand away. "It's not broken. You'll live."

"Thanks for your concern," he says in a dry tone, and I stifle a giggle.

"I *was* concerned." Abby wraps herself around him, holding him tight. "Love you, D. I'm glad you're home safe."

"Love you too, little bug."

The way they love one another warms my heart.

She thumps him in the arm and glares at him. "If you ever keep shit from me again, *Andrew*, you'll get more than a thump."

"So much for not being pissed," Drew mutters under his breath.

"Go talk to the others. I want a word with Athena." Abby gives him a gentle nudge.

Drew casts a glance at me, his eyes full of conflicting emotions, and I can relate.

My head is a mess over this guy, and I have no clue what's going on or where things stand with us. "I'm fine."

He nods and slowly walks away, looking back over his shoulder at me in a way that sends blood racing faster in my veins.

"Has something happened between you?" Abby asks, and I'm forced to drag my gaze from her brother.

"No." I blow air out of my mouth. "Yes." I yank the hair tie from my head, letting messy waves tumble around my shoulders. "I don't know."

Her eyes narrow. "You were spying on my brother, and if you're seducing him as part of some nefarious plan, I'll—"

"I'm not. What I feel for Drew is confusing as fuck, and I can't explain it, but it's genuine."

"I want to believe that, but you haven't been truthful with any of us."

"Would it help if I said I wanted to be honest, but my hands were tied?"

She sighs. "I'm angry with you, but I know the way these assholes operate, and I'm giving you the benefit of the doubt for now."

"It's probably more than I deserve. I enrolled in yoga class purposely to meet you and Demi, but every interaction we've had has been genuine, and I never meant either of you any harm."

"Just my brother."

"I wasn't told the truth. I've been manipulated by my own fucking father, and I still don't know why."

Pain and rage dart across her face. "Unfortunately, I've got some experience with manipulative asshole fathers. I'm sorry that's happened to you too."

"He's used my brother to control me for the last fifteen years, and I'm tired of being his lackey. It was all for nothing anyway." I lean back against the wall and wrap my arms around myself. I need to check in with Arlo. He'll be home this week, and I want to find out how things went for him at HQ. I'm hoping he might have changed his mind, but it's a tentative hope at best.

Abby is staring at me expectantly.

"I was trying to shield my brother from the world we live in. Dad promised if I did the things he asked of me he wouldn't force my brother's hand, but he lied, and I'm just so sick of all the bullshit."

Sympathy splays across her face. "As someone who would do anything for her brother, I get it. I hope there's some way to protect Arlo."

"I fear it's too late." I push off the wall. "I am truly sorry for deceiving you, Abby. I'm sorry for all of it, but please believe me when I say how much I love you and Demi and your entire family. Spending Thanksgiving with you was the best day I've had in years, and none of it was fake."

Her lips kick up. "We thought the joke was on Drew that day, but really the joke was on us."

"Yeah, I'm so not touching that."

"We're all waiting on you two," Baz says, materializing at the end of the hallway. "And if you don't get your pretty asses in here stat, Manning and Salinger are going to rip one another apart and probably destroy your house in the process, Abby."

Abby rolls her eyes. "I'd like to see them try." She shakes her head. "Lord save us from alpha males."

"Preach, girl."

We share a smile, and I get the feeling things will be okay between us. I truly hope so at least. I'd hate to lose her friendship because I've come to value it highly.

Baz turns on his heel, and we run to catch up. When we enter Abby's living room, Ares and Drew are all up in one another's personal space, the former smirking, the latter snarling.

"I swear I can't leave you alone for five seconds, D, and you're causing trouble."

"Just like when we were kids," Charlie says, flashing us a grin.

"Back down," I say, pushing my way in between the two hotheads. "What are you arguing about now?"

Kai chuckles. "You, what else?"

"Ares has just informed us of the connection between you two." Xavier is grinning from his position on the couch alongside his husband.

"It'd be entertaining if I wasn't tired as fuck and dying to see my kids," Hunt drawls, stretching one arm out behind his husband on the couch.

I turn my ire on Ares. "Why would you go there?" I wave my hands in the air. "This will only distract us from the important things we need to discuss."

"I've tried telling him that, but he never listens to me," Knight Carter says, lifting his gaze from his cell.

"What's the story?" Abby asks, curling into Kai's lap on the other couch.

Drew

"The CliffsNotes version is our moms became best friends after their mutual marriages to powerful men, aka our dads. Ares was born four years before me, and his parents named him Blade. Mom had trouble conceiving, so she was overjoyed when I was born. I already mentioned how she'd picked the name Athena for her firstborn daughter when she was a little girl. Apparently, Blade was enamored with me as a baby and always wanting to hold me and feed me my bottle. Our moms swore it was true love, and they hatched a plan to marry us off to one another when we got older."

"It was the done thing back then," Jase explains. "But not now unless it's a personal choice."

I glance at Knight without conscious thought. Of the four Luminary leaders, he's the only one who didn't get to marry for love, and I've always felt it was grossly unfair. Everyone and their granny knows how he feels about Bree, including his bitch of a wife. Rumor is she's fucking Knight's despicable younger brother even though Knight is faithful to her despite not loving her.

"So, what happened?" Abby asks. "And why do you go by Ares now?"

"We had to flee overseas and take new identities," Ares finishes explaining. "Mom named me Ares as the natural match to Athena, and when we returned years later, I didn't even remember my birth name." Ares smirks at Drew, and it's so incredibly juvenile and petty.

"You lied," Drew says, taking a few steps back.

"I thought we'd already established that."

"You lied about every fucking thing."

"Not everything, and don't act all innocent. You've been lying your entire life. To yourself and those around you."

His nostrils flare, and I fear I've gone too far, but it all seems so blindingly obvious to me now. I instantly regret that little outburst because I see the hurt he's hiding from others, but he can't hide it from me.

Ares chuckles, and I see red, whipping around and punching him in the gut.

There's a collective intake of breath, and I probably shouldn't have done that, but I don't feel sorry.

Fuck it.

Might as well own it.

I straighten my spine and lift my shoulders. "I'm not apologizing. You're acting like an immature brat, and I know that's not who you are. Drew has suffered enough. Stop trying to hurt him. He's been hurt enough." I stomp away from Ares and stand beside Drew, making my feelings known.

You could hear a pin drop in the awkward silence that ensues.

"You're forgiven," Abby says, her voice projecting loud and clear. "And I might just have a teeny-tiny girl crush on you."

"You've got balls of steel, Martin," Baz says, grinning. "If anyone else did that, they'd be facing the gallows."

"That's a tad dramatic. We've mostly left those days behind us."

"If the theatrics are out of the way, can we get down to business. We need to be on that plane in two hours, and time is running out," Knight says.

Abby climbs off Kai's lap. "I'll get coffee while you start, and help yourself to food." She gestures toward the large dining table where plates full of pancakes, fruit, pastries and muffins are laid out.

Kai and Xavier walk into the kitchen to help while everyone else grabs plates of food and takes a seat. Drew pulls two velvet-backed chairs from around the table over to the area beside the couches for us, and we sit side by side with plates on our laps.

Drew

When everyone has finished eating and we're all settled in the living area, Knight clears his throat and begins explaining. "We know you're all wondering who we are, but there is only so much we can tell you. The first thing you need to know is we are not your enemy, and we have no intention of hurting you or your loved ones. We're trying to keep you safe."

"We warned you to back down seven years ago because you were interfering in something connected to our world, and we wanted to handle it ourselves and to keep you protected from the kind of attention you have now attracted," Jase adds.

"Were you warning me off too?" Xavier asks Ares. "I recall a few times I was shut out of things and received anonymous messages telling me to butt out."

Ares nods. "I wanted to tell you, dude. I haven't liked keeping this part of my life from you, but it wasn't safe to drag you into it. I did what I could to keep you safe."

Xavier and Ares share a look loaded with emotion and unspoken words.

"Were you involved in what happened to Jane?" Drew asks, tensing beside me. My fingers thread through his like it's the most natural thing in the world. His palm curls tightly around mine, and his touch feels like my superpower. Like I could do anything as long as he's holding on to me. I'm enjoying a silent freak-out over those thoughts as Ares's gaze drifts to our conjoined hands, and he frowns.

I don't know why he seems to dislike Drew. I know he's completely in love with his wife and there has never been anything more than casual friendship between us. I only got to know him when we were adults when he returned to Lowell with Daphne and his little sister. It's probably just a clash of personalities, and both men want to prove they have the bigger balls.

"No," Ares deep tone bounces off the walls. "We weren't aware of her until your investigation led to Lowell."

"That put you on our radar, and when we discovered what you were doing, we reached out to overseas contacts until we found her," Baz says.

"What about her parents and her younger brother?" I ask because Drew said he hadn't been able to find any intel on what happened to them.

"We haven't been able to find anything on her parents," Ares says, rubbing his hands on his denim-clad thighs. "Which leads us to believe they never left Lowell."

Knight leans forward, clasping his hands on his knees. "We can't be sure, but we think some of the remains we found on my family estate years ago might have belonged to Silas."

"No," I whisper, clamping my free hand over my mouth.

Pain slices across Knight's face. "My parents were monsters, and I suspect they were involved in what happened to the Ford family."

Drew's grip on my hand tightens, and a muscle clenches in his jaw. "Were Hamilton and Mathers involved?"

"We have found no elite knowledge or involvement, and it seems unlikely," Ares says. "The organizations rarely crossover."

"My mother was an evil bitch who lusted after boys and young men right under our noses growing up," Knight continues. "She's dead now, as is my father, but she caused untold pain and suffering. We believe Silas ended up in her clutches."

"What about Jane's parents?" Abby asks in a soft voice.

"We haven't found any trace of them," Baz confirms.

"When we assumed leadership positions in our world, we uncovered a massive amount of corruption perpetrated by some of the previous leaders. Rhett Carter, Knight's dad, was the worst, and he very nearly took full control of everything," Jase says. "He had set up illegal sex trafficking rings in South America, and we've been working tirelessly for years to weed them out and shut them down."

"We know what you did, and we thank you for it." Knight stares solemnly at Drew.

"You were helping me," Drew says, and Knight nods. "I often wondered why things always seemed to go so smoothly. Why none of the locals I hired on the ground ever turned against me or how I was able to procure the supplies I needed without being discovered. How none of my planes were ever stopped."

"We realized pretty quickly there was no deterring you," Ares says with a hint of respect in his tone. "So, we did what we could to help."

"Where did you find Jane's body?" Drew asks, and I press in close to his side.

"She lived in Spain for the last three years of her life, imprisoned by this sick prick in a secluded mansion that served as his vacation home," Knight says.

"We hoped she might still be alive," Jase solemnly says. "But when we invaded the house, we found that prick and all his men lying in pools of blood, and the thirteen girls and women he kept chained in the basement were all dead with their necks snapped."

A sob rips from Abby's throat, and Kai lifts her into his lap, circling his arms around her and holding her tight.

I don't think Drew would appreciate a show of affection like that, so I just keep close to his side and hold his hand firmly, letting him know I'm here for him. "Someone knew you were coming," I say.

Ares nods. "Carter had spent years building a network of loyal supporters all over the world. We know there is a still a core within our society who are loyal to him and his ways.

Those who hate the changes we have brought in, and they are biding their time to strike."

"This goes no further, Athena," Knight says, drilling me with a look.

I bob my head. "Of course, you have my loyalty and my confidence. Always."

Abby stops crying, lifting her head and staring curiously at me.

"We have a few specialist teams tasked with hunting these supporters down," Knight says. "We have eliminated many of them over the years, but we know there are more."

"We had plans to ask you to join one of these teams," Ares says. "But I think that ship has sailed." His gaze lowers to where my hand is wrapped around Drew's.

"So, you think these people are behind what happened to Jane?" Xavier asks.

"We do because it's got Carter's signature all over it," Ares says.

"How did the Fords end up in Lowell? Who did they know there?" Charlie asks.

Knight rubs the back of his neck. "We don't know. The trail has been wiped clean. There is literally nothing showing them in Cali after they cross the border into Prestwick. It's like they disappeared."

"And everything and anything connected to each member of the Fords has been erased from the internet and government systems. If you go looking, they literally never existed," Baz adds. "The only proof is their legacy in Rydeville and their house. We imagine that's only there because you got to it first, Drew."

"How is that possible?" Charlie asks. "I know it's not that challenging to wipe stuff from the internet, but wiping official identities is top-level shit."

Drew

Ares's smug grin reappears. "We are top-level shit, Barron. Forget your pathetic little elite club because we run rings around you. We own you."

Drew, Charlie, Kai, and Sawyer all exchange wary looks.

Ares chuckles. He really is an asshole. He just can't help himself.

Knight clears his throat, letting his gaze bounce around the room. "There is nothing, and I mean, literally nothing, the Luminaries can't do."

Chapter Thirty-Two

Drew

"Except find out what happened to my friend and her family," Abby says, narrowing her eyes to slits as she stares at the four men.

It's a valid point.

"This happened before we came into power, and we can't find something that isn't there. With the traffickers, there were leads to follow, but there is nothing to go on in relation to the Ford family. We have spoken to hundreds of people who might have known back then, but no one remembers seeing them," Knight says.

Athena removes her hand from mine and sits upright in her chair. Her eyes are pained when she looks at me. "I think I was wrong earlier." Tears pool in her eyes. "I think my father *is* involved."

"We suspect as much," Jase says, but neither of us are looking at him. "Although we haven't found any evidence we can use to move on him, we suspect he is one of the group loyal to Rhett Carter. But we don't know if he was directly involved or he's just trying to cover it up for someone else."

"What do you know?" I ask, swiveling in my seat so I'm facing her. Our knees touch.

"I was fifteen when the Hanks family from Wyoming came to stay with us. Dad said David Hanks was an old friend from his Stanford days. His wife was Susan, his eldest daughter Francesca, and they had two younger kids. A boy, Justin, who was about seven, and a baby, Florence." Her chest heaves. "Francesca was seventeen, and she had the most beautiful blonde hair and gorgeous blue eyes. She was really pretty, and I remember being envious of her wardrobe."

All the air is sucked from my lungs, and I couldn't say a word even if I wanted to. I'm vaguely aware of Abby hopping up and dashing to the sideboard.

"She was super sweet and always nice to me, especially when my stepmom was being a cunt." Her eyes flit to Ares for a split second, and I grab her hands, keeping her attention focused on me. I do not like that asshole, and why is he so invested in Athena? I want to wipe the arrogance off his face every time he looks at her.

"Here." Abby thrusts a photo album in Athena's face. "This is Jane. Is it the same girl?"

A heavy weight sits on my chest as I look at the open page. It's a picture of Jane and me, taken a few months before I sent her away. She's sitting in my lap, laughing at something I'd said, and Abby had captured a sneaky photo.

I haven't looked at our old albums for years because the thought of it always hurt so much.

Now, the overriding sentiment is sadness and anger. Jane's life was snuffed out from her before it had really begun in the most heinous way.

Silent tears roll down Athena's cheeks, and she nods. "Yes, that's her."

My head drops to Athena's shoulder, and her body shudders as she cries. Abby is sobbing again, and Kai gets up, coming over to hold her. My arms go around Athena's waist as hers land on my back.

No one speaks, and the only sounds in the room are that of the two women crying.

After a few minutes, Knight clears his throat. "What do you remember, Athena? How long were they living with you, and how did they leave?"

She crawls into my lap and wraps her arms around me. I cling to her, inhaling her scent and the feel of her warm body against my cold one. I'm still processing, and my head is a mess.

"They were with us for like six or seven months. Then one morning I woke, and they were gone."

Rage charges through my veins, and I want to tear her father limb from limb.

"I was upset," she continues, holding on to me tighter, no doubt feeling the anger hardening my muscles and strengthening my resolve. "I considered Francesca a friend, and I was so in love with baby Flo. I was suspicious too because I really didn't think they'd disappear without saying goodbye. But Dad said they were running from some men who wanted to do them harm and we had to tell no one they'd been staying with us. I bought that because they hadn't left our house or the grounds the entire time they'd stayed with us, and Francesca had said they needed to lay low though she didn't explain why, and I didn't pry."

"I'm going to kill him," I growl.

"I'll help you," she coolly replies, and the look in her eye is completely sincere. "If my father was involved in what happened to Jane and her family, he deserves every bit of pain coming his way."

I set Athena down on the ground and stand. "Let's go now." I'm done waiting to have my revenge.

"Woah, wait up." Knight climbs to his feet. "No one is going near Amos Martin until we have proof and then there are legitimate channels we need to pursue. If he's guilty, I promise he will be punished."

"Fuck that." I square off with him. "That asshole is not going to jail. He deserves to die a slow, torturous death."

"I like you," Baz says, standing beside Knight. "And I wish we could give you his death, but we can't act above the law. We can't say we are changing things and then make exceptions when it's personal to us."

"If we go there, we're no better than our predecessors," Jase says, also standing.

"Then turn a blind eye," I say. "Let us do this and lose the trail."

Ares rises from his chair, and I shoot him a daggered look, preparing to deal with his shit when he surprises me. "Didn't think we'd ever find common ground, but I'm with Manning. If we find irrefutable proof Martin is involved, let's hand his ass to Drew and let him do his worst. It still won't come even close to payback, but it's something."

"It's too personal for you." Baz clamps a hand on Ares's shoulder. "You can't be objective."

"And you can?" Ares quirks a brow.

"None of us like this," Knight says. "But we can't jeopardize our reputations and everything we've sacrificed for one man."

"You said you eliminated others who were core Rhett Carter supporters," Abby says. "So why can't Amos be eliminated if he's guilty?"

"Because there's too much of a trail from Drew to my father," Athena replies.

"And if he's going to this much trouble to hide his involvement and to silence you, Drew, you can bet he has provisions in place should anything happen to him."

"This is fucking bullshit," I roar, shucking out of Athena's hold. "If that bastard is responsible for this, he needs to die!"

Athena takes my hand and steps up beside me. "I'm with Drew. If my father has done this, he deserves a gruesome death. What if there is another way to play this?"

"What do you have in mind?" Ares asks.

"We set a trap and let someone else take the fall for his murder." She squeezes my hand. "We go ahead with the Petrov play, and we make it easy for Amos to know what we're up to. We shadow his every move because my father won't show up to the meet himself. He'll either send me or his backup. We have a team ready in Lowell to swoop in and grab him. Then we stage a very public shoot-out between him and Petrov, and we feed it to the mainstream media. We show them both dead, but in reality, my father and that fucker Emil will be alive and enjoying Drew's and my hospitality at the hotel."

Anderson snorts out a laugh, and my lips are fighting a grin.

"It could work," Ares says, nodding. "Our members will buy it because it was out of our hands."

"Except our handprints will be all over this." Knight drags a hand through his dirty-blond hair.

"As would be expected when one of ours is involved in a very public takedown of a known felon," Jase says.

"Amos will look like the hero taking out the big bad sex trafficker," Baz says.

"No way," Athena responds before I can. "We spin it so it's two sex traffickers trying to eliminate their competition. There can be no scenario where my father looks like the hero. He needs to be shown as the villain he is."

"I hate to play devil's advocate," Hunt says, "but we're all assuming Athena's father is the guilty party when he may have only played a part in it. We don't know he didn't hand the entire family over to Rhett and his wife and they did the rest."

"Hunt has a point," Charlie says. "It seems like Rhett might be the guilty party if he was running trafficking rings, and it seems his wife was involved in Silas's death."

"That doesn't exonerate Amos," Anderson says.

"And if he's still doing Carter's bidding years after his death, it seems likely he knew what was going to happen to the Fords whether they died at his hands or not," Abby adds.

"I could ask him," Athena says. "When I'm home for Christmas. I'll spin it so he has to give me an explanation."

"He'll lie, Thena," Ares says, and I instinctively tuck her closer.

"I think we need to go home and reflect on it until we devise an appropriate strategy." Knight walks right up to me. "I understand why you need to do this, and while it makes me nervous, if we can find a way to do this so you get to end him, we'll do it. But we need to ensure he's guilty first." He eyeballs me in clear warning. "We need your promise you will not take matters into your own hands until we've formulated a joint plan."

"Where did you take the kid?"

"To a safe house we have in the city. He'll be well looked after and heavily guarded," Knight confirms.

"We've already sent the communication to Petrov, and we'll handle setting up the meet," Baz adds. "That's something we can't delay too long on because Petrov is not known for his patience."

"We might have to do the exchange and set a different trap for Amos," Jase says.

"Let's not go over old ground," Knight says. "We need to leave, or we'll miss our flight."

"You need to hold tight, Manning. Think you can do that?" Ares says.

"Yes," I say through clenched teeth.

Ares barks out a laugh. "I've seen kids lie more effectively."

"Fuck you."

"I'm strictly a pussy worshipper, so you're flat out of luck, dude."

Athena rolls her eyes before turning to me. "I know you have no reason to trust me, but I'm asking you to give me the benefit of the doubt. Promise you won't go kamikaze, and I'll work to prove my father's involved."

"You seem sure about his guilt. Why is that?" Jase asks.

"I didn't think he'd be involved in sex trafficking, but it seems too obvious to not be the truth. There is little love lost between him and me, and I'm sick of his manipulations. He's starting on Arlo now, and I swore months ago that I'd do everything in my power to protect my brother—even killing my father if that's what was needed."

"Cold, but I love it," Xavier says.

"It's one thing to say it and quite another to do it," Knight says. "He's still your father."

"He's a piece of shit. And if he sold Jane and Vera to sex traffickers and Silas to Cleo or even stood by and did nothing knowing it was going to happen, then he's already dead in my eyes, and I won't lose sleep over his death." Her eyes lock on mine. "I meant it when I said I'll help you. But Knight is right. We need to bide our time, gather our evidence, and form a rock-solid plan. My father isn't to be underestimated. If you try to go off by yourself, you could end up hurt or worse."

"You've waited this long, D. You can wait another few weeks."

"Okay." I eyeball the four assholes. "I promise I won't make any solo plans or moves. We'll decide the best course of action together."

"Huss speaks highly of you," Baz says. "Don't make a mockery of the man."

"What's Robert Huss got to do with this?" Anderson asks.

The four men trade knowing looks.

"You might as well tell them," Athena says. "They'll only go straight to the horse's mouth, and you'll put him in an awkward position."

"Huss is our man in the elite," Baz confirms.

"Are you saying he's your spy?" Hunt asks, and Knight shakes his head.

"He's our employee," Jase supplies.

"What exactly does that mean?" Charlie asks.

"It means we control the elite." Ares inspects his nails like he's bored. "Like we control every other sub-organization in the world." That smug grin is back, and my jaw pulls tight as I glare at the arrogant fucker. "You didn't really think you were in control, did you?"

"So, you guys have been pulling the strings all along?" Abby's voice elevates, and she's about to go nuclear on their asses.

"Not all along," Knight says, looking mildly apologetic. "Think of it like a pyramid scheme. We're at the very top, then we have the elite and other organizations like them, and underneath them are governments and official entities. We're committed to ensuring every organization in the pyramid is held accountable to a similar set of rules and laws."

A bitter laugh tumbles from my sister's lips. "Well, that's a fucking joke. Where the hell was the governance when my father was running around killing anyone that crossed him, blackmailing important people for shits and giggles, and hurting innocent women and children just 'cause he could?"

"We weren't in charge then," Baz says.

"Like we said, Rhett Carter was a fucking monster, and he didn't much care about those in the lower levels," Ares says. "He was going to wipe them all out anyway if he got into power."

"Jesus, I need alcohol." Abby flops down on the couch.

"It's eight o'clock, Firecracker." Kai drops down beside her.

"It's wine o'clock somewhere," Athena and Abby say together before they both laugh.

"Any other secrets you care to share before you leave?" I ask, pulling Athena back against my chest. I rest my chin on her head and fix the asshole with a glare.

"Nothing much." Ares smiles. "Except Huss has you and your friends earmarked to succeed him and the elite board when he retires."

My jaw hits the floor, and I don't need to look at the others to know they're stunned speechless too.

"But it's no biggie." Ares shoves his grinning asshole face all up in mine, slamming his hand down so hard on my shoulder it's a miracle he didn't break the bone. "We can discuss it another time."

Chapter Thirty-Three
Drew

"I want to ask you something," Anderson says as the four men are ready to leave.

"Make it snappy," Knight says.

"Did you kill my father and William Hamilton?"

"Yes," Ares readily admits.

"I thought you said you don't go around eliminating people anymore?" Abby asks what we're all thinking.

"They were elite, and our hand was forced," Jase says.

"You're starting to sound a lot like your asshole predecessors," Charlie says, affronted like the rest of us.

"I didn't mean that how it sounded. Just that elite are a separate entity, and we aren't under the same scrutiny when it comes to how we handle the other organizations."

"Sounds like hypocritical bullshit," my sister says, calling them out on their questionable morals.

Have I mentioned how much I worship the ground my twin walks on?

Kai is staring at her like he can't wait for all of us to leave so he can ravish her, and that's as far as I'm letting that thought go.

"You're a bunch of ungrateful assholes." Ares folds his arms and glowers at us. "Truth is, we saved your asses."

"*Again*," Jase drawls.

"We found out at the last minute that Hamilton had hired a contract killer to assassinate Atticus Anderson in Lake Garda and a way to lure Atticus's sons to Italy so they could take the heat. We know why too." Knight trains his gaze on Hunt. "After we deal with this, we want that file your father has hidden."

Hunt opens his mouth to say something.

"Don't," Baz interjects. "That tape relates back to things that happened in the past. Things that are no longer relevant but have the power to collapse the entire world, and I'm not being dramatic when I say that."

"As long as that tape is out there, it's a threat to all of us and a threat to your father. If our enemies knew of its existence, they would come for all of us. This isn't up for debate. We'll help you with this, and you will hand that tape to us," Ares says.

"What do you plan to do with it?" I ask, holding Athena tighter and trying to ignore the semi forming in my pants at the way her ass is pressed against my crotch.

"Destroy it," Jase says.

"Now, if there's nothing else, we'll—"

"So, you killed Atticus?" Kai asks.

"Actually, the sniper did before we could get to him," Baz supplies. "But we took care of Hamilton and the sniper, buried the evidence, and ensured you and your brothers didn't take the fall for it."

"Feel free to thank us any moment now," Ares says, and I bare my teeth at him. He needs to get the fuck out of my face.

"We owe you," Kai says.

Baz jabs his finger in Kai's direction. "You do. Don't forget it when we come calling."

"Athena," Ares says, jerking his head. "Walk with me." His eyes lift to mine. "*Alone.* I want a word in private."

I open my mouth to protest, but Athena turns in my arms and plants a hard kiss on my lips to shut me up. "I'll be back." She grins, swatting my ass and sauntering off after the degenerate.

"So, you two are a thing now?" Abby asks, her face lighting up like it's Christmas morning.

"Don't start. My head is fit to explode, and I'm not even attempting to touch that subject."

"Okay."

I arch a brow at my twin because she does not give up that easy. Abby scrambles off the couch and flings her arms around me. She doesn't speak, but she doesn't need to. I hug my sister fiercely, hearing everything she wants to say as she clings to me and quietly mourns.

"He wants to speak to you," Athena says, appearing in the doorway a few minutes later.

Abby shucks out of my embrace and touches my arm before returning to her husband's lap.

"Are you okay?" I ask Athena when I reach her.

"Not really. Today's been a lot."

I tuck her hair behind her ears. "Yeah, it has." I walk past her and out to the door where Ares is waiting. The other three are already in their SUV, eager to get home.

"Let's hear it," I say, folding my arms and staring at the man.

"Don't hurt her." He fixes me with a sober expression. "Athena is like a daughter to my mother, and I'm protective of her because she's good people and she's had a pretty shitty life."

"Message received." I turn to go back inside before spinning around on my heel. "Oh, by the way, touch her again, and you're a dead man." I flash him a dark grin.

"You really are a raging asshole."

"Takes one to know one I guess," I toss over my shoulder before walking off.

"You have a lovely home," Athena says, turning slowly around my large living room with appreciation on her face.

"Thank you. I like it." I deposit my bag and her two large ones at the door.

"It's not at all what I imagined."

"Which was?"

"I thought it'd be clinical with white walls and furniture and devoid of personality, but the whole place screams you, and it's stylish, luxurious, and homey at the same time."

"I worked with Alex Kennedy on the interiors. She designed Abby and Kai's house and my mom's too."

"All three look very different, but now you say it, I can spot her signature style."

"Do you want something to eat, or would you prefer to see your room and freshen up first?" We stayed at Abby and Kai's, talking with the guys for hours after the four men left, trying to wrap our heads around everything we learned and come up with ideas on how to trap Athena's father into giving us the final answers we need. Then we stopped at her apartment briefly after we left my sister's house so she could change and grab her things.

"Are you sure you're okay with me staying here? You seem like a guy who likes his own space."

"I do, but I'm fine with it." If you'd asked me even a week ago if I'd ever invite a woman to invade my private space, I'd probably have put a bullet through your skull for even daring to ask.

But I'm more than okay with this.

I like the thought of her roaming the floors of my home. Swimming in my pool. Walking in my gardens. Cooking at my stove.

I cut my thoughts off before I decide to check myself into the psychiatric ward at Parkhurst.

"If you want me to leave, I'll go. I'm capable of looking after myself, and I seriously doubt my father will take a potshot at me."

"We agreed it's safest for you here. Besides, he'll love it. It's proof your mission to seduce me is working." Athena was much more forthcoming on the trip back from Abby's house, filling me in on what her father asked of her and other stuff.

There's an understanding between us now, and we've both agreed to start over and work together as a team.

I never expected to like it as much as I do.

"I don't ever want to make you uncomfortable, Drew, so if you need space or you want me to go just say it. I want there to be nothing but truth and honesty between us from now on."

"Sounds good to me." I lift her bags. "Let me show you to your room. I'm gonna grab a quick shower, and then I'll make us something to eat."

"Something smells delicious," Athena says forty minutes later when she wanders downstairs. Her hair is freshly blow-dried and she's wearing yoga pants, an oversized sweater, and slides.

"Don't expect much," I say, plating the spaghetti with shrimp in tomato sauce. "I can cook, but it's definitely not Michelin standard or anything close to it."

She hops up onto a stool at the island unit, and I set a plate and silverware down in front of her. "I'm shocked there's something you're humble about."

Laughter rumbles from my chest. "I guess I deserve that."

I fill two glasses with water and give one to her before sliding onto the stool beside her with my food. We eat in companionable silence, and warmth swells my chest when she eats every single bite.

"That was yummy, and you can cook for me anytime." She pats her flat stomach through her sweater.

"You're welcome. It's the first time I've cooked for a woman in a long time," I admit as I scoop up the plates and silverware and take them to the dishwasher.

"It's the first time any man has cooked for me. I could get used to it," she admits.

I stack our dirty dishes and head to the coffee machine and turn it on. "How is that?"

She props her elbows on the counter and her pretty face in her hands. "Told you I haven't dated much. In college, the couple of guys I dated were the kind who ordered pizza and called it dinner, and later, the guys I was forced to date barely knew how to boil an egg."

"Forced to date?" I ask, removing two mugs from the overhead press.

"Most of those guys you've seen in photos with me were guys I seduced on my father's instructions. Men he had a grudge with or someone he was planning to rip off, and he needed insider intel."

Anger swirls in my gut as I fix two coffees. "I didn't think it was possible to hate your father any more than I do, but you've just proven me wrong."

"He's not hard to hate."

"Cream or sugar?" I ask.

"Neither. I prefer it black like my soul." She waggles her brows, and I just stare at her like an idiot, wondering if this is what it feels like to fall.

"You're so alarmingly like me at times it's freaky," I admit when I snap out of it, handing her a mug.

"I feel like a fraud most of the time," she says, slipping off the stool when I tip my head for her to follow me into the living room.

Nightfall is crawling across the sky outside, painting it in shades of dark gray with striking purple streaks.

"In what way?" I ask when we are curled up on the couch, each of us tucked into an end with our bare feet resting on the leather.

"My life has never felt like my own. My father has held me hostage, and I've done things I didn't want to do. Things I'm not proud of."

"I can relate," I say in between mouthfuls of coffee.

"You were making the world a safer place, Drew. I was committing illegal acts in my father's name for his personal gain, and honestly, I'm embarrassed I let him control me for so long. He played me perfectly. Using my feelings for my brother to hold me to ransom, and I'm so freaking mad."

"We'll make him pay."

"I want that."

"I know you do."

Her features fall, and I know where her mind has gone.

"Don't say it. I can't think about it or talk about it again today."

"I'm so sorry, Drew." Tears cling to her lashes.

"Don't apologize. It's not your fault. You're not responsible for your father's actions."

"I know what the board thinks, and I know why they need

us to hold off for now, but I think my father did it. It's the only thing that makes sense to me."

"Guess we'll find out soon enough."

She bites on the corner of her lip, and I can see the question in her eyes.

"Say it."

"You must have really loved her to continue searching for her killers after all this time."

"It's my fault she died." The bitterness of those words sinks deep, seeping into the dark pit inside me that houses my guilt. "I sent her to her death when I should have kept her by my side."

"It is *not* your fault." She drains the last of her coffee and sets her mug down on the end table before scooting over beside me. "You were doing what you thought was right. You were trying to keep her safe."

"Well, I fucking failed," I hiss, setting my half-drank coffee aside. "I put her in the path of predators, and she lost everything because of me." I stand, needing to get out of here.

"I'm sorry. I shouldn't have brought it up." She reaches for my arm. "Please don't go."

"I just need some space." I storm off in the direction of my home gym and take some of my frustration out on the new bag I just installed. After, I cool down in my pool, and that's where Athena finds me.

"Do you mind if I join you?" she asks, and I shake my head. My eyes almost bug out of my head when she toes off her slides and strips off her yoga pants and sweater before diving into the pool in her bra and underwear.

My dick likes it a lot, but I tell him to calm the fuck down. It's a reminder I've missed two weeks with Vixen at the club and I seriously need to get laid.

The thought settles like coagulated milk in my gut.

Vixen is an incredible lay, but the thought of fucking her now just doesn't appeal to me, and I think I know why.

Athena glides through the water like a sea goddess, and her skill and strength is evident. I swim lengths with her, and it's not long before we're in silent competition, flying through the water as we try to outpace one another. She's a formidable competitor, propelled by long toned legs, but she's injured, and after a while, it becomes obvious she's hurting herself to keep up with me. Briefly, I consider slowing down on purpose to let her accept all the glory, but she'd hate that, so I power forward, cutting through the water and claiming the crown.

"I'd beat you if my arm wasn't hurting like a bitch," she says, flattening her back to the wall beside me as we float in the warm water.

"I'm happy to challenge you to a rematch when you're fully recovered."

"You're on." She grins, pushing wet strands of hair off her face.

"You're a very good swimmer."

"I wanted to swim professionally, and my mother encouraged me, but after she died, Dad put a stop to all that. He told me it wasn't becoming for a woman of my position."

"I'll add that to the list of reasons I have to kill your father."

"I blocked most of his bullshit out," she says, staring off into space. "It was the only way I could survive, but now I've decided I'm done being his lackey, I'm remembering all the reasons I hate him. I know Knight thinks I'll regret it if I kill him, but I honestly won't." Her eyes lift to mine. "If I was a bigger person, I'd rise above it and just cut him out of my life, but screw that shit. He's a conniving prick, and I won't shed a tear over his death."

Chapter Thirty-Four
Drew

I heave a sigh as I roll over in bed, rubbing my tired eyes as I will sleep to come. It's been the same these past three nights. My brain won't switch off no matter how exhausted I am. Waiting for news is the slowest form of torture. Xavier submitted our suggestions to Ares, and they are reflecting on them and checking out some stuff on their end. Until they come back to us, it's a waiting game, and I'm gradually going insane. Usually, work is a great distraction, but that's not helping this time. I can't concentrate for shit.

To be this close to getting the answers I have craved for years is bittersweet. Now I might finally know what happened to Jane and her family and I might finally have my revenge, I can't help wondering what next? What will I do with my life now I no longer have this quest?

It's these kinds of thoughts that have me tossing and turning in bed. I'm just about to call it quits and get up when my bedroom door opens and a slim silhouette slips into the room.

"I know you're awake," Athena says in a soft, raspy voice that stirs things down south.

I sit against my headboard and turn to face her in the dark. "What's up?"

"Can I sleep in here with you?" she asks, tiptoeing toward the bed. "Not to do anything. I mean not like that. I just want to be held, and I want to hold you."

I should say no. I plan to, but that's not the word that trips off my tongue. "Okay." I lie down on my side and peel back the covers, silently questioning my sanity because this is the very definition of insanity.

Athena slips into the bed wearing an oversized T-shirt, and I can't decide if I should be grateful or disappointed. I know she has sexy nightwear as I saw a bundle of silky lace things when she was folding her laundry earlier. She moves next to me, setting her head on the pillow and turning on her side to face me. There is scant space between us, and I'm conscious I'm only wearing boxers the same time I'm wondering if she's wearing anything underneath that shirt.

Her big eyes find mine in the dark in silent question.

I lie down flat on my back because I'm already going to hell anyway and might as well embrace it. "Come here," I say, opening my arms for her.

She scoots right over, resting her head on my chest and her hand on my stomach. Her body presses up against me, and I'm instantly hard. Like full-on stiffy trying to poke a hole through the comforter.

I seriously need to get laid. I inwardly groan the second that thought lodges in my brain. I can't even think about Vixen when Athena is in my bed, in my arms, and obsessively occupying my thoughts like she has been since she moved into my house and edged her way into my heart.

"I haven't been able to sleep since Sunday because I keep thinking of everything, and I'm so confused."

"Join the club, sweetheart." My arm wraps more firmly around her back as her fingers dance softly over the ink on my chest.

"My father needs to die, and I want to be a part of it, but what if I lose Arlo?"

"You don't have to be involved. I want to be the one to end him anyway. The obvious solution is you sit this one out, and Arlo doesn't need to know you had any part in it. I'm comfortable being the bad guy."

She props up on one elbow, leaning her other arm on my chest as her face comes closer. It's seductive torture at its finest. My cock jerks behind my boxers, and I urge the beast to calm down.

"See, that's another issue. You're not the bad guy, Drew. Not the way you think you are, and I don't want that for you. You already carry such a heavy burden."

"And killing the man responsible for her death will free me of it." I trace circles on her back through her T-shirt. "I know you understand that."

"Yeah. I do." She sets her head back on my chest and eases her body back down onto the mattress. "It all goes round and round in my head, trying to drive me mad."

"I keep asking myself what now. What will I do when it's over? It's all I've thought about for fifteen years."

"You get to live your life."

"What does that even look like?"

"I can relate. I've had similar thoughts. I don't know what I'll do when my time is my own and I'm in full control of my own destiny. I want it, but I'm terrified at the same time."

"Yeah." I kiss the top of her head, holding her closer. "I get that. It's the same for me."

Silence descends for a few minutes, but it's not awkward. Her touch on my skin feels so incredibly good, and I could stay like this for eternity and die happy.

Her lips brush against the underside of my jaw as her arm slides across my stomach. "Drew," she whispers before dragging her hot mouth along my jawline.

"Yeah," I croak, trying to control my natural urges, which are tempting me to strip her out of that shirt, pin her underneath me, and drive my aching cock into her warm heat.

"You make me feel alive in a way I haven't felt in years." Her arm curls around my side as her lips continue their exploration, and my entire body feels like it's on fire.

I should lie and shut this down, but I can't lie to her when she's giving me her truths. And I'm sick of running. Tired of fighting emotions I think I shouldn't feel. "I feel the same way about you."

My head tips down as hers tips up and our mouths meet in a soft, sensual caress. I move on my side, keeping her flush against me as I angle my head and deepen our kiss.

And it's everything.

Everything I have been denying myself for fifteen years.

Everything I am done denying I need.

My inner beast is dying to be set free, but this isn't what this moment is about, so I restrain him and kiss this woman the way she deserves to be kissed. Worshipping her mouth before gliding my tongue between her lips and savoring the taste and feel of her. Athena's leg slides between mine, and I know she feels my erection straining against my boxers, but she makes no move to touch me there, and I'm purposely restricting this to kissing.

Because right now, despite how my body is reacting, this is what I need. What I think she needs, and I want to take care of her. To make her feel loved and wanted because I think that's been sorely lacking in her life, and her happiness is important to me.

We kiss slowly, deeply, intensely. My hands roam her back over her shirt, and her hands cup my face and brush my neck.

Eventually, we break apart, and she smiles before resting her head on my chest and closing her eyes.

My eyelids shutter, and I follow her into sleep.

When I wake the next day, Athena is still in my arms, awake and staring up at me. We're wrapped around one another, our legs entangled in each other and the sheets. The comforter has moved down, showcasing the boner tenting my boxers and openly saluting her.

"Morning," she says in a sleep-drenched tone. "We appear to have slept through the alarm, and we're late for work."

My fingers thread through her messy hair as I smirk. "Lucky I'm the boss." Her eyes seem different today, conveying a mix of vulnerability and trust. "How about we take the day off and spend it together?" I say before I can talk myself out of it.

"That sounds good. Got any ideas?"

"We could workout, swim, go for a walk, watch movies, read, cook. Take your pick. I'm open to other options too."

"I'm down for that." She props up and briefly brushes her lips against mine before easing back and peering deep into my eyes. "I don't want anything to be awkward between us because of last night."

"Nothing feels awkward to me."

The smile that appears on her face makes me feel like I've won the lottery. "Nor me. I like you, Drew. I like you a lot."

I clasp her face in my hands. "I like you too. It terrifies me, but I'm not running away from it."

Her smile grows wider, and while I don't want to diminish it, I promised her honesty, and I intend to stick to it. "I can't promise you anything, Athena, except to follow this road and see where it leads."

"That's enough for me," she says, and I sincerely hope she means it.

Athena and I are glued at the hip the next few days, and I'm surprised how much I'm loving doing mundane shit with her. We workout, swim, cook and watch back-to-back gangster and action movies. Neither of us has gone into the office since Tuesday, taking Wednesday off and working from the house yesterday and today.

I lean back in my office chair, pressing send on the message to cancel my session with Vixen tonight. I need to end things properly with her, but I don't want to do that by text. She's different than the other women I've entered into arrangements with at the club, and she deserves more respect.

Though Athena sleeps in my bed every night and we kiss up a storm before falling asleep in one another's arms, nothing else has happened, and I'm shocked at how much I'm not pushing for more. Especially when my balls are bluer than blue. I'm jerking off at least twice daily, always to thoughts of the beautiful blonde who is tearing down my walls and decimating every obstacle I've placed in her way.

"Drew." Athena pops her head through the door of my office.

"What's wrong?" I ask, tossing my phone on my desk and standing. Her eyes are red-rimmed, her face contorted in pain.

"I can't talk about it yet. I just wanted to let you know I'm going out for a walk. I need some time to myself."

I walk to the door and pull her into my arms, alarmed when I feel her body shaking against me. "Are you sure I can't help?"

Tears cling to her lashes when she peers up at me. "Not with this," she chokes out over a sob.

"Let me call Abby," I suggest.

She shakes her head and shucks out of my arms, swiping at the tears rolling down her face. "This is something I need to face alone for now. I promise I'll tell you. Just not now."

"Okay." I shove my hands in the pockets of my jeans, feeling utterly useless. "Call me if you need me."

"I will." Her sad smile is apologetic as she walks off, leaving me wondering what exactly has happened to cause such a reaction.

I spend the night alone in front of the TV, worrying about Athena. She texted me earlier to say she'd gone back to her apartment and she'd see me tomorrow. Now, I'm thinking I did something wrong. Something to push her away, and panic is setting in.

I'm staring up at the ceiling in the dark, unable to sleep, when the door opens, and my head jerks around. Relief pours through me as Athena pads softly across the floor. I open my arms as she crawls under the covers and gets into bed.

"I missed you," she whispers, wrapping herself around me like a koala. Not that I'm complaining.

"I missed you too. I'm pretty sure I won't ever be able to sleep again unless I'm holding you."

A sob rips through the air, and I hold her close, pressing a fierce kiss to the top of her head. "I wish you'd tell me what's wrong."

She sobs louder, and I let it go, holding her as she cries into my neck and her body shakes against mine.

At some point, we fall asleep, and when I wake the

following morning, I panic finding her side of the bed empty. A quick investigation proves she's in her room in the shower, so I pull on sweats, a white shirt, and slides and head down to the kitchen to rustle up some breakfast.

"Hey," she says.

I glance over my shoulder from my position at the stove. "I'm making omelets."

She hurries over to me, wrapping her arms around me from behind. "I can't believe you ever thought you were the bad guy when you're the best guy I know."

"That doesn't say much for the company you've been keeping." I switch off the heat under the skillet and turn around with her in my arms.

She giggles, and though an air of sadness still clings to her skin, her eyes are clear, and she appears to have stopped crying. I don't mention it, preferring to let her broach the subject.

"I love living here with you. You take such good care of me, and I haven't felt this protected or this wanted in forever."

I bundle her in my arms, pressing her face to my chest. "It's not a chore. We have slotted easily into cohabiting. Not too bad for a guy who's never lived with anyone but family before."

She peers up at me. "You didn't live with Jane?" I shake my head. "I thought since you were engaged and due to be married at eighteen it might have been different."

"I see my sister has been whispering in your ear," I say, helping her over to the island unit and onto a stool.

"She hasn't told me much more than that, and I wouldn't ask. I'd prefer you talked to me about her."

I slide omelets onto two plates and carry them to the table, followed by OJ and coffee.

"What do you want to know?" I ask as I cut into my food.

"How did you two get together?"

I talk in between eating and drinking. "I had always known

Jane through Abby, but I was about fourteen when I realized I had feelings for her. I asked her out on a date, told her how I felt, she admitted she felt the same, and that was it; we were together."

"Wow. It seems like you were meant to be." She avoids looking at me as she sips from her glass.

"Things were easy with Jane but also super complicated."

She tilts her head to one side, and wavy strands of hair cascade around her shoulders. She's so fucking beautiful, and I don't think she realizes it.

"In what way?" she asks.

"I had to keep so many secrets from her and do things I didn't want to do, things I could never tell her, and it ate away at me."

"I've heard about some of the elite initiation rituals. We had similar things in our world until our new board got rid of them."

"Then you get it."

"I do."

I don't stop to question it as I unburden myself. I've been stowing these things inside for a long time, and I want to tell her. She won't judge me because she's come from a similar situation, and it's refreshing to talk to someone who understands.

"Part of the reason why I never told her was because I knew she'd end things with me if she realized the full extent of what I'm capable of."

"What you did with that MC at fifteen is legendary around these parts." She waggles her brows and grins before popping a piece of omelet in her mouth.

"That grin is disturbing."

She laughs, and I'm glad I seem to be distracting her from whatever is troubling her. "I told you I see you, Drew, and I meant it."

"Well, taking out an entire MC because the son of the club

president made a pass at my girlfriend wasn't exactly a moment of pride, but I had to pick something as my main initiation task, and I was completely ruled by my emotions back then."

"I heard you killed thirty men, and when you ran out of bullets, you slayed them with your hands."

"That's a bit of an exaggeration. Charlie and Trent were with me, and it was more like twenty men, but yeah, I went full feral on them." I chuckle. "To this day, all the local MCs fear me and Charlie." The smile flees my mouth as I remember the night before the slaughter.

She says she *sees* me, so let's see how she feels after I tell her this. "I had already chosen my target for my initiation. The task was simple—to kill a man to prove I was worthy to belong in the elite. It was such bullshit, but I had to do it. My plan had been to take that guy out, not the entire MC. But the night before it was going down, my father took me to his basement dungeon club for the first time." Bile crawls up my throat, but I force the words out. "I'd heard rumors of what it entailed, and I was hella curious, but he'd never let me go there until that night."

"What happened?" Her eyes are glued to my face, her attention laser-focused on me.

"I was engaged to Jane by then. But her father had insisted on a virginity clause in the arrangement, so we weren't fucking at that point. I'd lost my virginity at thirteen at Parkhurst, but I hadn't had sex since I made Jane mine. My father wasn't pleased, so he took matters into his own hands."

I bite down on my lower lip as I thank fuck that asshole is dead. Right now, I feel like digging up his bones and whaling on them.

Her hand lands on my arm, and there is nothing but compassion in her eyes when she stares at me. "You can tell me anything, Drew. I guarantee I've heard worse, and I would never judge."

"I know that. This is still hard to admit because I've never told a soul about that night. Charlie doesn't even know."

"You can trust me with your secret."

"I know that too." I lean in and kiss her, just because I feel like it.

"I hate myself for that night."

"What did he make you do?"

"Fuck the slaves he had caged in his dungeon."

Chapter Thirty-Five
Athena

"I'm sorry he forced you to do that, Drew." I don't know what else to say. Any other words would seem flippant. I know Drew would never have willingly done such things, but telling him he's not the monster he thinks he is won't help. He's entitled to feel what he feels, and I'd be the same in his shoes.

"I wanted to kill myself when I returned to my bedroom. I stayed in the shower for hours, scrubbing at my skin, trying to wash the sin away. I hated myself, and I wanted to murder my father. Instead, I wiped out an entire MC, and it still didn't purge me of the disgust and guilt and self-loathing I felt." He looks away, and my heart bleeds for him. "I wish I could say it was the last time it happened, but it wasn't. And it wasn't just slaves. When we were at Parkhurst, we were expected to fuck the elite women there."

"And Jane never knew?"

His eyes are glassy when they lift to mine. "How could I tell her? She knew nothing about Parkhurst or that side of the elite. She had no idea of the man she was in love with. I let her love a lie because I was too terrified to lose her. Loving Jane kept me sane. Without her light, I would have succumbed to the dark a long time before I did."

I want to say it's not all bad in the dark and trying to suffocate large parts of who you are is never a smart plan, but this isn't the time, and who am I to tell him he shouldn't feel guilty for doing what had to be done to survive?

"I was a selfish prick. I should have cut her loose and let her find someone worthy of her love. If I had, she'd be alive today. But I couldn't let her go. I loved her. I needed her. I needed to be the version of me I was when I was with her. She was so good and pure, and if she knew the monster that was hidden beneath the mask I wore, she would've run a million miles away from me. Jane would not have understood the things I did. She would have held me accountable, and she would've been right."

"I don't agree." I take his hands in mine. "These hands have done unspeakable things, like my own. I spent many years thinking as you do until I realized I wasn't to blame. My father was. Our society was. If you'd told me you did those things and you loved it, without any remorse or guilt or shame, I would say, yeah, you're responsible." I raise his hands to my mouth and kiss the tips of his fingers. "But you have suffered for the things you were made to do, and you have tried to make amends. It wasn't always about Jane. Your quest to bring traffickers down was much more than that."

He bobs his head, and I clutch his hands, holding them against my chest. "I have tried to atone for my sins, but the guilt is always there." He takes his hands back, running them through his hair. "Jane died having no clue who I really was. She died at the hands of a monster just like me."

"No." I stand and push myself in between his thighs, refusing to accept this. "It is not the same. It's not in any fucking way comparable. As a kid, you became the monster you were forced to be to survive. And later, you became that monster again to wreak vengeance on the true monsters of the world." I clasp his face in my hands, staring him straight in the eye. "You are a motherfucking hero, Drew Manning, and there is nothing you could tell me that will ever change my mind."

His lips claim mine in a possessive, greedy kiss as his hands lower to my ass, and he pulls me in close. His hard length pushes against my pussy through my yoga pants, and I'm instantly soaked. This isn't like any of the nights where we've kissed until our jaws ached and fallen asleep wrapped around one another.

This is a different beast.

It's all raw need and lust, and I want to give in to it, but I can't.

Two things have to happen before we can go there, and I know it might never happen when that comes to pass.

Reluctantly, I pull back, and my pussy practically weeps.

"Athena," he growls, grabbing my ass and pulling me back against his body.

"We can't." I flatten my hands on his chest to keep distance between us. "I want you. I want you so fucking badly, but there is something I need to tell you first, and it can't wait."

I needed a day to process my feelings, but I'm nowhere near ready to handle the myriad of emotions the news has raised to the surface. My eyes well up again. This is going to destroy him and possibly end this thing between us before we've even gotten started. But I promised him honesty, and I intend to give it to him.

"I'm freaking out," Abby says when our four guests are finally here. I didn't want to tell Drew without backup because he'll need it, and I'm not sure he'll want me to stay when he learns the truth.

"Same," Demi replies. "What's going on, Athena?"

"I think we need alcohol for this," I say, looming over my two new friends as they sit side by side on the couch in Drew's living room. I'm nervous, and I'm sure everyone can see my hands shaking.

"Hey." Drew places his hands on my shoulders. "Whatever it is, we'll deal with it."

Tears pool in my eyes. "I'm so scared you're going to hate me," I whisper.

"That's impossible." He pulls me into his arms, and I willingly soak up his comfort, savoring the feel of his muscular arms protecting me in case it's the last time I get to feel this.

For the millionth time, I curse my father and vow to make him pay for all the heartache he's about to cause.

"I've never hated you even when I led you to believe I did."

"There's a first time for everything," I murmur pressing my lips to one side of his face. I ease out of his arms and pull my big girl panties on. I'm making this all about me, which isn't fair.

He kisses me in front of his sister, his cousin, and their husbands—his best friends—and my heart rejoices while equally splitting down the middle.

"Stay here," he says when he breaks our lip-lock. "I'll get wine and beer from the fridge." He pecks my lips one more time, trying to reassure me with his eyes, but I see fear there.

"We'll come with," Charlie and Kai say, following Drew out of the room.

"You look so good together," Abby says, smiling softly before her brow creases. "I want to grill you about that, but I'm seriously freaking out right now." She grabs my hand and pulls me down in between her and Demi. "You've got to give me something because I'm imagining all kinds of horrific things."

"It's not a bad thing," I say, dabbing at my eyes with the hem of my shirt. I didn't bother getting changed, and I'm still in my casual clothes. "At least I hope Drew doesn't think so."

The guys return in record time and distribute the drinks. I get up and sit on the other couch beside Drew, needing to be close to him when I tell him. Abby slinks into Kaiden's lap in one of the large chairs, and Charlie sits beside his wife on the other couch, sliding his arm around her shoulders. Everyone can sense I have big news to deliver, and anticipation is rife in the air.

I gulp back a healthy mouthful of crisp white wine as I feel five pairs of eyes boring into me, wondering what the fuck is going on.

Time to put them out of their misery and rip the Band-Aid off. "I want to say first that I had no idea, absolutely no idea, about any of this until I learned the truth about Jane and her family and realized the Fords were the people I knew as the Hanks."

"That was last Sunday," Abby says.

"I didn't raise my suspicions with you because I needed to be sure. I wasn't about to drop a bomb if I wasn't completely on the right track."

"That's what you spoke to Ares about as he was leaving," Drew surmises.

I nod. "That and I asked him to push that funding through for Moonlight."

"That was thoughtful," Abby says.

I knock back more wine and eyeball Drew. "This is one of the things keeping me up at night." And one of the reasons I wouldn't let him fuck me in the kitchen a couple hours ago.

When we go there, *if* we go there, there will be zero secrets between us.

"What I didn't say last week was my bitch of a stepmother

was pregnant when our visitors came to stay." I take Drew's hands in mine, and I honestly feel like puking. "I didn't realize Jane was pregnant too, not until she confided in me one night a few weeks after she arrived."

"What?" Abby cries out.

Drew's face pales as all the blood seeps from his skin. His hands are ice-cold against mine, and his limbs are rigidly still. He stares at me as if he's looking through me, and I forge on, hoping he hears me through the shock. "Jane was heavily pregnant the last time I saw her and due any day. It's why I was so worried she hadn't said goodbye, but my father reassured me she'd gone somewhere safe to have her baby." I chew on the inside of my cheeks as fresh anger blooms in my chest. "He lied. My stepmonster lied. It was all a ruse."

"What are you getting at, Athena?" Charlie asks, casting troubled glances at Drew.

Drew is stiff as a rock, and my heart is breaking for him.

"I don't know if Cadance was ever pregnant or if she was and her baby died in the womb or was stillborn because the records have been altered. Arlo's birth certificate verifies Cadance and Amos Martin as his parents, but it's not true." Tears prick my eyes as I stare at a shell-shocked Drew. I let one fall free before I pull myself together. "The Luminaries helped me run DNA tests, and the results are irrefutable." I squeeze Drew's hands. "You are Arlo's biological father, Drew, and Jane is his mother."

Chapter Thirty-Six
Drew

You could hear a pin drop in the room after Athena delivers that news, and then everyone talks at once, asking different questions, but I don't hear them. And I can't speak. Emotion is clogging my throat and sitting on my chest, compressing my lungs until they're so tight I can't breathe.

"Breathe, D." My sister peers up at me from the floor with tears in her eyes. She rubs my hands and my arms, but I don't feel it.

I'm numb, or I'm feeling too much.

I don't know.

I can't think straight.

"Come on, D." Abby grabs my face in her hands. "Breathe with me. In and out. Nice and slow."

My body cooperates even if my head is still floating in another realm, struggling to grasp the magnitude of Athena's revelation.

Arlo isn't her flesh and blood.

He's mine.

Mine and Jane's.

My head drops to Abby's shoulder, and I cling to my twin as emotion swells and swells inside me until it explodes. Rage blasts from my body and rips from my mouth as I'm twisted and torn into multiple fragments. I fling my glass across the room, roaring as it shatters against the wall. I jump up, narrowly avoiding pushing into Abby and Athena as I run across the room and out into the hallway, not knowing where I'm going, only that I need to hit something.

I skid to a halt in the hallway and ram my fist into the wall, over and over, as venom spews from my pores and a cloud of self-loathing shrouds me in darkness.

"Drew, please," Abby cries. "You're bleeding. Please stop."

"We've got you," Kai says, grabbing my shoulder.

"This won't help." Charlie hauls me back as I buck and shout, fighting against their hold. Rage has a vise grip on my body, and it won't let go. My buddies struggle to contain me as I give in to my emotions and let them control me.

"Look at him," Athena says, appearing in front of me. She thrusts a cell in my face. "Look at your son. Look how beautiful and precious he is."

I stare at his picture, and I'm choked with emotion. "He has her hair," I croak.

"And your eyes," Athena adds.

"He's a perfect mix of both of you," Abby says, wrapping her arms around my waist.

"You should have told me last week." I don't even have the energy to glare at Athena now the rush of anger has faded.

"I wanted to, but I needed to be sure. I didn't know if my gut was right or if my heightened emotions were leading me astray even if it was Arlo's eyes that planted the idea in my head in the first case." She rubs at her chest as she hands her cell to Abby. "I didn't know what had happened to your baby,

Drew, and I didn't want to give you false hope. I understand if you can't forgive me."

I can't even think about that now.

"Those fucking cunts stole your baby," Anderson says through clenched teeth.

"Fuck what the fucking Luminaries want," Charlie spits out. "I say we leave for Lowell now, and we grab those pieces of shit and force the truth from their lips."

"You can't," Athena says. "Not yet."

"You've got to think of Arlo," Abby says. "Drew." She turns around and presses her petite frame against me. "I know this is a huge shock, and I know your natural instinct is to swing into action and make those assholes pay, but you've got a son, and we need to consider his feelings."

"Arlo has to be at the center of what we decide," Demi says, moving over to hug Athena.

"D, you're a father. I just can't." Abby's face is swimming in emotion.

"He doesn't know me. I've lost fifteen years of his life. He loves that monster he calls a father."

"He won't when he discovers the truth," Athena says, her voice cracking at the end. I know this must be hard for her too, but I only have enough strength to keep myself standing.

"None of this would've happened if I hadn't sent her away." My hands clench at my sides. "Why the fuck didn't she tell me she was pregnant!?" I yell.

"She didn't know," Athena says. "She only found out after she got to Lowell. She tried to contact you, but your cell was dead. She sent emails but those bounced back too."

"Why didn't she contact me when she couldn't reach Drew?" Abby asks.

"I told her father to make sure she had no way of contacting anyone. I thought I was protecting her." I shove my bloody fist into the fist-shaped hole in my wall until Athena pulls it away. "I'm a fucking asshole!"

"Go hit your punching bag if you need to, but please stop hurting yourself. I can't bear it."

"And you're not an asshole. None of this is your fault," Abby says.

"It is." I flex my injured hand, welcoming the stinging pain. "It's all my fault. You realize what this means?" My gaze drags around my friends and family. "This is the reason why Jane died. Why Vera was sold into slavery. Why Silas was sold to that sick bitch. Why Jane's parents are MIA, rotting in some shallow grave most likely." I jab my finger in Athena's direction. "Your prick of a father did it all to steal our baby. If I hadn't knocked her up, if I hadn't sent her away, none of this would've happened. They'd all be alive."

Athena

I can't stop crying. My heart is shredded into pieces, and I don't know what to do, where to go from here. I don't do this. This isn't me. "I'm sorry," I sob as Demi and Abby console me on the couch. Drew has been gone for hours. Charlie and Kai are with him, and I'm glad he has their support because he clearly needs it. Watching him fall apart like that destroyed me. His pain is my pain, and I'm in agony for him. For me. For Arlo. For Jane.

"Don't apologize," Abby says, handing me another tissue. I must have nearly used up the box by now. "You are entitled to your feelings just like Drew is entitled to his."

"This is just as hard on you," Demi says.

I blot the moisture at my eyes and blow my nose. "No. It's way harder for Drew. I've had the privilege of growing up with

Arlo, of loving him. He might not be my flesh-and-blood brother, but he's my brother in all the ways that count. Drew lost the girl he loved and the first fifteen years of his son's life at the hands of my father and his conniving wife. I want to riddle their manipulative asses with bullets and then resurrect them so I can do it all over again."

"What has Ares said?" Abby asks. "Is this enough to go after your father?"

"Yes and no." I pull a hair tie off my wrist and yank my hair up into a messy bun. "Dad never fathered an heir; it's clearly why he stole Arlo. The one thing our society is still anal about is the purity of our familial connections. Our family is a master's family and masters are part of the upper echelons. Having a pure-blooded heir is important. That prick has been fabricating medical reports and tests for years. That's an offense in itself. Arlo was training at HQ, so we were able to get a sample from him directly, rather than using one of the DNA samples on file. It was done covertly so Arlo isn't aware of anything yet."

Tears gather in my eyes again, and it feels like my tear ducts are broken. "I haven't cried over anything since I was a little girl, and now it's like the dam is broke."

"It's understandable given the circumstances," Demi says, squeezing my shoulder.

"And you can't trap emotion forever. It will always find a way out," Abby says.

"So why not arrest Amos now and force the truth out of him?" Demi asks.

"He could be arrested for this, but it's not enough to hold him for long. If we show our hand too early, he'll go to ground and take any remaining evidence with him."

"Great." Abby sighs. "So, we still have to sit tight. That won't be easy for Drew."

"He'll do it for Arlo," Demi says. Her indisputable confidence in him is heartwarming. Why doesn't he see himself the way others do?

"How do we tell Arlo this?" I scrub my hands down my tired face. "This will devastate him. He hates Cadance, so he won't care about her, but he's going to feel so betrayed. The man he believes is his father trafficked his birth mom, which led to her death, plotted to kill his birth dad, and was keeping him in the dark for years. The only good thing is he is now free from Luminary responsibility because he's not blood."

"He'll have elite responsibilities," Demi says.

"But they're minor unless he wants more active involvement," Abby says.

"What do we do next?" I ask as Abby's cell pings.

"Hold tight, I guess." She frowns as she reads her cell. "Drew is staying at Mom's tonight, but he wants you to stay here."

"I don't see how that's possible. I think my presence will hinder rather than help."

"Athena." Abby takes my hands. "Your father's sins are not yours. You have been deceived too. Drew won't blame you for this."

"I could be a constant reminder of all he's lost."

"You won't be." Determination radiates from her eyes. "I know this is asking a lot, but please don't leave him. If you leave and something happens to you, he won't come back from it this time. I know my twin, and he wants you to be safe. Needs you to be protected. Your father believes you are playing your part, and you can't give him any indication it's not true because it'll all come out then, and everyone will be in danger."

"Okay. You're right."

"You can tell me to butt out, but I know what I saw earlier. I know you have feelings for one another, and this will have thrown Drew, but please don't give up on him." Abby wears her heart on her sleeve as she pleads with me. "His walls will go back up, but if you've shattered them one time, you can do it again."

"I don't know if that's true, but I care about him a lot, and I won't abandon him even if things aren't the same between us again. Drew and Arlo need me, and I won't let them down."

Chapter Thirty-Seven
Athena

Drew has withdrawn into his shell, and he won't speak with anyone. He's throwing himself into work, and he spends hours every night in the gym working himself into a state of exhaustion before going to bed alone. He has completely shut me out, and after the first couple times I tried to get him to open up, I stopped trying. I can't push him. He needs to deal with it in his own time in his own way, but it hurts.

We are tiptoeing around the house, trying to avoid one another, and I have cried myself to sleep more than one night this week. It's a world away from how things were when I first moved in, and I'm lamenting the loss like a death.

That's how it feels to me.

I had shared parts of myself with him, and I know he did the same with me. Now it's gone, and I'm grieving.

Plus, I'm worried about Arlo.

This will hit him so hard, and my heart aches for him.

When the time comes, I honestly don't know how I'm going to break the news to him, and it will have to be me because

Drew is a stranger, and we need to tread carefully when we introduce father and son.

But nothing hurts more than the message I've just received.

Beast wants to meet Vixen for a session.

It all clicked for me recently—all the little things my subconscious had registered. I know Drew is my beast, and I really should have figured it out sooner.

There is no man more perfect for me, and I've already lost him.

Perhaps it's my punishment for the heinous deeds I've committed in my father's name.

I planned to talk to Drew about it after the Arlo revelation. I didn't think it was urgent because Drew has been canceling for weeks. I stupidly believed it was because he'd caught feelings for me too and the thought of fucking anyone else repulsed him.

He's obviously gotten over it.

Gotten over me.

Because he's ready to get Vixen under him again, and it crushes my heart.

I should message and tell him who I am, but that's not what I do. I confirm I'll meet him there, and I go to my apartment to get ready.

If this is all I get now, I want one more time with him where I know whose hands are touching my body.

It will be the last secret between us.

When we're done, I'll tell him I want to end our arrangement, and I'll never step foot in that club again.

I am there before him this time, and I wonder if he'll stand me up. As I kneel naked in front of the cross in the dark room, like he instructed in his message, I can't work out if that will make me happy or sad.

The door clicks open behind me, and I bow my head, keeping utterly still as he walks into the room. My heart is thumping against my rib cage, and my throat is dry. My core pulses with need, and I want to feel him inside me, but now the moment is upon me, I don't know if I can go through with it. Not when I know his identity, and it would be the ultimate deception. I'm just about to speak up when he beats me to it.

"Vixen."

"I'm here," I whisper.

The air distorts behind me, and butterflies swoop into my chest as my heart beats out of control.

"I shouldn't have come," he says in a pained tone. "I thought I could fuck my feelings away. Lose myself in you and forget about all the shit in my head, but I can't do it. I can't do it to her."

My breath stutters in my throat, and I want to speak up, but the words lie idle on my tongue.

"I met someone," he continues. "Someone who turned my world upside down. Someone who makes me feel things I have never felt before. It's all fucked up now, and I don't know where we stand, but I know I can't do this. It feels like the worst betrayal, and the only hands I want on my body are hers. I'm sorry. I—"

"Drew." I get to my feet and turn to face his shadowy form. "It's me."

He sucks in a gasp. We stand facing one another for a few beats until he walks away. Pain glides between my ribs, slicing and dicing its way up to that mushy lump in my chest that used to house my heart.

I hiss and squeeze my eyes shut as the lights flip on.

"Look at me," he commands in a booming voice.

I blink my eyes open, forcing them to adjust to the brightness.

And then he's there. Right in front of me. Naked and glorious and hard as fucking steel.

"How long?" he growls.

"I only worked it out recently," I truthfully admit. "Long after our last session." His gaze slowly trails over my body from my head to my toes, and it's like being caressed with a flogger as his gaze soaks up every inch of my skin. My nipples pebble as he lingers on my breasts. His nostrils flare, and a little precum seeps from the tip of his impressive cock.

I conduct my own inspection as he drinks his fill, greedily raking my gaze over every dip and curve of his toned abs, the ink covering his bulky biceps and muscular arms, his powerful thighs, and the giant straining cock pointing toward me, the crown glistening with the evidence of his arousal.

Desire charges through me, and as our gazes connect, we move as one, crashing into one another with explosive passion. Drew devours my lips like a desperate man sucking the last of the oxygen from a tank. I whimper into his mouth as he slams me against the wall, pressing his hard length into my stomach and rotating his hips. I dig my nails into his shoulders, shoving him back against the spanking bench as I nip and bite at his lips and claw at his magnificent body.

Drew growls as he moves his lips from my mouth to my neck, sucking my skin and marking me. My pussy pulses with need, but he slaps my hand away when I reach for his cock. "Now, now, Vixen, you know who's in charge."

"Bite me, Beast," I snap, furious to be denied when my need is extreme.

"Gladly." He dives in, and I shriek when his teeth sink into my shoulder. Then I'm lifted, and my legs go around his waist as he walks toward the table on the other side of the room and smashes me against the wall beside it.

He's like a wild animal as he thrusts his erection against me and paws at my breasts, tweaking and tugging my nipples until they're stinging. I scream when he bites down hard on my left breast before sucking my flesh into his mouth. Blood seeps under my fingernails from the imprints I've just left in his shoulders.

Thrusting my hips up, I moan as his shaft presses against my core but doesn't slip inside. "Want something, baby?" he asks, grazing his teeth against my nipples and squeezing my ass cheeks hard.

"Your cock. Please, Drew. I need you."

I scream again when he uses his body to keep me secure against the wall so he can shove three fingers inside me. His lips meld to mine as he roughly finger fucks me. I protest when he removes his fingers, but the wicked glint in his eye tells me he's up to something.

Liquid lust gushes from my pussy as he roughly throws me down on the mat on my back.

"Spread your legs, bend your knees, and raise them to your chest. Show me my cunt," he demands, shoving his fingers in his mouth and licking my pussy juices.

"Drew."

"Quiet!" he snaps, narrowing his eyes on me. "You don't speak unless I give you permission or you need to use a safe word, and it's Beast."

I get into position and remain quiet.

Drew drops to his knees, holding nipple clamps and a leather flogger. He sets them down on the mat and lowers to his stomach, putting his face all up in my pussy. He parts my folds with his fingers, and he's utterly still as he studies me.

It's the hottest goddamn thing I've ever experienced, and I gush because I have never been so fucking turned on.

"You're such a dirty whore, Vixen," he says in a gruff tone, swiping one finger through the juices gathered at my entrance.

I cry out as his tongue darts out, licking up and down my slit.

He slaps my pussy hard, and I bite on the inside of my cheek to trap another cry. "Are you my bad girl or my good girl tonight?" he asks.

"Bad girl," I rasp in a breathy tone. "Always bad."

A wry chuckle leaves his lips as he lifts to his knees. "Such a beautiful bad girl," he says, leaning over me to put the clamps on. "Do you want me to hurt you, slut?"

"Yes, Beast."

He tugs hard on the clamps, and ripples of pain skate across my sensitive flesh.

He moves back between my legs and slowly inserts the handle of the flogger into my pussy, wearing an arrogant grin. "You've been a very bad girl, Vixen, and you deserve to be punished for concealing the truth." He fucks me with the flogger, increasing in speed as I writhe beneath him, so turned on I'm dripping all over the mat with juices running down my thighs.

"Fuck, you're so wet." He rips the flogger out and slaps his hand over my cunt several times.

Without warning, he flips me over onto all fours and pushes my head to the mat. "Safe word."

"Green."

He stretches my thighs wider and rubs the length of his cock up and down my slit. Positioning the tip at my opening, he leans over me, covering me with his warm body. "I can't be gentle, Athena. Use your safe word if you need to."

"I don't want you to be gentle."

Screams tear from my throat as he drives into me in one vicious thrust while keeping his hand on the back of my neck and forcing my face into the mat. Drew fucks me like he's trying to kill me, slamming his dick in and out with violent strokes, while squeezing my neck and fully controlling my body. He keeps up this punishing pace until I fall to pieces, screaming as I come all over his exquisite dick.

"Stay in position," he instructs as he pulls out, driving his fingers inside me and scooping up my cum. He smears it all over my ass before pushing three digits into my puckered hole, stroking my walls until I relax. Moans tumble from my chest as he plunders my ass, fucking me hard as he bites and sucks on my back.

Drew sits back on his heels, pulling me upright with his dick lodged in my ass. One hand creeps up my body from the front and wraps around my neck while the other holds my hip to steady his movements as he fucks up into my ass and chokes me. Every time I see stars, he releases his hold to let me breathe while savagely screwing my ass and digging his fingers into my hip.

The hand around my neck loosens, trailing down my body, yanking on the clamps, and smoothing over my stomach before he plunges his fingers inside my cunt and arches his hips, driving his dick so deep in my ass I almost black out.

I'm a writhing mess as my orgasm whips through me, obliterating all sensations except for singular pure pleasure.

Drew wraps his arm around my waist and lifts me up a little as he slams his dick in a couple more times. Then he pulls out, shouting as he flips me over onto my back and comes all over my chest. Ropes of cum streak across my tits and my stomach, and I close my eyes and open my mouth, gathering the last few drops on my tongue.

When we're sated, we stare at one another as the magnitude of what we've just done hits both of us.

Drew scrambles to his feet, grabbing fistfuls of his hair, and I watch with mounting horror as he paces the room, waging some inner battle. Pushing up on my elbows, I sit cross-legged on the mat, watching him self-destruct as I swirl his cum across my skin.

"This was a mistake," he says.

"Why?"

"Why?" He barks out a laugh. "Take your fucking pick!"

"So that's it?" I ask, climbing to my feet. "You're just going to hide behind your walls and shut me and everyone else out again?"

"I'm trying to protect you!" he roars. "Nothing good will come of this."

"I love you," I say, admitting it to him and me at the same time. "I see you, and I love you. Every single broken part of you speaks to the broken parts of me, and together I know we can be whole." I walk toward him, pleading with my eyes when I see him retreating.

"You can't love me." He steps back. "My love is toxic. I destroyed one woman I loved. I won't make the same mistake again. This ends here, Athena. There is no future for us."

Chapter Thirty-Eight
Athena

I'm still fuming as I drive from the city back to Rydeville. I'm cursing Drew and planning all the things I'm going to say to him in my head. He wants to be a coward and walk away from us? Fine. It's his fucking loss. But he's going to hear a few home truths because he needs to man the fuck up and be there for Arlo.

His car is outside the house when I drive up. I'm bristling with anger as I slam my car door shut and storm inside his house. I'm giving him a dose of tough love, and then I'm packing my shit and returning to my apartment.

Drew is in his study with the door open, staring moodily out the window at the bleak darkness outside, nursing a whiskey in one hand.

I stalk inside, waiting for him to swivel on his chair before saying, "Fuck. You." I glare at him with every ounce of hurt and pain swirling in my chest. "You don't get to fuck me like that and then reject me and treat me like trash."

"I didn't—"

"Shut your mouth." I dart forward and grip his chin,

spewing venom from my eyes. "You've had your say. Now it's my turn. You're going to sit there and listen, and when I've said my piece, I'll pack my stuff and get out of your miserable, pathetic life so you can get back to wallowing."

His eyes darken, and a muscle pops in his jaw, but he remains mute, which is a wise choice, 'cause I have a rifle in the trunk of my car, and I might be tempted to blow his stupid head off.

"You're a coward, Drew Manning, and I'm glad you showed me your true colors because I don't date cowards. You have stuffed your feelings inside for fifteen years and never processed your emotions. You've got the emotional intelligence of a teenager because you're still stuck there in your head, pining after your childhood love, and stagnating in a dark pool of guilt because you refuse to face your demons head-on."

He lifts his whiskey glass to his lips and takes a drink, looking at me with indifference.

I bark out a laugh. "You don't fool me with that face. The only person you're fooling is yourself. And I get that to a degree. I've done the same. I purposely self-sabotaged this mission because I didn't have the balls to just tell my father to go fuck himself and seek the truth for the right reasons. Maybe someone should have sat me down and given me the hard facts, but at least I've woken up now. You're still clinging to the past even when you hear the bullshit leaving your mouth."

He knocks back his drink and grips the arms of his chair.

"Here's what everyone else has been afraid to tell you. What you had with Jane was fucking fantasy land, and you're hanging on to that fairy tale by your fingertips because you know if you let it go you'll have to face the truth that you've wasted years of your life romanticizing a dream."

"You don't get to pass judgment on my relationship. You weren't fucking there!" he shouts, scrabbling to his feet.

"I don't need to be there to see what's fucking staring me in the face!" I put my face all up in his. "Wake the fuck up, Manning! Do you really think you'd still be with her? She didn't know you, Drew! You hid all the true parts of yourself from Jane! The fact you hid it from her speaks volumes, but you already know that."

"You're twisting my words."

"And you've got a real problem keeping your mouth shut."

"You don't get to shit all over her memory just because you're angry with me."

I shove him in the shoulders, kinda wishing I had my gun. "I'm not angry, shithead. I'm fucking furious!" I step back and take a deep breath before I do or say something I'll regret. "I'm not shitting on Jane. I adored her, and I can see how you fell for her. I'm not disrespecting the love you guys shared, and I'm glad she had that before her life was ended so cruelly. I'm pointing out if things had been different, if she hadn't left Rydeville, if she'd stayed here, you would not be together. Or if you were, it's because you were still hiding, and she was refusing to accept the truth. You'd both have been miserable."

"You don't know that."

"Maybe I don't." I step up in his personal space again. "But you do. Don't admit it to me, Drew, but at least admit it to yourself because you will not move forward until you do."

His chest heaves, and pain glimmers across his face as he averts his eyes.

"You need to get your shit together because Arlo is going to need you. He will be shaken to his core when this comes out. His whole identity and everything he thought he had planned for his future will unravel overnight. He will need us to be strong, and you can't bury your head in the sand any longer. You need to face your truths, and it starts with Jane."

Silence descends for a few beats, and I use the time to calm down. Shouting won't help, and I need to get through to him for Arlo's sake.

"You were only kids, Drew. She was your first love, and your relationship was cut off in its prime. That was so unfair to both of you, and what happened to Jane is horrific. It kills me, and I didn't know her like you did, so I do understand. But you can't keep beating yourself up forever and using this as a shield. You're hiding behind your guilt, punishing yourself repeatedly, and using it as an excuse because you're fucking scared of opening yourself up to someone. Scared your heart will be broken again. Terrified of failing the people you love so you lock your emotions up and keep people away, and that is no way to live, and you cannot do that with Arlo."

"Do you really think I don't know that?"

"I don't know, Drew, because you've shut me out all week and refused to speak to me, and you don't get to do that. You and me are done, but we still need to work together to support Arlo. He's all that matters now, and you need to man the fuck up for your son."

"What if I'm not enough? What if I'm a terrible role model?"

"You are enough if you let yourself be, and you can't be any worse of a role model than the man he thinks is his father."

"That's reassuring." Sarcasm is thick in his tone.

"If you want someone to baby you, go hire someone because that sure as fuck is not me. I won't enable you to continue hiding, and you have a choice here, Drew. Drop the façade and trust Arlo with the truth of who you are. Be real with him in a way you haven't been with anyone for a long time."

"I've been real with you." His eyes bleed sincerity. "I've told you things no one else knows. I've opened my heart and let you in."

"Yeah, and then you shoved me back out and retreated behind your walls the instant things got hard. I'm not sure any of it counts."

"It counts." He steps right up to me. "I'm trying to do the right thing by you."

"The sad truth is I can tell you believe that." Against my better judgment, I cup his cheek. "But what you are doing is the opposite. I told you I saw the real you and I embraced it. You know I'm capable of protecting and defending myself. You made choices for me without consulting me, and then you left me at the club like I meant nothing. Like I was another sexual transaction and nothing more."

"That isn't true."

"I don't let others in, but I let you in. I told you I love you, and your response was to reject me and tell me we have no future."

"You know that wasn't the truth."

"No, Drew, I don't." I cross my arms around myself and step back, trying to protect myself as hurt trickles through my veins. "We promised one another honesty, and I was vulnerable with you, but you disrespected me. You lied or took the coward's way out, and you didn't just let me down, you let yourself down."

"You deserve better than me."

"Oh, please. Shut the fuck up with the pity party. I'm sick of hearing it. You don't get to push me away for this. If you don't want me, fine, tell me, hand on heart with complete honesty, my feelings are unrequited. But don't fucking push me away because you think you're protecting me. Or because you're still pining after the ghost of a woman who is long gone and the ghost of a relationship that would most likely not have endured. You have Jane on the highest pedestal, and no mortal woman will ever compare. I refuse to compete with a ghost."

"It isn't a competition. I have never seen you like that." He drags a hand through his hair, tossing messy strands over his brow.

His refusal to see the truth only proves how much he has been hiding behind this illusion he created in his mind. "Because you're lying to yourself. You know I'll never take a back seat to any other woman. It's all or nothing for me. Face up to your past, Drew. Do it for yourself because you need to learn to love yourself before you can love anyone else. You're Arlo's dad, and I want you in his life, but you must get your shit together first. Prove you are the man I know you can be, and then come and fight for me. Until then, you can fuck right off, and I have nothing else to say to you."

I turn around and walk off as Drew calls after me, begging me to stay. I almost face-plant into Abby when I exit the door into the hallway. "Don't ask me to stay," I snap as I walk around her and head toward my bedroom. "There is much I'm prepared to do for your brother, but being his punching bag isn't it."

Her eyes jump to the obvious marks on my neck as I stride into my bedroom and pull my two bags out from under the bed.

"Please don't leave," Drew says, materializing in the doorway.

"I can't stay here." I don't look at him as I walk into the closet and start yanking clothes from the rail.

"I'm sorry for everything," he says, leaning against the wall at the entrance to my closet. "You are right. I'm a coward, and I'm pushing you away sinstead of facing my feelings and confronting my fears. They're deeply entrenched, and it's my go-to default setting."

"I'm glad you're admitting it," I say, pushing past him into the bedroom. "But you don't get to spout pretty words and everything is magically okay." I throw my clothes into the first bag. "You need therapy, Drew, lots and lots of it." I stuff the clothes in haphazardly and tug the zipper closed. I straighten up and look at him. "I don't mean that facetiously. I have no issue with the man you are. I love all your strengths and flaws, but you don't, and that's part of the problem." I hold his beautiful face in my hands. "You need to let go of the guilt and let go of Jane. You need to process all those pent-up emotions. I can't do the heavy lifting for you. You've got to do it alone."

His eyes shine with remorse as his hands land on my waist. "I'm so sorry for leaving you like that. For not taking care of you." He presses his mouth to my ear. "I didn't use a condom, but—"

"I'm on the pill, and we're both clean." The club requires every member to submit monthly test results.

"Let me look after you now," he pleads. "I'll run you a bath and get you something to eat and—"

"Stop. Don't do this. Please." Hurt splinters through my words.

He looks deep into my eyes. "I love you. That's what I should have said." His brow presses to mine. "I love you, Athena. Please be with me. Please don't leave. I promise I'll do better."

His vulnerability almost cracks through my defenses. He is opening himself up and bleeding for me now. It's a good start, but it doesn't change things, and until he comes to terms with his emotions, he can't say he loves me for sure, and I can't afford to take it at face value. "I wish I could believe that, but you don't know your own mind, and you said it yourself. This is your default mechanism." I ease back, still holding his face, letting *my* vulnerability show because I'm done holding back. "I want to be with you more than anything, but until you've dealt with your past, there isn't a future for us. And as much as

I want to be selfish, I can't. Arlo is the priority, Drew. Focus on him, not me."

"I can focus on both of you, and we'll be a better support to him as a team."

"We can support him together without being together like that," I say, easing out of his hold.

He follows me back into the closet. "Please, sweetheart. Don't do this."

"We need time and space, Drew, and I genuinely think this is for the best."

He doesn't say anything else, standing by his sister in the door of the bedroom as I move between the closet and en suite bathroom gathering my things. When I'm all done, he takes my bags and walks off as I take one final look around, ensuring I've got everything.

Abby is uncharacteristically quiet as we walk out to my car. Drew pops the trunk and stows my bags before turning to face me. When he pulls me into his arms, I don't protest, hugging him close while wishing it didn't have to be like this even if I know I'm doing the right thing for everyone. "Please be careful," he says. "I know you're capable and strong, but if anything happens or you need me for anything, please call me."

"I will." I offer him a sad smile as I shuck out of his embrace.

"I'll call you later," Abby says, hugging me quickly. "Drive safe."

Chapter Thirty-Nine

Drew

"You can say I told you so," I say to my sister the following morning as I join her at the island unit. Abby stayed here last night, but we didn't talk because I was emotionally drained after Athena left and in no state to discuss anything. I set a plate of bacon, eggs, and toast in front of her. "I deserve it."

"You're hurting, and that would be an asshole thing to say."

A wry smile pulls at my lips. "It wouldn't be the first time you indulged in some tough love."

"Seems like Athena delivered plenty of that." Abby picks up her silverware. "I'm not sure it's wise to pick more flesh from your carcass."

"How much did you hear?"

"Most of it," she admits before scooping up a forkful of creamy scrambled eggs.

"I really fucked up." I gulp back a mouthful of coffee.

"It's not irretrievable. She loves you." A happy smile ghosts over her mouth. "And you love her, and nothing about that was final. For what it's worth, I think she's doing the right thing. You need to do this for you, and it's your best chance at a future relationship with your son and with her."

"As much as I hate this, because I already miss her so much, I need to man up for Arlo and focus on him."

"It is possible to do both," she says as I tuck into my breakfast. "But you definitely need to handle the Jane stuff. Athena may not realize it, but she needs that closure as much as you do."

I frown. "I'm not following."

"She needs to be the center of your world, Drew. You need to fully let Jane go so you can give your heart to Athena."

"A part of my heart will always belong to Jane."

"Maybe. Maybe not." She shrugs. "I think Athena will be fine with that once you've laid her ghost to rest. You haven't grieved properly for Jane, Drew, and I think things will look a little different when you do." Abby puts her hand on my arm, peering at me with equal amounts of sadness and resolve. "I am so fucking angry and sad at the fate Jane suffered. She didn't deserve it, but enough with the guilt, D. This isn't on you, and I'm done letting you punish yourself. Jane's dad made the call to leave Rydeville, acting on the information you provided, but it was still *his decision*. He did what he believed was right for his family. You didn't misstep or trust the wrong person; her father did. But he's not to blame either. Fate wasn't in his hands or yours. It's time to forgive yourself and let go of the past to focus on your future."

A pounding on the front door cuts off any reply I might have made. I stride down the hallway with Abby chasing my heels, frowning when I spot a frantic-looking Sawyer Hunt peering at me through my door cam. "What's wrong?" I ask the instant I open the door, panic trickling through my veins when I spot Xavier sitting in the passenger seat of Athena's car.

"Ares called us after he called Athena," Hunt confirms just as Charlie's car turns into my driveway. "We called the others. It's better to update everyone together."

Kai hops out of Charlie's car and stalks toward us as Athena climbs out of her car and runs toward me. Fear is written all over her face as she clutches her cell to her chest. "He's not answering." Her tone is borderline hysterical, and she's visibly trembling. "Arlo always answers my calls unless he's at practice, but I know he's not."

"This is about Arlo?" My brow puckers as fear creeps up my spine.

"Didn't you tell him?" She looks at Hunt.

"There wasn't time." Hunt pins me with a sober expression. "It looks like Amos is on to us, and he might be in the wind."

"He won't hurt Arlo, right?" Abby says, falling into Kai's embrace when he reaches us.

"I don't think so, but if he's unhinged, who knows what he might do." A pained whimper accompanies Athena's words, and I don't care we're not together, I pull her into my arms and hold her tight.

"We'll get him back."

"Let's talk inside." Xavier wears a grave expression.

When we're all seated in my living room, Xavier and Sawyer begin explaining. I keep my arm around Athena's shoulders as they fill us in. "Emil Petrov showed up at a private airfield in North California late last night," Hunt says. "From what Ares and the board have managed to piece together, he was there to meet Amos. Most likely lured with the promise of retribution."

"How the fuck does Amos know about our play?" I ask.

"Ares mentioned an element within the Luminary society that is still loyal to Rhett Carter. We know Amos is part of that group, and he obviously has someone feeding him intel," Xavier says, leaning back in his chair and stifling a yawn.

"But this was contained intel." Kai rests his chin on Abby's shoulder.

"They have a mole within the inner ranks," Sawyer says, flicking a piece of lint off his pants.

"Let's stay focused. It doesn't matter how it happened. What matters is Amos killed Emil and he's pinned it on you," Xavier confirms.

"A bunch of Bulgarian mafia are on a plane headed in this direction," Hunt adds.

"Let's set up a welcoming committee." Charlie cracks his knuckles.

"Fuck the Bulgarians. Give them the kid, tell them the truth, and send them on their merry way. We've got more pressing matters, like finding my son."

"Salinger and the others raided Amos's house. Looks like they all left in a hurry. They clearly had help because there is no trace of them anywhere," Xavier explains.

"And the tracker I had on Arlo's cell has been disabled," Athena says.

"Your father figured you were playing him," I surmise, and she nods.

"If anything happens to him, I'll die, Drew. I'm so worried."

"We'll figure this out and get him back." I'm as worried as Athena, because Amos Martin is clearly a psychopathic asshole and nothing is off-limits. If he suspects we know the truth, then my son's life is in danger. We need to find Arlo and find him fast.

"Ares is setting up a specialist team to interrogate those closest to the family and their technologists will use every piece of tech at their disposal to find leads," Xavier says.

"It's not enough," I growl, standing and bringing Athena

with me. "They don't get to call the shots this time. Arlo is my son, Athena's brother, and we're not sitting around twiddling our fucking thumbs. We tried it their way and look what happened?"

"I'm with you. We need to head to Cali and search for them on the ground," Athena says.

"They could have already left the state," Xavier says.

"Or us running off without thinking it through is something Amos is banking on. It could be a trap," Kai adds.

"We have to do something." Athena smooths a hand across her chest.

Charlie eyes the evident bruising and finger marks around her neck and lifts an eye in my direction. I shake my head, because now isn't the time to get into all that.

"Keven and Zayn are at the office with a few trusted colleagues to conduct our own recon, but I'd like to speak to Ezra," Xavier says. "We should bring him in on this."

"He's at the hotel." While I couldn't tell him everything about the Luminaries and the things they confided in us, I did confirm he wasn't in danger and it was safe to go home. But he's really spooked, and he wanted to stay at the hotel. He can move there permanently for all I care. It's not like I'm going to have much use for it going forward. "Why don't we all reconvene there? Tell Keven and Zayn to meet us at these coordinates." I send a pin to Daniels.

"I suggest we pack a bag and come prepared," Charlie says. "That way if anyone gets a lead, we're ready to head out."

"How are you holding up?" I ask Athena as we walk from the parking lot of the hotel along the corridor toward the old lobby.

"I'm not, but at least we're taking action. I need to do something to distract me. I've been writing down places that asshole might go and listing some of Arlo's friends. I thought I could check them out while you update Ezra and the tech teams."

"Sure. I'm worried too. Scared your father will hurt him to hurt me."

She lifts her face to mine as we walk across the lobby. "Or hurt him to hurt *me*."

I lead my friends to my basement lair, securing the door behind Keven Kennedy as Ezra steps out of the office and says hello.

"You should audition to be the new James Bond, dude," Kai says, smirking as he slaps a hand on my shoulder.

"I am seriously fucking impressed," Kennedy says, stepping into my large office and scanning all the tech and evidence boards.

"Same." Athena plants her hands on her hips. "I was dying to get inside for a look, and it doesn't disappoint." She's dressed in a black bodysuit with a gun belt strapped around her waist and knives secured around each thigh. Her hair is tied up in a ponytail, and she wears an expression that tells everyone she means business.

She's my every wet dream come to life, and that's definitely not an appropriate thought to be having at this time.

"You should ask for a tour of the interrogation room," Charlie says, waggling his brows.

"No, thanks," my sister says. "I don't need any nightmares." She insisted on coming with us, and as Demi has taken the kids, there was no logical reason Anderson could use to keep her away. I don't mind. Abby has a cunning mind we could use, but I know there's no way Kai will let her step foot on a plane to come with us.

Ezra has cleared the maps from the table so everyone can

sit down. Charlie comes with me to grab coffee and water from the kitchen and then we join the others at the table and update Ezra before discussing options. My gaze wanders to Athena. She's seated at my desk making calls to Arlo's friends on a secure line while searching location coordinates on some specialist Luminary tech site.

Getting up, I grab a fresh mug of coffee and take a seat beside her. "Any luck?" I ask, sliding the mug to her as she ends a call.

"None of his friends have seen him since yesterday morning. Everything was normal, and he gave no indication anything was going on."

"It's possible Amos took him under false pretenses."

"Manning!" Xavier shouts, and I glance over my shoulder. His cell is out in front of him, and his eyes contain a new spark.

Athena and I get up and walk over.

"That was Ares," he says, repocketing his cell. "They got a tip-off. Amos was spotted with Cadance and Arlo at a gas station two hundred miles south of Lowell. It looks like they're avoiding the coast road and taking the lesser traveled route. The Lums have alerts out at all airfields and ports in Cali, and they are deploying men to go after them now."

"We need to get in the air," Athena says as I pull my cell out of my pocket and begin typing a message to my pilot. I'd rather not use the Manning Motors jet as it broadcasts our arrival, but time is of the essence, and I'm guessing Amos knows we're gunning for him anyway.

"Already on it," I confirm as my fingers fly across the keypad.

"Oh, and he also said they dealt with your little Bulgarian problem." Xavier smirks as he turns on the TV and flips to CNN. "His words, not mine."

The news headlines state an unidentified private plane has exploded over the Atlantic Ocean. Search and rescue is heading to the site of the crash, but survivors are not expected.

"Shit." Zayn smirks as he leans back in his chair with his hands behind his head. "They don't do things by half."

"What about Petrov's son?" Athena asks.

"On his way home to his grandparents," Xavier adds.

I'm glad he's safe, but he's not the teenager I'm worried about. I'm itching to get in the air and get to my son. "If anyone needs extra weapons, come with me. My pilot is heading to the airfield now, so we'll leave shortly."

Everyone trails after me into the lower basement, and I'm grateful they have all agreed to come. We don't know what we're facing, and the more backup we have, the better.

"Jesus, D," Abby says when our feet hit the ground. "This place gives me the creeps."

"I think that's the intention." Kai grins.

"And it reeks." She wrinkles her nose as I punch in the code on the wall-mounted keypad.

"Death usually does." Charlie winks at Abby.

"Gross. I'm sorry I said anything."

The thick iron door creaks as it clicks open. I push inside and switch the light on. "Take what you want."

"Fucking hell, Beast." Athena's eyes pop wide as she surveys the tables and cubbyholes crammed full of weapons and supplies. "I think I've died and gone to heaven." She smiles for the first time in days, and my useless heart crashes wildly against my rib cage.

"Beast?" Charlie arches a brow. Trust him to pick up on that.

Before it gets all kinds of awkward, Athena's cell vibrates with an incoming call. She frowns as she looks at her screen. "I don't recognize the number."

We all share a look.

"Put it on speaker," I say, and she nods as she swipes her finger to accept the call.

"Thena?" a male says in a low tone. "Can you hear me?"

She grips my arm tight. "Arlo, are you all right? Where are you?"

Chapter Forty
Drew

"I'm okay, but I can't talk for long," he says.

That's *my son*.

My flesh and blood.

The boy who was stolen from me already sounds like a man, and I'm choked with emotion.

My heart is pounding frantically as I listen to Arlo speak for the first time. "Dad took my cell and my tablet away for my fucking protection." Derision is clear in his tone, and my lips twitch.

Abby appears at my side, clutching my free arm and smiling through glassy eyes.

"But he doesn't know I have a burner cell." Pride flows through his words and blossoms in my chest.

"I didn't either," Athena mutters.

"It's a recent development but forget about that. Dad has lost his fucking mind, Thena."

My nails dig into my thighs every time he calls that thieving asshole Dad. Not only has Amos Martin deprived Jane of life and me years of my son's life, but he has deceived Arlo in the most despicable way. My heart aches for my son. He's about to have the rug ripped right out from under his feet.

"Where are you?"

"We're in some creepy old church at a graveyard in the fucking boonies. The back part has been converted to living quarters, and we're holed up here. I've sent a pin to your cell," he adds as Athena's phone beeps with a new message. "I watched him entering the codes to the front gate, the church door, and the alarm system. I sent you those too."

Anderson grins, thumping me in the arm. "Smart kid," he mouths.

"I'm getting on a plane shortly, but it'll be hours before I get there. You need to keep me updated. but be careful he doesn't see. He can't know you've been in contact with me."

"I'm not an idiot, sis, and I learned a lot at HQ."

"I know you're not, but don't underestimate Dad, Arlo. There is much you don't know."

"What's going on?" he asks, lowering his voice further. "I heard Mom and Dad arguing earlier. She was saying he needed to kill you now and it wasn't good enough he'd dealt with Manning. What does that mean? Why are they talking about killing you?"

I guess Amos hasn't turned on the news or made the connection between the plane explosion and the Bulgarians he set on my tail, which is good.

"I learned the truth about something he did," she says, looking up at me. "He has figured out I know, and he wants the secret to die with me."

"What is it?"

"I'll tell you when I see you. You'd better go."

"Hurry, Thena. I don't like this. He's talking like we're never going back home. We left with none of our stuff 'cause I think he was caught off guard. But he has a friend organizing a plane for us. We have to lie low until tomorrow, and then we're going overseas. He wouldn't tell me where. He told me I was to forget about you because you'd betrayed our family and now it was just the three of us."

"He's lying. Don't believe anything he says, and I promise I'll explain everything soon. I'll be there as quick as I can," she says, "and I'm bringing friends. Ares and the board are helping too."

"Dad must be in deep shit if the Lums are involved."

"He is, but you can't let on you know any of this. Act normal. Like your usual moody, hormonal self," she teases.

"Funny, sis, and don't worry about me. I know how to play Dad and how to wind the bitch up."

"Stay safe, Arlo, and don't take any risks. I'll get you out of there."

"I know you will."

"Love you."

"Love you too."

The call ends, and Athena and I look at one another. "He's amazing," I say.

"He is. He's smart, and he has good instincts, but he's been quite sheltered. He's still out of his depth, and we need to get to him stat."

I take her hand. "Let's go then. We're not waiting for Ares and co this time. We're getting him out of there ourselves."

The journey to Cali was fraught with tension and concern, but we're now only one mile out from the church where Arlo is with Amos and Cadance. Ares's men got here hours ago, and Xavier had to talk Ares into holding off. It didn't make sense to attack them in broad daylight when the cemetery was open to visitors. We need to sneak up on them under the cover of darkness and get Arlo out before we attack.

Daniels managed to get Ares to agree, but the asshole was vocal in telling us it was a mistake to wait. Athena has been in contact with Arlo via text using one of my burners, and he's under strict instructions to delete the message thread every time. He's primed and ready for our call.

I'm so grateful for the relationship he has with his sister. There hasn't been a single hesitation. He didn't for one second believe the bullshit Amos was trying to fill his head with. He told us he purposely threw a tantrum at dinner when Amos started spouting crap about Athena, and it gave him an excuse to lock himself in his room and tell them to leave him alone.

We all had a little chuckle at that. I'm glad he's resourceful and accepts the plan with no argument.

The strategy has been pre-agreed with Ares's crew over the phone, and we're all itching to get our hands on that sick prick as we pile out of the two vans that met us at the private airfield. To pull this off, we need to get Arlo out the same time we bust through the door and grab Amos and his wife. Both things must happen simultaneously. While Athena and I want to be the ones to rescue Arlo, we know it's safer if Ares's men get him out of here while we deal with the two adults.

"There aren't any cameras," Ares whispers as we all converge at the high wall behind the closed gates. "My men scouted the area, and we had drones sweep the place. The only security is the ones Arlo mentioned." Ares is the only Luminary leader here tonight. I'm guessing this is below his pay grade and he's only here for Athena and Arlo, maybe Xavier too. I'm under no illusion he's here because of me, but I'm grateful he's here all the same.

"It's sloppy," Athena whispers. "We must have forced his hand if this is the best he could do."

"Agreed," Ares says. There's an unspoken truce between us tonight. Getting Arlo to safety and dealing with Amos and Cadance are the goals, and we're united in that.

"Are your men ready?" I whisper as Athena approaches the keypad beside the gate.

"Yes. Let's do this."

Everyone splits up into their assigned teams as Athena punches in the code, and the gates open with a loud click. We're far enough away from the church for it not to be heard.

"Let's go." I slip between the gates and turn right in the direction of the church. We creep en masse toward the red and cream stone structure, splitting up when we get close. Two-thirds of us head toward the front doors of the church and the rest of the men to the rear. They will get Arlo out and keep watch outside for any unexpected visitors or threats.

"Send it," I tell Athena when we are in position at the front door.

She presses the button to send her pre-written text to Arlo telling him to climb out through the window now as Ares inputs the code to the front door. The alarm blares two seconds before we push inside the church. Zayn moves to deactivate the alarm system while the rest of us race around the pews toward the door at the side of the altar.

"He's safe," Ares says, pressing his earpiece. "My men are taking him to the car now."

Relief washes over me, and it's like a switch has flipped in my head. Cold determination replaces the blood flowing through my veins as I charge through the side door into the hallway that leads to the living area at the back.

Athena shouts a warning as a gun goes off when I round the corner, but I barely feel the bullet graze my temple as I let out a roar and lunge at the man readying to shoot me again. Amos and I tumble to the hard floor, throwing punches and wrestling before I land a solid punch to his face, knocking him out cold.

"You stupid whore!" Cadance, I presume, screams, and I turn in time to watch Athena headbutt her stepmother. Cadance shrieks, stumbling over a chair and yelling as she falls awkwardly to the ground before passing out.

We drag them to their feet and shove them into chairs.

"Let me look at that." Athena presses her fingers to the side of my head.

"It's only a scratch."

"It's more than that." She shows me bloody fingertips.

"I'll live, unlike them," I growl, watching with anger burning my insides as Charlie and Ares strip Amos and Cadance down to their underwear before tying them securely to the chairs.

"How do you want to play this?" Ares asks as Athena presses a wadded tissue to my temple and forces my hand to hold it in place.

I can tell it's killing the god of war not to say something, but he's behaving for a change. I'm glad they're letting me lead. Ares, Athena, and I have a vested interest in seeing this asshole dead, and my claim isn't stronger than theirs. But I have waited years for this moment, and torture is basically my middle name.

By the time I'm done with him, Amos Martin will be begging me for death.

There's gonna be a tank full of piranhas with his name on it by the end of tonight.

"Manning." Ares reclaims my attention.

I toss the bloody tissue to the ground and clench and unclench my hands at my sides. "I want answers now. Then we kill the bitch and take him with us. I have a nice room all lined up at my hotel."

Athena goes to the sink with a large bucket, filling it with cold water and adding the bag of ice she finds in the freezer. Except for the men outside standing watch, everyone is in the room, and we stand back as she throws the ice water over her father and stepmother. Cadance screams like she's being murdered when she comes to while Amos shouts out a grunt before narrowing his eyes at his daughter.

Athena turns to me, and I nod. She gets to start the show.

"Father. Gold digger," she purrs, running the tip of her finger around the edge of a serrated knife. "I'd say it's good to see you, but I'd be lying."

"You can't do this to us!" Cadance screams. "Your father has powerful contacts, and they'll kill you if you touch us!"

"Shut up, Cadance," Amos barks, piercing me with daggered eyes.

"Don't tell me to shut up," she screeches, and we all collectively cover our ears. "I'm in this mess because you never listen to me! I told you to kill them weeks ago, and you dismissed me!"

A squeal leaks from her lips when Athena presses the edge of the knife up under her chin. "What did you expect, cunt," she says, nipping her skin. A trickle of blood seeps from the flesh wound, and Cadance whimpers. "You're a woman. Only good for one thing, and you couldn't even do that, could you?"

Chapter Forty-One
Drew

Cadance screams when Athena slashes her panties, and the lace scatters like dandelions on the wind.

"What are you doing?" Horror washes over the stepmonster's face as she tries to move her arms to cover herself, but it's futile because Charlie's rope-tying skills are legendary, and there's no way that bitch is getting out of that chair alive.

"Quit your sniveling." Athena kneels. "No one here is interested in your used-up cunt." She drags the tip of the knife across Cadance's belly and lower into the top of her bare pussy. Bile crawls up my throat, and I hope she finishes whatever this is fast because I'm seriously grossed out by Amos's wife's skeletal frame.

Athena straightens up, glowering at her stepmother. "As I thought. No evidence of a cesarean, and everyone knows you're too selfish and lazy to push." Athena prods her knife into the swell of Cadance's surgically enlarged left breast. "You were never pregnant." She snips her bra through the middle, and the straps fall to the side, exposing Cadance's naked chest to the room.

I have never found the female form more unappealing, especially when she starts that whiny sniveling again.

"The bitch is defective," Amos snarls. "Just like her predecessor."

It's hard to stand by and not react to that, but Athena's got this.

"Say that about my mother again. I dare you." She steps sideways, standing in front of her father.

"She was a failure in every regard. Couldn't get pregnant, then she does, but it's a fucking girl. I screwed that bitch daily for years after you were born, and she never got pregnant again. She knew the importance of an heir, and she couldn't deliver the only thing I needed of her. The happiest day of my life was the day she was diagnosed with cancer, but she couldn't even die right. The stupid whore was recovering, but I took care of that." The look he gives her is pure evil, and I don't say that lightly.

"No." Athena gasps.

"It's true. I injected her with poison every day for months until she finally died."

Athena slaps him across the face before raising her knife.

I dart forward and snatch her wrist midair. "Not yet," I whisper in her ear. "Think of all the fun we'll have with him back at the hotel. You can go to town on him then. Pay him back for your mother's suffering."

Slowly, she lowers her arm and falls back against me. My arm curls around her waist protectively as Amos snarls.

"Another fucking defective female. I sent you to seduce *him*, and you let him seduce you instead," he hisses. "So goddamned weak. You're a slave to your hormones just like every other woman in my life."

"Stop saying that," Cadance says in between sobs. Yep,

we've progressed to that. "I'm not defective. My tests were all perfect."

"You lied. My daughter was right about one thing. You are a gold digger."

"I didn't lie," Cadance screeches, glaring at her husband, and we step back, silently agreeing to let this play out and see how it might work to our advantage. "I didn't fake the tests! Why would I when I have wanted to be a mother my entire life?"

"You're the defective one." Athena says in a calm tone, now fully back in control as she points her knife in her father's direction. She steps out of my embrace and thrusts her shoulders back. "You're shooting blanks." She throws her head back and laughs. "I bet my mother could've had tons of children with other men. Maybe I'm not even yours." She tilts her head to one side. "Wouldn't that be like winning the lottery."

"Hate to break it to you, sweetie, but I had paternity confirmed when you were a baby. Unfortunately, you're mine."

"But Arlo isn't." I step forward.

Athena nods, casting a subtle glance at her stepmonster, but I'm already on the same page. I crouch in front of Cadance, keeping my gaze glued to her face because being this close to her scrawny body already has my skin itching like a thousand fire ants are dancing on my flesh. "I just want the truth," I say, softening my tone and forcing a seductive smile on my lips. "Give it to me, and we'll let you go." The lie floats easily off my tongue. "We know Amos is the mastermind behind everything that happened to the Ford family. He will pay the price for those sins, but you don't have to. Why should you suffer for his fuckup?"

Amos grits out a harsh laugh. "He's playing you, honey. Don't tell him shit because it's all lies. We're going to die with the truth buried deep inside us."

"Manning isn't the one telling lies." Ares steps forward holding his cell in front of Cadance's face as he scrolls through multiple photos showing Amos with other women. Some are sexually explicit while others are him on dates with much younger women, wining and dining them, filling their heads with more of his bullshit I'm sure.

"He was getting ready to trade you in," I say as she openly sobs. "He was planning to poison you next."

"Don't listen to them, darling. It's a ploy to get you to speak, but you're smarter than that. Don't fall for it."

"He called you a gold digger five minutes ago," Athena reminds her. "And he's been calling you defective for years, blaming you for not giving him an heir when it was his fault all along. We don't like one another, Cadance, but this advice is given freely and without malice." Fire dances in Athena's eyes as she stares at the woman she hates. "Don't let him win. Take back control and show him who the real boss is."

Athena drapes a large bath towel over Cadance's shoulders, covering all her exposed private parts. Then she dabs at the tears streaming down her face and sweeps her hair behind her ears.

She's damn good at this, and I have to figuratively beat the beast in my pants into submission because he wants to get hard for her.

"It was my idea at first," Cadance says in a quiet voice, and I know we've got her.

I unfurl to my full height and shove my hands in my pockets as I brace myself for the truth.

Amos starts shouting and cursing and threatening her, and my patience is all out. I punch him in his mouth before slamming a knife into his thigh, being careful not to hit the artery. Can't have him bleeding out before I've made him suffer. Blood seeps from the wound in his leg, and he hisses, cursing me between gritted teeth before Ares shoves a wet, dirty dishrag in his mouth to shut him up. He secures it with thick tape, muting the bastard. He isn't going to give us anything anyway. That much is obvious.

But Cadance is a gullible bitch. I think she thinks with Ares here she's protected, so she has no issue singing like a canary.

"Jane was really shocked when she first discovered she was pregnant, so really we were doing her a favor." She smiles sheepishly at me, hoping I'll buy it. I have visions of wrapping my hands around her neck and choking the life from her, but I've had a lifetime of role-playing and fifteen years patience, so I stuff my true feelings down deep inside and encourage her to go on with a nod.

"I wore a prosthetic stomach, and we hired an ob-gyn who was willing to go along with the ruse. We attended appointments, and I took vitamins and everything. I even chatted with Jane about heartburn and back pain, and she didn't suspect a thing. No one did."

"You faked it good," Athena says in a voice devoid of emotion.

Cadance smiles like it's something to be proud of. "My idea was to buy the baby from Jane's father, and we'd help them to escape overseas where your father would never find them, Drew."

Amos shouts, but the words are muffled through the mouth covering. I know she's lying. She's not very good at it.

"I could tell Jane's dad wasn't pleased about the baby, and I knew we could have sold it to him. But Amos said it was too risky. He said if we wanted to make it believable Jane had to disappear, and unfortunately that meant he had to make her family disappear too."

Amos is apoplectic, thrashing around on the chair and glaring at his wife.

"Amos considered going after you too, Drew, but it was clear you didn't know Jane was pregnant with your baby, and there had been no contact between you." She pins me with puppy-dog eyes. "That's when Amos found the men you sent to watch over the Fords. He killed them all but kept their cell phones. He used to laugh when he was replying to one of your texts."

I dig my hands into my thighs through my pocket. "Whose idea was it to traffic Jane and Vera and sell Silas to Cleo Carter?" I ask, wanting to be done with this so I can get to the killing and maiming part of the night.

"That was your father's idea."

I blink several times as I stare at her. "*My* father was involved?"

"That doesn't make sense," Anderson cuts in, coming up behind me. "Michael Hearst arranged a marriage deal for Jane and Drew. Why would he do that if he wanted her dead?"

"I only know what I overheard that time he showed up at our house. Apparently, he only agreed to let you marry Jane so he could get to Amos. He had discovered Ford and Amos were friends at Stanford, and he'd heard rumors Amos was part of a more powerful organization. He wanted an alliance, and he knew Ford was the way in. Except Amos was never going to ally with a lowly elite," she scoffs. "Amos was furious when he showed up uninvited at our front door. It seemed Ford had called him. He was worried Amos was planning something, and he wanted to get Jane to safety, but he never should've called your father because he sold him out. Hearst made a deal with Amos. He'd help to make the Fords disappear and let us keep Arlo so we could pretend he was our son and heir as long as Amos helped him get control of the elite and one day he would propose him for elevation to Luminary status."

The vein in Amos's neck is visibly throbbing, and I hope he

doesn't have a heart attack. I'm not volunteering for mouth to mouth, but someone will have to do it because he's not going out like that.

She cackles. "Hearst was such a fool to fall for it. No one gets elevated. Especially not the bastard son of a whore and an adulterer. He wasn't even elite blood. Amos agreed because it served him to have Hearst do his dirty work. He was always planning to murder him when the time was right, but fate took matters into hand."

Shocked silence greets her words.

"If it makes you feel any better, handsome, your father never had any intention of letting you marry Jane. She was a means to an end. He always planned to kill her to get her out of the way. She wasn't worthy of his son, that's what he said. He was enraged when he discovered the pregnancy. He said it would ruin everything and he wasn't pureblooded enough to be your heir, he—"

I lunge at her and swipe my knife across her lips, needing to stop the vitriol pouring from her self-serving mouth. The howl that spills from her throat is music to my ears, and I shed my skin, becoming the beast. No one stops me as I rip the towel away and stab her repeatedly, slashing across her chest, driving my knife deep into her stomach, and tearing strips off her arms.

Amos has gone still, and a deathly hush ghosts over the room as I gut the bitch, savaging her pussy last as I plunge my knife repeatedly into her treacherous cunt.

Her eyes are full of fear as the life force slowly ebbs from her mangled body. I'm covered in blood as I get all up in her face, pressing the knife against her throat. "You stole my flesh and blood from me. You helped to seal his mother's fate, and you stood by and did nothing as your husband and my father killed Arlo's grandparents. You didn't deserve a place in my son's life. You had the opportunity denied to me. You could have loved him. You *should* have loved him, but you chose to treat him with disdain." I spit in her face as I press the knife into the flesh at her throat. "For that, you deserve to die. Rot in hell, gold digger," I say as I dig the knife in and drag it across her throat ending her life.

Amos stares at his wife with sick satisfaction gliding across his blood-spattered face. I rip the tape from his mouth and yank out the rag. "Got anything to add, you piece of shit?" I rip his boxers to shreds, leaving him shivering and naked and exposed.

"I won." He smirks. "Arlo will never love a savage like you. I don't care what blood flows through his veins. He's *my son*. You can do your worst, Manning, but it won't matter. You can't eradicate fifteen years of me loving him and him loving me. I did Arlo a favor selling his whore mother overseas and wiping out her family. But the biggest favor I did him was keeping you away. You have too much of your father's tainted blood in you. You were never capable of being the father Arlo needed. The father I became for him. So, go ahead, do it. Kill me. It will only cement his hatred for you forever."

"Liar!" someone yells from behind, and ice replaces the blood flowing in my veins.

My eyes meet Athena's, and I see the same shock staring back at me. Our heads whip around at the same time, and she screams "No!" racing past me to get to her brother, but it's too late, and we're too far from him.

"I hate you!" Arlo roars before pulling the trigger.

Chapter Forty-Two
Athena

The shot is on point, and it rips cleanly through Amos's forehead, leaving a nice, neat bullet hole. His head falls back, and his glazed eyes stare vacantly at the ceiling. I can't even be mad I didn't get to torture him because my every thought is consumed with Arlo.

My brother drops to his knees as I rush toward him. The gun slips from his fingers, clattering loudly on the patterned tile floor. I sink to my knees in front of Arlo and pull him into my arms. He falls lifelessly against me with dried tearstains tracking down his cheeks. I hug him close, pressing kisses into his hair as I fight tears. I didn't want this for him. I didn't want him finding out the truth like this. And I never wanted him to shoulder this burden.

It should have been on Drew and me. We wanted to do that for him.

I'm rubbing his back and dotting kisses into his hair while the others swing into action around me. Calling in a cleanup crew and deciding how to cover it up so no one ever finds out what Arlo did. My brother is numb in my arms, and I'm really starting to worry when a sob flees his mouth, and his arms finally go around me.

Drew is there to prop me up from behind as Arlo falls apart, clinging to me with a desperation that stabs holes in my already fragile heart. His agonized sobs speak of untold pain, and I silently swear to do anything and everything to help him get through this. Fuck everything else. The only thing that matters is my brother.

Drew is a silent comfort standing guard over us as all the men finally exit the house giving us some privacy.

I don't know how long we stay like that, but when the cleanup crew arrives, I know it's time to leave.

"Arlo." I rub his back as I gently ease him off me. My shirt is soaked with his tears, and more keep falling from his eyes. "We need to go."

"Don't leave me," he says in a hoarse tone. "Please don't leave me."

"Never." I smooth my hand over his hair, wishing I could take his pain and alleviate his suffering.

But like I told Drew, Arlo will have to do the heavy lifting.

Drew's arm extends, and he offers his hand to his son.

The tears stop flowing as Arlo looks up at Drew, his gaze running over his features, before lowering to the offered hand.

My heart is in my throat as I watch father and son. Drew is wearing his emotions on his face, along with a lot of blood, but I like he's not hiding who he is from Arlo. There is no shielding my little brother from the evils of the world any longer. Not after today.

A messy ball of emotion sits on my chest as Arlo takes Drew's hand. Drew offers me his other hand as he helps us both to our feet. I clamp a hand over my mouth as father and son stare at one another. Arlo is almost as tall as his dad though not as broad. Their eyes are a carbon copy of one another, and they have the same shape face. Seeing them together like this, I don't know how I missed the resemblance before.

Guess if you're not looking for something you don't see it.

A lot like me with Beast. Deep down, my subconscious knew he was Drew, but I didn't connect it until I was ready to process it.

Just like I knew deep down I was sabotaging my mission on purpose because I'd had enough, and I'd finally found someone worth risking it all for.

"Are you really my dad?" Arlo asks.

Drew nods. "Yes. I only found out a few days ago."

Arlo looks at Drew and then me, and the look of vulnerability on his face guts me.

"It's okay," Drew says as Arlo leans into my side. "We don't need to talk about anything tonight. I just want to get you two somewhere safe. Somewhere you can clean up, get something to eat, and try to grab some sleep. Everything else can wait."

I smile at Drew, squeezing his hand. I know what I told him, and I meant it, but I don't know if I have it in me to stay away from him right now. He still needs to deal with his shit, but I think he needs me as much as Arlo does, and I want to be there for both of them.

"That sounds like a plan. What do you say, Arlo?"

He sniffles, rubbing his nose against his sleeve. "I don't want to go back to that house. Everything is fake. Everything was a lie."

I gently clasp his face. "You don't ever have to go back there if you don't want to, and not everything was a lie. My love for you was and is pure."

His Adam's apple bobs in his throat as more tears fill his eyes. "We're not even brother and sister."

"Yes, we are." I press a fierce kiss to his brow. "Our DNA doesn't matter." I place my hand over my heart and then over his. "All that matters is what we feel, and I love you more than life." I peer deep into his eyes. "You are my brother, and I am your sister, and I love you so fucking much. You are everything to me, and we're going to get through this. I am not leaving you. Wherever you are is where I will be. That is a solemn promise. You are not alone. You have me, and you have Drew."

And a whole other family who already love him and will welcome him with open arms, but that's too much for him to grasp right now.

"Let me know if you need anything else. There are plenty of towels and toiletries in the bathrooms, and I left some clothes that should fit Arlo on his bed. Someone will bring food up to you shortly. There's a small refrigerator behind that cabinet with cold drinks." She points at a dark wood dresser tucked against the wall in the corner. "I hope you get some sleep."

"Thanks, Mrs. Stewart. We really appreciate all you're doing for us," I say.

She waves her hands in the air. "We're all family, sweetie." She nods at Drew. "Nice to meet you, Drew. I'll see you in the morning." Baz and Jase's mom closes the door, leaving us in the suite that is ours for the night. It has three en suite bedrooms and a large living area with a fireplace, two couches, a large-screen TV, and a small dining table with four chairs. It looks out over the rear of the Stewart family estate, but there isn't much to see of the magnificent gardens in the pitch-black night.

We couldn't go to a hotel given the circumstances, and it was too late to fly back to Rydeville. If I'm even returning there because that decision will be my brother's. The Stewarts offered to take everyone in because they have plenty of room and the estate is in a secluded private location. We all parted ways when we got here, and everyone has been shown to their suites. It's been an exhausting day, and we're all beat.

"I'm worried about him," Drew says when we hear the shower turn on in the bedroom Arlo has claimed.

"Same." I stifle a yawn.

"I understand why he did it, but I hate that for him. I fear it'll always follow him around."

"I know." I rub at my tired eyes. "I feel the same."

Drew moves closer, leaning in slowly before kissing me softly and sweetly. He pulls back after one kiss. "I love you."

"I love you too."

"I need to shower before the food gets here."

I drag my gaze over his blood-soaked form and smile. "You really do." A smirk tugs up the corners of my lips.

"What's that look for?"

I look over my shoulder to ensure Arlo is still in the shower and lean in as I whisper, "I was just remembering how you butchered the gold digger. I've never seen anything hotter."

"You have issues, Athena."

I giggle, and it's a miracle I can. "Tell me something I don't know, and pot, kettle, black, Mr. Manning."

"Guess that's why we're so drawn to one another."

I press a kiss to my hand and place it against his cheek. "Go shower, and I'll meet you back out here in a few."

By the time I return ten minutes later, the food has arrived, and Drew and Arlo are staring awkwardly at one another from across the dining table.

I sit on a chair in between them and grab a few slices of pizza and plonk them on Arlo's plate. "Try to eat something."

"I'm not hungry."

"I can relate, but Mrs. Stewart went to a lot of trouble, and you need to keep your strength up."

"Can I put music on?" Arlo asks, and Drew instantly hands his cell over.

"I have Spotify. Knock yourself out."

Arlo selects one of Eminem's albums, and we don't talk as we eat, none of us overly hungry but making an effort to get some food down.

After we finish eating, I make peppermint tea at the tea and coffee station in the room, and then Arlo says he's going to bed.

I give him a few minutes to get settled in bed before I knock on his door and slip inside. He's lying on his side under the covers, curled up in the fetal position, staring out the window through the open curtains. I perch on the edge of his bed and brush hair back from his face. "I'm here for you."

"I know," he whispers, clutching my hand.

"Want me to sleep in here with you tonight?"

"I'm not a little kid anymore."

"I know, Arlo. I'm not offering because I think you're a child. I'm offering because you've been through some pretty heavy stuff today, and if it was me, I'd welcome your comfort. I want you to lean on me, but I won't force you. If you'd rather be alone, that's fine too."

He twists his head and looks up at me. "I don't know how to feel, Thena." Tears shine in his eyes. "One minute, I'm numb, like I feel nothing, and then it all hits me like a freight train, and it feels like I'm drowning and I can't breathe."

I rub his shoulders. "That's totally normal. You've been through a huge ordeal, and you're in shock. It's going to take time to process your feelings, but how you feel is never wrong."

"I don't know who I am anymore," he whispers, and I lean down and hug him.

"I know who you are. You're the best little brother and one of the coolest guys ever. You're one of the good guys, Arlo. Don't let what happened today change that."

"I killed my father." He sniffles. "The man I thought was my father," he corrects. "I heard the things he said. He was a monster. I should feel good about ending him, so why do I feel guilty?"

"Because you're a good person forced to do something you never should've had to do. We were going to take care of it because we didn't want you to have to handle this."

"I didn't make a conscious decision to do it," he explains, flopping onto his back and staring at the ceiling as he talks. "I stole a gun and gave those guys the slip on purpose so I could sneak back in and find out what was going on. I knew it was some serious shit, like I knew you'd try to protect me from it. I never guessed it was anything like that. I was upset at first, and then I got so mad when I heard the way he was speaking to you and talking about my birth mom and about *him*." He pauses for a second. "My real dad." His eyes flit to mine. "I saw him killing the gold digger, and I was cheering him on. I wanted to be at his side, sliding that knife between her ribs and soaking in her blood. Still think I'm one of the good guys now?"

"Yes," I say without hesitation. "There are different shades of good and bad, and I know what's in your heart, Arlo. It's pure, just like your mom's was."

"You knew her?"

"Only briefly." I run my fingers through his hair. "You get your hair from her too. She was a sweetheart, and she already loved you so much."

"I hate Amos," he snarls. "I'm not sorry I killed him. I'm only sorry he didn't suffer more." He turns on his side, facing away from me.

"I'll get changed and come sleep with you."

"I want to sleep alone," he says. "I don't need to be babied."

I want to protest, but I don't want to start an argument. "If you change your mind or you need me during the night call out for me."

He doesn't reply, and my heart bleeds. "Goodnight, Arlo. I love you."

I'm closing the door when he says it back.

"I fear he's too much like me," Drew whispers from just behind me, and I almost jump out of my skin.

I swat his chest. "What have I told you about creeping up on people like that?!"

"Sorry not sorry."

I roll my eyes, taking his hand and dragging him away from the door. "At least you're not denying it this time."

"You left the door open a little, and eavesdropping was too tempting. I feel so useless. I want to help but I don't know how."

"You need to give him time. He's guarded even with me, and you're still a stranger." I run my fingers through the stubble on his cheeks. "He's in for a rough time, Drew, and I don't know how this is going to manifest. Being a teenager is fucking hard without going through something as traumatic as this."

"I know he may not want me around. I know it might take time for him to warm up to the idea of me, even as a friend or your partner, but I want to be where he is too. I won't force it. I can get my own place and let him set the pace, but I don't want to leave either of you."

"What about work?"

"I can work remotely, and they can manage everything else without me."

"What about Abby and your friends? Your mom and your nieces and nephews?"

He wraps his arms around my waist. "They'll be right where I left them, ready to welcome us home when all three of us are in a position to go back to Rydeville."

"That might never happen, Drew. Arlo might want to stay in Cali, and if he does, then that's where I'll be."

"My home is wherever you two are." He shrugs before leaning down to kiss the tip of my nose. "For the first time in years, I know what I want, and I'm free to pursue it. And before you say it, I'll sign up for therapy. I'll put in the hard work and deal with my shit. I'll set a good example because our boy is gonna need therapy too."

"Do you mean that?"

The playful expression leaves his face. "I do. You were right about everything."

"I usually am," I tease.

"I'm not wasting any energy disputing that. I will bow before you and humbly accept defeat. You knew what I needed to do before I figured it out myself. I'm done hiding and running from my feelings. What happened today has given me the closure I needed, but more than that, it has highlighted how short life is, and you truly don't know what's around the corner. I don't want to waste another second of my life. I have found my true purpose in you and Arlo, and I want to be there for you both in every way conceivable."

His lips brush my cheek, igniting a fire in their wake. "Jane was my first love and a lifeline when I desperately needed it. A small part of me will always hold love for her, and she lives on in Arlo. But I love *you*, Athena. It's a deep, intense, eternal love I have never felt before. No woman has ever seen every side of me and accepted me as I am. You are the first and hopefully the last. You have seen it all, and by some miracle, you still want me. Only a damn fool would turn that down."

He takes my hands and lifts them to his lips, kissing my knuckles. "I fucked up. I'll definitely fuck up again. But if I promise to work on my demons and swear that what I feel for you is pure and true and more precious than any love that has come before, would you give me another chance? Will you let me prove my love for you and Arlo is the real deal and allow me to become the man you need me to be?"

Butterflies swoop into my stomach, and my heart pumps with adrenaline and excitement and a million other emotions. What lies ahead will not be easy for any of us, but I feel like we can get through it if we stick together, and I want this man by my side.

It's time we both stopped fighting what we feel for one another and fully embrace what it means to be in control of our destiny. "Yes, Drew. I will give you another chance, and I already know you are the man I need. You just need to start believing in yourself."

Epilogue 1
Drew

The last seven months have been eventful to say the least, but I wouldn't change any of it. Not even the harrowing, heart-wrenching, soul-sucking challenging parts. Arlo, Thena, and I are all in therapy and working our way through our issues one at a time. In a way, it has helped to bring me closer to my son even if there is still a lot of work to be done in our relationship. Confronting my feelings after all this time is overdue but difficult. I never realized how emotionally stunted I was because I kept pushing everything away instead of facing up to it. But I'm an adult now, and I'm putting in the hard work for me, for my son, and the woman I love more than life itself.

Athena and I chose to put the brakes on our relationship, and while it's killing me being around her every day and not being with her in the way I want, it's for the best. This way, Arlo and I get to focus on our recovery with Athena's support.

Athena and I might have cracked a few times. Grabbing stolen kisses and making out like horny teenagers when the all-consuming need for one another combusts. But we haven't had sex. With each other or anyone else. We're committed to one another and faithful. We've agreed to wait to restart our romantic and sexual relationship when the timing is right.

I'm not sure how Arlo will feel about it, and we'll need to tread carefully so we don't undo any of his progress.

It's been really hard for my son. Trauma combined with teenage hormones does not make it easy, but I'm proud of him for trying. We have witnessed every gamut of emotions with Arlo. He has phases where he's angry and reckless and hellbent on destruction. Skipping school. Arguing with his friends. Messing around with girls and showing up drunk on several occasions. Other times, he withdraws into a shell, and we struggle to get him to come out of his room. When depression hits him hard, he is silent, closed off, and in so much pain it's palpable.

We're trying to guide and support him while giving him boundaries that protect his fragile mental state. It has led to confrontations, and he won't accept any attempt I make to discipline him for his safety, so a lot is resting on Athena's shoulders. But she gets on with it and at times she is the only one he will listen to.

It's hard seeing my son struggle and not being able to do much to help, but Thena reminds me it's a step at a time, a day at a time, and I'm building the foundations of our future relationship now.

"Drew." Arlo calls my name, yanking me out of my head.

I glance over my shoulder. "Yeah, buddy?"

His lips curve at the corners, and the dimple pops in his left cheek, reminding me of his mother. Jane had a dimple in the exact same place. "You've just been staring into space with your hands on that case for the past few minutes. You completely spaced out, dude."

"Guilty as charged." I toss him a smirk. "I'm almost packed

anyway." Now that school is out for the summer, we're heading to Rydeville for a month. Arlo was the one who suggested it, and we were more than happy to agree. I'm looking forward to chilling out with everyone and hopefully showing Arlo some of my old stomping grounds.

"Thena said the car will be here in ten minutes and to get your ass in gear."

"Okay. I'll meet you at the front."

He salutes me before strolling out of my bedroom and out through the front door of the guesthouse on the grounds of Athena's property I now call home. Arlo refused to return to the Martin family home. He said there were too many bad memories, and we both agreed. Thena bought this place a few blocks from the private high school Arlo attends in Lowell. They live in the main five-bedroom house, and I live here. It's the best of both worlds. I get to see them every day, yet we all have our own space.

I work remotely but travel to Rydeville once a month for a few days for in-house meetings and to catch up with family and friends. Arlo and Thena travel with me sometimes. My family welcomed them warmly, and some of the happiest moments I've shared with my son are when we've been at my mom's or Abby's and Kai's place. Arlo is great with his younger cousins, and they worship the ground he walks on.

It's been good for him.

Good for all of us.

It's been torturous having to return to Cali after weekends filled with activities and laughter, but Arlo calls the shots. We go where he goes. Period.

Thena's business is still located in Boston, and she hired a manager to oversee the office while she works from Lowell, so we're managing to make it all fit. It feels a little weird to say life has never been better when we've dealt with so much traumatic shit, but I honestly have never been happier or felt more settled, like I'm exactly where I should be, living the life I was always meant to be.

"Is Vera meeting us at the graveyard?" Arlo asks, removing his headphones and lifting his gaze from his cell shortly before we're due to land at the private airfield just outside Rydeville.

"I believe so," I say. Vera is doing so much better these days. I think Arlo literally saved her life. Her nephew has given her a purpose and a reason to prioritize her healing, and she's made so much progress she's finally ready to reclaim the life stolen from her.

Arlo loved her from the moment they met. That first meeting was emotional in the extreme for everyone. They have a special bond I'm envious of even though I'm super happy they have one another. They talk regularly on the phone, and I think it's good for him to have someone to talk to who is closer in age to him.

Arlo won't talk about Amos. At least not to Thena or me. I hope he's discussing it with his therapist because that's a heavy burden for a sixteen-year-old to carry.

"Are you coming to the house with us after?" he asks, eyeballing me.

"I would like to, unless you both want privacy for the first visit?"

We plan to head to the Ford family home after the graveyard. It will be Vera's first time there since she was a baby, and Arlo wants to see where his mom grew up.

"I'd like you there," he quietly replies. "Both of you." His gaze drifts to Thena. She's asleep with her head on my shoulder.

"You got it."

———

The memorial ceremony in the crypt is emotional but joyous. Arlo and Vera cling to one another as the harpist plays soft music while Jane's parents are laid to rest beside her. The Luminaries suggested we dig up the back garden of the Martin house a couple months ago, and we found what was left of their bodies there. It was intel offered by the mole after they discovered his identity and stopped him from putting Amos's posthumous plans into place.

All our family and friends are here, crowded behind us in the crypt. Lavender diffusers scent the air comingling with all the flowers in the stone room. We couldn't find any trace of Silas among the remains Knight Carter had reexamined, so we don't really know what happened to him. I'm sorry I couldn't reunite Jane with all of her family, but I hope they are out there together somewhere.

"Come stay with me tonight," Mom says, looping her arm in mine after we leave the crypt and make our way through the cemetery. "I've missed my boys," she adds, messing up Arlo's hair as he walks past with Talia and Jane hanging off his every word. They hero-worship their older cousin and love when he comes to visit.

"Love you, Gramma," he says, darting in to kiss Mom's cheek, and my heart swells to bursting point.

"Love you too, precious boy," she replies before the girls pull him away.

"How's he doing?" Mom asks.

"Better. The good days are outweighing the bad."

"And how are things progressing between you and him?"

"They're good. He's starting to confide more in me. I'm

trying to be open with him, and I don't shy away from telling him the truth even if he asks me something hard. Teaching him to drive helped too. I feel like it's brought us closer." He got his permit the second he turned fifteen and a half, and we bought him a Range Rover for his sixteenth birthday.

"I know things have been challenging, but I've never seen you happier, Drew, and that makes me so incredibly happy."

"Things are good." My gaze automatically gravitates toward Athena. She looks to be in a deep conversation with my sister, and I wonder what that's about.

"You need to make her yours. It's time."

I arch a brow at my mother. She's been on her best behavior since I sat her down and explained the agreement Athena and I had come to. There's been no more talk of weddings, but I hope to give her the opportunity to help plan ours one day. "You know why we're waiting."

"My grandson is smart, and trust me, he knows."

Alarm bells ring in my ears. "Has he said something?"

"No. But the boy has eyes. Everyone can see the love and longing between you. Talk to Arlo, and then get your girl, Andrew."

***

I'm still mulling over Mom's words an hour later as we explore the Ford home with Vera and Arlo. The couple I've been paying to maintain the place greeted us when we arrived, making a fuss over Arlo and Vera and helping to settle any nerves. Athena and I are holding back, letting Arlo and his aunt lead the way.

"Is this hard for you?" Athena asks as we trail Arlo and Vera upstairs.

"It's a little nostalgic, but I've been here before. I oversaw the renovations, and I pop in from time to time to ensure all is good."

"You're such a good man, Andrew Manning." She clings to my arm and snuggles into my side.

My arm goes around her shoulders as we walk up the sweeping staircase. "I'm trying."

Athena stops on the steps and beams at me.

"What?"

"You didn't refute it." Tears fill her eyes. "I'm proud of you, you know?" She presses her body up against me. "You've been going through hell since December, opening old wounds and dealing with your demons, but you've never faltered, and you've been so strong for me and Arlo. I love seeing you find all the true parts of yourself, Drew, and I fall more in love with you every day."

I want to kiss her so freaking bad. Our mouths are inching toward one another without even realizing it.

"Are you coming or what?" Arlo shouts, and we spring away from one another like we've been electrocuted.

A cheeky grin lifts his mouth as he stares at us from the top of the stairs. "Get up here already."

"I worried this would be too emotional for him, but his joy is obvious," Athena says as we hurry up the stairs.

"I'm sorry I didn't suggest he come here sooner. I think it's helping to see all of this. To help make Jane more real in his mind."

"You've talked to him about her. So has Abby. He's seen the photo albums. I think he needed to be at this point to see this and feel joy not anger or sadness."

Thena and I have talked extensively about Jane. I wanted to know all about her pregnancy and the months I missed out on. Knowing Jane thrived during pregnancy and she was excited and happy helps. She had plans to find me once things blew over, and that helped too.

I would never have forced Athena to share her stories if she wasn't comfortable talking about my ex. But she's confident of my feelings for her and not threatened by a ghost. She has specifically told me to talk freely about Jane and not to worry about upsetting her because she's assured of her place in both our lives.

"You're probably right," I admit, breaking free of the thoughts in my head.

"I know. I usually am."

I bark out a laugh before pressing my mouth to her ear. "I really want to kiss you right now."

"That's all?" She shoots me a saucy wink, and just like that, I'm hard.

"Not funny, sweetheart." I adjust myself in my pants, glad the other two have already gone into Jane's room.

"I think we should talk to him about us when we return to Cali."

"Mom said the same to me at the graveyard."

"The voice of wisdom has spoken, so it's settled." Mom and Athena get on like a house on fire, and I love how close they've become. Mom mothers Athena without suffocating her, offering maternal support that's been lacking in Athena's life since her mom was brutally murdered by her father.

"You've got to see this." Arlo snags my elbow and pulls me into Jane's room. I left it exactly as it was, figuring Vera could decide if she wanted to redecorate this room in time. It's had a fresh coat of paint, but otherwise, everything is as Jane left it.

It's like stepping into a time warp.

Arlo drags me into the side room where Jane did all her artwork.

"Look at all this." Vera turns to me with tears in her eyes, but she's smiling. "I never knew my sister was so artistic."

"Jane loved painting and making her own jewelry, but her specialty was handmade cards. We all got one on our birthdays and at Christmases. I think I still have some of them in a box at my house. I'll give it to you later."

"That's what I wanted to show you. Come on." Arlo snags my elbow and drags me over to the desk beside a large shelving unit where a box is sitting. "These are all for you," he says, carefully removing tons of handmade cards from the box. All have my name on the front, and they are a combination of birthday, Christmas, and anniversary cards, but there are other specific ones that bring a lump to my throat. A card for our wedding night. A pregnancy reveal card. One for the birth of our first baby, and many more highlighting milestones one would celebrate in a normal marriage.

"I'm not surprised she'd do this. It's just like her, but I had no idea these existed."

"She really loved you," Arlo quietly says.

"Did you doubt it?" Athena asks, squeezing his shoulder.

He shrugs, looking directly into my eyes. "You were so young, and I know I was a mistake."

"We *were* young, but we loved one another. You were an accident but never a mistake. You were conceived with love, Arlo." I take a chance and wrap my arm around him, forcing words out over the lump in my throat. "Never doubt you are wanted. Jane was excited to bring you into the world, and I have loved you from the second I discovered you existed. You're my son."

Tears stab my eyes, but I don't shove them aside like I once might have. I want my son to see me vulnerable. To know it's okay to show emotion as a man. It doesn't make you weak like my father had drummed into me.

It makes you strong.

I thump my closed hand over my heart. "You're all the best parts of me and every loving, pure, good part of your mother. I love you more than I can express. Jane would've showered you with love and affection if she'd had the chance."

What I don't say, what I know now without a shadow of doubt, is that my sister and Athena were right. Jane and I would not have lasted the distance. These cards prove it conclusively. Jane wanted the white picket fence and two point five kids. She visualized a fairy tale. She wanted Prince Charming, and I've always been the Beast. I couldn't have given her that life without losing key parts of myself, and if I'd shown her those parts I would've shattered her illusion. We would have been there for our son, but I don't believe we would still be together.

Jane was my first love, and it had an end date.

Athena is my forever, for infinity and beyond.

Letting go of Jane has been one of the hardest parts of my therapy, but it's been the most freeing. I cherish the time I had with her. I will always look back on those years together with fondness, and that's how I choose to remember her. She's been an important part of my life, for many reasons, but she's my past and Athena is my present and my future.

I've let Jane go. I'm letting her rest in peace.

"I'll always be sad I never got to know her," Arlo says. "And I'll always hate those assholes for taking that life from me, but I'm glad I've got you, and Thena, and Vera, and Gramma, Aunt Abby and Uncle Kai, and all my cousins, and everyone." Tears glisten in his eyes as he removes a frame from his backpack and hands it to me. "Abby gave me that. She thought I might like to have it by my bed, but I won't put it up if it'll upset you or my sister."

Drew

His gaze jumps between us as Athena peers over my shoulder, looking at the framed photo of Jane and me. It was taken the night of her sweet sixteenth. Her parents threw her a big party here, and it was a great night. There was a formal dress code. Jane is wearing a pretty pink ballgown, and I'm in a tux. We have our arms around one another, and we're smiling at the camera like two lovesick teenagers.

It's the perfect photo to give Arlo.

It captures the perfect moment in time, when there were no elite, no murderous fathers, or sick predators. Just two teenagers wrapped up in one another, losing themselves to reality in each other's arms. The love between us is undeniable, and it's a precious keepsake for our son.

"Abby already mentioned it to me, and I'm fine with it." Athena hugs Arlo. "I've told you before you can speak about Jane morning, noon, and night if you like. I loved her. Because she was a wonderful person who brightened up my life at a time when I needed it but mostly because she gave me you." Athena kisses her brother on the cheek before peering deep into my eyes. "And she brought you to me too. I could never hate her or feel jealous of her when she's given me so much. I will forever be grateful for Jane Ford, and I never want any of us to forget her."

Vera sobs, and I pull her into my arms as Arlo moves closer with Athena still wrapped around him, and we group hug with tears in our eyes.

"So, you're finally admitting it then," Arlo says after we've all wiped our tears and separated.

Thena and I share a look.

"You think you've been all secretive and shit, but you stare at one another with puppy-dog eyes nonstop, and it's seriously gross."

Vera howls with laughter, nudging her nephew in the ribs.

"Jesus, Drew." He rolls his eyes and points at his sister. "What are you waiting for? Kiss her already!"

Epilogue 2
Drew – One Year Later

"**Y**es, Beast. Just like that," Thena cries out as I bring the paddle down hard on her bare ass. "Again. Harder," she whimpers, and I oblige.

Seriously, how is this my life?

Things really don't get much better than this.

Last summer before we left to return to Cali, Arlo asked if we could move permanently to Rydeville. After discussing it at length with him and his therapist, we made the decision to relocate full-time here. The Luminaries accepted Thena's cousin as a replacement for her as head of the family, on the condition she makes herself available where the need arises. They are also keen for Arlo to get on the elite track, but agreed to leave that discussion until he turns eighteen. He's had enough upheaval in his life.

Moving here was the right choice. It was the fresh start my son needed. There are no bad memories here, and he doesn't feel left out like he was in Lowell when his friends were getting more immersed in the Luminary lifestyle and he was on the outside. He has settled in well at Rydeville High, and he'll be a junior in August. He's made new friends, found plenty of female admirers, and embraced our big boisterous family life.

We're closer than ever, and I've cut back on my working hours so I have time to spend with my son and my one true love. Now that Petrov's network has been shut down in Europe and the Luminaries have fully taken over tracking down other trafficking rings, I have more free time than ever and I'm making the most of it. Athena and I attend every one of Arlo's games. The three of us have weekly movie and pizza nights, and in the summer, we spend lots of time on the beach and enjoying barbecues with the whole gang.

Arlo and I visit our therapists once a month. I'm still working through all the repressed trauma from my youth, but I have new coping skills now and two amazing reasons to continue fighting the good fight.

"Red," Athena says, and I stop with the paddle raised midair.

"Shit, did I hurt you?"

She laughs. "No, silly, but I need you to fuck me again now. Arlo will be home in an hour, and I'll need to shower. I'm covered in your jizz."

The best part about being our own bosses? Getting to take the afternoon off on a whim to engage in kinky fuckery.

I had an extension built at the back of my house, and we moved the master suite to the rear of the property as far away from prying eyes and ears as possible. Our private dungeon is hidden at the back of our walk-in-closet behind the long rectangular mirror. Thena and I picked everything together, and I love nothing more than getting lost in my girl in here for hours.

"Good point," I say, spreading her ass cheeks and lifting her butt up on the spanking bench. I lean down and lick a path from her ass to her cunt, burying my nose in her honey scent before driving my cock into her pussy without warning.

"Agh," she cries out.

"Arms in front," I command, and she stretches forward, gripping the top of the bench. "This will be hard and fast because that's just the way my slut likes it, right?"

"You really are my perfect beast," she purrs as I slam in and out of her, groaning with pleasure as her tight walls hug my hard cock.

I lick my thumb and push it into her ass as I fuck her cunt like I'm a dying man. "I'm your *only* beast, Vixen." I plan to drill that point home real soon.

"Forever and ever," she pants as I fuck the breath from her lungs.

I screw her against the wall in the shower as we clean up after our marathon spontaneous session because I'm insatiable for my woman, and she's the same with me. We get dressed in record time, checking our watches as we rush out of our bedroom and head toward the kitchen. We like to be there for Arlo when he returns from a therapy session. While his moods are more stable these days, we still check in.

Athena slams to a halt in the doorway of the kitchen, and I almost crash into her from behind. "You're home early," she says, tucking her wet hair behind her ears.

"And you brought visitors," I add, spotting the two women in the kitchen with my son.

"Found them on the doorstep," he says. "Like two lost puppies."

"Strange thing." Abby smirks, propping her arms on the island unit. "We rang the bell repeatedly, and we tried both your cells, but there was no answer."

"It gets even more curious," Demi says with a mischievous

glint in her eye. "They were showering in the middle of the day."

Arlo bursts out laughing. "They were up to kinky shit in their secret sex room."

My mouth trails the ground as Abby's and Demi's eyes pop wide.

"What the what?" Abby's gaze flicks between me and Thena. "You've been holding out on me, sis."

"How do you know about that?" I ask my son.

Arlo rolls his eyes as he opens the fridge and grabs a protein shake. He wants to bulk up and he's eating protein to beat the band. We work out together in our home gym every day, and the three of us go for a run most evenings. Most mornings, Athena and I swim laps in the pool.

"Come on, Dad. I'm not blind or stupid. And I'm not a little kid. I've had sex. I—" He straightens up, looking at the faces of the four shell-shocked adults all staring at him.

"You called him Dad," Thena says in a choked voice.

My heart is presently trying to burst its way out of my chest. I'm drowning in the sweetest emotion. The urge to grab my son and hug the shit out of him is riding me hard, but he's not one for overindulgent PDAs, and I can already tell he slipped that out there on purpose.

Arlo's cheeks pink a little. He shrugs. "It's who he is. No need to overreact."

I can tell he doesn't want to big deal this, even if it is a big deal, and I want to shout it from the rooftops. "Do we need to have the sex talk again?" I ask, deliberately switching the subject.

He shoots me a look of relief before it transforms to horror. "Hell, no. I'm still recovering from that last awkward convo, and for the record, I'm cool with whatever you two do in that secret room in your closet, but I never *ever* want to hear about it, and I have zero interest in seeing your kinky sex den.”

“Well, I want a tour,” Abby says, and Demi is bobbing her head. My twin straightens up. “Like right now.” She moves around the island unit. “You don’t mind if I take pics, right?” she asks Thena. “I’ve been trying to convince Kai we need a sex room.”

I’m grateful when the three women leave, and I don’t have to listen to any more of that.

“You should see your face.” Arlo chuckles.

“I want to know about my sister’s sex life as much as you want to know about mine.”

“Valid,” he says. He looks over my shoulder to ensure they’re really gone. “When are you going to ask her?” he whispers.

“I’m trying to find the perfect weekend getaway so it can be romantic and something she can tell her girlfriends.”

“At this rate, I’ll be old and gray before you propose.” He leans back against the counter. “Forget about all that shit. Thena won’t care. Just make her that lobster pasta she loves with those mini chocolate lava cakes. Get champagne and flowers. I’ll help you cook, and you could do it in the sunroom one evening.” His eyes light up. “We can get candles and those twinkly sparkly lights and string them up over the roof.”

“Are you sure you’re okay with this?”

“Dad.” He enunciates the word as he rolls his eyes, and I wonder if it will always feel like fireworks are exploding in my chest every time he calls me that. “We’ve been over this. I’m happy you’re both happy, and that’s all that matters to me.”

“You might get shit at school.” His sister will be his step-mother, and I know full well how assholery teenage boys can get.

“I couldn’t care less if I do. I’ll level anyone who says

anything about Thena." His eyes blaze with protectiveness, and my love for him is this massive bubble of emotion and pride.

"You make me proud to be your father, Arlo. So fucking proud."

"Shit." He rubs at his eyes. "I thought all the emotion left the room when the women did."

I walk over and pull him into my arms. "Nothing wrong with showing emotion, son." He hugs me, and then we clap one another on the back and break apart.

"And your suggestion is a solid one. If you're free to help me this weekend, I'll ask her then."

A wide smile spreads over his mouth. "I'll keep Saturday free, and I'll stop by the store Friday night and grab the groceries we need." I love that Arlo has embraced my love of cooking. Athena loves it too because she dines like a queen.

"There was something I wanted to ask." He rubs the back of his neck in an obvious tell.

"Shoot."

"I want to be a Manning too."

My heart swells to bursting point. "If you mean that, I can make it happen in a few days."

"I'm sure, Dad. Thena will be a Manning when she marries you, and I want to take your name too." He doesn't need to state the obvious.

"I would love that." I'm overwhelmed, and I cling to him when he pulls me into a hug this time, not hiding the happy tears coursing down my face.

Drew

Athena

"Oh my god, Drew," I gasp when he leads me into the sunroom. Now, I understand why he booked a spa day for me, Abby, Demi, and Nessa, and why Arlo is having a sleepover at Olivia's.

The table is beautifully set with a centerpiece of white roses and candles. Overhead, rows of fairy lights cast a magical glow across the room. A fragrant scent lingers in the air and soft music plays in the background.

"What's all this for?" I ask though I think I know. My heart pounds wildly in anticipation, and I stare at this man with so much love, hoping he can see it.

I never thought this life would be for me, but I love every second of it—even all the tough times. Drew is my perfect match in every way, and I hope he's going to propose because I want to spend every day of my forever loving him.

"Fuck it." He lowers to one knee in front of me. "I have dinner made. All your favorite things. I have champagne too. Arlo helped me."

My eyes cloud with happy tears. That only makes this more special.

"I was going to do this after we'd eaten, but I can't wait a second longer." He takes my trembling hand in his. "Athena, my beautiful, sexy, sweet, kindhearted, ballbuster, badass warrior, dream woman. You are the love of my life and the owner of my heart and soul. Everything I have is yours and everything you have is already mine."

I almost choke on a laugh, and I can barely see through my tears.

He flips open the box, revealing an exquisite pear-shaped diamond set over a platinum band. It's expensive but not ostentatious. The angles are sharp with just enough softness to round them out. It's absolutely stunning, and I couldn't have made a better choice if I'd picked myself.

Warmth mushrooms in my chest as love for this man pours into every nook and cranny of my being.

"Our souls were forged together in the dark, but we emerged brighter than flames," he says. "I love you possessively, completely, eternally. Please be mine for always. Marry me, Beauty. Let me be your Beast forever."

"You already are." I hold my hand out for the ring. "And yes, Drew. Yes, I'll marry you. Of course, I'll marry you. It's only ever been you."

Emotion crackles in the air as he gets to his feet and slides the ring on my finger. Then he clasps my face in his large palms and kisses me passionately as my heart jumps for joy behind my chest wall.

We're sporting matching grins when we break our lip lock and I can't stop smiling as I cling to my man and stare at the stunning ring on my finger. We hold one another close as I lift my hand, and the ring sparkles under the fairy lights. Drew takes a pic and sends it to Arlo first before sending it to our family group. The text simply says:

She said yes.

Those words do something to me, and I grab his shirt, muting our phones as they start pinging like crazy with messages from our loved ones. "Can you keep the food warm?" I ask, sliding my hand between our bodies.

A wicked glint darkens his eyes. "What are you up to,

sweetheart?" He groans as my hand dives behind the waistband of his pants, heading toward the promised land.

"I'm hungry for something else first," I purr, reaching into his boxers, my fingers finding him already hard for me.

An excited giggle slips from my lips as he hoists me into his arms and slams us up against the wall. My legs go around his waist as he grinds against me. "Don't you know I can't ever deny you anything you need?" His fingers wind through my hair, tilting my head back.

"I only need you. As long as I have you, I'm happy."

His fingers crawl under my dress and up along my inner thigh. "Then I'm about to make you happy forever because I'm yours now and every day after that until the end of time."

Then he starts making good on that promise, and those are the last words spoken for a very long time.

And that wraps up the Rydeville Elite Series! Thank you for taking this journey with me, and I hope you are happy with how everything ended for Drew and all the characters.

But this isn't the last you've heard of them! Drew, Athena, Arlo, and all the main characters will appear in the Rydeville Elite Epilogue. This is an optional, multi-POV novella set in the future, coming in 2024. Available to preorder now from Amazon.

Want to read more about Ares, Jase, Baz, Knight and the world of the Luminaries? Check out my Dirty Crazy Bad Duet. Available free to read with Kindle Unlimited. Also in audio, paperback, and hardcover.

Dirty Crazy Bad Series

• Dirty Crazy Bad Prequel – free on all platforms
• Dirty Crazy Bad 1
• Dirty Crazy Bad 2
• Dirty Crazy Bad: The Complete Collection (includes exclusive bonus content)

rivalry escalates, Ares seems determined to use me as a pawn, and I'm trapped in the middle. It doesn't help that he's hot AF, knows exactly how to push my buttons, and my body hasn't gotten the memo he's off-limits.

I wish that were the least of my worries.

Pride. Wrath. Lust. Envy. Greed. Gluttony. Sloth.

My life turns upside down the moment the dark secret society of The Luminaries is revealed to me.

Everything I thought I knew was a lie.

Now, I have lost all control over my future, and a heart-breaking new reality emerges.

One where lovers become enemies, enemies become allies, and corrupting sinners to sin is my only way to survive.

Available now in ebook, paperback, hardcover and audio.

I didn't believe my fractured heart and broken soul could endure any more pain. Until Jared rocks up to the art gallery where I work, with his fiancée in tow, and I'm drowning again.

Seeing him brings everything to the surface, so I flee. Placing distance between us again, I'm determined to put him behind me once and for all.

Then he reappears at my door, begging me for another chance.

I know I should turn him away.

Try telling that to my heart.

This angsty, new adult romance is a FREE full-length ebook, exclusively available to newsletter subscribers.

Type this link into your browser to claim your free copy:
https://bit.ly/TITMHFBB

OR

Scan this code to claim your free copy:

About the Author

Siobhan Davis™ is a *USA Today*, *Wall Street Journal*, and Amazon Top 5 bestselling romance author. **Siobhan** writes emotionally intense stories with swoon-worthy romance, complex characters, and tons of unexpected plot twists and turns that will have you flipping the pages beyond bedtime! She has sold over 2 million books, and her titles are translated into several languages.

Prior to becoming a full-time writer, Siobhan forged a successful corporate career in human resource management.

Siobhan currently lives with her husband in Cyprus while their two grown-up sons reside at the family home in Ireland.

You can connect with Siobhan in the following ways:

Website: www.siobhandavis.com
Facebook: AuthorSiobhanDavis
Instagram: @siobhandavisauthor
Tiktok: @siobhandavisauthor
Email: siobhan@siobhandavis.com

Books By Siobhan Davis

NEW ADULT ROMANCE

The One I Want Duet

Kennedy Boys Series

Rydeville Elite Series

All of Me Series

Forever Love Duet

NEW ADULT ROMANCE STAND-ALONES

Inseparable

Incognito

Still Falling for You

Holding on to Forever

Always Meant to Be

Tell It to My Heart

REVERSE HAREM

Sainthood Series

Dirty Crazy Bad Duet

Surviving Amber Springs (stand-alone)

Alinthia Series ^

DARK MAFIA ROMANCE

Mazzone Mafia Series
Vengeance of a Mafia Queen (stand-alone)
The Accardi Twins
*Taking What's Mine**

YA SCI-FI & PARANORMAL ROMANCE

Saven Series
True Calling Series ^

---

*Coming 2024
^Currently unpublished but will be republished in due course.

www.siobhandavis.com